Anastasia

THE AWAKENING

by Nana Abraham

SETFIRE BOOKS

ANASTASIA: THE AWAKENING
© 2018 by Nana Abraham

ISBN: 978-1-7752729-0-8

DISCLAIMER: This is a work of fiction. Names, characters, businesses, places, events, locales, and incidents are either the products of the author's imagination or used in a fictitious manner. Any resemblance to actual persons, living or dead, or actual events is purely coincidental.

SETFIRE BOOKS
www.nanabraham.com

Contents

Prologue

DAVID SAT ON his bed, staring silently at his surroundings. His gaze darted across the polished wood that framed his bed as his fingers brushed the woven rich purples and reds of his bedding. He rose and began to pace. *So many mistakes…how will I ever find my way back?* The simpler times of his childhood and teen years were far gone—when all he cared about was worshiping.

Take me back to where I used to be.

David looked at his lyre. *When did things begin to change? How did I stray so far?* He hadn't played the instrument in years. His fingers gently plucked the strings as he hummed a familiar tune.

Regret and guilt burned through his chest. His eyes stung with tears. When lust threatened to drag him further under, he gave himself over to God. Desire for Him burst into his heart. *Why did I wait?* He put down his instrument and walked over to where his writing tools waited. As he began to write, tears welled up in his eyes. He mechanically wiped them away, not wanting to smear the writing on the page.

Lord God, I'm sorry for what I have done. Do not hide Your face from me. My days are consumed like smoke, and my heart is stricken and withered like grass, so that I cannot eat. Lord, I need You. Come to me.

He closed his eyes. A badly beaten and scarred man hung on a wooden cross. The needle-sharp points of a crown of thorns, moistened with blood,

---

5

pierced the rim of his head. As David gazed at the stricken man, His eyes drew and held David's gaze. Deeper and deeper those eyes penetrated his until David knew who He was and saw only what He saw. He was his descendant—the Son of God...

In blinding pain, He looked out on the crowd of people yelling and cursing Him. Some of them clutched each other as they wept. His arms stretched out on both sides of Him, beyond normal range. The rhythm of the hammer pounding nails into His feet had not faded from His mind as He hung there. *The people before Me did this—the people I served and cared for.* But in that moment, with His flesh split and peeling, He felt overwhelming love for them. This sacrifice was for them, and He would go to His death for love. There would be forgiveness.

David jolted awake and began to write.

Dogs surround me, a pack of villains encircles me; they pierce my hands and my feet. All my bones are on display; people stare and gloat over me. They divide my clothes among them and cast lots for my garment. But You, LORD, do not be far from me. You are my strength; come quickly to help me.

David was shaken by the knowledge that God would prepare such a sacrifice. God loved him and had forgiven him the moment he'd asked. Praise welled up from his very depths. His tears of sorrow turned into tears of gratitude and great joy.

He closed his eyes again. A lovely young woman leaned against a large red object with wheels. Her dark curly hair was gathered together. She looked peaceful in her sleep, but her swollen eyelids and the streaks down her face revealed that she had been weeping. He noticed a hopeless look about her. Her garments were unlike anything he had ever seen. The green fabric of her short dress did not look like the warm, soft clothing to which he was accustomed. As soon as the vision had appeared, it was gone. David was accustomed to seeing things he did not understand. Words flowed into his heart, and he wrote them down.

The remembrance of your name shall endure to all generations.

———

You will arise and have mercy on Zion, for the time to favor her, yes, the set time has come.

His God was faithful and always performed amazing wonders for the people He ruled. The girl he had seen came back to his mind.

He shall appear in His glory and regard the prayer of the destitute and not despise their prayer. This will be written for the generation to come, that a people yet to be created may praise the LORD. For He looked down from heaven to hear the groaning of the prisoner, to release those appointed to death to declare the name of the LORD in Zion...

CHAPTER 1

Eclipse

"*The partial or* complete obscuring of one celestial body by another. A temporary or permanent dimming or cutting off of light. A fall into obscurity or disuse..."

"*And we, who with unveiled faces all reflect the glory of the Lord, are being transformed into His image with intensifying glory, which comes from the Lord, who is the Spirit*" (2 Corinthians 3:18, BSB).

Ana

GOD, WHICH WAY? The crisp night air tightened the inside of Ana's nose. Above her, the moonlit sky looked velvety. The echo of her heels against the sidewalk emphasized the quietness she felt. She turned onto another street, peering into the darkness as far as possible—more streetlights, closed shops and no people.

Still no sign of her...and I have no idea where I am. Great!

She sighed.

I should just go home.

She felt deep in her jacket pockets. No cell phone, but enough change for the bus. The thought of giving up made her feel sick to her stomach. *She looked so frightened.*

She glanced into a darkened store window and saw with fresh eyes how low she'd stooped with her latest outfit. She looked in desperate need of attention. Her green skirt was too short, and her blouse was too tight. Her pinched toes settled into a numbing ache with each freezing step. *Stupid shoes.*

At least the street's deserted so no one can see me. I look like I just stepped out of a cheesy hip-hop video. What was I thinking?

Leaving her friends had been impulsive. But the pull to help had driven her out of the steamy warmth of the club to this—lost in the downtown core, looking for a random woman. After everything she'd seen and experienced, she needed answers. *There has to be a reason.*

A chill rippled through her spine. Only moments earlier, she'd felt warm. But once she'd resumed her search, the heat had quickly left her body. She clutched the edges of her pleather jacket to stretch it closer. Giving up on the jacket, she folded her arms across her chest for warmth. She moved closer to another window to examine her face. Tears had forced her eye shadow and mascara into the creases around her eyes. Her hair, once pulled back into a neat high ponytail, lay slack at the nape of her neck with freed dark strands, fighting with the final breezes of winter. If anyone had been out, at first glance, the person might have thought she looked like she had lost some sort of fight.

Ana rubbed the back of her hand over her eyes and glanced at her watch—2:15 a.m. Everything from earlier in the evening now felt like a dream. An eternity ago she and her friends had hopped into the car and headed for the club. Now, there was no turning back.

∽

Roving red and purple spotlights sailed over sweaty male and female clubbers jammed on the dance floor, highlighting them with pulsating color. They jumped and gyrated to the deafening music in the small dark room. Bartenders and waitresses squeezed through the crowd while young people weaved in and out of the room, trying to pick up or be picked up by a member of the opposite gender. It was 12:07 a.m.; the night had only begun at the Eclipse nightclub. Everywhere college students and the aged elite of high school milled about.

Ana sat alone at her table, staring blankly at her drink for a few minutes before refocusing on the dance floor. Waiting for her friends seemed to be the ritual lately. She scanned the room but didn't see them. *Maybe they're in the bathroom.*

While growing up, she'd always been told how wrong it was to be in clubs and to listen to "worldly" music. Initially, they'd practically dragged her to the Eclipse. But once the guilt had worn off, she started to understand the draw—the anticipation, dressing up and being someone else, even if only for a night. As the weeks passed, she'd started to relish the club seen—although she still wasn't sure what she thought about the Eclipse. *Is anyone really happy? Or is it all a show?* Tonight felt different though. No matter how much she tried to relax, her mind simply couldn't unwind.

The bass of the music vibrated through her as she peered at a few of her acquaintances from school. Transition time was on its way for all of them. First, the last hurrah of winter had ended the mid-February blahs. In another month the club would be sparse again, and the students would be settling in for the unpopular, but necessary, hermit lifestyle so common before finals. A frenzy of exams and papers would soon give way to the realization that another year of college was now completed. She wasn't the only one looking for distraction tonight.

Dree

In the corner Dree noted Incubus/Succubus weaving an intricate silk web of lust around a young man who eyed the women dancing near him. Dree recognized another demon, a spirit of murder, on a light-haired guy at the bar. He studied the other ancient spirits as they found new victims and piled themselves onto groups of clueless humans.

Dree himself preyed on a thin woman hunched at the bar. His powdery-gray celestial body clung to her in the unseen realm. He was still bony and weak from having gone months without a host; he had been looking forward to tonight. He concentrated his gaze on the top of her head and bore his words deep. Her shoulder-length blonde hair fell forward, creating a curly shield that prevented her from having to look at those who were around her.

My life sucks. No one's gonna want me. He pressed into her mind.

Dree used his power to make Cathy feel heavy all over.

She's mine! Dree thought exultantly. His travels through barren and dry land had almost caused him to disappear into the abyss before he'd found Cathy. Full of despair and sin, she was perfect. Months of watching her, easing his thoughts into hers and slowly trying to speak was finally paying off. Imposing his will on her had proved difficult at first, but lately her downcast mood and now the beers she had knocked back made it easy. She readily accepted his demonic voice as her own. I'll have plenty to feed on if I can persuade her to destroy herself! Then he would be even stronger to be able to find a new host and gain more worship. What she carried inside made her double the value.

આ

Ana stirred her Sprite with her straw. Her active thoughts pushed the music to a muted background. People danced everywhere, begging to be noticed—lost in their own created realities where they were the most important person in the room. Strobe lights added to the illusion by masking all imperfections as clubbers took on new personas, hypnotized by the music. Self-consciousness danced around Ana, mocking her silence. She wanted to dance, to let loose, to demand admiration from all, but something paralyzed her. *Maybe the guilt is back; I don't know...* All she knew was there was no way to belong. She sighed.

Susan and Megan finally strutted back to the table. Susan's hair, currently dyed red, fell in waves down her back. She had squeezed her voluptuous 5'8" body into skinny black pants and a shimmery loose tank. She tottered slightly in her heels as she leaned over to yell in Ana's ear. A waft of perfume, sweat and alcohol followed.

"You need to come dance and get your mind off Greg." She laughed. "I don't understand why you've been moping; it's not like you guys were dating or anything."

"Some of us think about more than just guys," Ana offered.

Megan's full deep-red lips broke into a smile. "Yeah, right. Come on," Her high heels made her short, toned body appear long and lean. "Have some fun, my little church girl."

"Yeah!" Susan punched a drunken patriotic fist into the air. "We are here for fun." She bobbed her pointed index finger at Ana like a parent's scolding a child. "We all know how much you love to dance!" She giggled and then grabbed her beer.

"I don't know; I'm not in the mood." Ana looked back at the dance floor. *They can probably see right through my excuses, but I don't care.*

Megan lost her ambition and sank heavily into the chair next to Ana. She kicked off her shoes to reveal small feet and painted toes. She leaned back and rested one elbow on the neighboring chair. Susan took the cue and grabbed a seat as well. Her thick eyelashes drooped for a moment.

Ana stared at Megan's heavily made-up face. Rarely did she go anywhere without makeup. She had carefully applied makeup to Ana's eyes before they'd left as well. "Don't you guys ever feel like there is more? But you don't know what it is?"

Susan squinted to focus on Ana. "Yeah, sometimes," she admitted.

Megan rubbed one of her temples. "Guys, I'm trying to rest a minute. Don't kill the vibe." She turned to Ana. "I'm personally going to make sure you have fun." She scanned the crowd. "But...there aren't a lot of good-looking guys here tonight," she noted. Her voice then lifted into a sultry tone. "Ooh, except that tall one over there. I think he's checking us out." She straightened in her seat as she sized him up. "He's cute," she added.

Susan's eyes widened as she grabbed her friends' arms. "Let's go dance!" she suggested.

Ana shook her head and took a sip of her Sprite. "Sorry, still not in the mood." She placed her glass on the table.

"Fine, suit yourself." Megan's voice was stiff. She lifted her short, brown hair off her neck with one hand and fanned herself with the other. "I didn't lend you my clothes so you could sit here and be bored, but whatever..." She slipped into her shoes, stood, and motioned for Susan to follow her.

Ana studied her friends dancing, feeling even more displaced. *What is it about tonight?* Maybe her friends did notice something weird too. Susan usually drank more heavily when she was trying to distract herself.

At times like these, she wished she could ignore her feelings and peel off the "church-girl" part of her so she could blend in better. But it never worked. She'd tried pushing boundaries, but it was impossible to do that and remain safe inside them. She had learned the hard way.

She knew she wanted something else—to be somewhere else... *But where?* Thoughts of home snapped her back to the reality of daily conflict with her mom. Thoughts of church stirred the ache of emptiness she was trying to forget because of Pastor Matthew.

I have nowhere else to be.

Dionysus

Dionysus' demonic eyes studied her with piercing hate. *I cannot afford to have **her** anywhere near my territory.*

Christians didn't belong in his club unless they were in rebellion. He hadn't spent years building deception, only to have *this* girl casually waltz in week after week.

Right now, he wasn't sure what to think. He'd seen Ana enjoying herself once before, but at this moment, he couldn't overlook her invasive light—dim as it was—that still emanated from her. All humans who were connected to God carried this particular light which shone brightly in and over them like a force field. Hers hadn't diminished enough for him to discount her although she did seem inactive. He needed something or someone to draw her in all the way. His evil eyes searched the crowd and found another set of eyes fixed on Ana.

⁊⋆

"Hey, do you want to dance?"

Realizing someone was speaking to her, Ana looked up to see the guy Megan had spotted earlier. He was tall and slender with black hair that waved and curled back over his head. He stood inches from her and smiled down as the strobe lights caused his eyes to twinkle. He extended his hand to her as he shouted, "I'm Andrew."

Caught off guard and suddenly tongue-tied, Ana stared back at him, searching for appropriate words as a flush of heat rushed to her face.

Andrew sat down and tried again. "What's your name?"

She hesitated. "Um…Ana…do I know you? You look familiar." She extended her hand to accept his earlier offered handshake.

Andrew shook her hand, and to her surprise, he didn't let go.

She was sure her heartbeat was now strong enough for him to feel as well.

"What school do you go to?" he asked.

"Second year at Ryant."

"I went there last year. Maybe that's why I look familiar." He finally released her hostage hand.

"Where do you go now?" she asked, relieved of the physical link.

"I'm not in school anymore. I'm working." He glanced back at the dance floor. "…so do you want to dance?"

She didn't want to seem like a hypocrite to her friends. "I don't know, I—"

"Come on! I can tell you *really* want to dance. Come on; I bet you're good too!" he added with a sly, handsome grin. Once again he extended his hand to her.

This time, she accepted his hand and allowed him to pull her up. She smiled for first time that night.

The music pulsated around them. The original uneasiness that had nagged at her suddenly became a strong nudge. She forced down the feelings and gripped his hand a little tighter as she followed him to the middle of the dance floor. From the corner of her eye, she saw Megan and Susan turn to look at her and then flash approving smiles before she quickly averted her gaze.

As she and Andrew began to dance, the uneasy feeling boiled with a vengeance and refused to be silenced. *Snap out of it.*

It's just dancing, she defended her choice in her mind.

She moved in sync with the crowd, trying to stifle the voice of her conscience. She loosened up, and for a moment, and felt protected from her raging thoughts. Andrew seemed nice, and she looked forward to getting to know him better.

Maybe this could develop into a thing.

"You're beautiful!" Andrew whispered in her ear as he pulled her closer. His gaze dipped purposely to scan her body but returned to linger on her mouth, before settling on her eyes.

Uncomfortable under his steady scrutiny, she focused past him. A sudden weight overshadowed her body. Everything in the room seemed to blur as her head spun. She closed her eyes to regain her equilibrium. When she opened them again, everything had changed. Distorted, frightening noise hammered from the speakers. A putrid stench rose from the dancing bodies, nauseating her. All around dark shadows hovered over them and lingered in every corner of the club. Some of the shadows swelled in size as they fell upon the dancers.

Her legs buckled, but Andrew reached out to steady her. His mouth moved in slow motion. She squinted, trying to make out his words over the painful noise that assaulted her ears. Puffs of black smoke circled where words should have exited his lips. She doubled over to ward off the threatening nausea.

As the noise reached a crescendo, she finally heard Andrew's voice.

"Are you okay?" His brow furrowed.

She looked up to see that the darkness and black smoke had disappeared. Everything was back to the way it had been. Ana took a deep breath and straightened. She offered a half-hearted smile and swallowed. "Um…yes, I'm okay." She held Andrew's arm as she looked longingly back at the table where she'd been sitting. She tried to sound casual as she asked, "Do you mind? I think I need to sit down."

"For a moment there, you looked like you were going to puke!"

She didn't respond to Andrew's comment. *What was that? A vision? I haven't seen one since—no, it couldn't be.*

As they headed back to the table, something caught her attention. "Hey, Andrew, see that lady over there?" she subtly pointed.

"What about her?"

Ana frowned, looking to the woman seated at the bar and back again. "Do you see something hovering over her—like a shadow?"

"A shadow?" He made a wry face. "Are you sure you're okay?"

"Yeah, I'm fine." She waved her hand.

What's happening to me?

"Are you sure you don't see that it's darker where she's sitting?" Ana asked.

"All I see is a drunk chick."

"Forget it. I'm going to go talk to her. I'll be right back, okay?"

"Whatever…" Andrew shrugged.

Ana crossed the floor toward the woman.

Is it real? Maybe it's a demon. She needed to know what she seeing.

The woman's head rested on her folded arms as Ana approached. *Is she even awake?* Ana couldn't help but feel sad as she watched her.

What can I say without sounding ridiculous? Excuse me, miss. Are you spiritually oppressed? Yup, no way not to sound crazy.

Ana tapped her on the shoulder. "Excuse me…"

❧

Dree looked up from Cathy in a panic. Through Cathy's eyes, he saw a young girl with curly black hair and a ponytail. She looked harmless, but Dree saw a dangerous truth.

A light bearer! I'm so close! Get away!

Cathy looked up. "Yes?"

Ana saw that her eyes were red-rimmed and dazed.

Dree remembered his power over Cathy. He frantically yelled into her mind. "Quick, run! She'll hurt you!"

"I was only wondering if you are okay?" the girl said.

"What do you want?" Irritation edged Cathy's voice.

Dree's implanted thoughts took root and grew until they consumed Cathy's ability to think or reason. Bolts of terror ran through her body, energizing her. She wanted to scream. *I have to get out of here!*

Cathy shouted loud enough to hear herself over her jumbled thoughts.

"Leave me alone! I haven't done anything to you!" She jumped off her seat, snatched her purse from the counter, quickly shoved her way through the crowd, and staggered toward the exit.

"Wait! I just—"

&

"Wow, what a speech!" Andrew joined Ana and stared toward the door. "Does she owe you money or something?"

Ana shook her head slowly. "I don't know her." Ana thought for a moment and then started walking toward the door. "I should go after her…"

"Why? You don't know her, and she obviously doesn't want to talk." He scooped her hand into his. "Stay here; I have things I want to say to you." He stared into her eyes.

She looked back at him. "But I think she's in trouble." Part of her wanted to stay with him, but another part of her was sad. She looked toward the exit and pulled back her hand. "I'm sorry…maybe another time."

If I ever see you again.

"Can you let my friends know I've left and will catch up to them later? They'll be back at my table soon. It was nice to meet you!" she said as she rushed out of the Eclipse.

&

Dionysus relaxed as Ana ran out the door. He smirked at the disappointment on Andrew's face.

Not the ladies' man you thought you were, hmm?

Andrew distanced himself from the lonely spot on the floor and went to the bar to order a drink. Dionysus pushed himself away from the bar, smoothed his suit, then headed toward the dark hallway that led to his office. *Not quite what I had planned, but good enough.* He turned to look back at his dominion before walking to his office. People were clearly enjoying themselves, oblivious to the world he was creating. *They're all asleep.*

CHAPTER 2

Awakening

"Besides this you know the time, that the hour has come for you to wake from sleep. For salvation is nearer to us now than when we first believed" (Romans 13:11, ESV).

1:30 A.M.

A S SHE PROCEEDED deeper into the downtown core, Ana soon left behind all evidence of the teenage clubbers. Without the context of the club to explain her attire, she felt out of place and exposed. Something about what she had seen in the club made her feel alive again, but the chances of finding the woman were slim to none. Her resolve to leave the warmth of the club waned with each freezing step she took. Still, she continued her aimless search until her desire to find the woman morphed into a frustrated anger—the same anger that always hovered over her, ready to pounce.

If I could just find her, I could help. How far could she have gotten? Who is she?

How could she help the woman when she didn't even know what she had seen? She glanced back to see if she had missed something.

Stop pretending.

As quickly as the thought entered her mind, she pushed it away.

Who are you doing this for?

Her steps slowed. "I don't know. God, what am I doing?" Her arms crossed over her chest as if to protect herself. Memories of the past year swept over her, filling her eyes with tears. Pastor Matthew was dead. No matter what she did, that reality crept in on her and dragged her into isolated pockets of self-pity.

Why can't people understand what it was like? Nothing should continue to move on. Where were You, God?

A tumult of thoughts rolled over and upon themselves, each pressing for its own spotlight. She didn't want to give in because such thoughts required expending energy that she didn't have. Stubbornness reinforced old walls in her mind, refusing to let her confront the truth trying to squeeze through open cracks.

Too late. Before she knew what was happening, the inevitable finally surfaced, hitting her head on, and the pain disarmed her. Beyond her questions and her pain, only God understood what she was going through. His love was the only constant she wanted to count on. In no way had pushing Him away helped ease her pain; rather, the terrible emptiness had only been magnified.

She found a curb between two parked cars on the street and sat down. With her elbows on her knees, she held her head in her hands and sobbed. Her temples throbbed from the pressure of blood behind her eyes. *Why can't I get it right?* She clawed at her chest, trying to grab what she felt would smother her. Her muffled cries intermingled with an inner pleading for help. "God, why am I here? I can't go on like this...I need You to help me!"

Instantly, in that old familiar way, she felt a calm, presence flow over her like warm oil. She still felt sad, but the hopelessness was gradually diminishing. God's presence soothed her. Tears continued to stream from her eyes, and she stopped trying to push Him away.

No matter how far away she had run, He'd been waiting.

"Come back," she whispered. "I'm sorry for everything I've done. I'm sorry for blocking You out of my life." She rubbed her tear-filled eyes, smearing her makeup. Desperation pounded in her heart. "God, I can't do this anymore."

Ana remembered the woman again.

What help can I offer when I am so messed up?

Still, she prayed, "Show me the way to You again. Help that lady I saw— wherever she is…"

Fatigue began to take over. She sniffled and closed her eyes, letting sleep claim her. The sharp bite of the cold seemed to soften.

∼

Sasson

Sasson, unseen by Ana, stood tall and shimmering behind her. He returned his heavy angelic sword to its sheath and crouched next to her. His gold and white body appeared as smooth as sculpted marble. His armor dissolved into his skin, giving him the appearance of a man—the custom for angels when dealing with humans, even though they would be invisible. On rare occasion, humans had been known to glimpse angels during special moments of revelation, so this change of appearance was merely precautionary. Even the angels seldom knew when their Master might split the spiritual veil to reveal their hidden activities. Their magnificent appearance, which was often a cause for alarm, would create less fear and impact in their terrestrial human disguise.

Sasson extended his large outer wings to cover and protect her from the wind and any external threat. He opened his other hand to reveal a small round package about the size of his palm resting there. The orb gleamed as if it had been polished with orange fire. He knelt behind her and opened his inner wings.

It's time. The long-distanced wait was now over, and Ana needed to know Jesus in a way she had never known Him from the beginning. Sasson's message for Ana was crucial to the fulfillment of her life's purpose.

He uttered an unknown language in her ear. With each layer of the orb he peeled, she would be taken deeper into visions of the past. What she gleaned from the past would help her understand her present.

In her sleep she whispered another prayer, "Help me to follow You."

At her words Sasson nodded and peeled off the first layer of the orb. Ana drifted into a deep trance.

~

Ana began to hear voices. Color and sound emerged all around her at once—like paint squeezed from tubes onto an empty palette. A lush forest of texture filled the space. She was a spectator to beauty unfolding before her.

A large throne burned violently at the center of the shimmering space. Evolving pictures of planets, trees, animals and other parts of creation orbited and changed within the fire. Precious stones embedded into the structure gleamed as a stream of fire from the throne cut across the light-gold crystal-looking floor.

Ana looked up. Above her, transparent crystal enclosed the atmosphere. Through the ceiling she could see the dark beauty of the universe sparkling with a heavy dusting of light reflected by distant stars. Palpable joy filled the atmosphere. Ribbon-like arcs of color suspended in the air above the heads of those in the courtyard.

Large flat-winged creatures flapped and brushed each other around the throne. The seraphim opened and closed their wings over their many eyes. Ana felt the soft breeze they created as they flew past her. The beauty overwhelmed her as melodic voices and distant bells echoed and floated through the air, part of a greater anthem. Ana did not hear words but felt the meaning within her. "Holy…Holy…Holy…" The words seemed to circle and overlap like the wings, taking the listener into a never-ending chorus of profound meaning.

Ana watched as a man draped in rich blue robes stepped forward and knelt. He bowed, touching his forehead to the floor. Tears dripped from his face and became small pools of light before they were absorbed into the surface of the sparkling floor.

"Father, I must go…" The Son spoke in a gentle tone. "It has begun."

Like the song, Ana understood His words, despite the cadence of the language she had never before heard or learned.

From the throne cloaked in thick, pure white clouds, the Father answered.

His voice reverberated like the primal sound of rushing of water. "Even so, some will still not follow."

"But for one, I will do it." The Son's voice was quiet but firm.

"I have made a way for You," the Father on the throne continued.

The love in his voice radiated through Ana, warm like the sun and permeated everything in the room.

"I have brought You forth from Myself, and We are the same. I am in You, and You are in Me. It will be difficult, but I have planned a perfect time for You so that this gift of redemption will not be forgotten."

"See! I have divided time. I love and honor You," He declared to His Son, "Go. I have given You all power!" The Father's voice thundered as streaks of bright lightning flashed from the throne to unknown places. The startled seraphim violently flapped their wings.

"Holy…Holy…Holy," the bells and voices resumed, answering one another. The stunning moment ended as suddenly as it had begun.

Sasson made sure that no one saw Ana, and no one disturbed her. He continued to whisper into Ana's ear and peel layers of revelation from the orb, which contained stories of people from both the past and the present. Ana was destined to cross some of their paths in the next season. Even if she didn't remember, knowledge of their lives would be a part of her. Some were part of that great cloud witnesses now watching from the bastions of heaven. For Ana to be transformed in her spirit, the timing was crucial. Her ability to grasp the love that Jesus had for her and all mankind would enable her to stand firm against what was coming.

Ana would know King Jesus in a new way. She had witnessed His glory and love in heaven right after Adam and Eve had given into sin, causing the Fall of mankind. Now she would see Jesus as He was—the first and greatest Intercessor. She was destined to lead those around her and to stand as a go-between for the city, praying God's desires into the land.

But first she had to experience why the earth needed intercessors so she could finally embrace her calling. Hers was to be a new beginning.

Ana could see nothing, but something was coming. The energy of the moment vibrated within her. Then the darkness was suddenly pierced by an agonizing scream. A new scene formed before her eyes—that of a young woman giving birth in a room. The room was mostly empty save for a sleeping mat in the corner and a cistern of water with some towels. The young woman, who looked younger than Ana, squatted in the birthing position. Her dark, wavy long hair was moist from sweat. Again she cried out. The voice of an older midwife spoke soft encouragements as she firmly instructed in her language: "Come on, one more push!" She crouched next to the soon-to-be mother, supporting the young woman with her arms and hands. The midwife's blue scarf slipped down to her shoulders. The young mother's face contorted once more as she focused a hard gaze on the midwife and pushed again. The woman's scream was followed by the shrill cry of a baby. As the scene went black, the sound of the baby's cry simultaneously filled Ana with both joy and sadness.

Moments passed, then in a quick flash she saw a large troop of angels hovering in the sky above shepherds who were tending their flocks in the field. The angels' robes and swords flashed with light that both encompassed and radiated from them.

The scene changed as noise from the bustle of people, animals and squeaking wheels came to Ana. She could smell and feel the heat around her.

"Your father and I have looked for You for days! Why have You done this?" The woman Ana had seen giving birth stared down at her son, who was now about twelve years old. A brown scarf covered her vibrant dark hair. The woman tried to look stern, but the tenderness in her eyes was impossible to miss. Even the scarf that framed her delicate features and hid most of her hair and shoulders couldn't mask her natural beauty. Her high cheekbones and soft-brown, almond-shaped eyes displayed a quiet wisdom. Under her dress, her stomach bulged with the promise of another child. Ana was drawn in deeper to Mary's thoughts.

"Why were you looking for Me? Didn't you know I must be about My Father's business?" the boy answered somberly.

Mary could see no trace of defiance in his face. He obviously did not understand her worry. Her hands rested motionless on her hips. She had nothing left to say to him.

She exchanged a helpless glance with Joseph. He shrugged.

How could He be so serious at such a young age?

She had often watched Him play with the other children, and then at a moment's notice, leave to go off by Himself to spend hours praying. He would crouch, face drawn in agony as He prayed and wept in the field. Another time after getting home from the market, she'd thought He was injured. She touched His shoulder, only to have Him turn and look right through her as if she were not there at all. She tried hard to be all that He needed although she didn't know what that meant. Sometimes she even wondered *if* He needed her at all. But her Son, as distant as He sometimes was, He was still a part of her.

Speaking to her husband of such observations had not helped. He had merely looked at her as if he were as confused as she was. One night before she fell asleep, Joseph whispered encouragement into her ear. "All will make sense eventually. I know it's hard," he spoke reassuringly, "but you're doing your best." He gently pulled her closer to him. With her husband's heart beating steadily against her back, she'd looked at her Son who slept in the corner. His dark lashes cast sorrowful shadows above His round cheeks while His rumpled, curly hair framed His peaceful face. *What does His future hold?*

She would remind herself of God's words spoken concerning His birth when He had given her this blessing. Joseph had done all that He could as well, but somehow it never seemed like enough. This child carried a burden, which neither of them could understand or explain.

The sound of creaking wagon wheels brought Mary back to the reality of the dusty path outside of the temple. The sun overhead burned. She placed her hand on her Son's warm hair and stared into His eyes.

Yes, He was hers— but only for now.

She turned on her heel with a pretense of confidence and began to follow Joseph who had already turned to leave. "Come along, Jesus. We have to make up a lot of time." The boy obediently followed his mother.

The arid day morphed into an evening full of ominous clouds gathering at the top of a hill. Ana heard the angry mob shouting before she saw the men and the women in robes and head scarves. The din of crying and yelling rose to a threatening, fevered pitch. The men on the crosses, devoid of hope, silently observed the people gathered to see them crucified. On the middle cross, words had been scratched into a wooden sign placed above the man's head. The man on the center cross looked out at the crowd, each breath an agonizing struggle. His flesh hung, torn and puckered in areas caked with blood. Purple bruises and blood smeared His face, making Him unrecognizable. Sections of His scalp were exposed where His hair had been torn from the root. A wreath of thorns encircled and pierced His head.

Ana had seen Him kneeling in heaven. She stared into His eyes. The painful expression on His face was the same she'd seen in heaven.

Just as the realization came, Ana was pulled into another vision of another life. The rhythmic beep of hospital monitors filled her with a deep sense of loss.

Beth awakened to the sound of beeping monitors and hushed voices behind the curtain. Her disoriented thoughts caught up as she straightened. She was still at the hospital, sitting beside her husband. Her stiff back reminded her that chairs were not made for sleeping. She looked down at her husband and remembered the day she had learned he was terminally ill. Every day since then had been a gift of time spent together. Now that he rested in the hospital bed, dying slowly, all she wanted to do was freeze time. Time was all she needed—and all she had left.

She tried not to think about burying him and missing him forever. She'd already spent many nights crying and blaming God for taking his life too soon. She touched the hand that rested on his chest and nestled her head close to listen to his heartbeat. She prayed again as tears filled her eyes and fell on his chest. Now, there was no time for blame.

§

While Ana witnessed these heart-rending scenes, a depth of sadness and grief overpowered her. She watched a slideshow of images as Jesus projected what He saw—families fighting, young children with guns, shouting and as they extended their weapons in the air, armies going to war; the poor and deformed begging, the whole earth revolting because of sin and destroying itself. Angels walking with humans. Demons hovering over the helpless and weaving lies. Chariots of fire surrounding an earthly army. Angels with swords fighting and pushing back demons in a great war in the sky. The pictures continued to flash faster and faster until they became a whirlwind surrounding her. She saw everything that had happened, was happening, and would happen in the future. The world seemed so broken, so sick. Never before had she thought about life outside of herself, and she didn't want it to end like this.

The heartache of hundreds magnified within her. The emotional pull created a pressure in her stomach that mounted until she was unable to bear it. She cried and screamed. The weight was too much for any human to handle.

Everything is crushing me!

Jesus was showing her the deeper levels of agony. Then blood dripped down from Him on the cross. When it struck the ground, an echo sounded like a thick blanket being snapped.

Jesus spoke into her mind. "I died for all of them. I died for you. How long will you deny Me?"

Another drop of His blood fell, hitting her skin. All at once brilliant light radiated through her. Soothing heat and a joy so intense took over and made everything she'd experienced only moments ago seem impossible. Ana reveled in the beauty.

"How long?" His voice boomed.

Ana became aware of how her choices had taken her further away from Him. The running had to stop. She continued to cry. "Jesus, I'm sorry I turned away from the truth. I'm sorry I rejected You. Please forgive me. I want to live for You. I want to see Your beauty in this dying world."

She continued to cry to the One who hung on the cross beyond the physical boundary of time and space.

When He finally answered, His voice filled with love. "I have many things to show you if you will trust Me. Follow Me and do not be afraid." His voice reverberated with such strength and clarity that Ana trembled. "I've given you power over all the work of the Enemy. Nothing will be able to harm you. I love you with an everlasting love!"

A massive river of love poured into Ana's heart and saturated her very being. She wished she could embrace Jesus and thank Him for His love—the love that was the only hope for the world. The strength of His love amazed her.

As the moments passed, blanket after blanket of peace and warmth engulfed her. The trembling continued and became more intense.

As Ana sat crumpled on the curb, Sasson finally finished unwrapping the orb. All that was left radiating out of his hand was light. As he placed the light on Ana's head, it dissolved into her.

When Ana awakened, she tasted the salty tears that had found their way into her mouth. Her body was warm, and her back felt like she had been stiff for a long time. She pushed herself up and dusted off her skirt. She tried to remember the direction she'd come from. *It's so cold. I need to get inside again soon.* It didn't make sense that she'd been warm a few moments ago. Maybe the cars had retained some residual heat. Her dream came back to her as she remembered the girl from the club. Assurance filled her heart as she asked God for direction again.

God, which way?

Sasson walked in step with Ana as he always did, knowing that now things would be different.

We can finally get somewhere.

He had guarded Ana for years. It seemed to him that humans could never make up their minds. One minute they prayed and asked for something special, and the next moment they gave up the gift in exchange for a worthless distraction.

He remembered great battles they had fought when she was a child and teen. Now that she was almost out of her teens, he found himself fighting demons that tried to attack her because of the places she went and the things she did. Even her night dreams were not enough to make her aware of what was happening. She either did not remember them or brushed them off as her "subconscious" mind playing tricks on her. Had she completely abandoned all the truths she'd once learned? Was she trying to throw away her destiny? Why would someone with so many God-given gifts waste time dabbling in filth?

The Lord of hosts had instructed the angel to allow Ana to see briefly into the spirit realm at the night club. She saw a glimpse of what he spent his existence fighting. That kind of revelation was actually a very rare occurrence. In fact, if humans understood what traps and spirits surrounded them, they would be afraid to leave their homes. And while the Lord occasionally chose some to see into that realm, such revelation was usually reserved for those living in the faith.

Nearly a year had passed since Ana had abandoned her life of faith. Sadly, she'd willingly closed her eyes to the truth, but God hadn't given up on her. As amazing as it seems, mercy and grace were always available to the people of God. They were incredibly blessed and didn't even know it.

After a long season of spiritual inactivity, Ana was being reactivated or "awakened" as the angels sometimes described it. Much was taking place in the city, and every available warrior was being called into action.

In a flash-like vision, Sasson saw her upcoming assignments, which closely resembled intersecting intricate paths, each one affecting the other. As she moved toward one or passed a test, he would lead her into the next one. He had confidence that because Ana had gone after the girl, she had now chosen the right path—and not a moment too soon. Much needed to be recovered in very little time. He couldn't help feeling excited about the future. New battles meant new territory!

As Ana prayed and looked at her watch, Sasson sought direction.

Left.

He moved away from Ana and closer to a nearby cat to use the animal to attract her attention.

Ana was startled by a cat's meow and slowed her pace, turning to the left. A low wooden sign, partially covered by a bush, revealed an entrance from the main street: MID PARK.

Maybe there was…must be a bus stop near the park… She decided to take a chance and turned in that direction. If she couldn't find the girl, then at least she could head back to Susan's place. There was no way they were still at the club.

"Here's hoping to no murderers," she mumbled and glanced behind her.

Though the trees from the park blocked out most of the light, she traded her visibility for shadows. She'd walked only a few steps when she spotted someone lying face down on the grass ahead. A pang of fear coursed through her.

Ana crept forward a few steps and searched furtively in all directions. As she neared the prostrate person, she recognized the curly blonde hair, blue jacket and black skirt. *The girl from the club!*

CHAPTER 3

Death

"Consider and hear me, O LORD my God; enlighten my eyes, lest I sleep the sleep of death" (Psalm 13:3, NKJV).

Cathy

CATHY'S HEART POUNDED through her rib cage as she ran. She glanced back without slowing her pace. Fear of what would happen if she stopped loomed over her. She made a hard right around the corner. A house came into view at the end of the street.

Kevin! He can help me! She bolted the rest of the way, stopping in front of the house. No lights were on, and some of the windows had been boarded up. She ran up to the doorstep and tried to open the door. *"Kevin! Kevin! I need you!" No signs of life stirred within. "Can you hear me?"*

Icy fear swept over her. It was here! Her body lifted as she made a feeble attempt to hold on to the front door handle. She opened her mouth to scream, but darkness folded in and choked out the sound. Her arms and legs flailed in the air before she fell into darkness. Thick blackness surrounded her, sucking the air from inside her. She was dying. She fell deeper, forgetting everything except the pain exploding in her lungs.

A hand firmly grabbed her shoulder, ending her downward spiral. Cathy gasped as the night air refilled her lungs.

"Hey! Are you okay?" The hand tightened its grip on her.

She opened her eyes and looked into the face of the girl who shook her. She pushed herself up. "Where am I?" she muttered. Heat rushed into her cheeks and lips, warming her face against the wind.

The girl frowned and carefully enunciated each word, "You're in the park. Are you okay? I saw you earlier."

Cathy squinted at the girl.

It was a dream?

The girl kept speaking. "I came over to speak to you at the Eclipse, and you ran away."

Cathy nodded as she remembered. "Yeah. Sorry—I wasn't feeling like...myself." Cathy pressed fingers over her closed eyelids. *What was I so afraid of?*

"What are you doing here?" the young woman asked in concern.

Her voice suddenly grated in Cathy's head. "I'm not deaf! Why are you yelling?"

The girl flinched. "Umm, I panicked when I saw you lying here. Glad to see you're fine." She stood and looked down at Cathy. "Don't you know it's not safe to be out here alone in the middle of the night?"

Cathy laughed. "Are you serious?" She gestured around them. "And I suppose your armed guard escorted you here."

Sasson stood nearby with his sword pressed against Dree's throat.

"No more speaking to Cathy," Sasson warned firmly. The demon lay sprawled on its back.

"Why didn't you show yourself at the Eclipse?" Dree taunted.

"You know why," Sasson said. Without their charges, angels rarely acted outside of their assignments unless it involved a life-or-death situation. "You tried to kill her...glad we got here in time."

"She fell," Dree sneered. "I was merely keeping her company."

"Your games are over for tonight," Sasson said.

The girl's face smoldered. "Just be happy that I found you and not some creep!"

Cathy sighed and lowered her head. *Creeps are the only ones who find me.*

She wanted to apologize for her attitude. "I really don't know why I'm here. The last thing I remember I was stumbling home." Her throat felt dry and gritty. She tried to remember her dream. Kevin's house. "Something was chasing me." She shivered. "...I'm so cold."

Seeing Cathy calm down drained the anger rising in Ana. "I was looking for you."

"You were?" Cathy stared at her in shock. "Why?"

"I don't know," Ana shrugged. "I felt like you needed help, and I had to find you. What's your name?"

"Cathy. What's yours?

Cathy? A rush of heat flooded over Ana. A familiar feeling nagged at her, but she ignored it and stretched out her hand. "Anastasia, but everyone calls me *Ana.*" As Ana shook her hand, Cathy shivered again.

Ana looked around. "It's really cold...we'd better get going. Do you know where the nearest bus stop is? I need to head east." *Spending so much time looking for this girl was silly. Cathy is fine. How very anti-climactic.*

"What time is it?" Cathy rubbed her eyes again and then stood.

Ana glanced at her watch. "Two thirty-two a.m., to be exact."

Cathy scrunched her face. "Sorry, the buses going east stopped running about an hour ago."

Ana threw up her hands. "How am I going to get back?" She'd never imagined her evening would turn out like this—stranded in a park with someone she scarcely knew. "I don't have enough money for a taxi, and my friends probably went home already..."

"Well, if you want, you can come to my place and call your friends. I live about two blocks from here."

"I...I guess that would work. Thanks."

"No problem. It's the least I can do since you came to my rescue."

~

As Ana followed Cathy home, a recollection of confusing images from her earlier dream flooded her mind…but she couldn't sort them yet. She needed time alone to pray and organize her thoughts. Things couldn't go back to the way they'd been. She was sure God still loved her and cared about every detail of her life. She wanted a strong, close relationship with Him again more than anything else. She needed to get focused spiritually.

She'd been compelled to find Cathy. Now that she was finally with her, she wondered if she had more to figure out. *What was that darkness I saw surrounding her? Why doesn't Cathy remember how she got to the park?*

Cathy lived in an old brownstone triplex three blocks from the downtown area. In the dark, Ana couldn't help but wonder about the safety of the neighborhood. The building's exterior hadn't looked promising. When she trudged up the three flights of stairs to the apartment, the stairwell didn't look much better. The peeling paint on the door caused Ana to hold her breath as Cathy unlocked the door.

The door opened to reveal a clean, open concept apartment, nicely decorated in cream and brown. Ana sighed with relief. "Nice place," she commented.

"Thanks." Cathy glanced around and then motioned toward the hallway. "Phone's in the bedroom if you want to call your friend." Cathy took off her shoes and tossed her purse on the couch. She grabbed her curly hair and rolled it into a knot before heading to the kitchen. "Can I get you anything? A drink?" she called back.

Ana popped off her shoes and peeled off her tight jacket. "Peppermint tea would be nice—if you any."

"Sure, feel free to stay the night if you need to by the way. I have some extra blankets in the closet," Cathy called back.

Ana appreciated the offer. "Thanks, I'll let you know after I make that call."

⚘

Cathy grabbed the kettle from the counter and filled it with water at the sink. She'd been so deep in thought she hadn't asked Ana more questions about herself before offering to let her stay. But despite having just met her, she felt safe in her presence. The earlier empty feeling of despair that had overwhelmed her was gone. She was glad to have company—even if for a little while. Her thoughts still felt blurry.

How much alcohol did I have?

Suddenly a wave of distrust shot through her. *She could be some kind of thief or worse!*

Cathy took a deep breath to calm down.

What's wrong with me? She came to find me. Everything's fine.

Ana emerged from the hallway and walked to the kitchen. "My friend Susan thinks I should stay the night. Good thing I called; she was worried." She came up beside Cathy. "Thanks again for letting me stay." She leaned on the counter.

"No problem. The couch is actually pretty comfy." Cathy handed her a steaming mug of tea.

Ana tilted her head. "If you don't mind my asking, how old are you?"

Cathy put her hands on her hips and turned her head to strike a model pose. "How old do I look?"

Ana squinted at her. "Not a day over sixty…" She grinned.

Cathy laughed. "Fine, I'm twenty-six. What about you?"

"I'm nineteen." Ana blew on her tea as they headed to the table. "So what do you do to afford all this fancy stuff?" Ana asked.

Cathy sat down across from Ana. "I'm a manager at the grocery store." Cathy took a sip of her own tea and then shook her head. "Some days are good, and some days…well, I contemplate shooting myself in the foot—so I can call in sick. Let's not talk about work. Makes me feel like I'm there right now. What do you do when you're not partying?"

Ana didn't know what to say. "I don't really party much. I'm in my second year at Ryant."

"Oh, yeah? I got accepted there a few years ago, but I didn't end up going." Cathy took another cautious sip from her mug.

Ana leaned in closer and rested her chin on her hand. "Why not? It's such a good school; anyone would kill to go there."

Cathy's seemed surprised at the question and shifted uncomfortably. "I'd rather not talk about that either." A few strands of her hair came undone as she shifted in her chair.

Ana felt like she was alone at the table as Cathy stared blankly into her cup. Finally, Cathy zoned back in and tucked her hair back behind one ear.

"It's a long story." Cathy pushed back her chair and stood. "You know what? We should get some sleep. It's really late, or early…whatever." She shook her head. "I'm exhausted, and I have to go to work in the morning." She flashed a weak smile.

Ana couldn't help but feel she had touched a sore spot.

"I'll get the couch ready for you," Cathy added as she walked away, mug in hand.

Ana sat at the table and stared as Cathy disappeared into the dark hallway.

~

Beth's hospital room faded out into a doctor's office. Ana stood in the corner. Cathy was stretched out on a table covered with a sheet and her feet in stirrups. A doctor and nurse hovered busily over her.

Beside the young woman stood two other beings. Ana could see the walls through them. One being absorbed all the darkness of the room, while the other shimmered and pulsated with light. Ana tried to see their faces but couldn't. The beings in the room apparently went unnoticed by the doctor and the nurse.

"Number one is here," The nurse concluded after some time had passed. She removed the tube that connected under the sheet. The dark being swelled as he rested his hand on the shoulder of the blonde woman in the bed.

The bright being placed a hand on the young woman's stomach and reached into her. He cupped his hands as light pierced through his fingers.

"Every good gift comes from the Father of lights," the being said somberly. A rush of wind and lights swept through her, ruffling her hair as it spoke into her spirit. "This one must return…" echoed the voice.

"All right, we're finished. Please wheel her into the recovery room." The doctor started to peel off his gloves.

"That's it, Cathy," the nurse told the woman. "It's done. You can wait until you're ready to leave and then go home."

Ana watched as Cathy solemnly and slowly rose from the table and sat in a nearby wheelchair.

Every good gift comes from the Father of lights.

The dream dissolved as Ana jolted awake. She glanced at her watch. *Four in the morning. I've only been sleeping for half an hour?*

Her mind began to process revelations from this dream she remembered from the curb. No way I'll forget that one again. But what about the dreams connected to those other people?

She closed her eyes and turned over on the couch to snuggle deeper into the blankets. The jogging pants and oversized T-shirt Cathy had given her smelled faintly of laundry detergent. No longer sleepy, Ana sighed. She stood and shuffled toward the kitchen in hopes of at least having another cup of herbal tea. Cathy probably wouldn't mind if she helped herself. As she filled the kettle, she heard a faint whimpering from down the hallway.

❧

In Cathy's room, Dree sank his sharp talons into her chest. He absorbed the empowering anguish that radiated from her chest to her fingertips. Tears streamed to her pillow as she tried to will herself to die.

Yes. Death will end what you're feeling so you'll never need anyone again.

Dree enhanced the self-destructive thoughts in Cathy's mind, and when her thoughts drifted to Kevin, he amped it up.

Kevin doesn't love you. No one ever loved you.

She glanced toward the nightstand at an old picture of the two of them.

Dree took advantage of her gloomy thoughts and played back a series of sad memories of Kevin. They'd fallen in love quickly—hanging out, clubbing, and becoming lovers. Their life together had been quite simple until she realized something was terribly wrong with him. First, she'd noticed his sudden mood swings. When he'd consistently come stumbling home early in the morning, with bloodshot eyes, refusing to talk, the unraveling had started. He would sleep all day into the evening, demand food, and then do it all over again. The nightly disappearances started to stretch into days at a time.

Her anger resurfaced as Dree intensified her feelings of frustration. Cathy saw herself accusing him of cheating on her. Kevin had flatly denied her accusations. When she'd threatened to leave, he finally admitted to having a drug problem.

Dree continued to speak negative thoughts into her mind: *It's your fault. You knew he had a problem, and you didn't stop clubbing before he relapsed. You weren't supportive enough. He couldn't withstand the pressure you brought into his life.*

She had learned that when he would go missing, she could do nothing but wait. But this time, weeks had passed, and she wondered if he would ever find his way home.

You didn't help him. He'll never come back home. Alone—you'll always be alone.

She wept, trying to shake off the hopelessness that overwhelmed her.

He won't be able to handle the stress you've created. If he doesn't come back, you should kill yourself.

Dree was winning, but he knew he was on shaky ground as long as Ana was in the house. He knew what she was. He was desperate to maintain his hold on Cathy at all costs, so he continued to press his destructive messages into her mind.

If he really loved you, he wouldn't have left you.

The weight of Dree's hypnotic words played over and over in her mind.

Maybe the reason he didn't come home this time is because he loves someone else. He must if he's not here with you.

Her chest burned as fresh tears streamed down her checks.

Dree sensed a shift in power and looked up. He was running out of time. *Death is the answer. Embrace it and let go.*

A low knock at the bedroom door distracted her from her depressing thoughts.

"Hey, are you okay?" Ana's voice was muffled through the door.

Wiping tears from her eyes, Cathy called, "I'm fine."

"I didn't mean to wake you up...I thought I heard crying."

"No, I'm fine. Go back to sleep," Cathy said.

"Cathy, can I come in?" Ana prodded.

Cathy stared at the door and sighed. "Yeah, come in."

The instant Ana entered the room, Cathy's red, puffy eyes clearly revealed that she had indeed been crying. Ana sat down on the bed. "Want to talk?"

Tears came to Cathy's eyes. She was silent for a few minutes. When she finally gained control of her emotions, she began to share. "My boyfriend left me, and I don't know what to do. My life is unbearable. It's spiraling completely out of control. I can't win—no matter how hard I try."

Tears streamed from her eyes. "I don't think I can do this anymore. I just want out." She began to sob as if her heart were breaking.

Ana felt sorry for her and searched for the right words. She hadn't expected Cathy to break down like this.

"I don't really know what to say," Ana started. "But when I saw you at the Eclipse, I felt an overwhelming sense of sadness. I can't imagine what you're going through, but whatever it is, I can promise that you have so much to live for."

She felt uneasy. She tried to quiet her internal apprehension and get in tune with God like she once had.

Jesus, what is it?

Quite suddenly, she knew exactly what Cathy needed to hear. "You know, God wants to heal the pain you feel right now."

"I don't know about all that. I'm not religious. I don't even know if I believe in God."

"God believes in you." Ana shifted her weight and stretched her legs off the side of the bed. "When I fell asleep earlier, I had a dream about you. I saw something very precious was taken from you, and an angel carried it back to heaven." Ana strained her memory to recall the rest of the dream.

Cathy's eyes suddenly grew wide and then filled with tears as she sobbed. "What...do you mean? What are you talking about?"

Ana's heart was beating fast, but she knew she had to continue on before she could change her mind. "I don't know. You were in a place that reminded me of a hospital. An angel took a package of light from your stomach, and when he did, he said, 'Every good gift comes from the Father of lights.' When he was gone, you were wheeled out of the room."

Cathy sniffled and wiped tears from her face. "How could you know about that?" She stared in amazement and shock at Ana. "Do you work at the clinic? Is this some kind of trick?"

Ana was confused by her response. "No. I…I don't know how I know. I had a dream; God showed me." Ana shrugged.

Cathy stopped crying and took a few deep breaths. "Do you know what the light was?"

Ana shook her head. She'd never seen anything like that before.

When Cathy spoke again, her voice cracked with emotion. "I think it was my baby."

Life

"...So that you may proclaim the excellencies of Him who has called
you out of darkness into His marvelous light" (I Peter 2:9, NASB).

A FEW MINUTES passed as they sat on her bed. Cathy tried to hold
back her sobs and finally spoke again. "Several years ago I decided
to have an abortion. I didn't tell anyone—not even my boyfriend at the time.
I thought having a baby would ruin my life." Cathy pushed her hair behind
her ear. "After the procedure was over, I was so angry and depressed that
everything became a blur. I never thought I would get pregnant as a teen."
She shook her head. "I never pictured myself having an abortion. I was a
mess inside so I distanced myself from everyone. I barely made it to the end
of my last year." She swallowed. "I know people say it's not a baby yet, but I
never believed that. I remember the machine and the tube that was used; the
whole process was so horrible—like a nightmare that never ends. Sometimes
I dream that I'm playing with my baby, and he's such a happy boy."

Her eyes lit up, and she smiled even though her face was soaked in tears.
"I can see his round, pink cheeks when he giggles..." Cathy stared off as if
looking at an apparition of her son. Ana shifted closer and patted her leg.

"When I didn't know what to do… I used to pray—please God, take care of my baby. And after the abortion, I just wanted to know where my baby was and if he was okay." Cathy's hands knotted the edge of her blanket. "I always wondered if God answered my prayers."

"I believe your baby is in heaven with God," Ana paused and shifted on the bed. "And Cathy, He wants to set you free from this guilt." Tears filled her own eyes.

Cathy's eyebrows furrowed. She stared blankly at Ana. "Why are you crying?"

"I don't know. Partly because of what you said, but even more because I can feel how deeply God loves you. He wants you to know Him and to be free from the weight you've been carrying all these years." She covered Cathy's hands with her own.

Cathy looked down at the knotted sheet she held and the hands covering hers. "How do you know that? I don't deserve to be free. I deserve this guilt. Maybe I'll just do it again." Her voice was harsh. Cathy looked down at her stomach. "This one's probably better off without a mom like me."

Ana followed Cathy's eyes, realizing the implication of her words. *Cathy is pregnant again!*

"Cathy, no matter the circumstances—your baby's life is a gift from God." Ana tried to make eye contact with Cathy. "God can and will forgive your abortion. His heart breaks when yours does because He loves you more than you can ever imagine. He died for you. He wants to take care of both you and your baby."

Cathy's eyes once again filled with tears. "Why would God care about me? After what I did?"

Ana looked down for a moment, searching for the right words to explain. "Parents love their children—even when they make mistakes, don't they? And whenever their little children are hurt, loving parents want to kiss away the hurt and make it better. That's the way God loves you—except His love is more intense and deeper than earthly parents."

Cathy was quiet before she finally spoke. "I'd like to experience that kind of love. But what if He rejects me?" she held onto the knot in the blanket.

Ana shook her head. "God won't reject you if you're seeking Him. I can pray for you if you want."

Cathy slowly nodded. "Okay."

When Cathy let go of the blanket, she joined hands with Ana.

Ana began to pray, "Heavenly Father, I come to You now in the mighty name of Jesus. I thank You that I met Cathy today. I thank You for Your love for her and that You have amazing plans for her life—whether or not she can believe it right now. I pray You would give her strength to trust You. Please show her how real and amazing You are so she'll never doubt it again. I know You love her and her baby more than she can even imagine, and that You will forgive her for everything she's done in the past. I pray, God, that You would bless her because You want the very best for her all the days of her life."

A wave of despair filled with regret came over Ana. She remembered the darkness she had seen hovering over Cathy in the club and knew it was trying to distract and derail her prayers. She found the words that had once been so familiar to her. "I…I stand against any work of Satan that would try to harm her or cause her to hate herself. In Jesus' name, amen."

❧

Dree witnessed a shimmer that quickly morphed into the angel he had seen earlier. The angel's sword was drawn, and his wings were fully open.

Fighting stance. Oh, no, not again…

Dree knew he had already lost his hold over Cathy. His scaly flesh quaked in the presence of the holy angel. Knowing his time was almost up, he removed his talons from Cathy and lunged with all his strength at the angel. The angel tossed Dree like a rag doll into the corner. Dree wished at this moment that he was at the Eclipse where he could outnumber and overpower this nuisance of an angel.

He scampered back and tried to bite the angel's leg. He just couldn't give up without a fight, but he'd been around long enough to know he was no match for him in his present weakened state.

Dree arched his back in pain when the angel's sword pierced him. He let go of the angel's leg and rolled out of the way. Dree sneered as Ana continued to pray, totally oblivious of what she was doing to him.

"Lord, help Cathy to trust and receive Your love and forgiveness." She opened her eyes and got Cathy's attention. "Cathy, if you want, you can ask God to forgive you, and He will. He's listening right now, so talk to Him."

Cathy nodded. "Dear God, I pray that You'll forgive me." Her voice broke. "I'm really sorry for what I did. I can't even imagine what it would be like to be free of this guilt. Heal me, please, and take away the pain I've been carrying. I do want to live."

An enraged Dree growled, and in a flash, he was gone.

સ

"Cathy, Jesus is God's Son, and He died for you on a cross and rose from the dead so you could be made brand-new and have a close relationship with the Heavenly Father. He's promised never to abandon you. You can give Him your life right now."

Cathy listened and then prayed again. "Jesus, please come and be with me. I need You." She remained silent for a moment and then said to Ana. "Did I do it right?"

"Yeah, you did. Do you feel different?"

"I do—lighter."

Ana opened her eyes. Cathy's countenance had changed; she looked peaceful and hopeful—for the first time since they'd met.

Ana smiled. "Wow, Cathy! You pray like a pro!"

"I used to pray at night as a kid." Cathy smiled back.

Ana stood to stretch her legs. "There's another part of God I didn't mention yet. God gave us the Holy Spirit after Jesus left the earth. He's here to teach us, comfort and encourage us. You can also ask Him to come to you now."

"*Holy* what?" Cathy giggled.

"Just close your eyes again and pray with me, okay?" Ana began to hum for a few moments. She raised her hands and with a smile, she whispered, "Holy Spirit, come..."

~

"You got here quickly," Sasson commented casually to the flash that materialized beside him.

"You know how it is!" He said as the light that surrounded him dissipated. "This is one of those events that was set in motion years ago but was only confirmed last week. So here I am! I am Yonah."

Sasson nodded. It was easy to forget that things were always in motion toward God's purposes.

Yonah looked at Cathy, his face filled with awe. Even though he knew she couldn't see or hear him, he spoke to her. "Welcome to the family, Cathy, daughter of the King, child of the Most High, Yeshua…" Yonah bowed as he mentioned the name of his Master. "You needn't worry because I'll be keeping a good eye on you again."

Yonah smiled at Sasson. "So it has begun."

Sasson chuckled, feeling lighthearted for the first time in a very long time. "I was beginning to think I would lose my place in Ana's life and be reassigned, but things are back on track now. I wish you'd been here earlier. You missed some powerful prayers," he motioned to the kneeling women. "They've been like this for a while now."

Sasson continued, "We have a lot to do over the next season. I was shown what was to come in order to get ready for tonight. The record of future events indicated that Cathy would hear the gospel tonight and possibly receive—clearly, she has. So we need to move forward."

Yonah nodded. "These two are now in place, and shortly others will follow suit. Those who are already going strong need to develop their giftings. We need all hands on deck."

Sasson nodded. "Once we meet with Kavo and the others, things will start to make more sense. Some of the humans have already begun receiving revelatory onars and are positioning themselves accordingly." Sasson paused briefly, considered and then added, "The visions and dreams have helped them realize the need to come into alignment with God's plan."

"And if the set-apart ones are not in place in time?" Yonah searched Sasson's face. "I have long waited to see the goodness which already exists in our realm played out in this temporal plain."

Sasson nodded, understanding exactly what he meant. Yonah didn't want to sound negative, but he'd had enough of seeing the worst that could happen many times over. "I too am eager to see this generation receive what has been stored up for them. But no matter how it turns out, we must not become impatient; we've waited too long."

As the ladies sang praises to God, Sasson started to smell the familiar, exquisite fragrance he'd known since ancient times. The soft, sweet scent drifted in and settled over the room. The weight of peace descended as they sang.

He's here!

Instinctively and without a word, Sasson and Yonah knelt and lowered their heads to the ground. Now that the Perfect Counselor was here, the time had come to rest and worship. Sasson was once again astonished at the incredible love of his Maker.

He loves them so much. He comes down just to be with them. God was singing over them, and they were answering him.

෫

Ana didn't want to stop singing because each word was a reminder of what God had done and what He would do in the future. She sang the songs so Cathy could hold those promises close to her heart. Plagued by thoughts of how she had closed her eyes to all God had done in and for her caused her to cry. Thoughts of Pastor Matthew and what had happened to him still hurt. But as she cried from a place of pain, the Holy Spirit's voice began to speak to her heart.

I love you, and I have been leading you back to Myself. You will not be moved from My plans for you. Receive My refreshing for the days ahead, for I have touched the tender scars and restored what has been stolen away. I love you; I love you.

⁓

The next morning came quickly. Ana awakened to the smell of toast and coffee. Because it was Saturday, she felt no need to rush. She had a fleeting memory of another dream where she saw Jesus walk out of a tomb. Two angels in white stood around, smiling at her as He walked toward her with open arms. She'd run into His hug where she felt incredibly secure and never wanted to leave. And even now after the dream had ended, she still felt as if she was wrapped in those same strong arms.

Ana flipped over on the couch again, hoping to go back to sleep in Jesus' waiting arms, but her stomach growled, demanding attention. After dozing again for a few more minutes, the beast in her belly began to roar. She rubbed her eyes. *What time is it?*

She peeked over the edge of the couch. Cathy was up, moving around in the kitchen. Ana rose and made her way over.

"Morning!" Cathy sang as she sipped from her mug of coffee. She was dressed and looked like she'd been up for a while, which Ana found hard to believe.

"Aren't you tired? You look so...alert."

"Well, it is eleven, and I have to be at work in thirty minutes." Cathy glanced at her watch. "Hey, help yourself to whatever you can find to eat."

"Thanks. Don't worry about me." Ana grabbed a mug from the cupboard. "I'll have some of this, then I need to get home." She poured herself coffee.

Cathy went to the front closet. "Last night was like...really cool!" She slipped into a black jacket. "I've never felt so happy in my entire life." She beamed. Her hair was neatly pulled into bun to go with her work pants and company shirt. She looked fresh—very unlike the drunken woman from the previous night. "I have to get going, but do you like...go to church or something? 'Cause if it was anything like yesterday, I'd like to go with you."

Ana's stomach churned. *Good ol' church.*

She looked down into her mug and shifted her weight to lean on the counter. "Sure, I guess we could do that. We can go tomorrow. Give me a call tonight when you get home."

"Okay, leave your number for me on the table. I have to run or I'll be late." Cathy shoved her keys in her pocket. "When you leave, just close the door behind you. It will lock automatically, and I'll see you tomorrow." Cathy waved and disappeared out the door.

Ana sighed aloud. "Oh, boy..." *How will I face everyone?*

Ana sipped her coffee, realizing she no longer wanted any. "I guess I'll find out soon enough."

CHAPTER 5

Confessions

"Confess your faults one to another, and pray one for another, that ye may be healed..." (James 5:16, KJV).

HOPING TO RETRACE her steps from the previous night, Ana tried to figure out which way was fastest to get home. When she finally found a bus stop, she stared off into space as she waited. The day looked dreary with the sun's hiding behind layers of dark-cream and gray clouds. Her skirt and jacket provided no more warmth than they had before.

"Ana? Wow!"

A voice startled Ana from her thoughts of returning to church.

"I haven't seen you in so long! How are you?" Ana looked up to see Leah, an old friend, walking toward her. Her straight brown hair flowed down to the middle of her coat and curled at the ends. Her glasses did little to mask her beautiful eyes.

❧

Sasson drew his sword.

The demon Sakron, who had been hovering over Leah, dropped to the ground with a chuckle. His faded, rusty armor appeared as Leah spoke.

47

Sasson noted the difference between their armor. Since the rebellion and their subsequent fall before the dawn of time, the fallen angels had been stripped of their automatic regenerating power. Forever cut off from the source of power, they were nothing more than old, distorted shells of past glory. Their only hope was to perpetually wander the earth, looking for hosts and trying to gain footholds in human lives for power. But even with a human host, they were always in deficit.

Only the anointed cherubs' armor radiated like the sun in pure gold and white that resembled polished ivory. Sasson felt his own armor begin to surface. He cautiously stepped back.

Sakron sneered, eyeing Sasson's drawn sword. "Brother, is that how you greet me?" Sakron hissed and then laughed.

"You are not my brother," Sasson replied in a no-nonsense tone.

"No, but there once was a time," Sakron said, "and a time coming when you will regret not turning with us."

"Never!"

Sakron flashed a crooked smirk. "The world is changing, and our age has finally come. Our kind will soon dominate the likes of you."

"We all know what the ancient books have foretold. Your time is only a fleeting moment, and then you will be destroyed," Sasson answered.

Sakron laughed and towered over Sasson. "Who will stop us? The feeble humans you rely on?" He moved closer to Ana.

Sasson stepped protectively in front of Ana and pointed the sword at Sakron's chest. "Their inheritance will never be yours."

Sakron grabbed the blade of the sword. "On what grounds do you draw your sword against me? I will crush you!" Sakron threatened, showing his jagged teeth. As he held the sword, his armor flickered back to reptilian scales as his power was drained. He grimaced the longer he held on. He tried to hide the pain, but Sasson could see the hot white light shoot through his hand, searing his lizard flesh.

"Stand back or I will call in reinforcements," Sasson ordered forcefully.

Sakron edged forward. "Ha, you have no grounds! Don't think I have forgotten the ancient laws."

"Stand down!" Sasson ordered, not budging.

"Fine," Sakron snarled as he pushed the sword back at Sasson. "I do not want your *little one*," he spat, eyeing Ana. Her inner light shone bright, bouncing off his dead eyes. "I have my own." He patted Leah on the head with his thick, scaly hand. His talons flickered into the gray image of a normal man's hand. He laughed. "This one has my full support—as long as I can control her."

"Your kind will have no footing here. Your kingdom is failing. Your lust for power will never be fulfilled," Sasson reminded the demon. "I was there when you fell from heaven, and I will be here when you are driven from this place."

Sakron circled around Ana, studying her from head to toe. "I remember this one. He put his mouth close to Ana's ear and growled. "You can't guard her forever." He snapped his teeth at her and then turned a taunting smile toward Sasson.

Sasson pointed his chin toward Leah. "Neither can you," he retorted.

Sasson looked toward Leah and felt pity. He knew this demon well. His methods were different from those of others. He had gained his power by living through his host and leading her into deeper darkness and deception. While other demons generally remained hidden, he knew that Leah was aware of what she did for Sakron—although he was sure she did not know the full extent of her captivity.

Leah had a dual future with King Jesus that existed only now in the book of promise—the Chazown. Every human started life with a blueprint designed by God, filled with the dreams and destiny God had planned for each person. The plans could be changed, but never corrupted. The Chazown would remain untapped potential if she never turned to Christ, and death cut short her life on earth.

Leah's destiny with God could be one of great power, but she would be destroyed if she didn't give up the life she was currently living. Sasson couldn't understand why anyone would choose evil over good, but he did understand that she had faced much pain. Her bitterness had driven her down this path. Still, hope remained for her—especially now.

Ana felt a shiver run up the back of her neck. "Leah, it's been a while."

Leah looked around. "I've never noticed you taking this bus before. Do you live around here?"

"Uh…I was visiting a friend I met yesterday." Ana had a thought. "We're checking out church tomorrow afternoon. Would you like to join us?"

Leah smiled sweetly, giving Ana's short skirt and obvious clubbing attire a quick once-over. "Did this *friend* happen to be a male?"

Ana's face flushed. "No, not at all! There was this girl—uh, never mind. So you in for church?"

"I've already made plans. Maybe another time?"

Although Leah was smiling, Ana felt as if she had somehow offended her. When the bus pulled up, Leah said, "Ugh! I just remembered I left my planner at home. I can't survive without it. Maybe I'll see you around."

Ana nodded and disappeared onto the bus.

By the time Ana reached her neighborhood, the sun had broken through. The gray clouds were giving way to a pale-blue day. She thought about the last twelve hours. A new feeling of purpose and excitement rose within her. Cathy needed her now. After all she had seen, she knew spiritual warfare was real; she would never be the same again. Cathy had almost never been helped. If she hadn't seen the darkness and gone after her, she shuddered to think if Cathy would have killed herself.

God had led her to Cathy, but how many more people out there need help?

Several children ran past her and disappeared around the corner, "Jailbreak!" one yelled. They were only playing a game, but how many people were trapped in a spiritual prison and didn't know it? She had been set free.

Sunlight trickled through the barren tree branches that hovered over her street. She shivered, hurrying up the concrete walk toward the side door of her two-story home. All she had to do to end this long adventure was sneak inside. The original plan had been to change before coming home, but she had left all of her stuff at Susan's. The last thing she wanted was for her mom to see what she was wearing.

Ana was careful as she unlocked and quietly closed the door behind her.

She kicked off her shoes then crossed through the kitchen and padded up the stairs. Safely in her room, she stripped off the accusatory clothes.

She hoped her mom was enjoying a slow day, too busy pampering herself to notice she was home, or better yet, maybe her mom was already out since it was well past noon. Ana knew she needed a nap to survive the rest of the day. She had much to think about and consider. Many things needed to change, starting today.

After choosing some pink flannel pajamas, she slipped into her welcoming bed. She felt immediate relief as her cold, aching feet touched the soft cotton, and her body heat warmed the sheets. Sleep intoxicated her, weighing down her eyelids like a drug. She had barely drifted into a dream when a knock on the door jolted her. *So close!*

As she buried her face into her pillow and groaned, the door creaked open and closed. Ana rolled over to look at her mom. Sandra stood with her back against the door. Her soft, black and gray curls covered her shoulders as her arms folded over her chest. Her large glasses perched on her nose were unable to hide the angry creases that had already formed on her face. Ana's nap looked less likely.

⁂

Aarao, Sandra's angel came in and stood next to her.

Sasson glanced at his old friend and asked, "What kind of day has it been for you?"

"You know—the usual—bitter thoughts, anger, happiness. It's been an all-over-the-place kind of day. I've been trying to get her to settle down and pray, but she keeps finding things to distract herself. She's worried... but, I heard you had a fun night."

"Not at the beginning! But yes. At the end it was quite refreshing. He came in beauty and splendor."

"Oh, for times like that again," Aarao said, looking at Sandra.

Sasson smiled. "Don't worry. More will come. I can feel it throughout my being."

Yes, I sense this." Aarao looked up. "How is she doing?" He nodded toward Ana.

"Ana's had a busy morning. She's not listened yet, but I'm hoping... I've been given much to tell her." Sasson stood behind Ana and touched her forehead. "She's asking questions, which is good."

Aarao smiled. "All right then! As always, I will try my best with her mother. Hopefully, this confrontation will not end badly."

❧

"Well?" Sandra accused.

Ana felt her mom's penetrating gaze like heat on her face.

"You know how sleepovers are," Ana sat up.

"Well, I called Susan's house last night, and her mom told me you all went out to a club. You now have three seconds." Sandra's tight lips disappeared further into her angry face.

Ana raised up her hands as if to fend off her mom's biting wrath. "Okay I did, but something great happened!" She hoped her enthusiasm would distract her mom from her disobedience.

Sandra stepped closer to Ana's bed. Her voice was low and steady. "Ana, are you listening to yourself? You lied to me. Not only did you lie, but you went to a club, and Susan's mom knew about it! We're supposed to be the ones with the open, honest relationship." She folded her arms again. "What kind of example are you setting for your friends about what Christians are like? Susan has more respect for her mom than you do for me, and she didn't even grow up in church."

Deflated, Ana sighed. "I'm sorry, Mom."

"Where, oh, where did I go wrong?" Sandra's voice sounded broken and teary. "I raised you the best way I knew how. I worked so hard." Sandra threw up her arms melodramatically. "I provided so you never needed anything after your father left." She paced the room. "I set a great example for you by being focused on living right..."

Ana sighed. *Here we go again. Death-by-guilt trip.* She rolled her eyes toward the ceiling as she clenched and unclenched her fists. *Forget the nap!*

Mom could go on like this for hours—rehashing small details of life, starting with her father's abandonment and her many struggles to make ends meet. Ana remembered the long, rehearsed speech from her childhood. *Blah,*

52

blah, blah…ends meet, blah, blah, father gone… As a child, she had thought "ends meet" was some kind of ground beef. She envisioned her mom's slaving over a big black pot stirring a brew like a witch.

She did feel sorry for her mom, and remorse always overwhelmed her during their arguments but, at this moment, something stronger than guilt changed her mind. "Mom," she interrupted, "I'm sorry I lied. I don't want to do it anymore. I'd like us to try and have a different kind of relationship."

Sandra shouted, "Ana, you've been acting crazy for months, and this is just the icing on the cake!"

"I don't want to fight with you, Mom. Please just let me have a nap, and then I'll explain everything." Ana eyes pleaded with her mother.

Sandra sighed in defeat. "All right, Ana. I'll see you downstairs."

Hours later Ana stretched and rolled over in bed to face the window. The sky had dimmed to early dusk. She hadn't planned to sleep so long. After she showered, she pulled on a pair of ripped jeans and a T-shirt and headed downstairs to the kitchen. Her mom sat at the table, flipping through a newspaper while a pot steamed on the stove.

"Well, hello there!" Sandra said with her gaze still on the paper. "I was beginning to think I wasn't going to see you until tomorrow."

"I guess I was more tired than I thought." Ana ran her fingers through her wet, curly hair and sat down to face her mom. The room was clean and organized. From the smell of baking chicken that filled the room, Ana guessed at what her mom had been up to. Her mom always cleaned or cooked when she was in a good mood, so she felt hopeful.

Where to begin?

Ana leaned forward and put her elbows on the table in front of her. She rested her chin in her hands and looked up at her mom. "Last night I was dancing at the Eclipse, when all of a sudden, I felt kind of sick…"

"Did someone put something in your drink?" Sandra interrupted as her eyes narrowed.

Ana shook her head and continued to recount the events of the night.

Sandra's frown deepened. Her anger was obviously on the rise even though she was quiet. Unable to maintain her silence, she finally yelled, "What were you doing at the club anyway? You put yourself at risk to find some woman you didn't even know? With all that's been happening in Tehly lately? Were you drunk? What if something had happened to you?" Sandra's face was stricken.

"Mom, just listen! I was totally safe, and you're missing the point!" Ana could feel her own emotions mounting. She was an adult too and deserved much more freedom than what she'd grown up with.

Sandra continued her tirade. "The point is that I raised you differently. I always hoped you'd never stray. I guess I failed. I never saw this coming. I told you about the young moms I work with. Did you learn anything—anything at all from my life experiences?" Sandra vehemently shook her head.

"We both know it's not that simple. You made all the right decisions, and Dad still left. No matter what you do, you can't guarantee that bad things won't happen. Life doesn't work that way."

Sandra's eyes pleaded. "Ana, is this about Pastor Matthew? You have to let it go. You can't live your life recklessly because of what happened."

Ana felt her heart start to pound. She didn't want to talk about Pastor Matthew. Ana sat back in her chair, almost ready to give up. She decided to try. "Please let me finish," Ana stated calmly to fight her own growing frustration. She didn't want to give into it—not with all that had happened. "Just hear me out."

Sandra nodded.

As Ana came to the end of the story, Sandra suddenly stood, causing her chair to screech backward and echo in the silent room. "I don't know how much more of this I can listen to..." Sandra walked away from the table, once again folding her arms across her chest.

Ana nodded, anxious to make her point. "Through this experience, I realized I never want to live that way again. I feel like I'm called to more than this. I see the pain around me, and I want to be a part of the answer. Of course, I know that Jesus is the only answer, but now that I see what's at stake, I don't want people to die and go to Hell."

Sandra squinted at her daughter, still shaking her head slightly.

Ana could tell her mom believed her. All she needed was more time to process the story. Her mom always could tell when she was lying. Plus, it'd been a long time since she'd humbled herself to apologize. If that wasn't a sign of change, then nothing was.

"I don't want you in nightclubs..." Sandra started.

"I'm done with them."

"You need to be honest with me all of the time—"

"You have my word."

Sandra surveyed her again, "I forgive you, sweetheart."

Ana's mouth dropped open. *What? This was way better than I expected...*

Sandra bent over to give Ana an unexpected kiss on the forehead. The tension in the atmosphere was suddenly gone.

"This is a very interesting story. You'll have to tell me more about Cathy later." Sandra sighed. "So which church will you be attending? Mine or the new one?"

Ana hadn't given it much thought. She'd forgotten about the changes while she'd been away. "The new one, I guess. I don't think I could handle being at Good News Remnant right now."

Sandra gave an understanding nod. "Okay, then. Dinner's ready." Sandra grabbed her purse and got ready to leave. "I'm working with a few new moms at the church tonight. I'll see you when I get home—if you're still up."

Ana watched her mom leave. Life with her was hard at times, but she never doubted her love. *Is it possible not to be absorbed in the sadness that permeated Mom's life—after the struggle we've been through together?*

Things were different now. They were financially stable, and she was no longer a child but her mother still seemed determined to be unhappy. Sandra's unhappiness was like an added feature built into the center of their home, always between them. Since they'd gone years with only each other to depend on, their respect for each other had grown, but the sadness was still ever-present—tugging at her, nagging her, threatening to drown her the way it was drowning her mother.

Ana had made her decision. *I will follow God again, but not like before, and not like Mom.*

―――――

Aarao

Aarao stayed in the church, waiting for Sandra. The danger of what could be missed in the next season made him ponder the years he had been with her. She had held onto so much pain, and yet she was a rich and beloved daughter of the King.

She blamed her husband for all she'd endured, but, in reality, she had imprisoned herself by refusing to receive Jesus' full inheritance which included the ability to forgive her husband. She had judged him with no mercy, no grace—the very things that had been freely given to her. And now she was judged with the same judgment she'd pronounced on him. Something so simple held her captive. Circumstances had to change before the season of Plinim came to a close. But try as he might, his words seemed to be knocking against a barricaded heart.

Sandra carried a worn look despite so many victories she'd experienced. She was strong, no doubt, and wise, but in this one area she was blinded.

―――――

CHAPTER 6

Isaac's Well and Ishmael

"Remove not the ancient landmark, which thy fathers have set" (Proverbs 22:28, KJV).

CATHY FOLLOWED ANA up the concrete stairwell to the second floor of the renovated warehouse. As she approached the door, she felt the steady vibration of the music.

What am I getting myself into?

A freshly painted blue sign over the doors read "ISAAC'S WELL."

Funny name for a church.

She glanced over at Ana, who reached confidently for the door handle. Ana paused before turning to Cathy. "I'm just going to be honest with you, Cathy. I haven't been to church in a long time. I've never even been to this building."

Cathy's eyes grew wide. "Really?"

"I didn't want to say anything to you, but my stomach's been roiling all morning."

Cathy laughed. "Mine too. But is something wrong?"

"It's a long story, I'll explain later." Ana took a deep breath and opened the door. The suction of air tousled Ana's loose hair as she walked in.

Cathy struggled to take it all in. The room was dim except for a few faint spotlights aimed at the stage. She scanned the faces of the people. Most looked to be about her age or younger.

The room was divided into rows of chairs facing the platform followed by square areas of open space. Fifty to sixty young people danced everywhere—some with their hands raised above their heads, others between the rows of chairs. Still others knelt or lay flat on the floor.

Ana seemed more relaxed and smiled. She whispered, "I don't know why I was so nervous."

Cathy nodded.

The dark-blue carpet softened the hard surfaces of the concrete room. From the distinctive scent, Cathy guessed that the carpet had recently been laid and the walls painted.

Ana pointed to some seats a few rows away and headed in that direction. Cathy ducked close behind, trying to be inconspicuous. Once they had reached their seats, Cathy followed Ana's lead again and stood. But after a few minutes of watching others who were clearly having good time, she felt somewhat self-conscious and sat down. She glanced behind her and wondered if being seated made her stand out even more. She stood up again.

No wonder everyone is happy here—the music is lively and positive.

Cathy found herself swaying to the music. She stopped. *What if people see me? Of course, they will judge me.* She looked around again and then glanced at Ana. No one except Ana knew her or her story. And since Ana didn't judge her, there was nothing to fear.

Her mind wandered back to Friday night. God had filled her heart with peace that she had never thought possible, and she was grateful. She smiled and started to sway and clap her hands—this time on purpose.

A team of singers on a small, low platform at the front looked like they were having the time of their lives. The lead singer spun around and jumped, her hair bouncing in time to the music. Cathy didn't have much experience with church, but it was clear to her that this place was very different from most.

§

Across the room, Sasson walked about the sanctuary. The Holy Spirit was manifesting today like rain. Droplets of radiant light rested on every angel and human being in the room. Some angels had opened their wings, extending them upward like a cup. Others knelt with their wings in the same position. Angels who had no wings extended their arms upward. Bright light glimmered on each of them as they waited for more instructions.

Sasson noticed his old friends and other angels of all sizes, each doing his own part. Nine-foot angels and small-winged heavenly creatures circled the room. Some were angels of revelation while others were guardian and specific warrior angels. The gathering of the saints always held an air of excitement for all of them. He could already see the marching orders for the week alighting on the angels like mini-flames.

Sasson smiled at the extra angels assembled with them. Some who were not yet assigned to anyone were simply attracted by the worship. His smile faded when he spotted one particular angel nearby. The angel crouched with his head bowed, wearing tarnished armor. He noticed deep scratches and cuts between his thick white wings. As Sasson neared, he placed his hand on the angel's back.

"Receive the refreshing, friend," Sasson gently said.

The angel nodded but didn't look up.

Sympathy filled Sasson's heart. He had been in a similar state only a few weeks ago, though not nearly as battered as this angel. Protecting his rebellious charge was still fresh in his mind. Safeguarding another meant going into dangerous territory, often with little covering.

§

Ana scanned the room as she listened to Mark preach the message. She recognized almost everyone. They'd been her friends before everything had gone bad. *Strange…not many people here are over the age of forty.*

Destiny sat in front of her. Destiny's deep caramel skin had often made people think she and Ana were sisters. But Destiny had her own three sisters and unique style. Today her light-brown braids with blonde tips fanned out down her back. She turned to flash a dimpled smile at Ana.

After the service was over, the sound system faintly played worship music as people greeted friends and packed up their belongings to leave.

Destiny caught up with Ana, threw her arms around her, and greeted her lovingly. "Ana, where have you been?" Without waiting for a reply, she turned toward Cathy. "Who's your friend?"

Before she could answer, Mark approached the group. He was only a couple of years older than most of the young people. His short, wavy hair promised brown curls if he would let his hair grow out. He was dressed in blue jeans with a gray cardigan over a white shirt.

He flashed his familiar big, open smile. "Well, well, well, who do we have here?" Mark extended his arms for a hug.

Ana laughed and stepped into his embrace. "Mark, what are you doing preaching here?"

"You haven't heard? I've been overseeing things here for a while. Good to see you. You've been missed." He extended his hand to Cathy. "And your friend is…?"

Ana smiled. "This is Cathy. And Cathy, this is my good friend Mark, or maybe I should say *Pastor* Mark."

Pastor Mark winked in a friendly manner. "Nice to meet you, Cathy. I hope you come again. You're always welcome."

Cathy stared back shyly, a faint smile on her lips.

He turned back to Ana to ask, "May I have a moment of your time?"

Ana nodded.

"Please excuse us, ladies, I need to have a word with this special young lady." He guided Ana away, leaving Cathy to chat with Destiny.

"So you've been here since…?" Ana started.

"Yes. Things were pretty messed up, but they're getting better," Pastor Mark answered.

Ana gazed at the people around the room and sighed. "I'm glad to be here. This new place feels really like home—like time hasn't passed at all—but in a good way."

"It will feel even more like home once you've been back for a few weeks. You are back for good, right?" Pastor Mark raised one dark eyebrow and peered at Ana.

She took a deep breath. "I am."

Pastor Mark held her gaze. "How have you been though? Really?"

"I'm okay." She felt like he could see right through her. "I think things are changing for the better. I've been wasting my time, but now I'm making things right with God. I had an experience the other day that really put things in perspective for me."

"That's good to hear, Ana. I'm glad. I've been praying that God would bring you back."

"I'm sorry I never returned your calls. I was avoiding everyone."

"Don't worry about it." His smile was comforting. "You've come back at a really important time. I have a lot I'd like to share with you. Can we meet some time for coffee or something? I'm sure Johanna would love to catch up with you as well."

"Sure." Ana agreed.

"I'll be in touch then."

Cathy appeared beside Ana as Pastor Mark left. "He seems nice; I like him."

"He's great. He's like an older brother to everyone."

Cathy looked around suspiciously and then whispered in Ana's ear. "So like…everyone here is so happy. I feel happier just standing here! You sure none of these people are high?" Cathy pretended to look around nervously. Ana laughed as she shook her head. "Let's go…"

~

Ana ended her call and turned up her music before flopping back onto her bed. Cathy's call was a reminder that she needed to pray. Days stretched on with no sign of Kevin. Cathy grew in her love for God, but her hurt was obvious.

Ana's stomach growled. She was so hungry that her stomach burned inside.

A three-day fast wouldn't kill her, but it was uncomfortable. Praying helped take her mind off food anyway. Whenever she felt hungry, she reminded herself of her longing for God. She wanted to glimpse heaven again so she could better understand more about His personality. The clarity in her dream life was also a perk. Fasting had a way of making her more physically aware of God's presence, which was thrilling.

She reached for her journal under her pillow and thumbed through to find a new page to record her thoughts.

> *God, I'm desperate, so keep me near You. I'm clinging to You. Everything depends on this, and I know it. I see Your dreams for me. Help me to hear Your voice. Take away my desire for evil things.*

The more time she spent with the Lord simply worshiping and praying, the more she realized how far she'd run. She looked at the bag on her chair which contained all the scandalous club clothes she had yet to return to Megan. A flyer for Eclipse was at the top of her of her full trash can. Since she hadn't thrown it away, she knew her mom must have come in to "clean." She smiled.

That she would ever try to walk away from God had never occurred to her. She mulled it over. She'd taken her relationship with Him for granted always assuming it would be there—as stable and steady as the people in her life but all that had been shaken. Nothing was sure except Jesus's love and the promise of blinding, worldly distractions, rendering her relationship with Jesus sterile. The false sense of security had distracted her from the all-out war for her soul.

"Father, the more I love You, the less room there will be in my heart for fake love. Help me to love You more. Make my desires as pure as Yours," she whispered. She prayed in tongues, overwhelmed with the Holy Spirit's energy coursing through her. *You love me, God; I just need to be obedient to what You show me and walk closely with You. I don't want the pleasures of false love. I want to experience Your real, enduring love without barriers.*

Ana closed her eyes and pictured herself catching the rhythm of His words by dipping her hand into a flowing, sparkling brook. The brook was always moving, and she simply had to jump in. The words "My daughter" pierced her heart in an instant, and then love's quiet beauty appeared and took shape, morphing into a multifaceted diamond. No matter which way she looked at it, it sparkled with truth that burned her heart.

She wanted to fast—if only she could taste of Him. He filled her emptiness. Pastor Matthew's smile flashed in her mind.

This is what he tried to tell me.

He had often said there was so much more than what he had taught her. The truth was that she had depended on Pastor Matthew to tell her everything. Now she wanted to open her hands, so God could personally fill them. *How long will this last?*

૪

Sasson worshipped next to Ana's bed, and Aarao was nearby as she prayed. A light breeze brought a perfumed scent. The melodies of heaven tinkled and softened the boundaries between the heavenly and earthly realms. Sasson could hear the faint whispers of "Holy" circling in the room. Working on this plain had its own adventures, but heaven had a beauty that could penetrate and transform their very being. God's presence was so pervasive in these times of prayer; who could resist transcending straight into the throne room? Sasson and Aarao joined in.

Sasson received vivid pictures of the trials prepared for Ana. He also saw pictures of the beauty awaiting her as her spirit became strengthened and perfected.

"You've been given instructions for her upcoming tests?" Aarao asked.

"I've only been told to hedge her in. She must identify and pass tests as she learns to depend on God," Sasson replied.

"What of the present?" Aarao said as he looked over at Ana.

"This is a time of blessing, refreshing and digging deep trenches so she can be filled. If she goes deep during this time, she will be well-prepared when the warfare begins. The days ahead are dark ones." Sasson towered over Ana. His armor flickered over his skin, as it often did when he spoke of battle.

"She's obviously been given the calling of a restorer and a protector. We need to align her with the others soon. With these ones, a battle is always looming on the horizon," Sasson continued.

"That must be the reason for the numerous tests," Aarao reasoned. He stretched out his wings, taking up the full span of the room. He then folded them back as he sat down.

Sasson sighed. "During the lifelong process of being proven, she'll understand who God has made her to be."

"Her rich heritage and inheritance will help. Let's stand in agreement that she will not fall victim to the same pitfalls as her mother," Aarao offered.

"The purposes and plans of God never cease. His word will not return void. They will stay at work in Sandra even now. But, yes, we do need to stay on guard. The Enemy will try to thwart the restorers in this city. Ana will help prepare the way." He paused and looked at her again. "She must succeed."

Aarao walked closer to Sasson and gripped his shoulder. "By God's power and love, friend!" Aarao drew his sword to meet Sasson's weapon as they had often done in the past.

"By His grace and forgiveness, brother," Sasson said as their swords touched and began to gleam brighter together.

～

The scent of roasted coffee beans permeated the air of the shop. Sasson hovered over Ana where she sat near the back with her friends. Mark's guardian—Kavo, and Johanna's angel—Rahos, hovered with Sasson while observing the three humans crowded around a small wooden table.

The large windows illuminated the shelves of books to borrow that lined the exposed brick walls. Other customers poured over books and steaming drinks.

As they talked, Mark told Ana about his new ideas for the church. He exuded an excitement that all of the angels recognized.

"Things are moving along well," Kavo commented. His large muscular frame took up the space between the two other angels.

Kavo remained a renowned leader and had been for many centuries. In another time he had led the invisible attack with myriads of horses and chariots of fire that had protected the prophet Elisha. For a leader such as Kavo to be reassigned to another country was quite unusual. Sasson suspected that Pastor Mark's involvement in the city would also eventually expand.

"What strategy is your charge planning?" Sasson nodded his head toward Pastor Mark.

Kavo soberly considered Sasson's question. He looked around the room at the other angels as well as the demons that accompanied some of the customers. "Follow me." He unfolded his wings and flew out through the roof of the shop.

"He is trying to gather the churches together. That he accomplishes this goal is imperative." Kavo finally responded.

Sasson and Rahos followed him until he landed just outside a nearby apartment building. Kavo walked a few moments, stopped and raised his hand. "I want you to listen. What do you hear?" Sasson closed his eyes and listened. He heard nothing.

Kavo spoke again. "Rahos, do you see that object sticking out of the ground?" He pointed to something jagged and brown jutting from the pavement.

Rahos nodded.

"Take a look below ground."

Rahos bowed to the ground as though he were praying and inserted his head in the ground like it was water. When he came up, his face was stricken. He tried to shake off what he'd seen.

"No, Rahos. What you have seen is very real. Sasson, what do you hear?" Kavo said.

Sasson suddenly thought about the strange vibration he had been hearing of late. "The sound of silence choking creation," he answered.

Kavo and Rahos were silent.

Kavo motioned for them to keep walking. "I know you've been out of the loop as of late, Sasson, but I figured you would realize what has been going on. The season of Plinim is ending in only a few weeks." He turned to face Sasson. "It's good that Ana has awakened and come back to the Lord right before the spiritual season came to a close. Now she has the opportunity to reap the rewards that have been stored up for her, but this city is crying out because of the distress within its gates. If the church is not positioned to receive the outpouring soon, the city will not be able to align herself for the end times. Only dark days will lie ahead of us. The sooner Pastor Mark can gather the churches in the city the better."

Sasson followed in step with Kavo. He was only permitted to see the written heavenly record of what was to come at crucial turning points. Even then, he could only observe what directly affected Ana. He pieced bits together, but like the humans, he was only part of a puzzle and needed the other angels for full revelation. "So the city will play a role in key events that will affect the world?"

Kavo explained, "Yes, Tehly city's specific prophetic destiny lies on a different timeline of prophecy than the church body, but all are of equal importance. The Annals say when the church moves toward her destiny of power, this city will be transformed. The Saints, the Holy Ones, need to be in place to receive the outpouring of power set aside for them now—before it's too late. Without the outpouring of power, they will not be ready to fight in the next season. Their spiritual bodies will not be mature enough and ready to withstand what is to come.

Kavo continued. "The violence has been prophesied to end, and the people strengthened. The prophecy also declares that many Holy Ones of great power will be sent out from here, but that is of no consequence now if we cannot complete the first step. Pastor Mark is trying to position the church body for the outpouring, but he is being met with great resistance."

Sasson listened as they slowly headed way back to the coffee shop. They passed by storefronts and buildings—some carrying the mark of God and others the mark of evil.

Kavo started. "Every kind of violence is on the rise. The body of believers in the city is disjointed. How can they move forward on the continuum as they should? As we speak, many fall from the ways of the kingdom, and time is running out." Suddenly Kavo sounded as old as he was. The grief in his voice was unmistakable. "I myself am weary of flying to and fro, alerting the brethren that we must bring everyone together again. These incredible people of faith do not realize the strength they have in unity."

Rahos continued where Kavo left off. Tears gathered in his eyes. "It's stubbornness. Every one of them has an agenda. Keeping the Holy Ones open has been very difficult. I have also seen the pain and the violence, but today was the first time I saw that…the underground rebel strongholds are growing. Rahos' eyes pleaded with Kavo. "Johanna can help with this. Why must we tolerate that underground?"

"Rahos, Johanna is learning and growing. As she grows, you will be made aware of more. Be patient." Kavo reminded.

Rahos shook his head. "Is it a ruling principality? Why are they calling more demons to the city gate?"

Kavo stopped walking and looked fiercely at Rahos. "It is unclear for now. All I know is we must do our best to prevent the scales from shifting."

"If that happens, it could take decades to uproot their work," Sasson added.

Kavo shook his head. "Discouragement is poison. Don't think its poison will not affect us. It is the cause of the lost ground."

As they continued to converse, Sasson received more truth. "If there is no reconciliation, then we are in for decades of this." Then he spoke as an oracle. "As the season of Plinim ends without the outpouring stored up for the saints, those born into the Spirit at this time will have great difficulty."

Kavo stared at Sasson. "The reconciliation will happen," Kavo declared.

"But there are those hanging onto the revelations—refusing to act on them," Sasson said.

Kavo was firm. "Those who have been waiting and praying have not given up. God will break the hardness of the others hearts."

"What would you like me to do?" Sasson asked.

"Keep Ana aware so she will press into God. Transformation will ensure that she's ready once everything else is in place. When the time is right, she will be given instructions."

"The division in the body of Christ was only the beginning, but the Enemy used it well." Kavo looked down calmly. "The church must unearth its true destiny if we are to succeed. I have passed this vision on to Pastor Mark, and he seems to fully understand his role. He has also been given direct access to the record of prophecy by God. I'm not sure of what he has seen, but it will come to light very soon."

"Good, then his leadership will help those with him." As they returned back to the entrance of the coffee shop, Sasson added, "I assume my charge also has an important role to play?"

"All of them do, Sasson. But before that, their hearts must be prepared for what is coming."

&

"Much has happened since you left," Pastor Mark continued. "As I said before, you've returned at an important time, and I really believe God led you back to help. What you went through a few weeks ago is remarkable. Maybe you and Cathy can share one Wednesday soon." Mark leaned forward in his chair.

Ana asked, "What happens on Wednesdays?"

Johanna answered, "Oh, that's when we hold the prayer and Bible study group we started a few months ago. We're trying to get more happening on different days of the week. Some are really new to the faith, and we need more time to teach them."

"Sounds good. Cathy would love that. She's so eager to learn that I can't even keep up with her. I've given her new books, Bible studies, and devotionals. She finishes them in a day! I'm running out of things to give her."

Mark smiled at Johanna. "That's great! We need more of that all around."

Ana sensed he had more to say. "So what's the deal? What did you want to talk to me about?"

"Well," Pastor Mark hesitated before firmly placing his mug on the table. "I wanted to know if you'd be up for teaching dance at the center. I know I'm asking out of the blue, but please consider it. They have an opening for some creative arts and are in desperate need of someone."

Johanna leaned in. Her long dark brown hair flowed over shoulders. "I could help, but I'm a bit too rusty to start a program like that right now. We both felt you would be perfect."

"I haven't even been back a couple of weeks, and you guys already have plans for me?" She laughed. "You must be desperate!"

Mark smiled, shrugging his shoulders. "Hey, you're the one getting all these visions. You didn't see yourself dancing in one?"

"Nope." She laughed. "Tell me when and where, and I'll think about it. Can I let you know in a few days?"

"Take your time. I've been praying about it for a few weeks now. I don't want you to just teach dance; I want you to teach worship dance. I think that is what Pastor Matthew would have wanted."

Ana's fingers tightened around her cup. She stared down and refocused her thoughts before glancing back at Pastor Mark.

"What about Pastor Matthew?" she whispered, feeling slightly afraid of what she was asking. She glanced toward the door. Part of her wanted to go through it, hear the chime behind her, and be safely away from her painful thoughts.

Pastor Mark glanced at Johanna before answering. "He was really interested in the community center before he died. I'm not completely sure why yet, but Wella mentioned that to me a few months ago. She told me to start looking into it. She was having a hard time but still made sure to I knew about it."

Ana swallowed a lump emerging in her throat. "I don't know how well I'd be doing if my husband of forty years was murdered at church…" In her mind's eyes, the awful scene replayed. She closed her eyes as the dull ache in her heart revived briefly. She caught herself and tried to focus on Jesus' love for her until she could blink away the tears that threatened. Pastor Matthew wouldn't want her to spend the rest of her life grieving. He would want something life-giving to come out of his death.

As if afraid to break the silence that had fallen on them, Johanna whispered, "I know, Ana; his death was hard on all of us." She gently took Ana's hand in hers.

"We all loved him and still miss him." Pastor Mark's voice broke before he cleared his throat. He wrapped an arm around Johanna's slender frame and pulled her close. "Wella spoke at the old church a few Sundays after the media circus quieted down. Even through her tears, she shone brightly with the love of God. She commissioned all of us to carry on the work Pastor Matthew started."

Johanna shifted in her chair and rested her chin on her hand.

Pastor Mark reached over to rub her back and then leaned closer to continue. "You can imagine why Pastor Steve blamed all of us. He said if we had just done what they were supposed to do instead of trying to bring so much change, then Pastor Matthew wouldn't have died…" He sipped his hot chocolate. "…since the guy who shot him was one of the new visitors."

Ana rubbed her forehead. The murderer had never been found. "I don't understand how he could have blamed us for something so random." Ana felt a rush of emotions. "I remember after Pastor Matthew died that church just wasn't the same. The anger…everyone pushed his own agenda. I felt desperate to get away, find a time to recuperate, but then, I just didn't want to go back. I focused so much on my own pain that I forgot about everyone else. But I did hear that you guys had planted a church." Ana's mind started reassembling the many events and emotions that had marked her year.

"Oh, you mean the *great split*?" Johanna noted sarcastically.

Mark frowned and then added, "That wasn't a church plant, Ana. I'm surprised your mom didn't tell you what happened."

"What do you mean?" Ana scooted closer in her chair.

Mark continued. "One day during the service, Pastor Steve was preaching about order and obedience. Anyway, the message was blatantly directed at some of the young adults, and Ishmael stood and argued with him right on the spot."

"In front of the whole church?" Ana shook her head. Ishmael had been one of the young leaders in training. He'd been an intense gifted speaker, but Pastor Matthew had rarely asked him to speak at special meetings.

"Then what happened?"

"As you can imagine, the service became tense. The atmosphere was emotionally charged after the murder; people were just waiting to take sides. You could feel the thickness in the room. Ishmael said he'd had enough of the old way of doing things and started talking about a fresh start. He said he was going to continue what Pastor Matthew had started and then invited whoever wanted to see changes to come with him. He walked out of the church, and people followed."

"Wow, just like that? That's horrible!" Ana fell silent as she imagined all of the work Pastor Matthew had poured into the youth—only to have this happen.

"So that was the beginning of the church. Glorious, wasn't it?" Pastor Mark's voice held a notable edge of sarcasm. "I didn't want to go with them, but I felt the Holy Spirit's nudging, leading me there to help bring everyone back together somehow. So we obeyed and left after a few weeks as well. For the most part, it wasn't as bad as I thought it was going to be in the beginning. The church functioned fairly well all things considered, and people even came to know the Lord. I stayed in the background."

"Ishmael preached each week and served as the overseer. I tried to talk to him about doing things properly, starting with asking forgiveness from the former church, so we could have the full blessing for a real church plant. He wouldn't hear of it, insisting they were the ones who should apologize." Pastor Mark stared into space. "He was so sure he could do things better, and that was his first mistake." He picked up his mug and took another sip.

"Some of the group that Pastor Matthew had been training felt convicted about the breakup and wanted to go back to the old church. He just shut them up."

"Why didn't you both leave?"

Pastor Mark shrugged. "We felt like we had to fix things or be there when it fell apart. It didn't take long for that to happen. People started noticing Ishmael acting strange. Everyone was confused when he stopped preaching the Word and started giving weird messages about finding your own truth and type of heaven. When he began to look haggard, everyone was already suspicious. People suspected he was addicted to some drug, but he tried to blame his appearance on the stress of starting a church. He didn't fool anyone."

Johanna shook her head. "The work was a mess, Ana. Ishmael had made sure that Jesus was no longer the focus of the church. He wanted it to be more like a social club."

"We gave up trying to convince him and started to pray. But as we gathered, what was happening became clear, and the results were devastating. One day Ishmael didn't show up for church, and no one has seen him since. Rumor spread that he was sleeping with some girl from the church, but no one really knows. The congregation was wounded and still wants answers."

Ana tilted her head in question. "So how did you end up leading?"

"Well, after Ishmael disappeared, what was left of the leadership team prayed and felt I should lead." Pastor Mark sighed and sat back in his seat.

Johanna spoke up. "Then we officially named the church 'Isaac's Well.' In the Bible Isaac re-dug the wells of his father Abraham. We realized we don't need to cut ourselves from the past to move forward. We need to work with those who went before us. There's absolutely no reason we can't reverse some of the damage that occurred. The church's name is our reminder of that goal."

Pastor Mark bit his lip in deep thought. "Listen, I don't want you to think it was all bad. Some good things did come out of all this, and thankfully, a lot of issues solved themselves as we got back on track. I've been working for the last couple of months to plan a special worship and repentance event—a *reconciliation,* if you will.

"I know God has a vision for this ministry. But the division that started this church is like spiritual baggage that we need to get rid of in order to end all of the disunity and community violence. God has been showing me that the roots of this church need to be cleansed."

"What's next?" Ana asked. All of a sudden Pastor Mark and Johanna seemed older to her. The reality of what they'd gone through hit her. While they had been fighting for truth, she had been running and trying to forget.

Pastor Mark bit his lip. "I've invited our old church to the new building, and I've shared with some of the leaders what I'm trying to do. I really want us to partner with our parent church. If we could officially repent and have them bless us and walk with us, it would be amazing. I've also asked a few of the churches in the city to gather with us on that day. I believe a reconciliation will bring honor to God. We've been praying and waiting for all of the leaders to accept our invitation."

Ana frowned. "What will you do if they decline?"

"I believe we're doing right. If they refuse, then there's nothing we can do." Pastor Mark stared through the space between Johanna and Ana. "The church plant is what Pastor Matthew was preparing us for, but this isn't the way he would have wanted it."

CHAPTER 7

Temptation

"But each one is tempted when he is drawn away by his own desires and enticed" (James 1:14, NKJV).

"COME ON, ANA! It'll be fun! You're always busy these days," Susan cajoled through the phone receiver. "Megan thinks you're trying to avoid us—because you're doing all that churchy stuff again."

Ana stood up from her desk and stretched as she held the receiver to her ear. She had been studying and realized she had lost all track of time. "No, honest. I've just been busy. My volunteering with the kids takes up more time than I thought it would, and I'm kind of helping this lady I met. I promise we'll go out soon. Maybe for dinner sometime?" She walked over to flop on her bed.

"Ana, what is wrong with you? That cute guy you met at Eclipse has been asking for you. Go out with him! How many guys would try so hard to get a girl's number when she runs away like you did? You're lucky he didn't think you were weird or something." Susan giggled. "Actually, he probably does think that!"

Ana could almost see Susan grinning through the phone.

"I thought you wanted to meet a nice guy and be in a relationship—especially after that creep Greg—" Susan tried again.

"Listen, right now I just need to keep things simple." What if I told Susan what had happened that night? Neither of her friends were Christians, but she had known them for years—both while she had served God and when she hadn't. She considered. They'd seen her in her best and worst moments and still loved her in spite of her apparent hypocrisy.

Guilt nagged at her. Her notebook and books on the table were calling her name again. "Okay, well, why don't we meet up later tonight for dessert or something? I could use a break."

"What about the party this weekend?" Her tone was the most serious Ana had heard coming from her in a while. "*He* invited you."

"Oh, my…he did?" Ana feigned excitement. "I wouldn't miss that for the world!"

Susan sighed. "I'm serious! I'm trying to live vicariously through you. If you'll just cooperate, we can both be happy."

"Not going. And let me remind you that you didn't want to live through me when I was talking to Greg!"

"Hey, you should have listened to the stories."

Ana groaned. "What stories? I heard nothing…well, Megan was the only one who warned me." Of course, at the time, Megan's friendly advice had sounded like jealousy. For Megan to discourage her interest in a guy had been so uncharacteristic of her friend that Ana had thought Megan had been interested him.

"Well, I'm warning you right now you should snatch up this guy!"

"So I'll see you later?" Ana changed the topic with a sudden craving for chocolate cake.

Susan sighed. "Fine, meet me at seven at Tom's Desserts. Don't be late. I'm sacrificing my diet for you! That's true loyalty, my friend. I'm taking a bullet for you."

Ana laughed. "Well, then I better get back to studying so that I will not be too busy to miss your great sacrifice."

"Finally, the mystery woman returns…"

Ana looked up from her menu to see Andrew grinning at her.

"Uh, hi?" Ana looked around and behind him.

"I was beginning to think I had only imagined you," Andrew responded. He scooted into the soft, plush red seat across from her. "Susan called and said you wanted to meet me here."

Ana's eyes opened wide. "No! I told her I didn't want to see you."

"Sorry?" Andrew ran his hand through his hair. His handsome smile faded.

"I mean…" She shook her head. "I mean, I think there's been a misunderstanding."

I'm going to kill her.

Andrew picked up the menu and casually started reading. After a moment, he set it aside. He was clearly holding back laughter. "Okay, I asked her to set it up. I wish you could see your face." He picked up the menu again.

Believing that Susan had actually tricked her took a moment to comprehend. She scoffed and glared at Andrew. "Listen, you seem like a cool person, but let's get one thing straight. If I wanted to go on a date—which I don't—I wouldn't need people to manipulate me to make it happen." She grabbed her bag and slipped from the booth.

He stood to block her leaving. "Wait! After all of my hard work, you won't even stay long enough to share a dessert with me? What's this world coming to?" He joked.

Ana was not impressed. She stalked toward the door.

He jogged ahead to block her way again. "Whoa! Hey, I'm sorry! I didn't think you'd react like this. Susan said you were easygoing…"

Ana sighed. "I'm sorry. I don't mean to be rude. I had a long day, and you caught me completely off guard."

"I know the feeling," he offered. "Please, don't blame her. She didn't mean any harm. I'm a pretty nice guy, and I just had to see the hot girl from the Eclipse again."

"That's just it; that wasn't—isn't who I am…I mean, I wasn't even wearing my own clothes…" Embarrassed, she looked away.

Andrew stopped her. "I don't care. I mean you're still beautiful, but that's not the only reason I had to see you. I don't usually do things like this. I just couldn't stop thinking about you—even after weeks." He glanced behind him at the door and shrugged. "Maybe you could take off the sprinting shoes for a couple of minutes so we could have a full conversation? I hear this is one of your favorite places." He pointed to the booth.

Ana looked over and then back at Andrew. She remembered how bewildered she'd felt in the club when he'd come over. His smile, the butterflies—there had been a definite connection and he was still tall and handsome. Even if she didn't want to admit it, part of her wanted to get to know him better. A few people in the restaurant were staring at them. She sighed and followed him back to their table.

"Ana," he whispered breathlessly as they sat down. "What's your last name? Who are you, and why do I want to marry you?"

Ana giggled, although she felt a little like he was serious. "I'm nineteen, I'm just a girl, and I think you're crazy."

He picked up his menu and smiled. "Just crazy about you."

"Wow! If you're going to lay it on this thick, we may have to skip dessert. I have a low *fakeness* threshold."

"All right." He extended his hand to shake Ana's. "I'm Andrew Norris, and what you see is what you get. Some people think I'm funny, and I work at a bank call center. I'm nowhere near as interesting as you are. The great lengths you would go to avoid a date astound me. I mean running out of a club in sub-zero weather after a girl you don't even know? That alone begs for a story. "

"If you play your cards right, I might tell you what happened after I left."

Andrew became serious and stared at her for a moment. "Hmm... I'm already intrigued, but I'll leave that for another day." His eyes twinkled. "Do you like to dance?"

"I do, but not in the way you think."

"You are just shrouded in mystery, aren't you?" Andrew laughed.

Ana smiled and studied him. His laugh made her feel comfortable like she'd known him for a long time. *Something else is familiar about him.*

"What'll you two have?" the waitress stood over them with a pad of paper and pencil.

Ana already knew. "I'll have the Chocolate Explosion, please. With some milk." She handed the menu to the waitress.

"Make that two Explosions," Andrew echoed, before casually tossing back the menu.

The waitress fumbled to catch it. Ana held back a laugh when she saw the angry glare the waitress shot at him before she left.

"One main thing you should know about me…" Ana started. "I'm a Christian."

Andrew shifted uncomfortably. "You mean like a Bible thumper?"

"No, I not in the habit of hitting people with Bibles…although at times, they can be used as a decent weapon."

"I bet."

"Well, Andrew, I can see I've now made you a little bit unsure of yourself. You don't believe in God?"

Andrew shrugged. "I do, but I don't do church. I just try to be a decent person. I'm not perfect, but who is?" He winked at her. "But I know you'll grow to love me."

Ana stifled a smile, slightly embarrassed. "Regained our confidence, have we?"

Andrew held her gaze and smiled, forcing Ana to do the same.

"One main thing you should know about me—I never lose my confidence."

Something was happening inside of her, and it wouldn't be good. He was funny and charming—a dangerous combination against what she wanted right now. Maybe he was someone she could fall for, but falling for someone was the last thing she needed at the moment. After all that had happened that night on the curb side, she didn't want to make the same mistakes. Maybe running out of the Eclipse away from him had been the right idea.

CHAPTER 8

The Chosen

"But you are a chosen generation, a royal priesthood, a holy nation, His own special people…" (I Peter 2:9, NKJV).

S ASSON STOOD IN the church classroom where the young visionaries from Isaac's Well and their angels had gathered. The angel was present at Kavo's request. Young men and women had come together at Pastor Mark's request. Their desks and chairs formed a neat circle facing inward.

Pastor Mark stood at the front. "Guys, I'm really excited about the churches coming together again. I just know God is going to pour out something amazing on us." He smiled at the people in the circle. "Some of the leaders of Good News Remnant are really interested in knowing how we've been doing."

Sasson surveyed his brothers who stood next to their charges. What amazing gifts and talents rested on each of the human beings!

Johanna interjected. "I'm a bit nervous. What if they come and don't like how we do things?"

Owen made a face under his glasses. "If they don't like it, they can leave! They probably think we're crawling back." A few nodded their heads at Owen's outburst.

Owen's angel named Edon, who was always dressed in full battle regalia, looked at the stocky young man and wrinkled his brow.

Sasson frowned. *The poison of division seeps into everything.*

"Relax, guys. This is supposed to be a forgiveness event. We're not crawling back. We're making peace, and I sense God's hand is all over this." Pastor Mark circled in front of the desk to get closer to everyone. "When I spoke with one of the pastors on the phone, I had the feeling that many of them are actually proud of us. Planting a church is hard work. Guys, some of our parents belong to that church, and some of us grew up there. Think back. They didn't kick us out; we left."

Sasson nodded and placed his hand on Pastor Mark. "We'll do everything the way we normally do it. We'll sing the songs we normally sing, and then Pastor Mike and I will do the service. After that, we'll go back into praise and worship."

Owen nodded. "Okay, Johanna and I will prepare the worship team. We'll have to practice this week to prepare for next Saturday."

Pastor Mark smiled at him. "Thanks, Owen. What else needs to be done?" At his question, Kavo nodded at Zeb, Daniel's angel.

"I think we need to get Ana back on this team." Daniel slouched over the desk. His red hair was bright against the light-blue hoodie gathered behind his neck. He uncrossed his basketball shoes and dug the tips of his sneakers into the floor. When he realized everyone had turned to him, he stopped doodling on his notepad and looked up.

Zeb whispered in his ear, and Daniel explained, "I had a dream a few weeks ago that made me feel like someone was missing. When Ana walked back into church, I knew she was the one. I've just been waiting for the right time to tell you guys."

Destiny looked at her friends. "She's only been back for a short time. Shouldn't we wait a while? Are you sure your dream didn't have to do with Will? He'll be back soon too."

Daniel shook his head. "When Ana came back, I felt something. She was the one."

Owen spoke next. "Nah, I agree with Daniel. When Pastor Matthew chose us, he picked each of us for a different reason. I know Ana belongs with us."

Destiny shook her head then searched Owen's face, "I just think she may need more time."

Owen waved his hand. "She's fine. I think she can handle being back. She's even started gathering people together again for prayer. It's not the same without her."

"I think so too." Pastor Mark sat down heavily on the desk behind him and looked down at his crossed hands. "But I also understand Destiny's concerns. I'll pray about the matter and speak with Ana again this week. She's been really busy mentoring Cathy, but I think she'd be thrilled to come back—especially if she knows how much we've missed her."

Destiny's eyes reflected concern. "Pastor Mark, I love Ana as much as you guys, but she was really close to Pastor Matthew—probably more than any of us. Has she recovered? She was MIA for a year…" She crossed her arms and leaned back.

Pastor Mark spoke. "No one ever fully recovers from something like that, but she's dealing with it. My conversation with her the other day indicated that she's ready to move on." He paused. "Let's keep her in prayer. If she's supposed to come back at all, God will quicken her heart to that decision. I'll approach her when we're all in agreement."

Johanna nodded. "I'll pray for her this week too." She closed her notebook and started to gather her belongings, then stopped. "Actually, let's pray now—for next Saturday and for all that God wants to do."

Sasson moved beside the other angels when Johanna and Owen got up to sing. As everyone joined in, Rahos stepped forward and began to stir a section of the air below them. A swirl of light and color appeared. Nearby another portal opened on its own in the air above Johanna.

Zeb stepped over to Daniel and laid his hands on his head.

Owen's angel Edon, with his hammer in hand, flew into the portal Rahos had created. Edon was one of the few angels who never morphed out of his armor. Whenever Owen began to worship, he would demolish the work of the Enemy. Edon always had to be prepared for that to happen.

Sasson turned to smile at Kavo. From the portal above Johanna's head, streams of bright, pure light poured over her. More light poured over Daniel, Owen, Mark and Destiny as it filled the rest of the room. Sasson could see each one of the human beings strengthened. Their gifts and callings were being energized. This moment was needed.

Johanna's ability to open portals and connect to heaven had grown. She often unknowingly shifted the atmosphere through her worship gift.

Sasson looked at Destiny. The light continued to stream, illuminating her. She trembled as her eyes stayed closed. Words! She received more prophetic words then she could handle. As a prophetess, she gave others direction that they couldn't always see for themselves. Her angel Towdah was always before the presence of the Lord.

Suddenly Edon came back through the portal. His armor was dented and smudged with dirt. Sasson and the other angels surrounded him.

"Where did you go this time?" Kavo asked.

"A remote area near the city's entrance. My hammer and I took care of business." He laughed as he twirled his hammer above his head. "The demons didn't know what hit 'em."

Kavo smiled. "Good, any towers of their work that can be demolished ahead of time will greatly increase our territory. We'll all be out there soon enough."

Edon stepped closer to Rahos and tipped his head toward Johanna. "Can you tell her to do that more often?" The light that had been pouring began to dissipate now as the group finished prayer and worship.

Rahos patted him on the back. "She has no idea."

Yonah

Yonah walked in step with Cathy as she made her way home from the library. He enjoyed guarding her. Things were going great. She listened every day and grew in obedience. The light that surrounded her showed her sphere of authority, and her power was also growing.

He looked further than Cathy could see. *Something's off. Something is on its way that will threaten to shake Cathy's faith.* He glanced at his charge again.

Obedience was pure power in his realm. If Cathy stayed on this path, she would become strong very quickly. Her innocent trust in God was admirable. Her gentle smile and childlikeness had stood strong over the years.

Yonah silently vowed to do whatever he could to protect her. He placed his hand on her shoulder and closed his eyes as they walked. He whispered in her ear, explaining to her spirit what was to come. Cathy grew tense. She was too far into her own thoughts to realize what he was trying to show her. Soon she'd see for herself and then hopefully hear what he'd said. Her inner light merged with his, shining brighter as they walked the last few steps to her home.

&.

The biting cold from early morning had warmed. Cathy's coat hung over her arm, just like all the other pedestrians who passed. A soft, spring breeze brushed through her blonde curls. It had been a good day with lots of reading and preparing for the baby.

Father, all of this is so new. I'll be a parent soon, but I feel like a baby myself.

Doubt started to creep over her as a strange pressure rose at the pit of her stomach. "God, help me…" she mumbled as she walked.

I won't be afraid; You will protect and help me—like You already have.

As she neared her building, she placed her hand over her protruding belly. "It's okay, little one." But even as she offered comfort, she knew the baby wasn't the one feeling apprehensive. She walked slowly up the stairs to her apartment, silently praying. "God, what's wrong?" When she reached the top of the stairs, she noticed the outline of a man leaning against her door.

"Hey, Cathy! I've been waiting for you."

Kevin.

CHAPTER 9

The Terror by Night

"Thou shalt not be afraid for the terror by night; nor for the arrow that flieth by day" (Psalm 91:5, KJV).

KEVIN SAT AT an odd angle on the edge of the couch. Cathy sat across from him on the couch and studied him while he ate the tuna sandwich she'd prepared and gulped the soda she'd brought him. He was so thin. Dirt mingled with his scruffy beard. She had prayed for him for weeks, asking God to bring him back, but now she didn't know how to feel.

This is all so surreal. His presence made the weeks of waiting and wondering seem like only a moment. All of her prayers revolved in her mind, followed by the word *"Answered."*

Is this the answer?

Her emotions shifted between relief, love and fear. *What is Kevin's mental state?*

Nukos

The demon called Nukos hovered, looking nervously from Cathy to Yonah. *Who is this angel protecting her?* His cold gaze was locked on her. The transformation already gave her a powerful radiance. *How could her light be this bright in only a few weeks?*

"Where is Dree?" Nukos spat toward the angel.

In the time Nukos had controlled Kevin, he had never seen this particular angel.

"Gone—like you will be soon." Yonah didn't turn to look at the demon.

Nukos snarled. *How could Dree let this happen? Cathy had been ripe with death.* "You think you can get rid of me that easily?" He sneered, exposing his jagged fangs. "Kevin is completely mine. There's nothing left that Cathy can do."

"Keep your pathetic lies to yourself. We both know that if Kevin were truly yours, he wouldn't be here right now. Crawl back to the abyss from which you came, demon!"

Nukos needed a plan to dislodge the cherub even if he had to do it himself. Then he'd drive Kevin into the streets again. However, if the angel had been there before Dree, then it might be more difficult to remove him. In the time the demons had been inflicting her, the thought that Cathy may have had an original guardian had never occurred to them.

Dree's weakness might have compromised both our positions. As long as I control Kevin, I can still wreak havoc in Cathy's life. I still have time to steal and destroy whatever strength she has gained.

❦

Kevin's looked up from his sandwich. "No hug?" As he examined himself again under her scrutiny, he took another big bite. He seemingly couldn't chew fast enough to answer to the loud growls coming from his stomach. Lettuce slipped from the corner of his mouth. "Maybe after I have a shower?" he mumbled between chews. "Sorry about my clothes."

Tears of guilt flooded Cathy's eyes. She walked over, threw her arms around him, and held him in a tight embrace. "I'm glad you're back. Do you want to see a doctor this time?"

Kevin put his free arm around her. "I didn't mean to scare you," he whispered through her hair into her ear.

"I tried looking for you, but I finally gave up. Your parents said I should move on with my life because you would keep disappearing until the day you die. But I don't want you to die!"

"Wow! My parents said that?" Kevin laughed. "I'd better go see them. They sound angry."

"It's not funny, Kevin. None of this is funny." Her voice was hoarse with sadness. "What are you going to do? You won't survive like this forever."

"I can't talk about this now." He stood up. "I need a shower first." He shoved the remainder of his sandwich into his mouth and left the room.

Cathy ran quickly to the bedroom and dialed Ana's number.

Ana listened in silence as Cathy relayed what had taken place. "I don't know what to do! He's in the shower now, and he might want to stay here. I haven't told him anything yet."

"Cathy, take a deep breath and calm down."

"No. I can't be calm right now, Ana. Don't ask me to be calm." Cathy was breathless and her voice shrill.

"Let me pray, okay?

Cathy sighed in resignation. "All right."

"Father, right now I ask You to pour Your love on Cathy so that she can feel it. Holy Spirit, what should Cathy do?"

After a few moments of silence. Cathy broke the silence. "I think God wants me to just listen to Kevin and forgive him for leaving."

"That's a start. Anything else?"

"I'm not sure yet, Ana. Thanks for that. I'll call you back. He just got out of the shower."

～

Kevin wore a pair of faded blue jeans and a green shirt he had found in the closet. Although the haggardness had not left his face, he looked more like himself. He sat down in the living room next to Cathy.

She placed her hand on his knee. "Kevin, I want you to know that things changed while you were away."

"Before you say anything, I want to tell you what happened to me," Kevin took Cathy's hand in his. "I started using crack again. One day when on the street trying to get money for drugs, I was planning to steal something to eat at a gas station…when a greeting card with a picture of a family caught my eye. I don't know why, but I couldn't get you out of my mind. I felt like you were calling me back home or something." After hesitating momentarily, he added, "I'm sick of doing this to you."

Cathy nodded. "Why didn't you come back sooner?"

Kevin shook his head. "I had no intention of coming back until that happened. I knew I had a warm bed at home and that you and my family were here, but I couldn't do it. It was like I didn't even know where home was. I was so confused. Then that day, I felt lighter—like I had power, and I could actually say 'No' to getting high. So I said no for a few hours, and then it was days. Then I got sick and tried to find somewhere I could rest and get better. I…I wanted to come home sober. Cathy, I'm finally done with all that stuff."

Kevin leaned forward and rested his elbows on his knees. He clasped his hands and looked down. "I'm not even sure how I'm here right now. I've never been able to do this before."

Cathy's heart filled with hope. "Kevin, I've been praying for you, and I know God's power is what brought you back. I had an experience with God. I can't even begin to tell you what it was like, but the best way I can describe it is like refreshing water being poured over my entire life and making me clean! I gave my life to Jesus!" Breathless, she paused and smiled, waiting for his happy reaction.

Kevin burst out laughing and then searched her eyes. "You're not serious?" He tried again, "Don't you have to be…like…a better person or something?"

"What's that supposed to mean?" Cathy said, immediately deflated. "Anyone can do it. Jesus accepts everyone who asks to be saved. The Bible says He hung out with sinners. He loves us and wants us to be in a relationship with Him."

"Well, I don't know about all that," he gruffly replied, but changed his tone when he saw her disappointed face. "Maybe you can tell me more later?"

She perked up. "Of course, I will!" Cathy grabbed his hands. "I know God brought you back here, and His power helped you say 'No.' But you can't do this on your own anymore. You need Jesus' help, and you need more support."

He frowned. "That's not for me. All I need is you. I want to be with you and be a family someday." Kevin cupped Cathy's face in his hands and locked eyes with her. "I want to marry you and be with you forever." He leaned in even closer, staring into her eyes. "You're the only good thing in my life. I'm not leaving you again."

Cathy's heart pounded at his words, but she felt like crying and didn't know why. She placed her hands over his and then slowly pulled them away.

Isn't this what I wanted? her mind screamed.

Kevin didn't seem to notice her sudden mood change. He looked around anxiously. "It's getting late, babe. Let's get to bed. I've missed you a lot!" Kevin stood and pulled her up from the couch by the hand.

Cathy pulled her hand out of his grasp and sat back down. "Umm, about that. Until we get married, you'll have to sleep on the couch. I'll make it nice and comfy for you," she said brightly.

"What?" Kevin rubbed his eyes. "Have you gone crazy? Cathy, we've already slept together—many times!"

"I know," she held up her hand. "But as a Christian, I'm not supposed to act like I'm married until I am married. And I don't want you to sleep in the bed next to me either because our being that close together will be too much temptation. I've already asked Jesus for forgiveness of everything I've done in the past because I want to be pure."

"Cathy, now you're talking about being pure? You've been brainwashed!" he yelled. "Who did this to you?" His face darkened in fury. "I'm going mess them up."

She stood and faced him. Her hands balled into fists. "I'm not brainwashed!" she said firmly. She glared at him as she spoke slowly and clearly. "I'm going to obey God because He says in the Bible that sleeping together outside of marriage is wrong. She pointed to the Bible on the coffee table. "I can show you verses on fornication being a sin if you want me to. You can stay here for now, but you need to find another place to live fast. For us to live together outside of marriage is not acceptable." *If we get married.*

She didn't want to upset Kevin or cause him to lose hope. Maybe he would change his mind and get help. She'd be happy even if he only did it for her. "Maybe you can move back in with your parents," she suggested. "I'm sure they'd be happy to see you."

"I'm not going anywhere. This is my home too. What kind of person would kick a man out of his own house?" He continued to yell. "Are you part of some cult?"

His anger brought tears to Cathy's eyes. *He doesn't have the right!*

"Oh, so this is your home now?" she yelled back. Tears streamed from her eyes. "It definitely wasn't when you left me here…when I had to had to take care of the rent myself…"

"I said I was sorry. Are you going to keep throwing that back in my face? That doesn't seem very Christian." He spat the words at her.

She flushed, feeling her own anger rising. "You know what? You're selfish. You've always been selfish." She turned toward her room.

Kevin grabbed her arm and forcefully turned her back toward him. When he saw her stricken face, his eyes widened, and he loosened his grip.

"Cathy, I'm sorry," he whispered hoarsely. His eyes were wild and red. "This is a lot to come back to, I'm still a bit cloudy. I didn't mean what I said. You're right—I can probably go to my parents' house—." He sighed. "This is your apartment. Whatever you want, but I think all this extra stuff is dumb."

Cathy's wiped her eyes. "All right, I'll get you some sheets for the couch."

∼

Cathy collapsed in her bed and stared at the ceiling. She'd purposely not told Kevin about the baby although she desperately wanted to. Her loose clothing hid the bump that grew daily. So far she simply looked like she had gained a few pounds. If he were going to make a decision, she didn't want it to be based on guilt or compulsion about the baby.

Will he stay this time?

This seemed like one of the other times he had shown up sick and dirty, expecting her to take care of him—except this time he was already sober.

"Thank You, Jesus. I know You're the One who brought him home. I pray that You'll bring him to an end of trusting in himself and help him to lean on You. I pray that any evil power controlling him will go away. Amen."

Yonah stood guard at the foot of Cathy's bed. He turned toward the living room and looked through the walls.

As Cathy prayed, blasts of white light pushed Nukos briefly, but he clawed into Kevin to hold on. He remained linked to Kevin's chest in the darkness. Nukos' hand had been revealed to Yonah; Kevin had received a message from God telling him to go home.

Nukos tauntingly shook his head and stared back through the wall at Yonah. Their eyes locked as the demon's lips curled around his fangs. Nukos wasn't going anywhere without Kevin. The demon still had legal rights to him and would continue to cause mischief.

Yonah silently gazed at Cathy as he placed his hands gently over her head to help her fall into a deep sleep. *No nightmares for you.* He couldn't say the same for Kevin with Nukos attached to him like he was. Until Kevin made the right decisions, Yonah knew he would have to protect Cathy from both of them.

Kevin

In the living room, Kevin stirred in deep slumber.

Kevin glanced at Cathy beside him as he drove her on the highway to work. She was so beautiful, and she was his. He jolted out of his thoughts at the sound of Cathy's screams and the car careening out of control. The tires skidded as he forced the wheel left and then right. It was hopeless. He had to save Cathy. In one moment and motion, he reached over to secure her, but before he made contact his seat belt released. Nothing held him as they impacted another car. He felt himself smash through the windshield. "Cathy!" He awoke abruptly, covered in perspiration.

The screams echoed in his mind in the darkness, when he thought he heard a mocking laugh in his ear. When he brushed at his ear to make the sound end, the laughter faded.

He shivered.

Just a dream.

His eyes closed again, and the heaviness of sleep overcame him.

☙

Thick green vines floated in the air around Kevin. Up ahead Cathy was almost out. She stumbled as she ran, grabbing and pushing anything that was in her way. She disappeared through a thicket. Kevin kept running, thankful that Cathy was safe. Low bushes scratched his legs as he ran from the wild barking. Sweat dripped from his forehead and his limps ached as he maneuvered his way through the jungle. How long had he been running? His feet pounded the soft soil.

He jerked his head at the ferocious snarl behind him. A strange, dull-gray and black creature bounded at him. Its sharp face through matted fur made his heart skip a beat. Unlike any dog he'd seen before, its eyes were pure black and cruelly fixed on him. The creature's claws scratched the earth as it vaulted toward him, toppling him to the ground.

Kevin rolled with the barking dog and tried to protect his face. Its saliva splashed his face; claws dug deeper into his chest. The animal's bark turned into a maniacal laugh.

Kevin suddenly awakened from the dream, but the laughing continued, growing even louder. He also realized he was unable to move. Stunned, he slowly tried to form, "Caaathy," but nothing worked. *I can't move!* He felt himself falling back further into the dream—into the darkness as he tried to say Cathy's name again. After a few agonizing minutes, he snapped out of it, and his body jolted to full consciousness. As he rubbed his eyes, a cackling laugh rolled around the room. He sat up and peered around the apartment.

Nothing there. It was only another dream. Probably a side effect from the drugs.

He collapsed back on the couch and pulled the sheets closer.

Andrew

Andrew drove home in silence. He had taken a girl home, and when he had told her after a mere ten minutes that it was time for him to leave, she had looked at him like he was crazy. Hers was certainly not the look he was going for, but his mind was all jumbled. First, a forgotten memory of his dad had flashed before his eyes. Then he saw Ana. He realized he missed her and wanted to see her again to talk to her and maybe even to hold her in his arms.

He couldn't remember ever feeling like this about anyone and definitely not a girl like Ana. She was cute, a raw beauty even, but she was different.

This night was taking a strange turn. He should be blasting music and feeling high. But right now, he just felt lonely. His thoughts raced. *What is my life about? What just happened? Ana.* He wanted her although she didn't seem like the kind of girl to trifle with. The thought of not being able to have what he wanted made him feel empty and desperate. He had no place for that kind of feeling. He accelerated to get home sooner where he could leave these thoughts as usual at the bottom of a beer bottle.

Leah

Leah sat in front of her bright computer screen. Sheets of paper and books lay strewn across her desk in a messy heap. She leaned back in her chair and yawned. The history of the city seemed long and complicated. She had been researching for hours but still hadn't found what she was looking for. She lifted her glasses to rub her eyes. When she rested her forehead in her hand, her elbows felt raw against her hard desktop. The bed called her name.

No sleeping tonight. Not even going to try.

Work had to be done, and that meant bedtime wasn't an option. It had taken her a bit of time, but she had finally pieced the dates together. Tonight was one of those nights when it would be safer to stay awake. If she continued to work, she would be less likely to have to face Dionysus.

She pressed her fingertips over her eyelids. His terrifying eyes flashed before her closed ones. His perfect, handsome face spoke volumes without a word. They told stories of torture and the destruction he had inflicted for centuries. They foretold the kind of future that could only await her. Her eyes snapped open, and she quickly turned to scan the room. Her heart took on its own quick rhythm as she tried to refocus.

Sakron is here.

She recognized his thick, murky presence in the atmosphere—something she couldn't see, but felt. Fear. Maybe tomorrow she would dream of nothing instead of demons prodding and cutting her. Years ago, when that supernatural door had been opened as a result of her curiosity, its evil arm had reached out and dragged her onto this path. Her formerly friendly spirit guides had eventually dropped the masquerade and revealed themselves as the demons they were. They would not stop harassing her. That's when Sakron had come. The desire for the simple life was far gone. Her fear had intensified so that she lived in a constant state of dread, making it impossible to be in a relationship with others. Terrified of awakening in strange places after being used by the demons, she set her thoughts on burying her fear of being trapped in the abyss without a body.

Leah pushed out her own memories and aligned her mind with Sakron.

I hate everyone here anyway. No one cares about me. They are all weak hypocrites. Soon, one by one, they will all experience what I go through every day. Then they will be the ones who are sick and in pain.

First, she had to familiarize herself with more rituals. She needed historical information to cast spells across wide tracts of the land. Without the injustice and crime, doing so would be impossible. The demons needed a legal right to be invited in and to set up shop. Human against human, violence and bloodshed provided the only access. The more violence, the more land they could take; the more land they took, the more violence they could influence. Sin that spilled blood was of the greatest value—highly prized. If things were too dry, she would need to spill blood herself. She knew where to enlist help if that need arose.

Leah swiped her finger over the mouse pad. Her eyes scanned the history of the community centre displayed on the screen.

Interesting.

She had already planted curses in the soil right outside of the building. The energy around the place felt different from what she had encountered before. She had been to other parts of the city many times but had never experienced what she did at the community centre.

Maybe this is why.

Something was coming. Leah reached up to massage her shoulders and then rolled her head to stretch her neck. Whatever it was, it would be big.

I have to prepare.

∾

Dree stumbled into the underground, clutching his sides. The smell of the dank earth was a welcome change from the atmosphere above. The ground squished beneath his talons. Without a host, he would be open for torment from other demons. Cathy was now being protected by her bright angelic friend, while Dree was stuck, hiding his failure. He lurched forward until he reached the gathering point at the front of the platform.

The darkness in the cavern thickened as hundreds of demons flooded in and began to stand in ranks according to demon types and positions. Dree glanced at the black wings that beat close to the roof. Bats and other winged creatures brushed through onto the various landings that decorated the smooth rock walls. Large and small, ugly and beautiful, furry and scaled, they jostled each other as they crowded into the dark space. Tunnels and passageways under the Eclipse echoed the scrapings and moans of the amassed demons.

A watcher raven rotated its head before it dug its fierce beak into its feathered chest. Its eyes, glowing red in the darkness, suddenly turned its stare upon Dree. Its glowing gaze instantly tore through Dree's fragile pretense. Dree ducked out of sight in quiet panic and moved deeper into the crowd, afraid the bird was gathering information for Dionysus.

No one must know!

He pushed into a group of humans who were now only vehicles for demonic use. They were called the *walkers*. The vacant look in their eyes was clear evidence of demonic controllers. Even though some humans willingly came to these meetings, they were still under enchantment, beguiled by demons masquerading as beautiful other world beings with higher knowledge.

If only I'd won with Cathy. Maybe she would have been here too, Dree lamented to himself.

A bump from behind sent Dree tumbling forward. He jumped up from the ground to see an armadillo-type skin disappear into crowd. *Sakron!* Dree spat. The demon took many forms, but he couldn't be mistaken. "Always late, but has to be at the front," Dree mocked.

"You're looking paler than usual," a familiar voice growled.

Dree turned at the voice. Nukos grabbed his arm and pulled him closer.

His claws dug into Dree's arm as he held him in a firm grip. "What did you do?" he growled. Nukos' grip tightened on his arm.

"N-N-Not my fault, a girl…" Dree winced in pain.

Nukos hissed in a mad rage. "Do you know what this could mean for us? I spent the night in Kevin's dreams. Cathy's prayers caused great interference."

Dree scurried backward and lifted his arms protect himself from imminent blows. Nukos reached down and grabbed his face, his talons slicing into Dree's scales. Nukos snarled into the demon's face, "If you can't hold onto what you've got, then you aren't worthy to stand with us. Maybe I should report you—"

"Please…no!" Dree shuddered. "Give me time. I'll get her back. I…I'll hang around, and when the angel is distracted, I'll get her. I just need a few suggestions to take root."

"Fine," Nukos shoved Dree's face away. "But you'd better hurry up. If I lose Kevin because of your negligence, I'll make sure you suffer my consequences as well as your own."

Dree's head snapped up at the sound of Dionysus' foot soldiers. Their march echoed from a nearby tunnel that led out to the platform. The soldiers were covered in gray scales and metal armor. They marched out, lined the front of the stage, and bowed low enough that their brown wings brushed the floor. Dionysus, wearing a suit, followed slowly behind them and stood at the center of the stage with his arms raised high.

Nukos backed away from Dree and dropped to one knee. Dree tried to control his shaking and bowed as well.

Dionysus's refusal to come in his own form was deliberate. By coming this way, he showed his hatred for the created. He would take the place of the humans. Even with his handsome human face and slicked-back hair, he still struck terrible dread in Dree's heart.

"Dream demons," Dionysus addressed them in a careful tone.

The room rumbled as Nukos and the other dream demons stood at attention. A demon in the form of a beautiful woman stood among them. While everyone watched, the demon flashed between the forms of a handsome man and a gorgeous woman and finally materialized into what looked like a huge oozing silkworm. A few chuckled.

Dionysus looked directly at the silkworm. "Incubus/Succubus, you have done well! You've bred lust strong enough to curse large areas of ground." Dionysus always spent more time addressing the dream demons because they interfered with one of the primary ways God communicated with humans.

He turned to address the rest of the demons. "Many of you may have been experiencing interference from the enemy. Do not be afraid. These are simply signs that our time is nearly upon us. The enemy is frightened because of the power we have gained." Dionysus clasped his hands behind his back and paced behind his kneeling fallen angels.

"Dream demons, block what you can. Lead the humans toward emptiness and themselves. Build our work. The earth will quake once more, but this time the humans will feel the wrath."

Dree stared at the adorned footmen.

Oh, to have my own soldiers.

Jealousy churned in his stomach until he could taste it in mouth.

Power.

From what he knew, Dionysus had started out much like him.

"She is coming," Dionysus said. The crowd erupted in cheers. Dree cheered, too, although he had no idea who "she" was.

"When she comes, the world will be our slaves again as we terrorize them like we did in the ancient world." Dionysus scanned the crowd. "Do you remember how God abandoned us? Exiled, exposed and without armor, we, the enlightened ones, were branded as rebels and left to crawl in the dust like slugs. Our skin adapted to this earth."

The demon crowd grumbled and growled as one.

Dionysus smiled. "But we will have the final laugh as the humans lose their inheritance. How will they lose it?" He crossed his arms and smirked. "They will give it to us."

The crowd howled with laughter. The walkers laughed the loudest. Dree solemnly gazed at Nukos who stood nearby.

Dree stared at the dusty rock and earth beneath him and remembered the moment they had fallen. Reestablishing their ranks had taken some time.

Final judgment. Bound here forever.

Yet Dionysus acted as if they wouldn't all have the same destiny—as if, in the future, none of this would matter.

Dree forced his mouth into a silly grin and growled to himself, "I should be able to rule too."

Dionysus grabbed a golden chalice and raised it toward one of the human hosts. The walker marched onto the platform. The apparition of a large demon covered in brown scales and fur emerged, momentarily stood apart from its host before reaching out, grabbing the man's wrist, and slicing it with his talon. The blood began to drip as the demon disappeared back into the body and held out the arm so Dionysus could collect the blood in the chalice he held.

In the moments that followed, a wild roar echoed throughout the room as demons attacked the humans among them, spilling blood and filth over the ground. The shape-shifting bears lumbered to the centre of the chaos to feed. Screams occasionally pierced the growing din as demons sliced, feasted, and tortured the bodies present. Some of the humans were whipped while others were severed. The blood was collected in the hopes of using it for ritual desecration at some other time.

"We will intermingle with the seed of the human once again," Dionysus shouted over the chaos. Lifting the chalice to his lips, he sipped. When he spoke again, blood still coated his mouth. "Knowledge of the Creator will dim, and we will have hosts without number." He lifted his chalice to toast the demons. "Another dark age of awakening is upon us."

Dionysus' reptilian eyes fixed upon Dree, and the lesser demon understood what their leader would not say—now was the time to rule because they never would again.

CHAPTER 10

Eyes Wide Open

"But God demonstrates his own love for us in this: While we were still sinners, Christ died for us" (Romans 5:8, NIV).

A NA STARED INTO *the magnetic eyes of Jesus on the cross. His gaze drew her deeper.*

In a flash Ana stood in the bedroom of a house. "Mom, I don't want to go to church today! I'm ti-i-i-red!" a dark-haired boy whined from the bedroom.

"Andrew, get yourself ready! I don't have time for your foolishness." His mom's voice called back.

"I don't want to go, and you can't make me!" He slammed the door.

His mother yelled from downstairs. "I'm sick of this. If your father were here, I wouldn't have to put up with this. No child of mine will stay home on a Sunday by any means."

Andrew kicked his bed. He missed his dad, and church was simply too boring with all those old songs. Anger at his mom pounded inside his chest. She cared more about church than she did about him. Andrew defiantly crossed his arms. Nearby, a book lay open on the floor. Beside it, green toy soldiers were still lined up from his last adventure. Why do we always have to go to church?

He thought about a song he had heard last Wednesday at prayer meeting. The melody replayed in his memory. "...When He was on the cross, I was on His mind." At church, the older women wore big hats and sang passionately—as if they too were in the choir. How could Someone who lived thousands of years ago have thought of him as He died on a cross?

Ana opened her eyes. Now awake, intense sadness weighed her chest. Jesus' love for Andrew had been real before Andrew was born. He'd seen him from the cross and died for him even though, as a child, Andrew's loneliness and anger prevented him from understanding God's love for him. *I've dreamed this before—that night on the curb.* There was a reason something about him had stayed with her the last time they had gone out. She marveled at God's overreaching love. Jesus had died for him even though right now, Andrew didn't have a place in his life for God. *I need to find a way to tell Andrew.*

The morning sun shone through Ana's window and cast playful mix of soft light and shadows over her bed and on the walls. She remained sprawled under layers of yellow and white blankets, with her arms nestled under her pillow. The Holy Spirit's warm, familiar tingling sensation drifted from the top of her head and lightly intensified over her body as she thought about the dream and God's love. She rolled over to reach for her Bible and read for a bit. After a while, she sat up to sing. The longer she worshiped the more she felt peace and joy about her future. Love welled up in her heart for God.

A picture of Andrew intruded into her mind. A different kind of rush flowed through the pit of her stomach. His attention flattered her. She didn't want to focus on how he made her feel. She was sure God had brought him into her life for a reason. Ana tried to push the picture of him out of her mind and then decided to pray about the dream. After all, thinking about him would only lead to liking him more—still a bad idea. He didn't believe in God the way she did.

He's available.

They would be mismatched, coming from different worldviews.

He likes me. What do I really know about him? It could be so easy...

She could almost hear her childhood Sunday school teacher's usual Val-

---

entine's Day warning to encourage the kids to pray and wait for person God would bring them in the future. She really did want to wait and not make the same mistake repeatedly. Selective amnesia was only fun until the problems started to catch up.

Ana grabbed her Bible again and flipped through the pages, but her focus was gone. Her eyes glazed over the page, and instead of reading, she pictured herself with Andrew. Theirs would be a whirlwind romance with gifts, surprises and passion. Then he would get bored with her. With no common interests, they would grow bored with each other. Or he would pressure her to go clubbing or being sexually intimate. After a while she would be exhausted from trying to change him. She pictured herself morphing into a nagging, haggard girlfriend with stringy hair, wearing a large muumuu to cover the extra hundred pounds she was sure to gain. Where would Andrew be then? That's right; he would be gone. A relationship with Andrew would never work. *But*, if he became a Christian, he could be perfect, and until then, maybe he would never pressure her, and everything would be fine.

Maybe.

That her mom was so suspicious of him didn't help either. She'd only seen him once and had already warned her not to let him give her rides.

I need to focus on important matters. Pastor Mark wanted her back on the leadership team, and she had agreed to host the prayer meeting at her house to get to the heart of the reconciliation issues. Everyone was still fighting. The previous date for the event had been cancelled with no future date in the works. Even she and her mom had squabbled over the subject when Sandra had said trying to have such an event was pointless.

Ana blinked and tried to clear her mind. She stretched her arms and legs under the covers and sighed as she stared at the ceiling. Beautiful swirls of gold in white covered the ceiling lamp shade. She closed her eyes for a moment to focus on what she remembered of the melody she'd heard in heaven during her visions on the curb.

Nothing.

She released a long breath.

Why do beautiful things always have to fade?

Her heart felt the same. People needed help, and she was going to be the one to help them. Anything Jesus wanted, she would do.

If I only knew what that was.

She pulled back her white duvet and scooted to the edge of her bed. The wooden floor was smooth and cold. She swept her feet beside her bed until they hit her furry bear slippers. Pushing them on, she headed to the bathroom.

∽

Susan stood in the front doorway of Megan's house. A fence encircled the side of the two-story structure. Megan's golden retriever stood on its hind legs, resting its paws on the low fence, and barked as Ana walked up the driveway. Susan flashed an "I-know-what-you-did-last-summer" smile, and Ana guessed the interrogation would begin immediately.

Susan grinned and blocked Ana's entrance into the house with her arm. "You've been ignoring my calls since I set you up on that cool date but you need to tell me everything right now!"

Megan's dog barked as if echoing the accusations. Ana laughed and ducked under Susan's arm. She pulled off her sweater and tossed it on the banister. "Oh, you mean the ambush you sent me into?" Ana said loud enough for Megan to hear. "I was waiting to tell you what happened in person."

Susan followed her inside. "I'm a genius, aren't I?" she beamed. "You can always thank me by paying for my lunch later."

"Oh, I'll be paying you back all right—but not with money," Ana joked.

"Whatever." Susan circled her hands to hurry Ana along. "So what happened?"

Ana felt her stomach turn over. She'd thought of what to tell them, but now all she could feel was heat crawling up into her face. "We had fun hanging out. That's it. Nothing will come of it."

"What? Why?" Megan's voice sounded muffled from upstairs.

"He's not a Christian," Ana said simply. She walked to the kitchen to get a drink. They wouldn't understand, and she didn't want to hurt their feelings.

Susan argued, "We'd never send you on a date with someone we didn't think you'd like. When I asked him, he told me he grew up in church—just like you."

Ana emerged from the kitchen and leaned against the wall with her water. "I appreciate the thoughtfulness, but it's more than that. He needs to have an actual relationship with God. He needs to care about that more than anything else in his life."

Susan stared at her like she was crazy.

Megan spoke her piece from the top of the stairs. "Oh, please, Ana! Grow up…just because he doesn't live in church like you do lately doesn't mean he's not good enough for you. Don't be so picky." She appeared at the top of the stairs in a crop top and a jacket thrown over her arm. "It wasn't that long ago that you didn't want to have much to do with church and God either. Besides we're friends, and I'm not a Christian."

"It's not the same. I was going through something, and I regret how I acted. But now that I'm trying to get back on track, I need someone who will have the same beliefs and convictions." She counted off with her thumb and index finger. "Someone who will pray for me and help me learn more about God's love through my relationship with him. I want him to be an amazing husband and father because he listens to God."

Megan groaned as she came down the stairs. "I can almost see you running through a field with him already. You're wearing a virginal white dress complete with a halo of yellow flowers around your head."

Susan laughed.

Ana rolled her eyes. *This was exactly what I wanted to avoid.* She walked back to the sink and put down her glass. On her way back, she quietly picked up her sweater. She loved Megan and Susan, but she knew if she pressed her ideals, they would feel judged. Hanging out was fine, but they simply couldn't understand the deep parts of her heart she longed to share with them. Lately, it was Cathy who "got" it. Even though she was a new Christian, she and Ana seemed to be on the same page.

Megan smiled at her. "It's pretty obvious why you don't want to date him."

"I already told you the reason," Ana said.

"No, not that. You're afraid to have an adult relationship with him. You're afraid to lose your virginity."

Ana shook her head. She reached for the doorknob.

Megan blocked her path. "You know I'm right; just admit it. Megan grinned.

"I'm not afraid. You guys both know I'm saving myself for marriage." Ana folded her arms.

"Ana, you need to grow up. No guy is going to want to be in a relationship with you if he's not gettin' some."

"The right guy will," Ana stated calmly.

"Yeah, like that worked out so well for you and Greg." Megan threw back and then moved out of the way so they could all leave.

Ana's face flamed. "Why does everyone keep bringing that up? He wasn't a Christian, and that's exactly my point. I'm not doing that again." She trailed outside and waited for Megan to lock the door. "I don't get you. One minute you're warning me about a guy like Greg, and the next moment you're telling me I should date another—who seems very similar I might add."

Megan smiled and patted Ana's cheek. "That's because part of me worries about you, and the other part of me wants to push you from the nest. It's time to grow up. But you're right. Greg was a sleaze."

Susan giggled. "Megan knows from personal experience."

Ana shot Susan a look. "What?"

"Never mind about that." Megan laughed as they walked down the path to the car. "Ana, no one like you exists anymore."

"Just because you don't know anyone else like me doesn't mean I'm the only one. I guarantee you I'm not. Don't you remember when we were freshman in high school—"

"Do you ever feel lonely or like you're missing out?" Susan questioned before getting into the car.

Ana rested her hands on the top of the car and faced Susan. "I guess sometimes I do feel lonely. But a relationship won't cure that. I don't want to make a desperate decision based on loneliness. I want the best."

"But what if there's no "best" for you later?" Megan got in the driver's seat and fastened her seat belt. "What if *now* is all there is? And you're giving up all this stuff, and later you have nothing. You end up alone. Are you willing to risk that for an improbable future?"

Ana fastened her own seat belt and stared out the window. "Well, if now is all there is, then I hope my decisions will give me options I'll be happy about in the future." Regrets were always attached to hindsight. Seeing regrets attached to decisions ahead of time was impossible. *The Lord knows I already have regrets, but none of them have to do with decisions I've made for Him.* Almost all of them had been moments when she'd tried to take an easier route apart from Him. If now was all there was, she wanted to use it to follow Him.

∾

Cathy stood sideways in front of the mirror and stretched her light purple blouse closer to examine the size of her stomach. Kevin was playing video games in the living room. He hadn't moved out yet, and at five months pregnant, she was finding it harder to disguise her protruding tummy. She tugged at the skin under her eyes and then rubbed her hands across her face. She looked flushed and puffy. She turned to look at herself from the back. The baggy clothes were getting annoying. She was surprised he hadn't already guessed. He'd asked if her new style was part of being a Christian.

It's time to tell him.

She pulled on the only pair of jeans that didn't squeeze the life out of her and quietly closed the bedroom door behind her. From the hall she heard Kevin's voice drifting from the front door.

"I will get you the money. Just give me a couple of days," Kevin whispered. He stood at the front door, but she couldn't make out to whom he was speaking.

"Man, Greg ain't gonna like that," a male voice answered. "What about that? It could bring a few bills."

Cathy's heart pounded. Kevin looked at his hand and shook his head. "Nah, man. I can't. My grandfather gave it to me; I'd never sell it. This here is love." He smiled in his confident, joking way, but from Cathy's angle she could tell he was worried.

The man at the door coughed. "Fine. I'll be back. You wait too long, and you're gonna have some scary, ugly-looking dudes after you."

"Yeah, I get it." Kevin waved the man away. "Just pass on the message."

As soon as the front door closed, Cathy walked into the room. "Who was at the door?" she tried to sound casual, but she couldn't hide the tightness in her voice. She walked over to the kitchen to grab some milk.

"Nobody. Don't worry about it." He went back to the living room, plunked down on the floor and picked up the video game controller. "Can you get me a soda while you're in there?"

Cathy poured herself a mug of milk and grabbed a Sprite from the refrigerator. "I don't like strange people showing up at my door, Kev. Can you please arrange to meet your shady friends elsewhere?" Her voice sounded higher in her ears. She rounded the counter that divided the kitchen from the living room with the drinks and sat on the couch next to him.

"Do you still have your savings? Or a couple hundred I could borrow for a bit?" he popped open the can and took a swig without his gaze ever leaving the television screen.

Cathy felt hot as her heart started to beat faster. Kevin only asked for money for two reasons, and one of them involved partying and disappearing for days. "I thought you said you wanted to change. You sound the same to me." She stood up. "That didn't take long, did it?"

Kevin blinked back at her in bewilderment.

Guilt crept over her. Maybe she was jumping to conclusions.

"Babe, what's up with you? I always pay you back when I get it."

"I don't want to waste any money with all the changes coming." She brought the mug to her lips to hide the quivering.

Kevin paused his game and turned to stare at her. "What changes?"

Maybe he knows.

He gently pulled her arm down to look into the mug. "Since when did you start drinking…what is that? Milk?" Kevin made a face.

"Since I found out I was pregnant." She let out a breath she hadn't realized she'd been holding. The silence in the room thickened. She felt light-headed. Finally, she said the words. "We're having a baby."

Kevin's visibly processed the information as Cathy waited. "What? Oh…" Kevin sputtered. He swiped his hands down over his scruffy face and then up over his sandy hair. He stared off quietly and then seemed to remember Cathy. His face broke into a wide-eyed grin. "This is amazing!" He jumped up and pulled her into a tight hug. The milk sloshed over the side of the cup and soaked into the carpet.

Kevin pushed her to arms' length to really look at her for the first time since he had returned. He rested his hands carefully on her baby bump. "How did I not see this? I'm going to be a dad!" He looked around and then back at her. "You're going to be a mom," he informed her.

"Yes, I know." Cathy laughed.

"I need a job." He turned from her and started pacing. Then he hugged her again.

As he released her, Cathy stared into his eyes and saw they were sincere. She hadn't anticipated his positive reaction. The anxiety that had mounted suddenly fizzled out of her. She took another deep breath. *He doesn't want me to have an abortion; he didn't even think of it. He wants to be a family!* His happiness touched a place in her heart that had long been broken. Hope started to tear through the wall fear had built. Kevin had always been different from most guys. He was so loving, and it made her want him even more.

He embraced her. "Cathy," he said low and soft in her ear, "I'm going to marry you, and we're going to be a family." He kissed her forehead and cheek repeatedly before his lips found hers.

Gingerly she pulled away. "We shouldn't…" she started, but then her lips were locked with his.

～

The doorbell rang. Someone was early for the prayer meeting. Ana ran down the stairs to answer it. Cathy stood in front of her with wide red eyes and a puffy face.

Ana was taken aback. "What happened?"

Cathy's voice was frail. "Is there like a confession thing I have to go to 'cause I did something bad?" She rubbed her face and pushed back her hair. "I…I don't think I can be a Christian anymore."

"Come inside." Ana beckoned.

Tears streamed down Cathy's face. She sniffled and wiped her nose with the sleeve of her loose, light-blue sweater.

Ana put her arm around Cathy's shoulders and led her up the stairs to her room. Once inside Ana closed the door behind them. She pulled out a soft chair for Cathy to sit on and then plopped onto her bed.

"I've sinned, Ana; I slept with Kevin again. I'm so sorry!" Cathy choked out. "I'm not good enough to be a Christian. I told you I'm horrible."

Ana whispered, "It's okay, Cathy. You made a mistake."

"No, it's not okay. How can he love me now? I promised him I wouldn't, and then I did. I gotta fix myself up before I can be a Christian."

"God's love for you was never based on your being perfect." Ana leaned in closer. "Cathy, you made a decision to follow Him, and that means He'll never leave you. He wants to help you make wiser decisions and to keep you from sinning, but you need to listen to what you know He's telling you deep down inside."

Cathy shook her head until her curls fell in front of her face. She tucked the loose hair behind her ears. "It's true, Ana. I knew it was wrong, but I did it anyway. I wasn't going to say anything, but then I couldn't take it anymore." She sniffled, swallowing tears.

"When did this happen?" Ana asked.

"A few days ago when Kevin found out about the baby, and he was so happy I pushed my conviction out of my mind. I feel so ashamed."

Ana slid to the edge of the bed to look directly into Cathy's eyes. "Listen, it's okay. Ask for forgiveness and then recommit yourself to God. It's hard at times, but you must trust that He knows what's best for you. He'll help you avoid sin. But you also need to be more careful. You can't play with fire, or it will destroy you. You need to tell Kevin to move out."

Cathy covered her face with her hands. "I know; I already asked him to, but I don't want him on the street."

"He'll be fine. You need to focus on yourself."

Her lip trembled as she looked at Ana. "Do you think God will forgive me for this?" Her eyes pleaded. "I won't do it again."

"I promise, He will forgive you." Ana took Cathy's hand again and squeezed it. "Don't worry, Cathy. I'm not going to let you go either. We're in this journey together. Let's pray."

Sandra

The basement was packed. Sandra looked in amazement at the large number of Ana's friends who turned out to pray for the reconciliation. Teens were spread out everywhere, praying fervently without a thought about who was around them. Even though chairs had been set up, some of them opted to sit on the floor.

Ana interrupted the prayer time to share a few words. "We're here to meet with God, hear and pray His purposes into reality. I believe as we pray something will shift in the heavens. The hindrances we've been experiencing to the reconciliation are real, but we aren't here to cast blame. Pray in the spirit and in whatever way you can because it's time to push past previous levels of prayer and go deeper."

Sandra smiled to herself. She'd never before seen Ana be this bold—not before Matthew had died and definitely not after.

Before Ana had finished, the room erupted into a low, but increasing, rumble of voices calling out to God in intercession. A few people began to kneel.

Sandra was shocked. She'd never even seen this kind of responsiveness in any gathering. The young people cried out for God's presence in their lives, their church, and their city. The kids' sincere, raw love and gratitude toward God was refreshing.

Her mind flashed back to the early days of her faith: to the all-night prayer meetings, tent meetings, and fasts. Those had been the best times of her life, and she missed those moments of excitement and expectancy. But here in her basement, something powerful was happening. She dropped to her knees as well.

Stand in agreement with them. They will need it.

A rush of heat caused goose bumps to form all over her body. God hasn't spoken to me like that in a long while! She had a strong sense that God was so pleased with their hunger.

All of her years of trying to be perfect and look perfect had robbed her of passion like this. She desperately wanted it back and to feel the years of sadness and disappointment lift off and disappear.

Sandra opened her eyes and scanned the room. Something was happening. The energy was unmistakable. The room rumbled as they continued to pray. God's presence was thick and tangible—so heavy that it was almost impossible to remain upright in her kneeling position. Sandra bent lower to the carpet and began to weep.

※

Aarao faced the other guardians in a large circle encompassing the room. His wings were open and overlapped with the others. He waited while a few messenger angels delivered specific words to individuals in the room. Aarao had another message for Sandra. *Would she receive it?* He observed her lying on the carpet. There was hope in her crying; her heart seemed tender, open and humbled.

One of the messenger angels landed next to Sandra. Aarao studied the gold flecks and feathers intermingled with the angel's ivory wings. The golden sash the messenger wore around his waist was reminiscent of the color of the sunrise. The angel made a final examination of the golden message rolled up in his hand and then held it directly over her. Sandra began to pray the message.

The sound of fluttering wings alerted Aarao that more messengers were coming. The room was already packed with them and more were coming? They alighted next to the people praying and gave scrolls of prayer mysteries. Aarao closed his eyes and received more instructions.

As people prayed the scrolls, person after person lit up like a white torch. Soon the room radiated like a large bonfire, and each new prayer added fuel to the growing flame. The atmosphere ripened.

Aarao touched Sandra's head and finally gave her what he had carried— messages about her own life, the church and the influence she would have over Cathy. He instructed her not to allow her heart to grow hard toward these young ones. Unity was the source of power.

※

After a while Ana raised her head to look around. Things were coming together in her mind. The original intensity of the prayer meeting had settled into quiet. Cathy sat nearby with her eyes closed. Some of the guys had stopped pacing and were silently leaning against the walls. Ana stood in order to share what was on her heart. "Guys, I feel that part of the reason we are having so much resistance to bringing the churches together for the reconciliation is because we haven't dealt with the stuff behind the disunity."

Pastor Mark nodded. "What are you sensing we need to do about that?"

Ana thought for a minute. "Well, if we are trying to host a repentance time, we need to start with ourselves. We weren't simply divided from our parent church; we were divided from each other at the onset of this church." She looked around the room. "I was one of those who left, and I'm sorry for running. I don't have a real excuse for what I did, but I can identify with maybe some of the reasons others left. I'll go first." Ana prayed out loud, asking God to forgive her. She started to cry. Then she turned to Pastor Mark and Johanna. "I'm sorry I let my grief get in the way of my relationships with you all, which resulted in my leaving for the wrong reasons. My offence prevented me from receiving the love that you offered."

"It's okay, Ana." Pastor Mark responded. "We forgive you."

He and Johanna stepped in closer and surrounded her in a hug. After they let go, Destiny stepped closer to hug her too.

"I also think we need to forgive Ishmael," Pastor Mark added. "His anger founded the church, and then he disappeared. I know some of you have felt abandoned."

A few people around the room nodded their heads in agreement.

Owen stepped forward from the wall. "Can I pray into that?"

Pastor Mark nodded.

Owen started. "I personally forgive Ishmael for going ahead of what Pastor Matthew was planning for us. I forgive him on behalf of all of us for being presumptuous and spearheading a church split. I also repent for those of us who followed in our own anger."

Elikai, a very tall muscular guy with dark skin and dreads added into the prayer. He was one of the regular prayer warriors from the church. "Even though we don't know what happened afterward, we also forgive Ishmael for taking off."

The room was silent. A few people were joining together into small groups to pray. Destiny stood with her arm around Ana's shoulder with their heads leaning toward each other. Ana knew they were going in the right direction. Hopefully, more would follow.

"I want to go next," Sandra spoke up. "I have to admit that I've been very judgmental toward you. As one of those who represents the parent church, I want to repent to all of you for not recognizing your maturity and for judging you because of your age and what happened."

"I want to agree with you in prayer for that too." Destiny said. She extended her free hand toward Sandra. "We did the same thing to you. We haven't honored where you guys have come from and what you've been through." She clasped hands with Sandra. "We have so much to learn from you, but instead, we've let pride block that."

Cathy stood and took Ana's free arm and joined them. Soon everyone in the room was holding hands. Sandra prayed and asked for forgiveness followed by Destiny.

As the energy in the room intensified, she could feel that something important was taking place although she didn't know what. She prayed in tongues again.

❧

Sasson was busy helping other messenger and guardian angels when he turned and noticed the intense beams of light that pierced through Ana. He stopped. Kavo, Yonah, Aarao and the others didn't seem to notice. This kind of thing had happened before but not to Ana. He hadn't received instructions regarding this situation. Everything seemed spontaneous. Orbs of light rose from her body and hovered. Within the orbs were keys—the keys for breakthrough.

Sasson watched as the keys to open up healing and authority over land were revealed to him. These keys had been implanted in her from the moment she had given her heart to God, but like all angels, he didn't know which ones were present until they were revealed. They'd been hidden directly in her spirit man. As Ana prayed, some of the keys were released. Sasson could hear the faint sound of mini-explosions.

Things are breaking open in the spirit…

Others' keys also materialized above their heads. Sasson watched motionless, afraid to disturb what was happening.

❧

Ana bent over consumed in prayer. The sound around her seemed faint even though she knew she was still with everyone in the basement. God's voice was clear.

I've called you to redeem the land. I am uprooting the sin of generations. You will be My messenger in this city. My people will turn to Me and be strengthened.

A vision came to her. Everywhere she stepped, the earth split and shattered like soil broken with a plow. Dark spirits sucked up from the ground and disappeared with howls of despair. Springs of water bubbled up around her feet and soaked the dry, pale dirt and rock beneath. In the distance wild trees and valleys lay before her bathed in the red hues of the setting sun. Ana opened her eyes, and her insides trembled. *What could it mean?*

❧

The spirit realm shook violently. Sasson could scarcely keep his balance. A deep rumble below them sounded like the earth was being torn apart. The sound was so magnified that Sasson's head swung from side to side to look at the others.

Did they hear it?

Something massive had been opened. What was it? He shot a glance at Kavo, who stared upward.

The heavy scent of spikenard and sweet spices drifted into the space above the angels. Kavo knelt as a rich cloud of gray smoke filtered into the room and began to spread. The other angels humbly and quickly followed suit. *He* was here. A strong voice blasted through the cloud like a perfect melody. *Come up here!*

Holy fear coursed through Sasson's body. The thick scent and heavy atmosphere were so much like the throne room that he had forgotten he was still in Ana's basement. A heavy pressure—heavy enough to feel uncomfortable but not enough for him to feel like he was being crushed—fell over him. When it was released, he was catapulted out of the room.

~

Sasson's robes ruffled and whipped as he zoomed through the cool darkness of the night sky. Stars and galaxies whizzed past him at warp speed. He was on his way to the King. There were two ways to get to heaven—in an instant or like this. Curious as to why he was travelling this way, Sasson swiveled his head to get a better look around.

The air was filled with pictures of Ana as a baby. Another picture followed of Ana as a toddler, smiling and running to her dad. Her wide eyes were filled with the trust and innocence he remembered so well from her childhood.

A moment later, the vision shifted to Ana at age ten. Serious eyes also held compassion and laughter. Even then her eyes held the mystery of her calling. Sasson had only finally known years later when God had marked her. In the next scene, she was dressed beautifully in her prom dress. *This is strange. Why the reminders of her physical journey through life?*

In the last picture that hung before him, Ana wore the whitest, most spectacular wedding gown he'd ever seen. Sasson's pace through the stars slowed, and he landed before the golden bowls in the incense room. In this room the prayers of the saints were collected and distributed. Two large bowls stood on separate golden pillars. Smoke steamed and hovered above each bowl, constantly filling. The floors and walls of the room were of gold and brass, and each wall held beautiful carvings and moldings of people and prayer movements that had touched heaven.

"Aren't they great? All of them?" Jesus' voice echoed off the metallic walls of the empty, dimly lit incense chamber. He crossed the floor toward Sasson and pointed toward the wall. A picture carved itself—without evidence of hands—upon a small part of the wall. At that very moment, an image of Ana, her friends and the prayer group were being imprinted there.

Immediately Sasson knelt and folded in his wings. "Master," Sasson said soberly.

Jesus smiled as His eyes twinkled with joy. "Sasson! I'm very pleased with My daughter Ana. She has turned her heart to Me, following willingly and allowing everything that has hindered to fall to the wayside." He pointed to the carving. "Look at her run in the spirit!"

His King's statement filled Sasson with wonder. Why would Jesus say this when Ana was still trying to figure herself out regarding Andrew? She was still making mistakes.

As if in answer to the silent question, Jesus' placed a warm hand on his shoulder.

"Ana is a prayer warrior—one of my best soldiers," Jesus said. "I've given her a spirit of warfare, and she will fight for My kingdom. Her prayers will always fill this incense room, and she will stand before My presence as she speaks. I will honor all requests from a pure vessel." Jesus tilted His head and gazed at the last picture of her. "Isn't she spectacular?"

"Yes, she is, Master, but I don't understand…"

The picture of Ana wearing the wedding dress took on a new appearance. Truly, she was radiant. Her gown was enhanced with clear pearls and diamonds, reflecting more light and reverberating with their own power and light.

Jesus answered, "In this vision, Ana is perfect because she's clothed in Me. This is what her spirit will look like in the time to come." Jesus pointed to the gems. "Those are her spiritual rewards created from the pressure of trials she will suffer and walk through. I will be with her through all of it."

Sasson nodded.

Jesus' eyes brimmed with tears. His voice was saturated with tenderness. "She is Mine; I love her, and she loves me." Jesus moved in front of Sasson.

Sasson could tell it was almost time to go. He stood.

Jesus placed His hands on Sasson's shoulders and faced him. "I want you to take special care of Ana. After the prayer meeting tonight, I want you to deliver a message for Me." He whispered the words to Sasson.

Outside of the incense room, Sasson emerged onto a wide golden platform. The sweet smell of the burning incense from the prayers of the saints clung to his robes.

Kavo and the others waited for him in the darkness. He could see them on the golden steps that led up to the place where they worshiped. The holy citadel seemed empty except for them.

Only the occasional falling star zoomed across the night sky and disturbed the stillness. Behind scattered dust clouds, bright galaxies rested against the backdrop of the night sky that looked close enough to touch. Molded pillars of gold stood evenly spaced, decorating the inner courtyard. Embedded sapphire, rubies and emeralds made an exquisite design in the smooth floor.

"We came as soon as you left," Yonah shouted as Sasson drew near.

Sasson smiled at his brothers. He noticed another large angel among them. The angel had two gold sashes crossed over his chest that formed an "X." Each sash was decorated with semi-precious stones. This angel represented the body of Christ in the city.

"We are very fortunate," the large angel said. He turned to Kavo. "The message to you is that your charges have done well. I have been told the season of Plinim has been extended."

Kavo took a step closer. "How is this possible?" His eyes were wide with inexpressible emotion.

The decorated angel lifted his face upward. "The saints have unknowingly given what was required to tip the scales. Their love and repentance will draw many into the secret place. The fervent prayers of the saints have been answered."

"Then there's still have time for the reconciliation?" Yonah's voice surged with hope as he glanced from the angel to Kavo.

"They've already begun the reconciliation," the angel stated.

Sasson took in what the angel was saying. If the reconciliation had already begun, then there was time for the saints to be transformed.

Kavo looked around at the group. "The polluted land is still hindering some of the leaders' decisions with its implanted lies. Once the full reconciliation happens, we'll be able to release more people into truth."

The large angel addressed Rahos. "There is more to the community centre than you imagined. The rebels are planning to take it over because it is one of the last original righteous foundations in this city. You must not let this happen. They would create much harm and suffering if they gained a stronghold there."

Rahos nodded and turned to Sasson. "Has there been any progress in starting a prayer covering in that spot?"

"Not yet. Andrew and his familiar spirit have been distracting Ana. I don't think she's even thought of it yet."

Kavo patted Sasson's shoulder. "Ana is on track. I am certain she will not be easily uprooted this time."

Sasson tried to grasp at the peace of the incense room once again. Much of what needed to happen depended on individual choices that would affect groups of people.

The decorated angel spread his wings and announced, "I am being summoned." He began to rapidly beat his wings until they were just a blur. He lifted from the platform around them, and in a moment, he was gone.

Kavo turned and started walking toward the east gate, and the other angels followed. As they approached, the smooth golden floor around them changed into the dark-blue stone of lapis lazuli. Streaks of gold and white made it appear much like the appearance of the earth from outer space.

"Where is Edon?" Sasson asked.

"You know what happens to him when they worship and pray," Zeb answered. "He's underground with his hammer, preparing our path for us."

"Dionysus has been working hard. No doubt he is behind much of the evil that is happening," Kavo stated.

Rahos added, "He fancies himself a ruling spirit and a terrorizing god—much like he was in ancient times complete with temple prostitutes and worshipers. The guise of the Eclipse affords him the power he needs to retain his foothold."

Kavo folded his arms. "He wants more."

Yonah flapped his wings. "He will eventually run out of options. He won't always be able to fit into each new generation. Humans will begin to see through the ruse. The temple has changed its face, but the spirit behind it is still there. The Eclipse will be exposed for what it is."

Sasson tried to bring back the focus. "What shall be done to prepare for the gathering?"

Kavo paused. "More prayer is needed. Press it on the hearts of those for whom you are charged to care." He looked at Aarao. "I saw what happened to Sandra as well. She is now equipped to fulfill her role."

Aarao nodded. "We will do our part."

Kavo continued. "The time has come for holiness to be planted back into the ground. The purity and unity of the saints will affect the land they touch." He turned back to them. "The hearts of the fathers must turn to their children to dispel the control of the Adversary's power."

Kavo spread his wings and nodded to the other angels. After a few quick steps, he disappeared.

"Let His mercy guide His people," Sasson said. The others responded in unison as each of them, in turn, disappeared in a flash.

~

Destiny took a sip from her water bottle and then stood. She leaned closer to Pastor Mark, "I'm sensing a few prophetic words I'd like to share, if that's okay with you." When he nodded, Destiny flicked her braids over her shoulder and went to stand in front of Sandra.

"This is a night of change. Something great has happened in this city that will not be stopped. Ms. Levi, I believe the Holy Spirit is speaking to you. He has given you the secrets of His kingdom, and it's not what you expected. He's giving you 'new vision' and 'new sight.' You will mentor the next generation, and through this, you will receive the healing for which you've been waiting."

Destiny turned toward Cathy. "Cathy, God says He is going to use you to train up other women in the Lord. He sees your heart and knows you are a pure vessel. Stay obedient to God, and you will be surprised at what God will do in your life."

Cathy's eyes filled with tears, but she quickly swiped them away before they could fall.

Destiny walked toward Ana and stopped in front of her. "Ana, God says you will be instrumental in redeeming the land in this city. He will use you greatly for His glory. He loves you and has never stopped. He wants you to know that."

A picture of Jesus on the cross from that night on the curb came to the surface. His love burned within her. He would have His way. The reconciliation would come.

CHAPTER 11

Hearts of the Fathers

"*And he shall turn the heart of the fathers to the children, and the heart of the children to their fathers, lest I come and smite the earth with a curse*" (Malachi 4:6, KJV).

CATHY CLUTCHED A stack of hospital towels. Her running shoes squeaked on the tiled floor. The air smelled like a mix of disinfectant, stale rubbing alcohol and sickness—not very inviting, but it didn't bother her. In a few more months, she'd be having a baby here.

She had been at Breaker Hospital a few times in the past for different reasons, but she had never imagined volunteering. Weeks ago she had bawled out her eyes and considered giving up on her walk with God because of how she had failed with Kevin.

Now she was here, and he was with his parents. Since the prayer meeting, Sandra had been helping her get her life on track, and this suggestion of volunteering was perfect. She loved taking care of people, although Kevin thought working for free was crazy.

Kevin's face popped into her mind, and her stomach lurched. Her smothering him and trying to help him many times always resulted in the same thing—a bruised heart and being taken advantage of. She could only hope that now that he was back, he'd realize his own need for God.

She smiled at the front-desk nurse. Maybe one day she'd be able to study to be a real nurse. Being a manager at the grocery store was okay, but somehow this work felt right.

Cathy heard banging. She followed the sound to the elevators. Nearby, a short older woman alternated between hitting buttons and pounding the glass window of the vending machine.

The woman's shoulders shook. Cathy rushed over, "May I help you?"

"Oh," the woman turned abruptly. "I'm sorry. I just wanted some chocolate, and this machine won't give it up!" She slammed the machine once more. When nothing happened, she leaned heavily against it and buried her face in her hands.

"P-Pl-Please don't cry." Cathy patted the woman's shoulder. "I've had some problems with this machine myself. I'll get you some chocolate from my stash." Cathy left and quickly returned with a chocolate bar. "Here you go."

The older woman stared at the chocolate before finally taking it. "Thank you, dear."

As she fiddled with the wrapper, Cathy studied her. The deep wrinkles in her face softened. *Why, she's lovely.* She had large, kind eyes. Her pale-black hair was streaked with gray—almost as if she had colored it that way on purpose. "I think I've seen you before. My name is Cathy."

"Probably so." The woman shrugged. "I'm always here. I'm Beth." She wiped off her hand and offered it with a weak smile. "Are you a nurse?" She glanced down the hallway toward one of the rooms.

"No, I'm just a volunteer. Are you here visiting a friend?"

"No, my husband is a cancer patient here." Beth's voice cracked with fatigue. "He was admitted about three months ago. The doctors say he doesn't have much time left." Tears gathered in Beth's red-rimmed eyes and rolled down her cheeks. She took a handkerchief from her bag and dabbed her eyes. Her body began to shake.

Cathy reached out and then lowered her arms. She wanted to hug her and tell her how wonderful Jesus was and that He could help. *But how can I?*

This poor woman wouldn't understand in the midst of her pain. Cathy placed her hand on Beth's arm and guided her to take a seat in a nearby section of empty, wine-colored visitors' chairs. She placed the towels on the small magazine table between them.

"Oh, don't let me keep you." Beth blew into the handkerchief.

"You're not keeping me. I'm done. I was only moving this stuff as a favor." Cathy motioned to the towels. "If you have a moment, I'd love to chat with you."

"I'm sorry, I'm normally more put together." Beth looked up self-consciously. "I haven't slept at home for days because I'm afraid to leave him. He's been worse lately, and I'm not sure what will happen." Beth massaged her temples with her fingertips.

"How many years have you been married?"

"Forty years. Stephen's all I have. I can't imagine losing him. This sickness crept up on us. We'd planned to travel for a year to celebrate our anniversary. I don't know why God would make something like this happen to us. We're good people."

"You believe in God?"

"Yes," Beth said thoughtfully. "I guess I do. Although sometimes I hate Him for doing this to us."

"I believe in God too. He loves us, and I don't think He wanted you to have to go through this suffering, but He will help you through it if you ask Him."

"Doesn't sickness come from God? I've prayed and prayed that God would take this sickness He gave to Stephen."

Cathy leaned forward to speak softly. "Sometimes bad things just happen. God didn't do this to you. I've been reading a lot of the Bible since I became a Christian, and Jesus healed people from sickness. The Bible says He did things to show us the heart of our Father in heaven, which means that God would want us to be healed too."

Beth stared into space. "I do remember stories of Jesus' healing when I was young, but then why are we suffering like this?" She pleaded, "I may lose him, and he's always been such a wonderful man!"

Cathy rubbed Beth's back. "Don't lose hope, Beth. I know God wants to help. He really loves you."

Beth lowered her gaze. Her brown eyes were soft under tear-soaked eyelashes. "I do so want to believe that."

"Why don't we pray together? I can meet you every time I'm here and pray with you."

Beth smiled tentatively. "You would do that?"

Cathy's eyes moistened. "It'd be my pleasure."

~

"God music again? Don't you ever play anything else?" Raquel, one of the girls from Ana's dance class, shouted over the music.

Ana smiled at them through the wall mirror. "What do you have against my taste?" She crouched and turned down the music.

Brad lifted his hand. "Well, the beat is good! Then it's all Jesus this and Jesus that!"

Ana laughed. "I'm quite sure this song doesn't even say Jesus. You guys are just being biased. You can bring your music as long as it's not about anything inappropriate with lyrics about sex or drugs."

"But all of my music has that!" Brianna threw her hands in the air.

Ana smiled. "Well, then, I have just the thing for eleven-year-olds." Ana clapped to get everyone to refocus. "Okay, let's take it one more time from the top. We've been doing this hip-hop choreography for a while now, so I expect you to follow the steps even if I change the music."

The kids groaned collectively but got into formation and completed the dance.

Ana reminded them. "Each of you needs to learn the steps for yourself. If you rely on the person in front of you, then you will falter when they do. Otherwise, good job today, guys! I'll see you Friday." The kids clapped and then scattered in all directions.

Brad scooped up his bag and stood next to her. "When do we get to perform this dance?"

"You're almost ready. We just need a little more polishing, and we're good."

"But where are we going to perform it?" Christy added while she tied up her street shoes.

"Hmm…if you guys are serious about performing, we have a something coming up at my church that this could be perfect for."

Christy smiled. "Cool!"

"I'll check with my pastor and let you know at the next practice. Till then, be good!" Ana slung her bag over her shoulder, but before she could get through the door, a red rose popped out in front of her face.

"Hey, gorgeous!" Andrew greeted in a deep, sultry tone of voice. His gaze swooped over her. "You looked great in there today."

"You saw our practice?"

"Yeah. Let me show you one more move." He put the stem in his mouth, twirled her once and then dance-dipped her.

A couple of kids from class clapped and hooted on their way out of the classroom.

Ana laughed. "Stop messing around!"

"I'm here to pick you up," Andrew said as he lifted her back up. "This is for you." He handed her the flower.

She scrunched her face and grabbed the flower before any more of the kids came out. "I don't understand what you're doing."

"I'm taking you out to dinner. I'll wait here while you change."

They drove in silence for a while until he finally turned to look at her. "Is something wrong?"

"No, I was just thinking." Ana stared out the window.

"About what?" He knew he had been pushing his luck lately.

"Oh, nothing."

He took a deep breath. "Ana, you're one of the most beautiful and talented girls I've ever met."

She shifted awkwardly and then laughed. "Thanks, but we need to get you out more."

Nervous. Of course, I am. But he couldn't let up. Not now. Tension was good. Tension might get him what he wanted.

———

"The first time I saw you at Eclipse, I knew something was special about you. I couldn't take my eyes off of you. I'll probably sound like a jerk, but I usually get tired of girls. But the more I'm with you, the more I like you.

Ana looked down at her clasped hands and said nothing. They drove up to the restaurant. He found a parking spot and turned off the ignition.

"Andrew, why are you telling me this now?" she whispered.

He turned to look directly at her and then back. He shrugged. "I planned to do this with a bit more finesse, but I couldn't wait." He placed his hands on the steering wheel and looked straight ahead. "I'm hoping you feel some of what I feel when I'm around you."

He regretted the words as soon as they came out of his mouth. *I sound like a lame sixth grader. Do you like me? Check yes or no.*

She answered, "I do like you, Andrew"—as if she had heard his mind. "You have many cool qualities."

Now was his moment. "I know we've only been casually hanging out, but I'm really attracted to you. I want you to be my girlfriend."

Ana sighed deeply.

His heart beat faster. Soon she'd be locked in his arms, and he'd be kissing that sweet face—

She shook her head. "I can't date you."

Andrew drew back as if he'd been hit. "What? Why?" But he already knew why.

"I'm sure that it would be fun in some ways, but it's a bad idea." Her face looked doubtful—a mixture of sadness and regret.

Maybe I still have a chance.

"How could it be a bad idea?" He shifted in his seat until he was facing her straight on.

Maybe she needed to look at him and see what she could have...

"You're amazing! I want to be with you. So what's the problem?" Andrew's face flushed.

She flashed him a look of pity.

Pity was not what he wanted to see. Desire, attraction, anger...

Ana hesitated. "We don't believe the same things, and we're coming from

———

123

completely different places… I honestly feel like we would make each other unhappy."

"You're not making any sense, Ana. A second ago you said it would be fun."

Her fingers rubbed her right temple. "There is a lot you don't know about me."

Now I'm giving her a headache? Maybe I should shut up.

But he couldn't stop talking; he wasn't used to rejection. "Like what? You're smart, gorgeous, kind—"

Ana interrupted. "I mean about my spiritual life. I can't share that with you. It's everything to me." She shook her head. "I'm sorry, this is my fault. I should have been clear about my feelings from the beginning."

"What do you want me to do?" Andrew slumped back into his seat.

"It's not like that. You can't just do what I say so we can be in a relationship."

He looked at her and then reached to caress the side of her face. He lightly touched a lock of her curly hair, like it was a rare jewel. She didn't pull away. "Look, why don't you just think about it?" He whispered in his most soothing voice. "I mean, like really, and if this isn't for you, I promise I'll accept your decision."

He reluctantly pulled his hand away and smiled. "Just let me take you to dinner tonight."

"All right," Ana agreed, and she bit her bottom lip.

Andrew smiled. The tiny glimmer of hope that remained was enough to keep him going.

～

"I heard the good news," Ana popped her head into Pastor Mark's office. She'd stopped by the church to pick up a box of dance flags for the kids and hoped she could speak to Pastor Mark about Andrew.

He smiled and waved her in. "So much progress since the prayer meeting," he said in relief. "Thank your mother for me. I don't know what she said or did, but everyone seems to be getting on board. We even finalized a date."

"Really? I'll tell her. She's been great lately. She's even taken Cathy under her wing." Ana set the box down and took a seat across from him.

"I'm looking forward to seeing these kids you told me so much about." Pastor Mark pointed to the box. "If you're getting them ready, I know they'll be great."

"They're already excited," Ana said. She slumped back into her chair. The band-aid approach seemed best for getting out what she needed to ask. "I need your opinion about something," she suddenly blurted.

"I have a few minutes. Shoot."

"So there's this guy I've been hanging out with. I met him a while back at a club right before that encounter I had with God. He's not a Christian, and he wants to date me. I know I should probably stop hanging out with him, but I feel drawn to him like I know him for a reason. He's pretty much said he feels the same way about me." She put one hand over her face in exasperation. "I don't know what to do. I know we aren't supposed to date—at least not now, but I don't want to cut him off either. I need to know if I'm doing the right thing for the right reasons."

Pastor Mark was silent for a moment. "Do you think there could be a greater purpose to your friendship other than dating?"

Ana nodded. "But I don't want to hurt his feelings. I know that I'm supposed to wait. I guess my friends are in my head a bit. I just want you to remind me I'm not alone in this."

"You're not alone. God is backing you up." Pastor Mark smiled sympathetically. "I get it. You want to honor God with your actions, and that's good. Choosing the right path even when you know what it is can be very hard sometimes. Pray for wisdom and ask for an opportunity to share God with him."

"I also feel like I'm supposed to tell him some things that I've been holding back. Our conversations usually stay on superficial matters," she admitted.

"Don't hold back what God shows you. Be friends with him, but there's no rush about getting into a relationship. Relationships can be a blessing, but at the wrong time, they can really hinder you." Pastor Mark paused for a minute and then continued, "When you care about someone, believing everything will just fall into place is easy. But sometimes it doesn't. Good relationships require a lot of work and communication. However, you both are in very different places right now."

Ana bit her fingernail. *That's all I needed to be reminded of. Shallow reasons for "Relationships 101" never really ended well.* When Pastor Mark and Johanna had dated, they had both gone through a lot; they were already both mature Christians. *I want a mature relationship like theirs. Their ability to hear God's voice and be submitted to Him has saved their relationship in spite of the trials and has helped their marriage flourish.* "You're right," Ana finally admitted. "Now all I have to do is tell him I want to be a nun."

Pastor Mark laughed. "I'll pray for you."

～

The night of the reconciliation had finally come. For a Saturday night, the auditorium of Isaac's Well was surprisingly packed. People of all ages and ethnic backgrounds filled the room. Even from the back of the church, Ana felt excited and uncertain about what would happen. The music and spotlights made it look like a concert, but it was to be so much more than that.

The praise and worship time Johanna and Owen led was almost over. They clutched their microphones and sang. Johanna's face appeared radiant when she tilted back her head as if to look in God's face.

Ana spotted Cathy entering through the back door. She noticed her face was drawn and haggard. Cathy waved and walked toward her.

"What's wrong? Why are you late?" Ana asked as Cathy joined her. The music slowed to songs about turning back to God as people around them raised their hands.

"I haven't seen or heard from Kevin in a week. His parents haven't seen him. No one has. I think he relapsed again." Cathy crossed her arms and looked at the ceiling as her voice shook, and her eyes filled with tears. "This is my fault. How can he follow God when I'm a terrible example? I told him I wanted to be pure, and then I just threw that all away when I slept with him again. He probably thinks I'm a big hypocrite. Why would he listen to me?"

Ana's heart broke for her friend. Kevin was his own person, but she understood why Cathy felt the way she did. "Don't blame yourself. You told me he's done this many times before."

Cathy shook her head. "I should have been strong for both of us. But I don't know how to help him. He's so stubborn." Unchecked tears rolled down her cheeks. "Should I pray for him or give him up? Do you think he left again because of the baby? Why didn't he just get help?"

When Cathy started to break down, Ana wrapped her arms around her. "Don't do this to yourself," she whispered as she held her close. "Making yourself sick is not good for you or the baby. It'll be okay. We'll keep praying for him."

Cathy cried on her shoulder before breaking away, her eyes pleading. "Ana, how many times am I supposed to go through this with him? He promised me..."

"He'll figure it out. If he doesn't, then God will show you what to do next."

Cathy sighed and stared up at the ceiling. "All right, I'll pray for him tonight. I've been so depressed that I almost didn't come at all."

"I'm so glad you did."

From across the room, Pastor Mark waved to Ana. Worship was about to end, and the kids were up next. "Let's meet and talk later, okay? I have to go gather the kids for their dance."

Cathy nodded and drifted away to find a seat. Ana hurried through the crowd to the side doors that opened into the hallway. Most of the kids were already assembled and stretching as she came in. The others trailed in behind her.

Ana tried not to show her jittery nerves. "Everyone ready?"

The kids all started chattering excitedly. She raised her hand to hush everyone. There wasn't much time. "Okay, let's do this!" As the music in the main room died down, she led them through the doors to take their places under the spotlights.

The music began, and Ana and the children moved effortlessly through most of the dance moves. The crowd shouted with excitement. Near the end, some of the kids started to lose focus and forget some of the steps. Ana was glad no one seemed to notice. At the end of the dance, the congregation stood and cheered enthusiastically as Ana and the kids held their final pose.

Pastor Mark took the microphone as the dance troupe filed to their seats. "Wasn't that fantastic? God is doing something great with the younger generation. Let's give them another hand!"

Pastor Mark continued, "Now I'd like to call Pastor Mike up to join me so we can begin the ceremony. Once Pastor Mike joined him on stage, he continued. "Some time ago, our church split off from Good News Remnant Church in response to discord that came from the Enemy. Today, we, as a church, repent for the disrespect that took place. We acknowledge that we stem from righteous roots but laid the wrong foundation when we left with bitter hearts."

Ana held her breath for a moment. *It's finally happening—after so much prayer.*

Pastor Mark continued. "We ask for your forgiveness, and we request a blessing as we step into a new arena of ministry in our church." Pastor Mark raised his hands high. "We dedicate our work into the hands of God. We step under the covering God ordained. We want you to pass down wisdom and authority that has come to you from God. We need your guidance and support."

Some of the crowd responded with "Amens."

Pastor Mike took the microphone and gripped Pastor Mark's shoulder. "We also repent for our actions that drove you away. We forgive you and, in turn, we ask for your forgiveness. We also extend our blessing to you for all future endeavors."

Tears filled Ana's eyes. She wondered if Pastor Matthew could see this from heaven. All the work that he had put into building for the future was now bearing beautiful fruit. Jesus was definitely smiling down on them. As Ana gazed around the room, she could tell she wasn't the only one who felt the enormity of what was happening. A few of the older women had their arms around some of the youth. Others had big smiles on their faces.

Pastor Mike lowered his head and began to pray. "Father, we ask You to remove anything the Enemy tried to plant from the origin of this church. We release peace and joy and Your mighty outpouring that the work You began would be completed in this church. We agree to partner with this church as they reach more people for the kingdom. Mark this place with Your fire and never let it depart from these walls."

Kavo

Droplets of fire roared as they fell upon the people in the room. Kavo nodded with pleasure. Something was shifting.

In the spirit realm, a structure of a magnificent building rapidly began to take shape. Translucent panels sparkled like ice and shimmered into the atmosphere. A rumble produced the base of the structure as it broke through the ground and grew upward. More crystal panels formed in response to more repentance and prayer. The structure superimposed over everything happening inside the church and grew so wide that it extended outside to the street.

Kavo and a few of the other angels delivered messages as the Holy Spirit continued to inspire prayers. The angels brought glowing packages to those praying.

There was no need for individuals to understand what happened in the Spirit realm. Kavo knew that as they unified and humbled themselves in obedience, their hearts would be forever joined into the finished work taking place.

Pastor Mark opened his eyes and hugged Pastor Mike. He placed his arm around his shoulders. "And now, Lord, would You seal these prayers as we, Your people, humbly seek Your face. In the name of Jesus, amen."

The people's voices combined in a chorus of shouts and applause. Kavo's heart surged with joy as more holy fire fell from heaven.

Pastor Mark stood side by side with Pastor Mike. "I'd like to end this reconciliation with worship and more prayer as we close. Find someone of a different age group to pray for and bless."

Johanna and Owen returned to the platform, where the rest of the worship team sat quietly behind their instruments waiting for their cue. Johanna leaned over and whispered to Owen, who nodded. They motioned to get the attention of the musicians around them and started clapping. The lead guitarist played a familiar riff as the rest of the team followed and burst into the intro for "My First Love" by Stuart Townsend.

Kavo positioned himself near Pastor Mark as both young and old found places in the sanctuary and began to pray for each other.

Energy charged through Kavo. People prayed fervently. Others wept. The atmosphere grew thick. Supernatural smoke drifted down over them, surrounding the angels with the distinct scent of spices and sweet flowers.

*

Ana danced, feeling a connectedness to the moment that she couldn't describe. She looked around. Suddenly she realized that everything felt different. They were on the verge of something monumental that was about to break through—as if the room were holding its breath. For a moment even the worship team hesitated. Ana was convinced everyone in the room could palpably feel the difference.

*

In the angelic realm, light pierced through the panels of the crystal structure, sealing it together. The structure glowed with its own source of light that filtered out into the city night. As the worshippers praised, more panels connected at a faster rate, and the structure towered higher.

Sasson and other angels twirled and swayed in dance as they saw traces of their home begin to appear in the room. They beat their wings as they bounded and leaped in exultation. The beauty of heaven, the gemstones that were built into the structures of the Holy City began appearing in greater numbers all over the floor in the spiritual realm and embedded in the walls. The room sparkled with color and light, but that sight was masked from human eyes.

An increasing number of angels from around the city materialized in the room after being drawn by the beacon of intensity created by the worship. Sasson danced. He was still in position near enough to feel the charge of power flowing through Ana.

He laughed as the congregation abandoned the chairs and rows, opting to spread out around the sanctuary and dance. Congregants of all ages, including little children, praised God with all of their might. An angel passed by some of the kids from the community centre. He carried a vial and poured the oil of heaven on their heads. The rare and precious oil would impart God's power and authority in the city. They were being given gifts of faith—gifts of the Spirit to help them fight. A time was coming when their own assignments would begin.

"I've never seen anything like this kind of freedom," Sasson said to Kavo. Kavo smiled. "I have, but only once."

Sasson was curious, but he didn't ask what his friend meant. The scene was so beautiful that Sasson did not want to miss a second of it. People lifted up colorful flags and banners and began waving them through the air.

Sasson noticed a woman waving a sheer gold dance flag. Her flag floated lightly as she spun and twirled it over her head. Her wavy gray ponytail swayed and bobbed as she danced. He recognized Wella, Pastor Matthew's widow. In the unseen realm, her flag was a deadly sharp sword cutting fear from the people in the room and freeing destinies and future generations into the purposes of God.

Ana had picked up a decorated tambourine beautifully strung with ribbons. She tapped out a rhythm as she sang. Sasson heard the heavenly message being played out through her hands. *Revival is here; God is here.*

The large angel who represented the body of Christ appeared, holding a gold package and opened it over Wella's head as she danced.

After a few moments, the woman suddenly broke through the crowd. She ran from the back, holding the flag above her head like a messenger of war. Her heavyset body seemed firm as she ran with purpose. Once she neared the front rows of chairs, smiles of familiarity replaced the confusion on a few faces. Wella kept running with the flag held high.

Two angels floated by her sides as trails of fire streamed behind them. They seemed to follow and lead her at the same time. She ran one lap around the room before she stopped close to the front row and headed straight for Pastor Mark.

She swept the hair away from her eyes as sweat glistened on her face and swallowed hard as she tried to regain her composure.

Sasson glanced at Ana to see if she had noticed what was happening. Her face reflected the delight that he felt.

Wella leaned in to whisper to Pastor Mark. He then handed her his microphone and raised his hands to attract his wife's attention.

Wella's original burst of stamina dissipated without any warning. She laboriously climbed up on the stage. Her eyes held a youthfulness, although her face was plump with age. A purity seemed to stream from deep inside her.

"Church, I sense that God wants us, as an older generation, to walk with you and to hold you up in prayer," Wella said as she tried to catch her breath. "An anointing comes from heaven as we walk intergenerationally. No more strife, no more competition between us or our churches. God wants to shift this city for His glory," she shouted. "Violence is coming to an end, and the things that have held our children captive are being broken—"

Everyone in the room interrupted with cheers and shouts to God.

After a moment, she continued. "We need to pray for you. God wants us to release something here because we're going to need strength for the coming days." She placed her free hand on her hip. "Many of you have let your love for God grow cold as you've been carried away by the spirit of competition and conflict." She wiped more sweat from her eyes.

"Disunity is not what God intended for us." She shook her finger at everyone in a scolding way, but smiled. "He has given us many gifts, and He promised He would come to help us. The book of Joel says He will pour out His Spirit on the young and old. We are living in that time, but we've been blinded by our own pursuits.

"As we sing the next verse of this song, allow the Holy Spirit to minister truth to you. We're going to make an old-fashioned fire tunnel." She motioned for people to come to the front.

"I want all of the older people to start the tunnel, joining hands and praying over the youth and young adults. After the younger ones go through the tunnel, we'll trade places so you can pray for us, okay?" She handed the microphone back to Pastor Mark and stepped down. She held out her hands for others to join her.

Johanna cued the band again. But this time Owen took over on the drums and banged out a new rhythm.

Sasson could hear what only the angels understood. In the spirit Owen prophesied on his instrument, summoning the other warriors.

———

Now that the praise was so thick, the throne of God emerged in front of their angel eyes. A deep vibration rumbled as Sasson and the others shook uncontrollably. An electric tidal wave of power passed through them.

Kavo called out to the others, "The outpouring we've waited for is here!"

The angels instantly assembled and stood shoulder to shoulder forming a barrier around the room with their bodies.

꒰ꔛ꒱

"What are we doing?" Cathy nudged Ana as she fell into the line behind her. "Who was that lady?"

Ana whispered back, "That's Wella, Pastor Matthew's widow."

Cathy stared at Wella for a moment before she impatiently asked, "And what are we doing?"

"I've heard about these before; my mom said they used to happen in the church whenever they wanted to impart something spiritually."

"What does *impart* mean?"

"It's like passing on some kind of blessing for the power of God to grow for a specific purpose."

"Oh." Cathy wrinkled her nose. She raised her hands to her waist and put them palm up as she got ready to go through the tunnel.

Ana smiled, glad that Cathy wasn't letting her circumstances keep her from trusting God. That Cathy could be so brave amazed her. She didn't know what she would do if the tables had been turned.

As Ana walked through the human tunnel, hands reached out and touched her. A heavy hand rested on her shoulder and slowly pushed her to the next person who would pray for her. One older man put his hand on her head as she stood in front of him.

He said, "And you will be a redeemer of the land back to God."

Something at the pit of Ana's stomach burned like fire as she heard his words. They reminded her of the night they had the prayer meeting at her house. She lost her balance for a second as the tunnel swam in front of her.

A woman's hand steadied her and patted her on the back. "Bless you, daughter! Run in the Spirit!" The woman laughed aloud until Ana felt herself giggling.

———

Ahead of her some of the young people from Isaac's Well danced to the beat of the worship as they walked through. Ana knew she couldn't dance now even if she wanted to. She wanted to cry with joy. As the members of Good News Remnant prayed for them, they looked like proud parents—like all the pain from the past had never happened.

Ana could hear more words of blessing and prophecy given to those around her. She tried to focus on what God was doing inside and felt a wave of new strength coursing through her—like she could conquer anything. At the end of the tunnel, Ana stepped to the side to get in position to pray for those still coming through the line.

"This is like the London Bridge game I used to play as a kid," Cathy said with a relieved giggle as she faced Ana, getting ready to join her in prayer.

Elikai came out of the prayer tunnel shaking and stood next to Ana. He spoke loudly in tongues. Then Daniel stumbled out of the tunnel, laughing hysterically.

"Elikai! That was amazing." Daniel exclaimed. He grabbed both of Elikai's shoulders. Elikai smiled and gently moved him forward so he could start praying and laying hands on more people as they came out of the tunnel. At the touch Daniel suddenly shook like he'd been electrocuted and fell to the floor laughing.

Ana jumped back so he wouldn't fall on her. She looked over at Cathy, whose eyes were as big as saucers.

Elikai bent to help Daniel stand, but his effort was hopeless. Every time he would touch him, Daniel shook more violently and laughed louder. Elikai finally gave up and focused on praying for others.

Ana tried to see everything through Cathy's novice eyes. This was very much a crazy sight. But for Ana this was almost like the amazing times she'd experienced before Pastor Matthew had died—when things had been really good. Everything was finally coming alive again.

Ana's heart burst as Wella finally came through the tunnel, shuffling and dancing toward her. Dual emotions of joy and sadness surfaced as she looked at her. This wonderful woman had lost so much but still had much about which to praise God. Ana threw her arms around her.

Wella squeezed her and kissed her cheek without a word before she moved on to the end of the line. Wella's eyes glistened with tears as she smiled. Ana imagined that just like her, Wella must have wished Pastor Matthew could be here too.

Sasson and the angels had stood together with their arms locked to brace themselves against the initial impact of heaven's outpouring. Their feathers were now drenched by the water that had poured from heaven. Sasson lifted his wings to shake off the heavy droplets. Water sprinkled and fell to the floor as gold dust.

Owen's angel, Edon, swung his hammer in the air above them. His armor began to radiate before he suddenly disappeared.

Sasson noticed his own armor coming to the surface. Surprised, he glanced at Ana. She prayed for people and danced like she had been doing a moment before, but something had changed. Before he could figure out what was happening, he was zooming underground on Edon's heels.

Sasson drew his sword from its sheath to prepare. He had never been sent into warfare like this before. Was it because of the outpouring?

Edon flew ahead into the dark tunnels of the city. His wings opened so wide that they brushed the sidewalls as he flew. He extended the arm that held the hammer so that as he passed, he could take down already collapsing evil structures that lay before him. His hammer glowed silver as he swung it from side to side with precision, aiming at demons perched on dark murky structures that jutted out from the walls.

Sasson had no choice but to follow Edon's lead. A screeching, clawing demon flew at him, but Sasson quickly used his sword to knock it out of the way. Edon turned around, finally noticing Sasson.

"Hey! What's Ana doing up there?" Edon laughed as he smashed the base of a tower so high that its peak could not be seen above them.

Sasson shook his head and knocked down another demon who didn't know what hit him. "What is this place?" he shouted to Edon.

"The strongholds of judgment and their demons," Edon replied soberly. "We need to take down as much of it as possible while we have this cover."

"Over here," Edon motioned for Sasson to follow. They landed at the mouth of a small cave. The rock was black with age and jagged all around. "The last time I travelled through here, I noticed this. I was hoping I'd be led back to it."

Sasson examined the gaping claw marks at the sides of the entrance. *This isn't going to be a peaceful exploration.* Whatever or whoever was trapped inside was probably still there. By the looks of the claw marks, it had used its nails to break its fall or had been forced into the cave.

CHAPTER 12

What Lies Beneath

"Now have come the salvation and the power and the kingdom of our God, and the authority of his Messiah. For the accuser of our brothers and sisters, who accuses them before our God day and night, has been hurled down" (Revelation 12:10, NIV).

KAVO FELT AND saw the effects of the Holy Spirit's presence inside the church as temporarily stunned demons and spirits of oppression were pulled free from their hosts with loud, agonizing shrieks and their angelic disguises unraveled. Demons of sickness oozed from a woman who stood nearby. He drew his sword to sever the last bit of the clinging demon. The demon's eyes glazed over as Kavo pushed it away. It finally disappeared out of the room.

Kavo looked at Rahos, Johanna's angel. A large demon had jumped up from its confused state to claw at Rahos. Shouting obscenities, the demon scrambled to hide behind its human host. "My master will not tolerate this disruption!" The demon pulled a dagger and started to jab at Rahos.

As Rahos charged forward to impale the demon with his sword, it dodged out of the way and managed to slice Rahos' wing with its dagger.

Kavo flew in, knocking the demon's legs from under him and issuing a stern warning: "Leave now before it's too late!"

The demon still clung to one of the pastors. Kavo recognized the man as Pastor Norman, the pastor of a neighboring church who had been invited.

The demon screamed and tried to dive back into Pastor Norman. "If I leave, I'm taking my human with me!"

Rahos intercepted the demon and sliced at his leg. "Get away from him. You have no grounds to remain here."

The demon grimaced and grabbed his leg. He looked over at Kavo in panic. "My human needs me to bring him the truth. This meeting is out of order. You are attacking me, your brother!"

Kavo held his sword very close to the demon's face. "You cannot hide here."

Seeing his bright reflection in the metal of the sword, the demon shrank back and gripped his dagger tighter until it grew into a sword. He began to grow as he pushed out his brown feathery wings until they were at full span. His voice changed from raspy and frail into a silky, strong tone. "Without me, this will fail. You need me."

Rahos took a deep breath. "The Lord rebuke you, religious spirit. Leave this place along with your deception."

Kavo moved to circle the demon from the back, his sword ready for any defiance from the religious spirit. He looked around the room. A few other angels were also busy getting rid of demons.

The religious spirit looked up and screamed in rage. Veins protruded from his neck as his leathery green skin stretched in fury. His brown wings flapped, and his gaze flashed from side to side. Two more demons similar in appearance, flew to join him.

Kavo turned to Rahos and gave him a nod before he spread his wings wider and lifted off the ground. Rahos and Kavo shouted a war cry as they dove toward the demons.

～

Sasson followed Edon into the dark cave. He took small careful steps, ready to defend himself. A spirit resembling a bat flew past them.

Edon stepped closer to one of the rock walls to stare at the markings and ran his hand over them. "These were made by humans. They're centuries old." He shot a perplexed look at Sasson. "Who could have done this?"

Sasson shrugged. He hadn't been told about anything like this before. "It's possible some possessed humans were dragged down here to make their home in the darkness."

Edon's hand squeezed his hammer and held it closer to the wall to further examine the writing. "There's something different about these markings, they—"

"Why have you come!" a voice hissed from behind them.

They turned to see that the voice came from a towering brown-winged creature. Its sharp beak pointed toward them, its tongue flicking in and out as it spoke. A person shrouded in a dark, hooded robe quickly retreated behind the beast and ran deeper into the cave.

Sasson watched Edon out of the corner of his eye. Edon's hammer was glowing, and he began to twirl it over his head.

"Why have you set up shop in the foundations?" Edon challenged. "Leave this place!"

The creature howled in displeasure and charged Edon.

As the bodies of Edon and the beast collided, Sasson looked down to see his armor suddenly shining brighter. He needed to help Edon; that was why he had been sent here. He rounded the demon and started taking swings at its wings.

The demon snapped and bit, refusing to submit. Sasson jumped onto its neck and wrestled it down as Edon beat its body with his hammer. The creature wings flapped as it squawked and tried to escape the two angels' reach. Screeching, it tried to dodge Sasson's sword, but Sasson thrust it through the thick skin.

Edon jumped up and began to spin until his body and face were a blur. He shot out at the demon, knocking it flat.

Without any warning, the demon withered and shrank in size until it disappeared.

"What kind of demon was that?" Sasson asked, breathless.

Edon frowned and shrugged. "Who knows what evil has shaped that creature?"

Sasson added, "Well, thankfully, at this point, it's too weak to cause much more damage."

"Any sign of the hooded person?" Sasson turned in both directions and then glanced back at the strange markings on the wall.

"No, it looks like they escaped. Let's get back to the church."

As Kavo fought the two demons, Rahos lifted his sword above his head to bring it down on the neck of the religious spirit.

The spirit rolled out of the way right before the sword would have struck its mark.

Rahos looked at Johanna. She was still singing and immersed in worship, unaware of the fight going on around her. Rahos opened his mouth, tapped into her song, and released a heavenly melody as he lifted his sword again.

The demon covered its ears in pain and then lifted its sword to block Rahos' swing. Flying to Pastor Norman for cover, the demon stumbled toward him as it landed and attached itself to the pastor.

Pastor Norman abruptly doubled over as if he had stomach cramps and looked around.

Rahos turned to yell to Kavo. "Pastor Norman!"

Too late! The two other demons followed suit and then disappeared as they nestled themselves into Pastor Norman. He hastily made his way toward the exit.

Kavo had only one other option; he bowed his head to communicate with Pastor Mark. The young pastor stopped dancing and looked around. He noticed Pastor Norman's hurrying for the door and jogged over to intercept him.

"Hey, Pastor Norman! I'm so glad you were able to make it. Leaving already?"

"Yes, I'm sorry, Mark. This atmosphere doesn't feel right to me. Something is terribly wrong. I feel the judgment of God on this. All this carrying on is not biblical. You've opened your doors to Satan's lying wonders."

Pastor Mark's smile faded. "What are you talking about? Don't you feel God's presence here? He's doing something awesome!"

Pastor Norman shook his head. "Mark, I'm very disappointed in the disorder you've allowed here. If you don't deal with it, you will see your church plant fall into the hands of the Enemy." Pastor Norman glanced behind him toward the doors. "I have to go."

Pastor Mark frowned as he watched Pastor Norman walk through the double doors.

Kavo and Rahos stood nearby and watched the religious spirit leave within Pastor Norman.

"So close," Rahos whispered. "At least he's gone." He shrugged.

Kavo shook his head. Religious spirits were dangerous on their own, but when they were attached to a pastor, they could wreak severe havoc within the church and the body of Christ. They masqueraded as spirits of light, but their sole purpose was to steer people away from trusting in God by putting their trust in themselves.

"Yes, gone for now, but still out there. Who knows what kind of damage he will do."

❧

Rahos looked around. As Johanna continued to worship, he could feel her spirit tapping into heaven. It was time to get to work.

Rahos turned to a section of seating filled with a few worshippers. He began to circle the area as fast as he could, until he was little more than a blur. Suddenly a carved structure with pillars arose and superimposed itself over the section of chairs. The smooth white alabaster framed the pool of water that emerged in the angelic realm.

The water in the pool splashed and washed over those within it. A five-year-old girl sitting nearby saw the angel as her spiritual eyes were opened. Rahos smiled and waved at her. She rubbed her eyes in doubt and looked around to see if anyone else saw it. She could see the pool. With wide eyes she slowly bent from one side and then the other, before dipping her hand into the air around the bottom of her chair. She stared at her fingers as if she could see water pour through them. "We're in a pool!" No one seemed to hear or notice her as she jumped out of her seat to play and wade in the invisible water.

As the people in the section of chairs danced with renewed vigor, a young man started to cry out to God. Rahos was immediately by his side and laid a hand on him. A row down an older man started to yell. "I'm healed!" he said as he stood up and threw his cane to the side.

People began to look up and gather around him when a young woman sitting a few feet away placed both hands over her ears and started to cry. "I can hear! I can hear!"

Rahos smiled at the confusion and joy on the faces of those within the pool. They seemed unsure of what was happening and broke out into spontaneous applause. The commotion grew as more people rushed toward the heavenly pool.

He turned and moved closer to Johanna but stopped short and looked up. A beam of white light pierced through the ceiling of the room and traced a path. Left behind was an imprint on the floor in front of her.

"A landmark," Rahos said as he walked over to stand next to Sasson.

Sasson knelt at the edge of the mark and stared.

Rahos continued. "This moment is branded into eternity. Now we are tapped into anyone in the past or future who would join this prayer of unity. This well of power will create a synergy into the ages." He placed his hand on Sasson's shoulder.

❦

Ana walked between people dancing in the aisles and found an empty spot near the back of the church. She sat down on the floor with her back against the wall, and her knees drawn up to support her elbows. The Holy Spirit nudged at her heart.

The kids she had brought from the community centre were scattered around the room; some were dancing. She spied a few crying as people prayed for them. Some were lying on the floor so still. It was all too unbelievable.

She knew she'd have a lot of explaining to do later. For now, she needed to hear what God was saying. As she bowed her head, a warm sensation descended from her head to tingle both her arms and spine. It was clear what she needed to do.

Can't I just wake up completely obedient to You—all at once?

Simple steps, one-by-one.

Now her decision needed to be followed with action. She sighed. *Will it always be this hard?*

Peace flooded her soul.

Cathy clapped along with the music, but her mind felt much further away than where she stood in the last few rows. She blinked hard to focus on where she was and what was happening in worship. She smiled slightly as she looked around at the joy on people's faces.

If only Kevin was here.

Her meager happiness ebbed away as her movements slowed, and heaviness descended on her.

Forgive him.

Haven't I forgiven him enough? He's still doing the same thing.

Forgive.

Cathy sat down and put her face in her hands.

I want to forgive him for all the hurt I feel. I need strength.

She sighed.

I forgive him for leaving me. I forgive him for the fights.

Tears flooded into her eyes. *Nobody wants me.*

I want you. You are Mine.

Cathy closed her eyes as tears slid down her cheeks. She saw herself walking down a street as a little girl, holding her father's hand. But the picture disappeared as quickly as it came. She sat silently during the praise and dancing around her.

Now forgive yourself.

I'm not angry at myself.

She shook her head, denying the words in her heart and then realized it was true.

"I forgive you, Cathy," she whispered to herself. Her insides shattered like cascading falls as her silent tears exploded into loud sobs. As she crumpled to the floor, someone's arms encircled her and pulled her into a warm embrace. Sandra's hushed voice was warm in her ear.

She barely registered Sandra's words before her earlier vision came alive and morphed from a still picture of her father into a vivid moving picture. The scene changed from a street to a meadow of flowers. Her dad's hand changed to a another man's hand. She held the hand as he laughed. *This isn't a memory.*

"My Cathy," the man appraised. *"You are so wonderful and caring."* Love radiated from His eyes.

Cathy smiled back. Although she had never met this man, she felt completely safe.

He reassured her. *"I have many beautiful plans for you, and I promise I will always be here for you."*

With every word, new strength filled her. The man laughed and lifted Cathy's small hand so she could jump and skip. She felt like she was flying; her girlish curls bounced as her laughter bubbled. Each time she jumped, she sailed higher over flowers and rocks in the meadow.

When she opened her eyes again to the scene in the church, she was still laughing.

Sandra sat close by, looking puzzled.

Cathy felt lighter. The heaviness she had carried had lifted. The pain inside was gone, and she didn't feel like worrying; instead, she felt like laughing.

Jesus is strong and has everything under His power.

Suddenly, everything was so funny that she laughed hysterically, unable to stop and doubled over. Satan's number was up. She was still laughing as she clutched her stomach and shouted the name of Jesus.

Somewhere between bouts of laughter, she managed to see Ana coming closer to sit next to Sandra. Sandra's perplexed face broke into a smile, and Ana started laughing too.

Cathy's face was wet with tears and sweat. The issues in her life that caused pain seemed suddenly ridiculous next to Jesus' ultimate beauty and authority. She laughed at that too.

―――

How could I have worried about anything before?
Everything was hilariously ridiculous.

～

Kavo blew the ceremonial ram's horn, long and loud, interspersed with short sounds, heralding the new season that had been ushered in.

He shouted, "The saints have stepped into what we have long seen in our realm. The season of Milcamah is here. A season of warfare has begun."

Two other angels lifted their horns and repeated the original blasts. In response, a mild rumble reverberated back through the structure, growing from the center of the room.

Hours later, with the building empty, the shining tower remained, faintly echoing the beautiful sounds from the saints' worship. Kavo walked through the midst of the towers. The large crystal panels reflected the activity and beauty of heaven, and from where he stood, he could see pictures of the people there, angels flying within the walls, and the incense room.

This is what they are capable of.

Kavo knelt and ran his hands over the smooth surface and sturdy foundation that had been laid. Heat seemed to emanate from it, although to the touch, it was as cool as ice. Much had been accomplished, but more remained to be done. Today's resounding victory could not be hidden. No, this building would send a message loud and clear throughout the city.

CHAPTER 13

The Invisible Kingdom

"That which is born of the flesh is flesh; and that which is born of the Spirit is spirit" (John 3:6, KJV).

DIONYSUS PACED UNDERGROUND at the Eclipse. He couldn't take it anymore. He had to see the wreckage.

He opened his gray wings and flew through the layers of tunnels. He exited through an alleyway and folded his wings back into his body to resume the look of a normal man as he landed. He looked around in disbelief.

This cannot be happening!

They'd been so close.

Dionysus eyed the jutting crystal structures with disgust. They had torn through several parts of the street and surrounding buildings that made up the skyline in the entertainment district. Pieces towered over him, while others were barely visible from the ground. Everything in the earthly realm went on as usual. People walked and cars drove through the enemy structures that were only visible in his realm.

Dionysus walked a few feet and stood in front of a structure that only reached his knees. In awe, he ran his hand gently across the sharp points and flat surface. The crystal caught and stung his flesh. Suddenly aware of his position, he made a fist and grimaced in pain. The burn of his seared flesh mirrored the hatred burning within him.

I will not lose ground so easily.

He knew these crystal structures well. They had first appeared after the crucifixion of Jesus—right after the great shaking that had taken place in the inner depths of the earth. But for the last while, they had been far less beautiful and clear in the city than they were now.

What have those Christians done to make these structures reemerge with a dazzling new brilliance?

He smoothed his burned hand over his business suit and looked around. People continued to scurry down the sidewalk.

With each step through the downtown core, he surveyed the damage done to his own buildings and monuments. Some of the new structure renewed by the power of that horrible church gathering sprouted like weeds that had contemptuously pushed his own work right from the ground.

He ground his teeth as he thought of the community centre. Once he attained it, he'd be more powerful. It's roots were deeper than the Eclipse. What happened to the community centre was personal.

When the goddess returned to take her rightful place, he'd be given this city. Together, they would increase their influence. Humans would be their slaves, and interfering anointed cherubs would be forever banished.

He examined his neat, dark-blue suit. He'd never expected to need these types of bodies. The great rebellion had promised power and far more glory, but instead, they'd been abandoned to shame and powerlessness. Still, his human body did not deteriorate as it would have without his takeover.

Dionysus turned back in the direction he'd come. He shuddered to think of what the future would hold if these people tapped into more of the ancient power. He'd seen it before and never thought it would happen again. But here it was right here before his eyes. He rubbed the back of his neck.

Not now—not when it was almost time for victory.

He remembered Jesus' commanding demon spirits to leave human bodies without a word. When Jesus walked into a town, spirits immediately flew into the abyss. Dionysus had fought with sword and stone against the holy people before Jesus came on the scene. Time had changed his weapons, but all that would be useless in a war with these new holy ones. He shook his head and tried to snap himself out of the horrors of the past. He hurried back, ducking into the alley where he'd exited.

A metal door came into view. He used his nails to pry open the heavy blue door barely wide enough to fit inside. The door slammed behind him. He stood in a dark stairwell, looking down at concrete steps that led deep into the underground of the city.

Dionysus' mind flashed back to the days before the crucifixion. He had beat Jesus. In the body of one of the soldiers, he had laughed and kicked Him. Jesus had taken pity on his host. With a simple glance, Jesus, whose eyes were always trained on the invisible, had cast him out of that soldier. Dionysus scoffed. If only he'd realized the truth then. He would have murdered Him sooner…before the cross. The Creator had sent Himself to die for the created ones, but they hadn't understood. Here in this time, the prophecies made sense. These humans had to die. That was the only way to stop what could otherwise ruin his plans.

Within the underground tunnels below the sewers, Dionysus found his way back to his office.

"Sakron," he called. The cement office around him lay barren. His hands flickered back and forth between his primal form and that of his host.

Sakron materialized behind him.

Dionysus turned. "How could this happen?" he demanded.

Sakron looked grave. He opened his mouth to explain, but nothing came out. He shrugged sheepishly. Dionysus turned a cold gaze on him.

"We still have many roots in this city. The bright ones will not be able to undo what is already in progress." Sakron explained.

"What of the temples?" Dionysus' human eyes morphed into green holes with black slits edged by yellow.

"Our worshippers are still compelled," Sakron answered.

Dionysus nodded. "Good." As long as those who gathered at the movies, the Eclipse and other places still received his messages, they would maintain a steady stream of power coming from the demonic breeding grounds to get things ready. He chuckled as he pictured Christians subjecting themselves to his own carefully crafted mind control. The same messages of years ago still brought in converts daily.

There is no God. There is no Hell.

He laughed out loud to himself.

You are the master of your own universe. If you're good enough, you'll live happily ever after.

"Make sure our movies continue to gain popularity, especially among the young. We must distract and hinder the prayers of the saints." He came around his desk. "If we can taint those, we can still manage our plans."

Sakron nodded.

Dionysus lips curled involuntarily as he stared off into space. If they could plunge the world into spiritual darkness by once again hiding the truth for long enough, he would eventually realize all of his dreams. He walked over to what looked like a fire pit in the corner of the room. He lifted his arms and began mumbling a chant.

Fire whipped into the space. From the middle of the fire, the slim figure of a woman rose before him. A large, burgundy hood covered her head and gave way to thick, flowing robes. She pushed off her hood. Long, shiny, black hair fell free as she bowed slightly.

"Priestess." He bowed as well.

"Dionysus." Her voice was faint and airy over the sound of the fire.

"We will need you to enter the city to prepare for the Great Lady sooner than we had planned." Dionysus turned toward Sakron as he began to disappear from the room. "We have some troublemakers for you to deal with."

~

"This walk with God keeps getting better and better!" Cathy gushed as she and Ana returned to the church the next morning. The reconciliation had gone deep into the night. Ana had gratefully accepted Cathy's invitation to spend another night at her place after she had called some of the parents to pick up their kids from church.

"Just when I think I've experienced or learned something cool, something even better happens! Last night—unbelievable! I didn't even know I could be that happy!"

Ana laughed. Cathy's excited chatter made her feel a tinge of jealousy. *Laughter?* Her life seemed like a constant flow of tears. But she was happy for Cathy nonetheless.

"You looked like you had a lot of fun," Ana finally said when Cathy paused for a breath.

"I was laughing and speaking in that weird language I heard at the prayer meeting but different—I didn't want it to end. Sandra told me it's called tongues—*glossolalia.*"

Ana looked at her in surprise. "That's great! You were given your spiritual language. I have it too. I use it to strengthen myself spiritually."

"How do you do that?"

"I basically just start it and stop it whenever I want. I focus on God and let it roll off my tongue. I use it to pray into things."

"Why not just pray normally?" Cathy asked.

"Well, you can. It's just a different type of prayer. I find it helps me feel more connected to God." Ana paused for a moment in her explanation. "Praying in tongues builds up your spirit man. You remember we talked about being three parts? Spirit, soul and body?"

Cathy nodded.

"Well, your spirit man also needs to exercise and to connect with God. When I pray and worship in tongues, it helps me hear God speaking to me and to stay focused in prayer when my mind tends to want to wander."

As they neared the church, Ana started singing a melody in tongues to demonstrate her explanation. Cathy joined in, though tentative at first and then stronger as their voices beautifully harmonized, only adding to the serenity of the morning.

"So now that I have it, I can use it any time?"

"That's the way it works. The only way it would disappear entirely is if you deliberately chose not to use it. If that ever happens for any reason, just tell God you're sorry for neglecting something He has given you and then start again."

"Good to know, thanks."

"Any word from Kevin yet?" Ana asked. As they approached the church, people were arriving both on foot and by car. She turned to look at Cathy's profile.

Cathy frowned, "No, nothing. I'm still going to pray, but yesterday I felt like somehow everything would turn out okay."

As they stepped through the doors of Isaac's Well, Ana gasped. Three times as many people were there than normal. Some of the local television stations were also there. Obviously, word of the previous night's events had spread through the city. A few people already knelt at the altar. The atmosphere inside was electrified and expectant.

People from neighboring churches chatted and waited for the service to begin. From the excited talk around her, Ana pieced together some of the events that had taken place during or after the service. Many had been healed, and some had left the service so full of the Holy Spirit that they had to be carried out.

Ana scanned the crowd during the service that day. Many worshiped while others watched. She could not deny the dual atmosphere, which made her feel uneasy.

৵

Leah squirmed uncomfortably in her seat at the back of the church. Her attention was on the tangible heavy presence in the room that greatly threatened her power. For the first time in a long while, Sakron was not with her. She knew that once she entered the church building, he would not join her. He had awakened her in the middle of the night, furious about something that had taken place with the potential to ruin his plans. He had assigned her to attend the service today to spy and find out what was going on. Anger coursed through her fingers and veins.

Why did she have to come back?

Over a year ago, she had accomplished her assignment against the young pastor Ishmael. But completely unknown to her, another stronger leader had taken his place. Worse than that, he was married, meaning the process would now require an entirely different approach.

More sleepless nights!

Leah seethed as she listened to some of the testimonies from the previous night's service. *Delusional.*

Still, she allowed a tear or two roll from her eyes whenever she felt people were watching. At the end of the service when Pastor Mark asked if any of them wanted to come up to receive Jesus, Leah made her way to the front. She brushed the tears from her eyes and looked down at the floor. Her fingers fumbled with her hair. For the work that she had to do, she needed to be on the inside…and this time it had to be believable.

After service Leah had almost reached the door to the outside before a hand tapped her shoulder. She turned to see Ana with a big smile on her face.

"Leah!" Ana said as she leaned forward to embrace her. "I'm so glad you decided to come."

Leah smiled sheepishly and shrugged her shoulders. "I just felt it was time—you know."

"That's great. Just like when we were kids, remember?"

Leah was surprised Ana had brought up their childhood. Over the years she had come to believe Ana had put the past behind her—as if they had never had a history at all.

"Just like old times," Leah agreed, beaming.

And this time, you will be the one who's destroyed.

~

As Ana crossed the community centre parking lot, she noticed a couple of parked cars. Usually, the parking lot was empty on Saturday because dance was the only program held at that time.

The hallway of the community center was basically quiet except for some faint voices that drifted around the corner. She peered down an adjacent hall. A young man with straight light-brown hair and a woman in her late thirties or early forties accompanied Mr. Stucco.

Using his arms to gesture widely, Mr. Stucco directed the dark-haired woman's attention to different parts of the building structure. Her business suit looked crisp and neat. She nodded and concentrated on what Mr. Stucco was saying. The young man was not much taller than the other two but stood

152

out with broad shoulders and a slight, but muscular, build. He wore a bored expression but listened as well. Mr. Stucco looked up.

"Oh, Ana, do you have a moment? I'd like you to meet Ms. Woodstock."

Ana quickly crossed the distance between them and reached out to shake the woman's hand. The moment their hands touched, Ana suddenly felt her vision go dark for a split second. A woman's scream echoed inside her mind followed by a sick feeling that washed over her. She shuddered.

Ms. Woodstock's face held a curious look as she gripped Ana's hand.

Why is her hand so cold?

Ana offered a weak smile, unable to muster more.

Ms. Woodstock finally released her hand and turned to smile at Mr. Stucco.

"Mr. Stucco has kindly agreed to give me a tour of the premises; he told me about all the good work you do here with the kids," Ms. Woodstock explained. Her smile was tight and forced.

Mr. Stucco continued, "Her company is interested in helping with a renovation project." He looked at the young man who was with them and then spoke to Ana. "And this is my nephew Will who acts as our custodian and takes care of the place for me whenever he's not away at school."

Will smiled. "Nice to meet you, Ana."

Ana smiled back but didn't offer her hand. Though she swallowed hard, she couldn't seem to get rid of her earlier nausea.

Ana studied his face. He seemed kind and quite attractive.

"Well, I'd better get to class," she said before turning away.

"Have a good one," Will called after her.

She found the classroom was buzzing with chatter when she finally arrived.

"Did you see me? I was shaking; I think I freaked out my parents. I couldn't stop telling them about what I was seeing."

"Not me, I went straight to my room when I got home."

"Did you see that lady fall over?"

"That was so scary. I thought she was dead."

Ana listened as she leaned down and slipped her gym bag off her shoulder.

A week had gone by, and the kids were still talking about the reconciliation. She'd anticipated a lot of questions. "Hey, everyone! How was your week?"

A tumult of voices rose as everyone tried to talk over each other. "Sean's not here," Christy piped up over the others. "His mom wouldn't let him. He got grounded."

"Oh?"

"He was still shaking when he got home, and his mom thought he was doing drugs or something. She didn't believe he was at church."

Ana bit her bottom lip and scrunched her face. "I'll have to call her," she noted. "You're probably wondering what happened at church last week, huh?"

Some of the kids nodded their heads.

"And how come it stopped?" Brad shouted.

"Well, what some of you saw and experienced is called *manifesting*." She sat down on the floor in front of them and motioned for them to do the same.

"Manafesto…" Raquel tried to repeat as she and the other kids sat down cross-legged.

"*Manifesting*. The word means 'to show or reveal.' What you saw was the power of God falling on people in a visible way. God is real, and when He touches people, it's sometimes like an electric shock. Sometimes our bodies react to His power."

"I was shaking…" Candice announced.

Ana explained, "Yes, the experience is different for each person. Sometimes God's presence is very peaceful, and at other times, it can be very intense."

Tanisha asked, "Isn't God always around though?"

"Yes, He's everywhere, but when He begins to touch people the way that He did the other night, that's a much different scenario. He shows His manifest presence in ways that can be felt and seen. It usually happens when people are seeking God together in prayer or worship."

Christy raised her hand. "Afterward I saw pictures of people in my head."

"What you experienced is called a *vision*. That's more of a picture of the past or the future."

"Am I a psychic?"

"No, not at all. As I said earlier, what you saw was the power of God at work. Don't let anyone ever tell you that God isn't real or that He doesn't have any power." The kids nodded in understanding before she continued. "Just as much as our God is real, He also has a real enemy whose name is Satan. In fact, the truth is that a war is going on between good and evil for each and every one of you. God wants you to be His children, while Satan wants to destroy you. And He'll do whatever it takes to bring you down."

"Can't God just *zap* him?" Brad questioned.

"Yes, He can, Brad, and He did. God zapped Satan right out of heaven."

Christy looked at her questioningly. "If I'm not a psychic, then what am I?"

Ana pondered her question before answering. "Well, Christy, you experienced God's true power. The Enemy has used people claiming to be psychics to keep people from trusting God's real power. Satan likes to imitate everything God has so that he can confuse people and take the focus off Jesus. What happened to you is called prophecy. It's spoken about in the Bible in the books of 1 Corinthians and Acts and all throughout the Old Testament. With this spiritual gift, people can speak the word of God or speak of the future that they couldn't have known about in any other way."

Christy smiled. "Wow!"

"Jesus told people about the future and about their lives right on the spot." Ana looked at the class. They had become more attentive than ever before. "Maybe we could meet for a little while at the beginning of each class and study the Bible together. What do you think?

"Let's do that!" Christy exclaimed, turning to look at her friends for their agreement.

Ana felt her excitement rise as she looked at their youthful faces.

This group is special. What does God have in store for them?

She remembered herself at that age. "Without realizing it, when I was your age, I got involved in things that were displeasing to God. Satan wants to distract us by making us fascinated with evil and horror. When I was little, I never knew that God had given me gifts He wanted me to use to do good things. Because I didn't realize He wanted to speak to me and reveal Himself, I allowed myself to get caught up in evil things."

"What do you mean?" Brad asked.

"For instance, how many movies have you seen with vampires or people practicing some form of magic?"

Raquel nodded. "A lot. I saw one yesterday."

"It seems normal watching some guy suck someone's blood, right? Especially when a hot guy is doing it, but it's pretty sick when you think about it."

Raquel slammed her fist into her palm. "I don't care what he looks like. A guy tries to bite me—I break all of his teeth."

Some of the kids started laughing.

Ana felt a familiar rush of heat overwhelm her as she spoke. *This is important for the kids to know.* "God wants to teach us and take us deeper into relationship with Him, but we must separate ourselves from the things that will keep us apart from Him—the barriers that will prevent our hearing what God wants us to know."

Christy spoke in barely a whisper. "Ana, I gave my heart to Jesus that night. I saw a picture of Him. He spoke to me, showing me how much He loved me and that He died for me." She looked around self-consciously. Some of the other kids smiled back at her.

"Oh, Christy, I'm so happy for you. This is the most important decision you'll ever make." As Ana hugged her, Christy smiled shyly. Ana felt tears burn her eyes. She cleared her throat and stood. "Okay, class! We'll talk more about this later. Let's get changed and ready to dance; I have some new moves for you to learn."

~

Ana gathered her belongings to leave as the last student trailed out of the class. She heard a heated discussion as she passed Mr. Stucco's office. His door was slightly ajar, and he seemed to be arguing with Will.

"Why don't you just turn the place over to me? You're getting too old to run it. You should be able to relax and retire. You know I can handle it; I've been helping you here for years."

"No! No, Will. We've talked about this before, and you know exactly how I feel about that."

As Ana quickly walked past the door so she wouldn't appear to be eavesdropping, Mr. Stucco noticed her and waved her inside. "Come in here, won't you, Ana?"

She peeked through the door of the stuffy office. "Hi, Mr. Stucco," she greeted him. "What's up?"

"I noticed a lot of talking in dance class today."

Ana's stomach knotted. Mr. Stucco was generally nice but very hard to read. She hoped she wasn't in any trouble. "We did a performance at my church the other night, and the kids had many questions."

He smiled. "That sounds wonderful! What church did you say that was?" Mr. Stucco raised a bushy eyebrow.

"Isaac's Well."

"I've heard of that church," he commented, scratching his head. "Will, isn't that the church you attend?"

"Yup, that's it," Will said with a sigh. He didn't look pleased about the change in topics or the interruption.

The old man chuckled. "Ana, did I happen to mention that Will's my favorite nephew?"

Will, who had been leaning casually against the wall, pushed away and walked over to where his uncle stood. He patted the old man's shoulder and flashed an enigmatic grin at Ana. "What he didn't say is that I'm his *only* nephew."

Mr. Stucco beamed. "Will takes good care of me. He's the son I never had."

Will laughed and slapped his uncle on the back. "But you do have a son. He lives in another city with his wife and kids."

Ana caught herself laughing as well.

"So you go to my church, Will?" she asked suddenly curious.

He tilted his head and studied her. "Yes, I serve on the leadership team there."

She glanced away. "I haven't seen you around…"

"I've been away at school," he interrupted. "I joined after the church plant. I'm happy to be a part of it all."

Ana glanced back at Mr. Stucco, who was now staring at them. Suddenly he busied himself with papers on his desk. "Don't mind me. I have to be going. I'll leave you two to get better acquainted." He gathered a handful of papers and shoved them into his carrying case as he stood to leave.

A little embarrassed Ana edged backward toward the door. "I have to get going as well."

Will stepped forward. "I'll walk you out," he offered.

"Sorry you had to hear all that," Will said as they stepped from the room. "My uncle and I can really get into it sometimes."

"You don't have to explain."

"Don't get me wrong. I love my uncle, but sometimes he's just so stubborn. That lady you met earlier doesn't simply want to renovate the centre. She wants to control it. She wants my uncle to sell it, but I don't trust her at all. I'm afraid my uncle will cave if she keeps the pressure on."

"I'm sure he just wants to do what's best," said Ana as they walked down the front steps. She marveled at how he seemed incredibly comfortable with her. She didn't know why, but she felt comfortable with him too.

"The thing is my uncle doesn't trust her either." Will rubbed his chin. "All of our roots are wrapped up in this place."

Ana nodded. "She did seem kind of strange. I had a weird feeling when I shook her hand."

Will turned and frowned. "It's strange that we didn't meet before I left for school. I feel as though I should have at least heard about you from someone other than my uncle. He tells me the parents love you."

Ana smiled. "Well, a lot was going on at church then. I missed a lot of it. There's definitely a lot happening now."

"I can imagine. Even away at school, I was having dreams about this place. I'll bet I have a lot of catching up to do."

Ana laughed, "I'll fill you in. You won't believe what's been going on…"

"Try me."

CHAPTER 14

Fallen

"*We are all infected and impure with sin. When we display our righteous deeds, they are nothing but filthy rags. Like autumn leaves, we wither and fall, and our sins sweep us away like the wind*" (Isaiah 64:6, NLT).

Wᴴᴱɴ Cᴀᴛʜʏ sᴛᴀʀᴛᴇᴅ her shift at the hospital, she noticed a note attached to the clipboard where she normally checked her tasks for the day. She read, "*Head nurse wants to see you.*"

Curious, Cathy hastily tracked her down.

As she approached, Lorraine smiled comfortingly. "Cathy, I wanted to check in with you to see how you're doing. I know how hard you've been try-ing to support Beth." She gently patted Cathy's arm. "Are you taking care of yourself as well?"

"I've been sleeping okay, but sometimes, it's a bit of a struggle." Cathy glanced down at her growing belly. "But I guess that's to be expected, right?" She smiled.

Lorraine squeezed Cathy's arm. "You're such a sweet girl. I hope that you'll stay here for quite some time." She glanced down at her clipboard and momentarily stared at Cathy with a questioning look. "Anyway, I wanted you to know that a young man admitted himself over the weekend. He's being treated for dehydration among other things. He said he knows you. I thought you'd like to know." Her eyes narrowed as she examined Cathy's face. "He's in room 305," she added, as she picked up her binder and turned to leave.

Cathy felt the blood drain from of her face.

After being missing for so many weeks, Kevin is here?

Cathy forced a smile to keep her face from reflecting the shock she felt. "Thanks for telling me, Lorraine." She quickened her pace as she walked toward the elevator.

Cathy entered the hospital room and walked quietly to the Kevin's bedside. Bruises lined his arms; his fingertips and thumbs were cracked and dirty, and he had open sores on his hands. The skin around his eyes looked dark and sunken, and he looked thinner than when she had last seen him.

He looks so helpless in his sleep.

The anger she'd been harboring drained away seeing like this. *He's here— alive—in front of me. At least he is safe for now.*

She stepped away from his bed and began to weep.

≈

The slight sound of sniffling awakened him. He forced his eyelids open to see Cathy standing halfway between the bed and door…uncommitted about staying or leaving.

"Cathy…" he hoarsely whispered. His arm felt too heavy and sore to wave her over.

Her startled gaze met his for only a moment before she turned to walk toward the door, wiping her face with her arm.

"Please don't go," he begged, straining to speak through swollen, cracked lips. The last thing he wanted to do was speak, but he needed to.

She stopped but didn't turn to face him. "Kevin, I have to get back to work now. I'm glad you're safe, but I can't stay." Still, she didn't move.

"Please, hear me out." His voice was hoarse.

Cathy turned around but made no effort to move toward him as she waited for him to explain.

"You were right. I can't do this on my own. I don't want to keep repeating the same stupid behaviors. Please help me." He tried to adjust his position but failed. "I asked them to put me in a program. I'm here because I realized I couldn't be what you and the baby need like this. I'm not strong enough to fight on my own. I need all the help I can get."

&.

Nukos hovered in the hospital room, studying Kevin's face. Dree had joined them in desperation the day after Kevin had left for the street. Despite having Kevin to feed on, Dree was in worse shape than he'd been before. Kevin was supposed to be dead, but for some reason, their plan to destroy him had gone awry. He'd been receiving positive messages from their enemy, and somehow he had managed to stagger home in a stupor and then checked himself into the hospital.

Cathy turned to face him. "Kevin, I'm having our baby. I don't know what I'm doing. How can I take care of all of us?"

His eyes were wide, desperate. "I don't expect you to take care of me. I just need your support until I get past this thing. I realized so much while I was away. I know I've said this before, but things are different now. I'm going to do whatever it takes to get past this addiction." He paused for a breath before adding, "I'm going to start going to group counseling and get individual counseling. The doctors told me a program here specializes in helping people with addictions. I'm going to do it all. Just don't leave me," he begged. He looked down at his hands and slowly shook his head back and forth in realization. "I know I don't deserve you and the baby, but I want to be a better man. I have to change my life before it kills me. I can't do this anymore."

Cathy shook her head. "Kevin, how do I know that you won't do it again? How am I supposed to feel when you keep choosing drugs over me? How is our child supposed to feel when it's born, and you're gone—or dead?"

Licking his lips, Dree hovered around Cathy's head, planting his thoughts in her mind. *Don't trust him; he doesn't deserve anything!*

Nukos was now by Kevin's bedside, planting his depressed thoughts. *You are alone, alone, alone...*

"I'm sorry," Kevin said as his eyes became red with threatening tears. "I can't promise you anything. I know I can't ask you to trust me—I can't even trust myself. All I can say is I'm going to do my best." He shrugged. "If the system is any good, then maybe it will help. I want to be what you need. I want to marry you and be a family, and I'm willing to do whatever it takes so that we can have what we always wanted and used to talk about."

Sadness crept into Cathy's voice. "My life is changing so much. I can't handle all this."

Dree stood on the floor next to Cathy, his lips only inches from her ear. *You can't, can't...*

"I understand," Kevin acknowledged then paused as he searched for the appropriate words. "You just take time to think about it. I know I don't deserve your forgiveness for leaving again, but I need you to trust me. *I* want to trust me too. I'll be here for a few days while they set me up with a counselor. My mind is so messed up that I don't want to be alone." He sighed. "Thanks for listening to me." He tried to smile at Cathy, but he felt a lone tear escape. He turned away and closed his eyes so she wouldn't see.

Cathy walked over to the bed and kissed him on the forehead. He opened his eyes as she walked away, feeling fear and despair overwhelm him.

If she won't stay with me, then what's the point? I should just give up now.

Kevin felt his eyes burn with fresh tears.

I'm always alone—and no wonder. I'm a failure. Not even my parents or Cathy love me anymore.

Nukos came in closer to weave more negative thoughts into Kevin's mind. Nukos noticed Dree mournfully watching Cathy leave.

He wouldn't risk following her. That bright lighter could be anywhere.

Kevin lay in silence as anger cascaded over his heart, protecting him from the pain. He was angry at himself and everyone else for abandoning him.

Try Jesus.

The thought came to him so suddenly that he repeated it out loud, surprising himself. Nukos looked up at Dree. *He* was interfering again.

What? No!

Jesus is the answer.

Nukos saw the struggle in Kevin's mind and scratched a talon across Kevin's face.

A stab of pain went through Kevin's head.

I feel awful.

He thought about leaving to get high. The craving to give in was so strong that he was giddy just thinking about it. He looked around. He could easily detach these tubes, find his clothes, and be out the door... *Nothing matters when I'm high. All I feel is pleasure. But after the high...* Another wave of sadness hit him.

Then what?

Every time he came down from a high, he was half-dead and felt like killing himself because he wasn't. *Maybe I should just do it. Everyone would be better off.* He looked down at his body. *I'm disgusting.* Who would want him now? Why did Cathy even care? *I don't deserve anything. I'm selfish. I'd probably sell my own kid one day to get high. It's pointless.*

He pushed himself up on the bed and sat up. Another pain ricocheted across his head.

Kevin sat in silence. Cathy had Jesus and seemed to be doing great. He expected that, even with the baby's coming, Cathy would be fine without him. She'd changed. She seemed to possess a strong confidence he'd never before seen in her. In the past she'd been insecure and so needy that he felt stifled. Now she rarely seemed unsure of anything. He felt annoyed at no longer being needed, but at the same time, knowing she'd be all right was comforting. Maybe she did know what was best. She'd mentioned Jesus a few times, although he hadn't wanted to listen. He'd acted stupidly. Maybe she was right about that too.

Maybe prayer will work.

"Jesus," Kevin said out loud.

Nukos jumped up in shock and flew toward the ceiling. Dree realized what was happening and put his hands over his ears and started to run to the far corner of the room.

Kevin whispered, "God, I need Your help. Um...please help me."

Beams of light filled the room. Nukos screamed as he felt a stray bolt of what felt like lightning pierce his thick skin. He tried to cling to the ceiling while batting away the light coming in his direction. He looked down and squinted at Kevin through his own panic.

This is a foolish thought, boy!

Kevin felt a bit foolish, but it was better than nothing. He waited for a moment. "Jesus, I want to do what's right. Please help me." He looked around the room. Nothing was really around. *I need to start reading too.* The next time he saw Cathy, he would ask for a Bible.

~

Stephen's angel and Yonah harmonized as they sang in their language over Stephen. *Haraoda,* as the song was often called, spoke of provision, including protection and healing. Stephen's angel rested his hand gently on Stephen's head. Beth sat quietly praying in a chair nearby.

Stephen slept. His dark-brown hair had turned white in places, but it was still thick despite his age. Even with the tubes protruding from his body, he looked peaceful.

Cathy came by and paused at the door. After a moment she walked in and gently placed her hand on Stephen's head, closed her eyes and prayed. When she opened them, her face was streaked with tears. Beth stood to join her.

"What's wrong?" Beth frowned as she studied Cathy's face.

Cathy waved for Beth to follow her from the room. Yonah followed them.

"My boyfriend's sick," she whispered. "He's been struggling with addictions for a long time. Now he's ended up here. He says that he wants to marry me." Cathy shook her head as she folded her arms across her chest. "But what if he never gets better? I love him, but he's unreliable and keeps leaving." Cathy pushed her hair behind her ear and rubbed her eyes.

"You've given me a great deal of hope regarding my husband." Beth reached out to take Cathy's arms. "Even though he isn't improving, I still feel more at peace than I ever have before. Don't you have faith enough for yourself?"

Unable to answer, Cathy looked down at her hands. "It's different. Your husband is sick and wants to get well. Kevin is stubborn, and he's broken my trust so many times that I don't know if I even want to trust him anymore." She blinked back the threatening tears.

Beth linked her arm through Cathy's and led her toward the end of the hall. "Do you remember when you told me that there's hope for everyone? I think that this is just hard for you because you're too close to the situation. I know the power of addiction is very strong, but while he's alive, there's always hope." She peeked back toward Stephen's hospital room. "Hey, I have an idea. How about each time you pray with me for Stephen, we go and pray for Kevin as well?"

Cathy squeezed Beth's hand. "I'd like that."

"Come on then, let's go."

$\sim$

"Kevin?" Cathy stood beside the bed with an older woman whose graying hair accentuated her delicate features. Her kind eyes twinkled.

Before Kevin had a moment to think, he smiled. *Cathy's come back.*

Cathy motioned toward the other woman. "This is Beth. I met her here. Her husband has cancer, and we've been praying for him. She suggested that we also pray with you. Is that okay with you?"

"Sure," Kevin said, sitting up slowly. He felt awkward.

Who is this woman who now knows I have a problem?

"Have a seat."

Cathy grabbed a chair and offered it to Beth. After she was seated, and Cathy sat balanced on the armrest.

Kevin said softly, "It's nice to meet you, Beth. I think I'd like to start reading the Bible. Cathy, can you get me one?"

Cathy's eyes grew wide. Then she squinted suspiciously at Kevin. "What? Um…sure. I think I have an extra one here in my locker. I'll get it for you before I leave."

"Great!" said Kevin as he beamed his delight.

Beth leaned in. "How are you feeling, Kevin?"

Kevin looked into her bright, warm eyes and felt like telling her everything. "Actually, I'm feeling somewhat better. The first few days were really bad. I've been really tired and felt sick…basically, I need a new body."

"Well, then," Beth chuckled. "We'll pray for that then." She patted his arm.

Kevin rolled over so he could face her. "Pray that I'll do the right thing. I just feel like smoking up when I'm bored and have nothing to do."

Beth's eyes looked sad as she smiled. "You'll be okay. Let's pray." Everyone bowed their heads and closed their eyes.

Beth prayed. "Heavenly Father, I pray for Kevin. I pray that You would fill him with strength to make the right decisions. I pray that You would heal his body, soul and spirit."

Cathy prayed. "Father, please give back to Kevin the years that have been given over to drugs. I pray that he would put his full trust in You and allow You to heal his heart from every hurt."

Kevin opened one eye to look at Cathy. Her eyes were closed. She looked really serious. He closed his eyes again and decided to pray. When a lull came, he said, "God, I pray that You would forgive me for trying to do this on my own. I need Your help."

❧

Nukos and Dree gagged on the waves of light that began saturating the room. Hovering had quickly become useless as the room filled. They had nowhere left to turn, and they could do nothing more to affect Kevin. Nukos spotted Yonah through the light and motioned to Dree that it was time to go. The waves of light had already drained most of their power. Nukos felt himself growing weaker and more disoriented by the second. His mouth and eyes were stinging with pain from the bright beams of light everywhere. Dree growled at Yonah before they disappeared. They'd have to try again later when Kevin was alone.

~

The sun's rays glinted off the cars passing through the busy downtown street. In the late afternoon bustle, Ana was immersed in her own thoughts. The trees were almost in full spring bloom, and their foliage seemed out of place among the backdrop of concrete high-rises. Light streamed through the branches, casting soft shadows across her path. She looked from storefront to storefront trying to find her destination.

"On time and lost, I presume?"

Ana looked up in just enough time to avoid bumping into Andrew.

She pushed her sliding gym bag back over her shoulder and smiled. *It's good to see him again.* It had been a while.

She glanced back over her shoulder. "I was wondering if I got off the bus too early."

He grabbed her hand and pulled her back in the direction she had just come from. She had unknowingly passed the deli. She felt guilty holding his hand—like at any moment someone would jump out and say "Aha!" She was relieved when he let go to open the door for her.

The small deli had a very old and worn-out atmosphere. The aroma of toasted bread, melting cheese and various cooked meats and spices filled the air.

As he led the way to the counter, he said, "I've been coming here for years, and it's still my favorite place. All my favorite sandwiches were invented here!"

Ana leaned against the counter, looking at the long list of sandwiches. "What do you recommend?"

Andrew stared up at the list. "Hmm, try the French toast ham and cheese with all the works."

She giggled, making a face. "Ew, that sounds gross."

Andrew laughed. "No, it's actually really good. They dip the whole sandwich into a French toast batter—minus the cinnamon, of course—and then fry it!" he said, putting his hands together. "And it comes with a side of fries."

"You're right; that does sound good," she admitted.

After Andrew placed their orders, he leaned backward over the counter and turned to her. "You're paying, right?"

Ana fumbled to find and take out her wallet.

He laughed and stopped her. "I'm just kidding! Of course, I've got it." He took out some money and placed it on the counter. "By the way, I was talking with Megan and Susan the other day about your church. We're thinking of visiting this Sunday." They walked over to one large open window and found seats.

"Really?" Ana couldn't hide her excitement.

"We want to know why you like it so much." The fresh air and occasional downtown fumes drifted in around them. The sunlight played across their table as the cars and trucks roared by.

Ana smiled. "I bet you'll like it just as much as I do."

"Let's not get ahead of ourselves. I only said I was visiting." He waved his hand. "Don't start planning my future there or signing me up to some club."

"Well, there goes my plan to sign you up for the pastoral team."

"There's a pastoral club?"

Ana laughed, "Don't worry! They wouldn't want you anyway."

"I'd be a great pastor. The first thing I would do is give myself a raise!"

"*Whatever*, Andrew."

Right then, the cashier delivered their meal to the table. Andrew grabbed his chicken sandwich and took a big bite. He looked at her. "So have you thought about my little proposal I mentioned a few weeks ago? You could be a pastor's wife." Andrew sang between chews.

Ana felt her stomach start to tense. "Yes." To distract herself, she grabbed her hair and twisted it to the nape of her neck. She kept her twirling the handful of hair "I've prayed about it, and it just doesn't feel right. I need to do things differently than I have in the past."

Andrew's face fell in disappointment. He tried to keep eating casually, but his annoyance was obvious. "It's because I don't go to church like you, isn't it?" He paused, as his jaw clenched and unclenched.

Ana could see he was growing angry.

"Ana, what about how I feel about you and how I treat you? Doesn't that count for anything?"

"It does, but we're in different places right now," Ana attempted to explain in an effort to soften the blow.

Andrew spoke sharply in reply, "You know, you should give a guy a chance. Otherwise, you'll end up old and alone." He took another big bite of his sandwich.

Ana's mouth dropped open at his sudden attack. She stared back at him before lowering her gaze. A tense silence forced its way between them. It didn't matter if he said the spiteful words out of hurt. *What if he were right?* She picked at her sandwich and finally took a bite. The sandwich seemed hard and slid dryly down her throat. Her appetite was gone.

She finally spoke cautiously, trying not to betray her feelings. "I want to know that I'm doing the right thing—not what I want in the moment. I don't feel that right now."

Andrew shook his head. "You're hiding behind God. Why don't you just say you don't like me, or there is someone else?" He put down his sandwich, sat back in his chair, and crossed his arms across his chest. "You're acting like a baby, Ana. It's time to grow up and see what's out in the big, wide world in front of you."

She shook her head, ignoring his comment. "Andrew, I can't explain to you how I feel. I just know that, at this point, it's not right for me."

Andrew leaned in closer. "Everything has gotten better since I met you. I want you to be in my life. I want to make you happy," he said softly as he reached for her hand.

She pulled away from him. "I am happy. Look, I don't want things to be awkward between us. I'd like it if we could stay friends."

He stared at her and finally dropped his gaze, as silence reigned at their table and made Ana restless. She realized for the first time that she had caused him pain. Shamed by her selfishness, she couldn't let herself off the hook. Over the last couple of weeks, the thought had never occurred to her that Andrew could actually get hurt. She hadn't thought about guarding his heart the way she had her own. She had only thought of herself. Andrew had been up-front about his intentions from the beginning, but she had continually lied to herself while enjoying his attention.

Maybe I am afraid of being alone. "I'm really sorry; this is my fault..."

"It's okay, Ana. Friendship is better than nothing," Andrew interrupted with an audible sigh. "I don't understand, but I'll let it go for now—but not forever. I know you're in my life for a reason." He stared out of the window and then turned back to face her.

Ana nodded. "I think you're right that I'm in your life for a reason." Ana picked up her neglected sandwich and took another bite.

He leaned forward. "All right, tell me more about this church of yours. How close to the front do I need to sit?"

~

Andrew sat in the seat with Ana on his left. Her friends, Susan and Megan, sat on Ana's other side. So far he was enjoying church. The singing part was really long, but some parts did something to him, stirring old memories. He glanced quickly at Megan and Susan. His gaze again caught Megan's—for the tenth time. He winked at her and then yawned.

What time is this going to be over?

There was a lot of chatter over on the other side of Ana. He wished he felt more comfortable talking to Ana during the service but conversing with her was impossible. He could almost feel his mom sitting next to him, ready to pinch him if opened his mouth. He'd learned long ago that talking in the service was a big no-no. He noticed that Megan and Susan didn't seem to get that memo.

When Susan tried to find the Scriptures that the pastor mentioned, Ana assisted her. Susan seemed to be enjoying everything too. Megan was the one who raised doubts in his mind. Every few minutes, a giggling Megan would nudge Susan to point at something in the room. From what he could see, Susan wanted to pay attention—even if Megan didn't.

I'm sitting next to Ana in church, what...?

In a zillion years he'd never have thought he would have come back to church. The way he remembered it hadn't been like this. I could actually get used to this. It isn't so bad. The music—the people were so into it. First, they were dancing like they had each won the lottery; next, during the slower songs, the people cried like they had—just won the lottery. During worship he had glanced over at Ana's profile. She'd been in her own world—hands raised with tears streaming down her face. Even he had to admit that an overwhelming sense of peace reigned in this place. When the musicians and singers ended the music and everyone sat down, he felt somewhat sad but couldn't explain why. *What am I missing?*

He looked over his Bible. It was old, but in mint condition. His dad had given it to him shortly before he had disappeared.

A part of him had died when his father had left. That stolen piece of his heart had, like his dad, never returned. Misery clung to him. Life held no real excitement anymore. Although he hadn't done much with life yet, he always felt like he'd already seen and done everything. He often questioned his sanity.

For so long he'd been numb, until now. Ana had brought something fresh and new. The only problem was that Ana seemed so completely fulfilled without anything he could actually put his finger on. She didn't need him or anyone else. He wanted her to need him like all of the other girls had. Ana had a peace about her that he craved for himself.

"Jesus thought of *you* when He made that painful sacrifice on the cross," Pastor Mark said as he was nearing the end of the service. Andrew looked directly at Pastor Mark; at this moment, he felt like the pastor was speaking directly to him. *Has Ana told the pastor about me?* But there were things he hadn't even told Ana—like how angry and hurt he had been when his father had left.

"God is a Father to the fatherless. He deeply cared about widows and orphans," Pastor Mark continued. Andrew wished his father was here now to see him in church. He would have been proud. His mind drifted to the many Sunday mornings his mom used to bully him into attending service. Okay, maybe she hadn't really been a bully. He smiled to himself thinking about how angry he'd once been. His mom had been doing it for his sake, but at the time, both she and everyone else had seemed like the enemy.

"Jesus loves you. He died for all of humanity, but He would have died for you alone." Pastor Mark's words resonated inside him. He used to wonder about this. *Does Jesus actually know me?*

"We used to sing an old song when I was a kid at Good News Remnant," Pastor Mark continued. "When He was on the cross, I was on His mind. As the band comes back to play that song, I want each of you to think about what God is asking you to do considering Jesus' sacrifice."

When the song began to play, Andrew's heart broke. Too many painful memories washed over him.

"We have an opportunity today to give our life to Him, to have Him lead us. Jesus' blood was spilled so that we wouldn't have to be enemies of God, but so we could be adopted as His children, cleansed from our sin, made brand-new."

Maybe I should just give God a chance. No. Then what? Nothing but rules would replace the things that keep away the emptiness. No, not yet.

Pastor Mark interrupted his thoughts. "What is God asking you to do in light of that sacrifice? This is your opportunity to come to the altar and give your life to God, so please come." Pastor Mark motioned to the front of the small stage.

As the song continued to play, Andrew eyes burned with tears.

Why am I crying?

The last time he'd thought of this song, he'd been arguing with his mom about not going to church. Then he remembered the women at church singing. His father's smile. His father gone.

The memories kept coming, but they were changing. He just saw his father smiling and gazed into his eyes. He loved him and would always love him. His father had thought about him and his future.

Ana put a hand on his back and whispered to him. "Andrew, I never told you this, but I had a dream about you a long time ago. I think I dreamed what I did because Jesus wants you to know that He was thinking of you when He died on the cross." Andrew felt tears coursing down his face. *This is too much. How does she know?*

Ana continued "He loved you that much. He loved you before you were born and into eternity. He loved you and was with you when you were young and hurt and angry about your dad. He doesn't want you to be afraid of trusting Him."

The song finally made sense. Jesus was thinking of him and had died for him and was now offering him a new life. Andrew felt the bitter loneliness inside of him start to ebb as he thought about Jesus. How comforted he felt was unreal. *I miss you, Dad. Is this what you wanted for me?*

Andrew dropped his head so that no one nearby could see him crying. He rubbed his eyes. *I can't be a Christian.* His heart started to pound. He knew he only had two choices. Ana's hand was still on his back. He didn't care that she had seen him cry.

Maybe I can do this.

He noticed Susan making a move to go to the front and decided to follow. He trailed slowly behind. As he got to the platform, the tears he'd tried to hide were streaming down his face again. Megan and a few other people crowded in the front too.

Pastor Mark smiled at them like a proud father as they came. People came to embrace those who had come to the front. Andrew felt exposed. No one was standing with him.

What am I doing here?

Andrew looked down and glanced to the side. Before he could look behind him, Pastor Mark was beside him, putting an arm around his shoulder and pulling him into a hug.

CHAPTER 15

Jericho

"*By faith the walls of Jericho fell, after the army had marched around them for seven days*" (Hebrews 11:30, NIV).

SANDRA AND CATHY worked side by side in the kitchen. Cathy tried to press the pie crust neatly into the baking dish.

"Try pinching the sides, like this," Sandra instructed and then demonstrated the technique.

Cathy tried unsuccessfully. Exasperated, she said, "Can't I just leave it like this? It's just going to get baked and eaten before anyone has a chance to see it. Besides, what does baking have to do with being a mom anyway? I feel like the karate kid."

Sandra laughed. She dusted her hands and then pressed them to her apron before grabbing another bowl. "Let's just work on the filling for now."

Cathy watched as Sandra started to pour ingredients into the bowl and begin mixing them with a large spoon. Cathy sighed and looked at her watch. "Kevin was supposed to be here by now."

Sandra looked up at Cathy. "Being late all the time is not a good sign."

Cathy shrugged. "He has a lot on his plate. Maybe he just forgot. He has to go to several counseling appointments. He is trying to make real changes in his life."

"Kevin is in a bubble right now. He's not working or dealing with life yet. If he can't remember simple things now, then how will he act when the baby comes?"

Cathy looked down and rubbed her abdomen.

Sandra continued. "You need to be wise and focus on you and the baby in the decisions you're going to make. I don't really trust Kevin."

"I'm trying to do what's best, but sometimes, it's hard to hear what God is telling me. I feel scared just thinking about it—like what will happen if we do get married."

Sandra stopped what she was doing and turned to face Cathy. "You're not seriously thinking of marrying him, are you?" She resumed stirring and then handed the bowl to Cathy. "As irresponsible as he is, I don't think he's ready to take that step in life. And don't get me started on how selfish he's been. You don't want to commit your life to someone like that and have him leave you on a whim. You and the baby would be hurt in so many ways."

"Trust me, he's trying. I'm just trying to be supportive and not give into my fears."

Sandra took the mixing bowl from Cathy and placed it on the counter. "Come have a seat." She took Cathy's hand, led her to the kitchen table and sat down across from her. "Your fears are valid. You can't trust a drug addict. He will say anything. He has mastered ways to lie and manipulate to get what he wants."

She sighed deeply before adding, "I don't know if I ever told you this, but Ana's father left when she was only a baby. I can't even put into words how hard life was for us. You have so much potential. I don't want to see you throw away your future simply to marry him. Has he made any effort to show you that he's ready to be a husband and a father?"

"Well, not yet. After all, I mean he just found out about the baby a short time ago."

"I don't think you should trust him, Cathy."

Cathy felt strange. She put her hands on her forehead and leaned over the table. "I don't know." Sandra meant well, but something about her tone didn't sit right with her. She sounded angry, and Cathy had no idea why.

Sandra sighed again. "I'm just trying to protect you so you don't have to go through the heartache of abandonment. I want you to be happy, and you don't need Kevin for that."

"I'll keep praying about what to do."

"What's there to pray about?" Sandra suddenly snapped. "Think about it, Cathy; use some logic. Do you want to get hurt again?"

Cathy sat back. *How much more hurt can my heart take?*

Okelani

Okelani watched Will pace around the room. As his guardian, he could often sense turmoil in Will. The room was dimly lit with only a desk lamp. The house was silent except for Will's low murmurs of prayer. He sat down and put his head in hands. Pastor Mark had asked Will and Ana to lead the joint prayer meetings between the churches. The more they had all come together to pray, the more Will sensed a burden for the community. He didn't understand what it was all about.

Okelani waited for Will to get settled in his spirit man so he could deliver the message God had given him.

Despite Will's physical absence from the outpouring, God had given Will his portion. This was home, and that meant that whatever happened here in the spiritual realm affected them too. Their preparation was also imperative to the coming battle.

Will finally relaxed and began to listen. Solid words formed in his heart. **Greater love has no man than this, than to lay down his life for his friends. Protect Ana.**

Protect her? How?

As Will began to pray for her, the uneasiness within him ebbed. This was it. He'd keep praying for her over the next few weeks if that's what God wanted.

Okelani put his hand over Will's head as Will prayed. There was confusion over Ana. Will actually wanted to know her better, but he had to wonder if he should stop thinking about her altogether, except to pray. Okelani was the only one who understood the spiritual element that pulled them together to work as a team. Their lives were linked in a way that Will would not soon understand. Will would try to ignore what he felt in his heart. His sensitivity had always made him cautious, and that was good. He would take his time before he acted, and that too was good because the timing had to be right.

Will prayed until tears filled his eyes. "God, I'll do anything You want me to do. Just help me to know what that is. Take away these feelings so that I can focus on Your work because I want to do Your will."

The walls of Jericho must come down. Worship and prayer will bring down the walls. If my people who are called by my name will humble themselves and pray, then I will hear from heaven, and I will heal their land.

Will opened his eyes and wrote in his notebook.

Take back the territory.

What territory do we need to take back?

~

Once the people had gathered in the sanctuary of the church, Pastor Mark called for their attention. The weekly prayer meetings had been growing, but new reports of violence in the area had been released. "I know you've heard about what's going on. Given what happened at the school, I thought it best we gather today to pray specifically about this incident."

Ana leaned over to whisper to Will, "What happened?"

"A stabbing—a twelve-year-old attacked another kid," he whispered back.

"That's crazy!"

Pastor Mark continued. "A few people have been coming to me with similar senses and dreams about our community, so I'm convinced that it's time we gathered to pray into it." He turned to Will and Ana. "You guys ready?"

Sasson and the other angels flew back and forth in the church. Now that the outpouring had taken place and the people were better equipped, the time had come to begin the outward work in the city. All that was needed was to make the holy people aware of what the King had ordained.

Sasson flew to Ana and placed an orb of light above her head. He watched as it sank in. He looked up at the other angels who swept through the room, carrying additional orbs. The Holy Spirit danced into the room like a whirl of smoke as people prayed. He took his time to caress the prayer warriors and whisper in their ears. He swirled and unfurled into their hearts and rested above others like He was pondering what to do next.

As Ana prayed, the Holy Spirit surrounded her. For a time, she remained silent.

Sasson examined the crowd of regulars praying in the church. They had been alternating prayer meetings between Good News Remnant and Isaac's Well. Ana and Will had done a great job of leading everyone in prayer. The Holy Spirit was clearly pleased with the cooperation of both churches. The scent of spices thickened in the room as He continued to retouch those whom He had already visited.

Sasson waited as they walked back and forth praying in the tongues. Some were sitting in chairs, listening and waiting for God to speak. The dots had to connect in order to move forward. Sasson moved closer to Ana and placed his hand on her head.

"I feel like we need to form small groups to pray and focus for a bit," Ana whispered to Will as he passed by. He nodded.

Ana spoke up. "Okay, everyone. Let's break into groups of three or four. We're going to focus on praying for the community." She joined hands with those closest to her.

After a few minutes of prayer, everyone regrouped to debrief.

Will started. "In my personal times of prayer, I've sensed that there are demonic boundaries and lies the Enemy is trying to establish in specific areas of the neighborhood. There are several spots including one near the elementary school." He pushed his hands into his pockets. "I believe that is why we've seen increased violence there."

Ana nodded and jotted down what he was saying. *Strongholds.*

Daniel was next. "I agree that something is there. When I walk by, I always begin to feel sad or lonely—no matter what mood I was in before. At first, I didn't notice it, but after a few times, the feeling has become obvious."

Ana glanced around. "Anyone else pick up on anything?"

Pastor Mark cleared his throat. "I feel that much has been going on behind the scenes. Maybe the negative stuff we're sensing at the school has been there longer and is more established."

Ana nodded, "Listen, why don't we go there and pray? Not everyone has to go, but I think it would be good if we could get one group to go out and one group to stay back and pray."

Will lifted his hand. "I'll go."

"Me too," a few others offered.

"All right, let's break into two discerning groups. Then we can try and sense what's happening."

Kavo whispered to Pastor Mark, who turned to Ana. "I think we should all go together and pray."

Ana nodded and turned to face the group. "New plan everyone; we go together. Grab your stuff, and we'll meet in the parking lot in five minutes."

A bright-orange sunset coloring the sky surrounded the buildings as they silently walked to the elementary school. The street was busy with a smattering of cars and people strolling to their destinations as Ana led the team from the church.

After turning down a few blocks, the group gradually started talking with each other. Destiny and Owen began to sing worship songs as they walked, and soon others joined in.

Ana quietly sang in tongues as she tried to listen in the spirit. Will stepped into the space beside her. As they neared the elementary school, Ana noticed that the excited chatter of the group become strained; silence began to descend on the group. The singing stopped, and everyone seemed to look more than a little hesitant as their pace slowed.

"Let's each pray here," Ana announced. "We'll join back together in a few minutes to share what we feel God is saying."

Will sat on a swing as a few others spread out. Some sat on the playground equipment, and some walked to the ball field. After about twenty minutes, Ana called everyone back together.

A young woman spoke. "I sense this cold feeling of dread as if something bad happened here."

Christy, a young girl from Ana's dance group at the community centre, added, "I'm getting a feeling that's really gross and icky."

Daniel said, "I just had a vision and saw someone planting curses in the ground."

Destiny raised her hand. "When I was praying around the corner, I felt a sudden jolt of fear like I was being chased."

Will volunteered, "Spirit of death? Maybe that's the stronghold here."

"All right," Pastor Mark nodded. "We've discerned a lot. Anyone getting what God wants to do here?"

Destiny nodded. "He wants to break the curses and release an outpouring of love and power. He wants to heal the children who have been affected."

Ana turned to Owen. "Let's spend some time praising God over this spot and then pray. Can you lead us in a praise song?"

Owen began to sing, and the others joined in.

Though difficult at first, Ana felt herself break through the sadness that had descended as everyone focused on praising God. Owen then led them through a few worship songs, as they exalted the name of Jesus over the land and poured worship out on that place.

☙

Sasson and the angels joined arms around the prayer warriors. Sasson exchanged glances with Kavo. *No turning back now!* The group would be exposed to the Enemy as they began to actively take back the land spiritually. The angel's job was to protect them.

As the company of angels linked arms, their light glowed and spread until it created a dome of what the angels termed as "hiddenness" around everyone in the group. The dome would remain in place until they finished praying.

☙

Daniel started in prayer. "Father, we ask that You break every curse that was planted on this ground. We lift up Your name in this place. We say that You reign here."

Pastor Mark continued. "Jesus, we plead Your blood over this land and ask You to reveal the schemes of the Enemy in this place."

As various people prayed out loud, the rest of the group listened and prayed in agreement. Some prayed in tongues while others sang softly.

Destiny spoke with confidence. "Father, we repent for the murders or violations that have taken place on this land in the past. Heal those who were hurt and allow Your justice to come to them and this place. We pray that the Enemy would no longer have his way here but that You would be glorified here in this place. Let Your name be lifted higher than any trick of the Enemy."

The group joined hands and continued to pray. The sun had fully set when Pastor Mark said the final prayer.

Moments later, he found Ana, "Hey, I need to speak to you and Will."

Ana waited for Pastor Mark and Will as she watched the rest of the group disperse on their way back to the church.

"What do you guys think?" Pastor Mark folded his arms and stopped walking.

Will kicked at the dirt. "We're not finished yet. I feel like we have only scratched the surface."

"That's exactly what I was thinking."

Ana shivered; the air had cooled once the warm sun had set. "I feel like unity is where God is leading us. Remember the overflow of power at the reconciliation? That's where God is taking us. We need to get other churches involved in prayer for the city. Our unity will break through in the Spirit. As we were praying, I thought about a prayer march like God's people did in the book of Joshua."

Pastor Mark nodded. "I agree; that's exactly what we need to do."

Will frowned as he remembered something. "Wow, I sensed that in prayer a few nights ago. I heard the words, 'The walls of Jericho must come down.'"

Something stirred within Ana's heart. She pondered the story of Jericho. "It could be like a prophetic act—like it was with the city of Jericho in the Bible. We could walk a route through the city going to key places God shows us. It could be a silent prayer march for six days that ends each day in a prayer meeting or something." She paused then added, "Then on the seventh and last day instead of the Israelites' trumpet blasts, we could have a huge praise party." She was surprised that she had come up with the idea.

Pastor Mark nudged Ana in the side. "I love it! See, that's why we missed you so much. I'm putting you in charge of the whole event. Will, you can work alongside Ana. Let's meet again tomorrow to discuss plans."

Ana reeled. "What? I can't possibly…"

Pastor Mark's hand was already up. "Ana, you will do fine. I'm confident that you can do this. Anyway, I need to get home, Johanna has been ill."

As they entered the church parking lot, Pastor Mark headed for his car and got in. As he started his car, he rolled down his window and called, "Start praying into the march. See you guys tomorrow.

Ana shouted back. "Let Johanna know we are praying for her too,"

When Pastor Mark had driven away, she turned to Will. "I don't want to lead this. I've never done anything like this before. I don't even know where to start."

"Oh, Ana, it'll be fine. I'll be helping too. We just need to decide dates and then get worship bands for the praise fest. We should start mapping out the area too. I'll do some research tonight."

Ana sighed. "You seem pretty confident about all this."

Will stared at her like he had just noticed something. "Are you afraid?"

Ana looked at the pavement. "Maybe…" She suddenly felt embarrassed. *Why do I care what he thinks?*

"What are you afraid of?"

Ana smiled sheepishly. "I don't know. I don't like being the leader. I'd rather be the support person—less pressure and no potential for failure involved."

"I've watched you, Ana. God made you a leader. Don't be afraid. He'll give you wisdom. I'll pray for you too, and as I said, I'm here to help. Plus, if God gave you the vision for it, then that must mean you're to be involved in it. My dad would always tell me that if God gave you the idea, He'll help you do it."

Ana felt comfort in his words. "Thanks, Will! I feel better after talking.

You're right. I shouldn't be afraid." Suddenly Ana yelled, "If God is for us, who can be against us! Right?"

"I'm fairly sure Satan is against us, but I see what you're getting at!" Will matched her outburst.

They began to laugh. Ana narrowed her eyes and threatened, "You know what? I hate Satan; He's going down!"

"Yeah, we'll bring him down together." Will smiled at her and then looked away suddenly. He folded his arms. "It's getting late. Do you need a ride home?" He turned toward his car.

"Thanks for the offer, but I have Mom's car. It's parked at the front."

"I'd be happy to chauffeur you to your car." Will bowed and gestured to a car that sat under a bent tree in the parking lot.

"The lazy-man way. Sure, thanks." Ana pushed short curls behind her ear and followed him.

"Remember when I told you I kept having dreams about this place?" Will said as they walked to his car,

"Yeah?" Ana said, only half-listening. Her thoughts were on Andrew—what he was up to now.

"I didn't know why. I thought I was just homesick or something. But now that I'm back, things are starting to make sense. God wants to do a lot in this city." As they stepped closer to his car, he opened the door for her. After she sat down, he closed the door and went around to the driver's side.

"You're right. I sense that too." Ana agreed, as he started the car. "Let's just hope we're not the only ones."

～

The familiar guttural voice grumbled in Leah's ear. "Get up!" Leah sat up. Her sweat caused her shirt and hair to cling to her skin. Sakron's presence brought only empty coldness. She shivered. *What's happening? Why is Sakron angrier than usual? This could mean pain for me.*

"My work has been exposed. You need to create more diversions and curse shields right now!" Sakron growled.

"Wait... What's going on?" Leah questioned as she glanced at the clock. It was two in the morning.

"Earlier the people at church broke down some of my curse shields. The coming battle requires us to have as many legal rights to the land as possible. The enemy has reinforcements on the way. I can feel the holy ones emerging." Sakron appeared in front of her.

"What should I do?" Leah asked. She threw off her covers and grabbed a sweater.

"I want you to unleash demons to attack Ana. Attack her relentlessly from every angle. You may not be able to touch her directly so use her friends. She must not accomplish this task that has been given to her."

Leah walked into the bathroom as Sakron continued to speak. "Much depends on her failure." As Sakron hovered nearby in a dark corner, his thoughts were as loud as words in her ears. "If we can keep her from this path, then many other people and things will fall with her."

"Now is the time to use those dedicated to me to destroy from the inside." Leah looked confused.

Sakron answered her confusion. "Some are not aware of their role and their compliance to me. Unless I state otherwise, do not reveal anything to them. In the meantime, they are my connections into the church. The time is almost at hand for the priestess to arrive."

"Priestess?" Leah asked.

"You will know her when you see her," Sakron barked. "Attend every prayer meeting, cause dissension and disunity whenever you see an opportunity. Those schemes will then take care of themselves so you can focus on the bigger matters. Your attempt to distract the pastor has failed. His wife is almost well, and he has already prayed through it and is more focused than before. We must look for another angle. If you break the prayer covering, you can go unnoticed for a far longer time…"

CHAPTER 16

A Call in the Spirit

"To open their eyes, and to turn them from darkness to light, and from the power of Satan unto God, that they may receive forgiveness of sins, and inheritance among them which are sanctified by faith that is in me" (Acts 26:18, KJV).

"I DON'T APPRECIATE the way you've been eyeing my food." Elikai covered his plate of loaded fries.

Owen tried to steal a fry as Elikai used his fork to defend his territory.

"Hands off!" Elikai warned.

Owen frowned. "I'm not feeling the Christian love at this table, brother." He turned to Will. "I'm glad you're back to model what real Christian charity looks like."

Elikai laughed. "You're only glad because he buys the food, and you can eat off his plate whenever you want."

"Whatever my reasons, I love him the same," Owen answered.

Daniel chimed in, "You're the one who wanted to cheap out on the food."

Owen feigned a look of annoyance. "I'm not cheap; I'm frugal."

Leah fiddled with the paper wrapping of a straw as she sat with the boys and continued to listen to them bicker in the diner. The bright turquoise vinyl seats gave the place a sixties feel. Hanging out with them like a normal teenager felt a bit strange. All they needed was a group nerd, and they'd be on their way to a nationally broadcast sitcom. But she wasn't going to let this "Saved-by-the-Bell" atmosphere distract her from the reason why she was present. She was picking up on some definite dynamics at the table. Andrew and Will both seemed to be trying to engage in conversation with Ana, while Megan was trying hard to hold Andrew's attention. For the most part, Megan's advances worked, but clearly, if Andrew had his way only he and Ana would be at the table.

Leah sighed. She needed to learn as much as possible so she could use the information against them. Sakron wasn't with her to feed her private information, but she sensed a similar presence resting over Andrew. She wondered if he were like her.

Destiny began, "We need to discuss a few things and pray about them over lunch. Many of us are receiving prophetic dreams and words of knowledge. We should start piecing together what God is showing us about the community and decide what to do…"

"Why do we all have to be involved?" Owen interrupted. "Pastor Mark put Will and Ana in charge of prayer for a reason. I don't think we should bore our new friends. Let's just have a nice peaceful lunch."

"We are leading it, but we could use your input," Ana laughed. "I'd also like to point out that your idea was to have this meeting now."

Owen rubbed his stomach. "Come on, you can't hold a man liable for the decisions he makes when he's hungry."

Destiny shook her head and rolled her eyes. "All right *Esau*, but we still need to discuss this stuff." She shifted in her seat. "We also need to find a way to get people more involved at church and with the community. We have a lot more people at church but not doing anything else. We need to motivate everyone if we are to move forward and help our city and end all this violence."

"There's nothing we can do about people being more committed." Elikai jumped in. "I think we should just wait it out. The crowds are curious. It's great having so many people coming out."

Destiny protested, "But we can't just settle for that. That we are effective as a church is far more important—even if we remain small."

Elikai shrugged. "We can't expect all of the new people to be involved in everything. Some of them are visitors from other churches."

He turned to Ana's friends. "What do you guys think? Are there things you want to get more involved in, like our prayer group?"

Susan looked uneasy. She nervously gathered her black hair with blue tints in her hands. "I'm already struggling with summer school and have very little time to devote to anything else."

Andrew shrugged. "Are you guys sure you want me to be more involved? I don't know anything."

Owen dramatically threw up both of his hands. "Guys, he's right. I mean, like do we really want newbie over here ruining everything?"

Destiny held up her hand to stop Owen. "Be quiet, Owen. They aren't used to your twisted sense of humor." She smiled at Andrew. "He's totally kidding. You'll have to forgive our friend. He gets a bit weird when he's hungry—and all the rest of the time."

Owen pushed up his glasses. "I'm not weird; I'm just stressed. You try leading worship with all these intense spiritual stuff happening. Without Johanna, it's doubly hard. There's so much pressure to perform. People have even started giving me song requests."

"Anyone know how Johanna is doing?" Daniel asked. "Who gets bronchitis, laryngitis and the stomach flu all at the same time like that?"

Leah shrugged. "Sounds rough."

Will patted Owen's shoulder "She's getting better. Pastor Mark has taken good care of her." After a brief pause, he added, "Owen, just do what you sense God is saying to do in worship. Nothing else matters."

Owen nodded. He turned back to Andrew. "I'm sorry, lots is lost in translation when I'm sarcastic. What I meant to say is that you're not going to wake up one day and know all you need to know about God. To grow, you need to be taught…"

Owen looked around the diner. "Hold that thought…" He got up and walked over to an older man who was sitting nearby.

"What's he doing?" Megan asked as she watched him sit down and talk to the man. "Does he know him?"

Destiny smiled. "I think he had a prophetic word for him. He's trying to increase his ability to hear God's voice by being obedient to everything he believes God is saying to him."

Megan looked puzzled. "What do you mean when you *say a word*?"

"Well, it's when God speaks to you about something either from the past, present or future. It can be a word of knowledge or a word of wisdom. It's one of the spiritual gifts God uses to give us information about someone's life or some advice or direction that will somehow lead a person closer to Him," Destiny answered.

Leah was intrigued. *How did they know about getting information that way?* She had only just learned how to get information from Sakron after years of practice and study.

Andrew asked, "Why?"

Destiny smiled. "God loves people and wants them to know He's thinking of them. My sisters and I love practicing on each other. Our dad always told us how important it was for people to hear God's voice."

After a few minutes Owen returned with a fake smile plastered on his face. "That did not go well."

Ana laughed and picked up her milkshake. "I'm sure it was powerful in the spiritual realm."

Andrew grinned and shook his head. "Wow! You guys are like superheroes with all these secret abilities no one else knows about."

"That is really cool," Susan added.

Megan made a face. "You don't believe this stuff, do you?" she whispered to Andrew.

Andrew nodded. "Sure I do. My grandma used to do stuff like this all the time; she wasn't a Christian though."

Will turned to face Andrew. "If she wasn't a believer, she might have been into some negative stuff. Did she used to contact the dead?"

Leah looked over at Andrew to hear his answer. *Maybe this is why I have sensed the presence over him.*

"It was creepy the way she'd tell us things. Sometimes I think I still see her." Andrew gazed into space.

Owen put up his hands. "Don't be alarmed, but we need to pray for you. Will, hold him down."

Andrew looked at Will quickly. "What?"

"He's kidding about the holding you down part." Will frowned at Owen. "But we should pray."

Elikai added, "Yeah, if she's dead, you should not be seeing her. Maybe she had a familiar spirit. Sometimes that kind masquerades as someone who's died."

"What's that?" Andrew asked.

Will explained, "Some people speculate that these spirits were from the line of the Nephilim, the race of giants spoken about in Genesis chapter six. People believe they were created when the fallen angels began to have children with the women of earth. The wickedness and evil created by these superpowers was spreading and intermingling with the people on the earth. Imagine those superpowers terrorizing humanity. So God flooded the earth in order to cleanse it."

Leah wondered about Sakron's origins.

Was any of this possible?

She suddenly started to feel vulnerable and uneasy.

Destiny asked. "Noah's ark and the flood?"

Will nodded, "Exactly. After the demon hybrids died, they were stripped of their bodies; they quickly tried to regain power by encountering people and families. Sometimes they even set themselves up as a 'family idol.'" Will turned back to Andrew. "That's why God warned people about idol worship and about sacrificing. They were sacrificing to these demons that gained power from their worship. Imagine a demon that comes out of nowhere, demanding to be worshipped. Even if it masqueraded as a long-dead relative, it could still get what it wanted. The spirits would have had access to information about the past. Someone who could contact someone like that would appear very powerful and get a type of worship too. They feed from human hosts, needing their worship and attention."

Andrew could no longer contain his curiosity. "But what about the future? How do they know what's going to happen?"

Will responded, "Remember, these types of spirits want to draw as many people away from God as possible. They don't really know all of the future, but they might know some things. However, because those spirits use their knowledge against human beings, it will never turn out good."

Susan looked around as if she could suddenly see spirits. "So these spirits just attach themselves to people and hang out?"

"Anywhere they can fulfill their agenda works well for them. Psychics then use these spirits to read a person's family history."

Megan asked, "How do you know this stuff is true?"

Will shrugged. "I don't know for sure; I'm just telling you what I've read. I like studying Bible mysteries," Will explained. "Daniel and I were looking into this stuff before I left."

Daniel nodded.

Owen said, "I still don't get how the spirits can tell the future." He grabbed an extra fork and dug into Will's plate of pasta.

Daniel chimed in. "Everyone has more than one potential destiny—the one God has for him or her and the one the Devil wants for the person. The Bible says death and life are in the power of the tongue. Telling you about your 'future' can be as simple as saying certain things will happen to you—whether good or bad. Curses spoken over a person's life can allow circumstances to be set in motion to make evil things happen."

Will took a sip of his soda. "To be fair, not all psychics know what they're doing to people. The Devil is definitely using them. I don't doubt that maybe God intended some of these psychics to be His mouthpiece and give true prophetic words, but they somehow got seduced onto the wrong path."

Leah felt a shiver run up her spine.

Will continued to eat, either unaware or ignoring the fact that Owen was helping himself to his food. "Or maybe they just never knew what was possible for them in God."

Ana announced, "I think I had a familiar spirit while growing up."

Both Andrew and Leah turned to look at her.

She nodded. "I did. I had many nightmares and reoccurring dreams as a kid. I always felt like something was watching me." Ana stared down at her plate. "Then when I got serious with God, things started to get worse and then it finally left. I'm glad it's gone."

Andrew was pale when he met her gaze. He looked around the table until his gaze finally settled on Will. "Um…Will, so when can I get this special prayer you mentioned?"

Megan popped a French fry into her mouth. "You're actually going to do it?"

Andrew shrugged. "Prayer can't hurt."

"You see, guys," Daniel said, tapping his index finger on the table. "This is why I always say we need to remember we're in a spiritual battle."

Destiny, Elikai and Owen groaned collectively.

Daniel grimaced. "Exactly what I'm talking about, people. How come every time I start talking about spiritual warfare, everyone groans? We are in a spiritual battle!"

Owen sipped Will's drink and then added, "'Cause that's all you ever talk about, Daniel."

"That is not *all I ever talk about*," Daniel said mimicking Owen. "Spiritual warfare is a vitally important topic that no one wants to address. The Enemy has been infiltrating everything, and, as people of God, we've been doing our best to ignore it all."

Will nodded. "Daniel has a point, guys,"

Leah suddenly felt anxious. "Infiltrate? You're making everything sound so intense and scary—like a military attack. I don't think we should be so paranoid."

Megan nodded. "This stuff creeps me out."

Daniel raised his hands to explain. "Back in the day, there was a lot of talk about spiritual warfare and ex-witches in the church; now it's like a taboo topic. What's everyone so afraid of?"

Destiny pointed with her fork. "It may not actually be fear that keeps people from wanting to discuss the subject. Sometimes it's more important to focus on what God is doing than on what the Enemy is doing."

Daniel defended. "Guys, I'm not talking about finding a demon under every rock. I'm simply talking about being aware and informed. I think people are scared and don't want to admit it."

"Scared of what?" Megan asked.

Daniel shrugged. "Scared of everything. Fear has been bred and marketed, and many people have bought into it."

Destiny narrowed her gaze and stared at him. "What do you mean?"

"Think about it. The horror shows on television, and, you know, the criminal stuff focusing on twisted minds. Let's face it. We love to be afraid. We're fascinated with evil—as long as it's not real. But what if it were real, and the Enemy just wanted you to believe otherwise? We've been conned, guys. If we don't do something, we'll be useless for real spiritual warfare because we're afraid of what's happening right before our eyes. Our community is being destroyed, and we'd rather watch television and play video games while pretending the violence and evil is not actually affecting us."

Leah forced a laugh. She wished she could turn the conversation to something else. *This was a train wreck.* "Thinking we can stop people from doing bad things in the community through prayer is ridiculous. If someone is coming at me with a knife, the first thing I'm going to do is call the police."

Ana looked over to Leah. "Prayer really *can* change the community. We need a strategy to combat the violence that has been occurring."

Elikai added, "And we have to stop being lazy and making excuses. If we want to see something happen, we need to do something. What's the point of having power we don't use."

"And if we rely on God, we'll know how to pray. We've already seen things shift." Destiny's fork dangled from her fingers. "God is taking us into a new place of warfare as we pray His truth over these matters. We're going to need different kinds of prayers to help spread the kingdom of God on the earth." She took another bite. "Let's start with Andrew. If there's something messing with him, we should get rid of it."

Will and Elikai reached over so they could lay their hands on Andrew's shoulder while Destiny, Owen and Ana stretched out their hands in Andrew's direction. Megan, Susan and Leah closed their eyes.

Elikai started. "Andrew, pray with me. I renounce all ties to demonic spirits in my life. In the name of Jesus, I command them to go."

Andrew closed his eyes and repeated the words.

Although Leah's eyes were closed, she suddenly heard a shriek. Startled, she opened her eyes to see a spirit clothed in torn rags float away from Andrew. Its heavy presence left with it. *How did they do that so easily? They can't even see what's happening.*

As they continued praying, Leah started coughing. "I'm sorry. I'll be right back."

Megan and Ana scooted out of the booth to let her out.

❦

Leah bent over to splash water lightly on her cheeks and forehead and then pulled a paper towel from the dispenser.

Megan and Ana came to check on her after her a few moments. "Feeling better?" Ana asked as the door swung closed.

Leah looked at her through the bathroom mirror. "I just needed a minute. I'm fine."

Megan looked skeptical. "You sounded like you were hacking up a lung out there. I don't blame you though. It was getting a little weird."

Leah smirked. "You're telling me."

Ana turned to Megan. "You and Andrew looked pretty cozy back there."

"We've been hanging out a bit more lately. You don't mind, right?"

"No," Ana said, shaking her head. "I'm just surprised."

"At what?" Megan smiled slyly. "Obviously, I'm the prettiest one. If you don't want him, I will take him off your hands."

Ana laughed. "When was this determined?"

Megan pulled out a tube of lipstick and turned to the mirror. "It's a known fact that I get the most attention."

"That's probably because you're the most aggressive." Ana leaned back against the sink as she watched Megan primp.

Leah kept busy rewashing her hands, while listening to the conversation. *This is gold!*

Megan replaced the lid on her lipstick and cleared a smudge in her eye makeup. "You're right, but we can't all be as virginal as you. I swear if we didn't take you out with us sometimes, I don't know what would become of you." She put the lipstick back into her purse. "If it weren't for girls like me, girls like you wouldn't be special."

Ana's face drained of color. "Why do you say stuff like that? No one is forcing you into a role. You can choose who you want to do and be."

"I act the way I act because I like who I am, and so do guys." Megan walked into the stall. "Andrew's more my type anyway, and he likes to party." She added with a laugh, "With our looks, our kids will be beautiful."

Ana stepped closer to the stall and spoke quietly. "Megan, why do I have the feeling you're upset with me?"

"Why would I be upset with you?" The toilet flushed, and she emerged and pushed past Ana to the sink. "You have two guys who are clearly interested in you, and you're simply oblivious to it all." She gave Ana a dirty look. "And I'd appreciate it if you'd keep your judgments to yourself."

"I'm sorry I'm not trying to insult you. I'm confused. You're upset because I don't want to be with Andrew, but you like him? Why did you guys tell me to go out with him in the first place?"

"We just wanted to add some excitement to your life. You needed it. You'd been moping forever." Megan grabbed a paper towel.

"No guy was going to get me out of where I was. Only God could do that."

"Here we go again about *God*. Can we just go back to the table? We can talk about this later." Megan pushed open the bathroom door.

Leah shrugged at Ana before she followed Megan through the door. *This is better than I thought it would be.* Leah now had an idea.

CHAPTER 17

Weapons of Warfare

"The weapons we fight with are not the weapons of the world. On the contrary, they have divine power to demolish strongholds" (2 Corinthians 10:4, NIV).

CATHY'S HAIR WAS gathered in a loose ponytail and with her light-pink mesh sweater, Ana thought the expectant mother looked younger. Her face was radiant with the glow of pregnancy.

Cathy continued, "I've had a couple of visions here and there, but I feel like they were more frequent before Kevin came back. Since he's been here, I've been busy thinking about him." She chuckled. "I tell him not to worry, and then I worry." She shook her head.

Ana sat cross-legged on the floor of her room. Cathy perched on Ana's bed in front of her.

"I understand. Even the best of us must fight worry sometimes, but as we focus on the truth about God, everything will work out as we continue to pray. If it doesn't, then at least we didn't give in to fear, right? Worry is a type of fear." Ana tried to reassure her friend, but she knew what Cathy had to decide was difficult. She didn't know what she would do in the same situation.

Cathy leaned back on her elbows, and her hair brushed the bed as she stretched her neck. "Any more pointers?"

"Yes. Keep pressing in with prayer. God loves you and Kevin, and as you wait on Him, He will work out things for His purpose in your lives."

Cathy nodded. "By the way, I hope you won't take this the wrong way, but I've been noticing that some things seem…a little off." Cathy pushed herself up so that her back was straight.

"Like what?" Ana leaned over to grab her journal and started flipping through it.

"Well, some of the people at church… Whenever I ask them what God is showing them in the Word, they give me a blank stare or make some comment about my being a new Christian. They say things to each other like 'Oh, she's really on fire, but she'll calm down over time'—like they're making fun of me."

Ana waved her hand like she was swatting a bug. "Don't worry about it. They do that to feel better about losing their once-fiery passion. I've heard people say that the longer you're a Christian, the less you'll care about spiritual matters. But that's not true—at least, it's not supposed to happen that way."

Cathy made a face. "Is that what happened to you?"

Ana shook her head. "No, what happened to me was different. I let hurts and disappointment hinder my relationship with Christ. I was so busy feeling sorry for myself that I stopped listening to Him. I'm very thankful He didn't stop trying to get my attention."

"Oh." Cathy looked down at her bulging stomach. "So how do I make sure that I don't stop following God? I could never survive if I fell away from Him—even for a second."

"The more you lean on God, the less room you will have to put your trust in other things. I started to lean on my pain and stopped trusting God." Ana paused. "Some people become distracted by events in life and forget how they originally felt about God. But take Wella for example. She's been a Christian for over forty years, and Pastor Matthew was just like her before he died." Ana smiled as she remembered Pastor Matthew. "He used to love to dance—just like Wella." She became quiet. "I really miss him."

"You'll see him again in heaven, and I'm sure he'll be dancing there," Cathy whispered.

Ana nodded as she flipped through her journal. "Let's talk a bit about hearing God's voice."

"As hard as it is to believe, you've probably been hearing God and not realizing it. We can potentially hear three voices—the voice of God, the Enemy's or our own voice. The key to listening is to let go of heart distractions and selfish desires when we pray." Ana touched her temple to demonstrate.

"Let go of anything that would keep you from missing what God wants to say. Then pray and ask God a question. Wait and listen for His answer. Sometimes God will speak to you right then or through dreams or throughout your day when you are quiet. When God is speaking, His voice is loving and compassionate. He will give us correction, but we won't feel condemned or hopeless."

Cathy looked concerned. "Okay, but how will I be able to identify the voice of the Enemy?"

"Satan's voice is forceful, and he'll never say anything good. Remember how you felt when you thought you weren't good enough to be a Christian? That's kind of what his voice does to us. His speaking to us makes us want to give up as he introduces doubt and unbelief in God. Most likely you will hear the Enemy's voice at some point in your day when something happens, and you have a decision to make—like should you let go of something negative or harp on it. That's a part of us too. I think, by nature, we are prone to want to do wrong.

"Anyway, the Enemy tries to draw us into listening to him by using our own desires, but if you are regularly reading the Word of God, you'll be able to recognize when the Devil is trying to influence you because you'll be feeding yourself with the Truth."

"Hmm…" Cathy said as she scribbled reminders in her own notebook.

Ana stood and went to sit next to her on the bed. She pulled her legs underneath her and faced Cathy. "Let's practice hearing God right now."

She took Cathy's hands in her own, then closed her eyes. Ana led in prayer. " Spirit, we welcome You into our hearts and ask You to speak to us.

I pray You would open our spiritual ears to hear Your word and Your truth. Block us from listening to the voice of the Enemy so we can hear and respond to Your voice. In Jesus' name, amen."

Cathy added, "Heavenly Father, teach me to hear You because I rely on your thoughts and direction. In Jesus' name, amen." They waited silently while still holding hands.

After a few moments, Cathy spoke, "I had mental picture of Kevin at church, and he looked happy."

Even though her eyes were still closed, Ana could tell Cathy was smiling by the sound of her voice. She decided to pray into that. "Father, we pray that You would strengthen Kevin. Help him to walk with You and never give up. I pray You would bless him with wisdom and a hunger for a deeper relationship with You."

As Ana was silent, a vision of Cathy's weeping in a hospital room flashed in her mind. A beautiful angel stood behind her with its expanded wings and a hand on her shoulder. Cathy seemed to radiate with light.

What does it mean?

This vision was different from the one she had seen months ago while sitting on the curb. This vision wasn't set in the past. She opened her eyes. Cathy looked so peaceful sitting in front of her. Ana didn't want to destroy what she was seeing. After a few minutes she spoke. "Cathy, I had a vision of you. I think you're going to go through a period of testing, but God has promised to fill you with His strength. After it's over, you will have grown and become spiritually stronger." She couldn't shake the odd tone from her voice.

When Cathy searched her eyes, Ana looked away.

"What did you see?" Cathy asked soberly.

Ana swallowed. She didn't even understand everything in the vision yet. Scaring Cathy was unnecessary, so she chose her words carefully. "I saw that you were sad, but that God had a beautiful angel watching over you. Then I saw you grow in a way."

"Oh," Cathy smiled faintly, and left Ana's explanation at that.

"Can we spend some time worshiping and praying for my friend Beth and her husband Stephen before I have to leave for work?"

"Sure." They joined hands again and began to sing and pray in the Spirit.

"So that's the plan?" Daniel asked.

Pastor Mark nodded and looked around at those in the prayer meeting. "Ana will organize and lead the march two months from now. It'll be full-fledged summer by then, so let's all try to get her some contacts to help make her job easier."

Johanna turned toward Ana. "I already have some contacts for you. I think many of the area churches will be interested in joining with us." She started to rummage in her purse, looking for the list she had made. "We can start making phone calls this week. I'm available whenever you need me."

"Great, I'm going to need your help with worship as well. We need about four other teams from other churches. We want the praise festival to continue for at least five hours. Each team will play for an hour."

Johanna smiled. "Got it."

Ana added, "I'll ask Mr. Stucco about getting a permit to hold the rally in the parking lot outside of the community centre. It's a great spot right on the edge of the ravine and forest."

Leah looked at Johanna and immediately saw that Sakron was right. Johanna was fine. She still looked a bit pale, but she was nowhere near as sick as she should have been. Leah would have to think fast, or this prayer march would go off without a hitch.

"The Lord knows that area needs prayer," Elikai joked.

Andrew piped up, "I don't understand why we're doing this. What can a parking lot sing-a-long do to stop the violence in the community?" He turned to look at Pastor Mark.

Will answered, "Psalm 149 talks about how our worship works to fight the work of the Enemy. Second Chronicles twenty tells that before the people of Judah went to war, they sent the worshipers first. All the worshipers did was praise God, who then set ambushes for Judah's enemies. The enemy ended up fighting among themselves and destroyed each other. That battle was won before God's people even had to fight."

Pastor Mark added, "The march will be much like the story of Joshua.

The Israelites took the city of Jericho by marching around it. God had promised them the city, but Jericho had fortified walls that they couldn't possibly breach. God gave them specific instructions to march around the city for six days in silence. On the seventh day they were to shout, and the priests were to blow their horns. As a result of their obedience, the walls of the city crumbled; Joshua and the Israelites captured the city. We are believing that as we march in prayer, God will bring down the evil spiritual strongholds the Enemy has been building in Tehly City," Pastor Mark concluded.

Daniel chimed in, "Many supernatural things happen during worship that we cannot see. Prayer and worship are some of God's most powerful and effective weapons of warfare."

Andrew nodded. "Well, I guess that makes more sense." He opened his Bible and started randomly flipping through the pages.

Ana rose and began to pace back and forth. "Anyway, guys, I'm open for suggestions for how the day will look."

Leah waved her hand. "I have an idea. Why don't we make it into a parade? We could ask all the churches to make floats to represent their churches. All the churches would want to get involved—you know, to get their names out to the public."

"That sounds like fun," Megan agreed.

Ana looked a little uncertain about the suggestion. "Um, okay. I don't see any harm in doing that."

Leah felt like she was on a roll. "We could get some of the local bands to play too. They could do some covers of songs that are at the top of the charts right now."

Elikai argued, "I think that would defeat the purpose. Most of the music out there is working against God's plan."

Daniel spoke next. "Elikai has a point. We need to make sure we're soaking the city in praise and worship. We should only include worship bands."

Pastor Mark nodded. "We'll stick to the worship bands."

Not wanting to appear too eager, Leah pretended not to care whether or not they agreed with her suggestions. "Well, shouldn't we believe that God can work through secular bands too?"

Daniel shook his head. "We can't involve those who have no relationship with God or spiritual discernment into spiritual warfare. That's dangerous for them and us. Those on the front lines in worship need to know what they're doing and why."

Leah turned away and rolled her eyes.

Pastor Mark stood up. "I think we need dancers as well, but Ana will be busy. What about you, Jo? Up for a solo?"

Johanna nodded. "I should be ready by then."

Owen raised his hand. "What about the kids who danced at the reconciliation? They were really good?"

Elikai spoke up. "The kids may have been good, but I don't know if we should have them dance simply because they were good. Like Daniel said, everyone involved should know what's going on and be able to prepare his or her heart for spiritual battle."

Will raised his hand. "Some of the kids have been coming to church regularly. They've even been at the prayer meetings, including the walk we did the other day to the school. I really think they would be able to handle it. You see them all the time, right, Ana?"

Ana nodded. "More than a few of them have made genuine commitments to God, and I've been teaching them. I think they could be ready."

Will commented, "Tell them what it's about and see if they'd be willing to fast and pray with us for the weeks leading up to the march. If they're up for it, adding them in could be powerful."

Ana nodded. "I'll ask them when I see them at the centre."

Pastor Mark smiled. "This was good! Ana, why don't you run with what we have so far? We'll plan to meet again next week. When Ana finishing recapping, we'll close in prayer."

꙳

After the prayer time, Andrew sat by himself, staring at an open Bible. Things were changing in his life. Here he was at a prayer meeting. It was crazy to even think about it, but the changes had been good. He was saving money now too. Partying all the time had cost him far more than he'd realized. He looked around the room and noticed Ana chatting with Pastor Mark and Will.

Whenever Will spoke to Ana, he found their interaction hard to watch. His feelings for Ana hadn't changed, but he had to cope with spending less time with her because of her church involvement. From his perspective, Will seemed like a good guy, but he was grateful that Ana didn't seem to noticed. Will was friend-zoned—just like he was. It was good too because Will appeared to be Ana's perfect match on paper. *I don't want to lose Ana to this wannabe Superman.*

He looked at Megan. She'd invited him over, but he wasn't sure if he would go. When he was with Megan, he didn't feel lonely even though she was very different from Ana. The only time Ana seemed to really notice him was when he was talking to Megan. *Jealousy can be advantageous.* Maybe he could snap Ana into realizing what she was missing. In the back of his mind, he did want to be careful. He didn't want to run the risk of ruining things with Ana. Megan was fair game if he wanted her, but messing with her would be suicide.

❧

"Hey, Andrew!" Leah flashed her most ravishing smile.

Andrew looked up from his Bible as Leah settled into a chair beside him and leaned in close. "You know, all this parade stuff doesn't make sense to me. I guess I'm so new to everything that I just don't get it." She glanced down and noticed that Andrew's Bible was opened to the book of Joshua.

Andrew stared at his Bible, as if he were trying to solve some kind of mystery. "I know what you mean."

Leah leaned forward again and rested her hand on her chin, then pointed to the Bible. "That book is Greek to me."

Andrew was barely paying attention.

Wow! Maybe I need to be more obvious.

"Maybe we could go for a drink sometime…" Leah suggested.

Andrew shifted uncomfortably.

"…and you could help me make sense of it. I'm sure you know way more than I do." She casually sat back in her chair.

Andrew scrunched his dark eyes and stared a Leah for a moment.

"Uh, maybe… I'm sure I don't know much more." He stood. "Anyway, I have to catch Ana before she leaves. Talk to you later."

Leah stared after him as he threaded his way across the room.

She glanced around and spotted Destiny collecting her notebook and Bible to leave, and she casually walked toward her.

"Hey, Destiny, what are you doing later?"

"Not much—going to go grab a bite to eat, and then I'll probably go home and read."

"That sounds restful." Leah looked around. "They must really trust Ana a lot to put her in charge of this prayer thing." Leah glanced at Ana who was standing across the room.

Destiny followed her gaze. "Ana's great. She's very dedicated—a hard worker. She's always been like that. A natural prayer warrior too." Destiny smiled.

Leah leaned in closer. "Hmm, but I heard she just got back into church. Where was she all that time?" She dropped her voice and whispered, "I heard...clubbing frequently."

When Destiny looked up from rummaging in her bag, Leah felt exposed. She decided to back off a bit. "I mean, I've just returned myself, but I wouldn't feel confident enough to lead anything. I'm only a baby Christian. I think someone like you should be leading. You seem to have been consistent for years, and you have many spiritual gifts too." Leah smiled again. "I remember how active you were in the church when I used to attend years ago."

Destiny looked at Ana and then back at Leah. "I can't take any credit for any gifts I've been given. It's only by God's grace that I'm here right now. You know, we all have our pasts." Destiny shrugged and sighed aloud. "Good thing God doesn't hold them against us." She raised her eyebrows. "I'm sure whatever Ana went through last year is behind her, but if you're truly concerned, maybe you should speak to her or Pastor Mark or maybe even keep her in prayer. I'm sure she could use it." Destiny slipped her purse strap over her shoulder. "Maybe we could hang out together soon—if you're up for it."

Leah suddenly felt uncomfortable. "Yeah, sure."

"Anyway, I have to go. I'll see you soon." Destiny waved and then walked away, leaving Leah standing alone.

Well, that tactic didn't work...

Leah looked around the room and spotted Megan and Susan in conversation. She tried to eavesdrop as she walked over.

"Even I've noticed you hanging out with him a lot lately," Susan teased.

"If Ana doesn't want him, then I don't see the problem," Megan argued.

Shaking her head, Susan said, "I don't know. Feels like you're breaking some kind of girlfriend code, and he doesn't seem that into you."

"Who cares? It's just fun. You're beginning to sound like old woman Ana over there," Megan laughed. She turned and noticed Leah. "Hey, what's up?"

Leah stepped closer at her invitation. "Oh, nothing, just another boring evening to look forward to. I wish I could be more outgoing like you. I just feel like no guys are interested in me." Leah fiddled with her hair. "Maybe if I went blonde? What do you think?"

Megan looked her up and down. "No, honey, the world has enough blondes. I can give you some pointers to get guys to notice you. You're very pretty. You just have to know what kind of clothes to wear to emphasize what you want them to see." She smiled as she straightened her own tight clothes.

Leah laughed and looked at Ana who was standing on the other side of the room with Andrew and Will. "Well, Ana doesn't need any help to get the attention of guys. I guess it's because she's so flirty. The guys just fawn over her. Look how she has them wrapped around her little finger." She looked back at Megan and Susan. "Especially those guys.

"Ana's the opposite of a flirt." Susan laughed. "I've known her for years, and she is just shy—shy—shy."

Megan winked at Susan. "I don't know, Sue. Our little Ana might just be growing up," she theorized.

Leah once again looked at Ana and smiled.

❧

Ana felt a hand slip behind her elbow and looked up.

"Hey, haven't hung out in a while. How about dinner tonight to catch up?" Andrew said as stopped in front of her.

Andrew's touch still affected her. His proximity and the smell of his cologne brought back a mix of emotions. She glanced past him and saw Leah, Megan and Susan talking and laughing across the room. They seemed so carefree. She missed feeling like that. "I think I'll pass today, but thank you. I need to start calling some of the churches and contacting the kids."

He frowned in annoyance. "All that can wait. There's no rush; you have two months…"

"I know, but I want to get a head start so I'll have plenty of time to pray into everything." She paused, "I don't know; I've been feeling really overwhelmed lately—sort of confused and upset when I least expect it. I think I need to rest tonight and spend time alone."

Will, who was still standing nearby, walked over to join them when he overheard her comment. "You haven't been feeling well?" His eyes searched hers for a moment. "What can I pray about for you?"

Andrew backed up and glared at Will.

When Ana looked at Will, she could see he was actually waiting for an answer. *He's so thoughtful.* She was touched by his request, but she also noticed that Andrew did not look happy. She turned back to Will. "Please pray for clarity of mind; it's like I'm in a haze."

She again heard Megan, Leah and Susan laughing and turned to look at them. She and Megan's eyes locked for a moment.

Will patted her shoulder. "I'll do that. Let me know if there's anything else I can do."

Andrew stared him down as he walked away.

"That guy irritates me," he snapped.

"Why?" Ana picked up her backpack. She hoped Will hadn't heard him.

Andrew's tone became sharp and impatient. "I don't know. He just does. Anyway, so do you want to come to dinner or not?"

"I'll pass, but thanks again," she sweetly replied.

"Fine, suit yourself." He turned on his heel and walked directly over to Megan and whispered something in her ear. Megan smirked and then the two of them said goodbye and left the group. Susan and Leah remained behind.

Ana felt her face flush. Last year she'd done whatever she wanted. Life had seemed simpler. Part of her wanted to feel that way again. She shook her head. *What am I thinking?*

After Megan and Andrew left, Leah stayed behind to chat with Susan. She had a perfect opportunity to keep an eye on Ana. Out of the corner of her eye, Leah was aware of Ana's every move. *I won't be satisfied until you're broken.*

CHAPTER 18

Wheat, and Tares

"...Their work will be shown for what it is, because the Day will bring it to light. It will be revealed with fire, and the fire will test the quality of each person's work" (1 Corinthians 3:13, NIV).

"I COMMISSION YOU... be everywhere." Pastor Mark spoke in a solemn tone as he preached to the congregation of Isaac's Well. "Let God use you anywhere and in all situations." He closed his eyes and began to pray. "Oh, God, don't let us be satisfied until we see Your power changing the lives of people all around us."

Kavo stood close by. The combination of Pastor Mark's humility and expectancy was weighty; even now he felt it stirring heaven and drawing the presence of God like a magnet. Although miracles continued each week, another divide was coming. Faith and skepticism grew side by side in the soil of Isaac's Well. This divide would separate the believing from the unbelieving. But something else was also influencing the people. He could sense a bitter fragrance surrounding some of the people during worship.

Pastor Mark continued. "Be a mouthpiece, a healing touch. Show love to your neighbors. Let's terrify the kingdom of darkness!" The congregation

207

cheered and clapped. As the service closed, Pastor Mark made an announcement. "Ana Levi will be heading up some prayer and fasting in preparation for our prayer march," he stated. "I encourage you all to get involved. The violence in our community will end through prayer!"

Sasson flew over to Kavo. "Sakron is using Leah to stir up more trouble."

Kavo responded, "I suspect someone greater than Leah is involved here. People becoming more distracted by idols isn't a coincidence. The outward worship cannot hide what is taking place in the heart."

Sasson thought for a moment. "I had hoped Leah would have realized her error. Surely she must know that Sakron hates her. Why does she hold onto her allegiance to him?"

"It's not too late for her," Kavo answered. "A part of her soul still remembers and hasn't completely given over to him. But we must focus on the saints here. Their hearts must let go of these idols before the battle begins, or they will become drained and distant. Already worship is being withheld based on whether or not these idols are fulfilling them. The truth of the invisible realm must pull down the failing kingdoms of men."

Sasson nodded. "I also sense confusion in Mark."

"Indeed, he feels what's coming but has no words for it. He wants to help everyone line up with what God is doing here, but he also doesn't fully understand."

Sasson lifted off the ground and motioned for Kavo to follow. "On the day of the outpouring, Edon and I discovered something underneath the foundations of the church. However, I thought we had dealt with it so there was no need to bring it up—"

"Show me."

~

As they landed next to the cave, Sasson noted the claw marks at the entrance he had seen on his previous visit. Everything still looked the same. They entered and looked at the markings on the walls.

After a few moments of studying them. Kavo spoke. "I've seen these before."

"What do they mean?" Sasson wondered aloud.

"They are spells that call down curses to allow hidden demon activity to operate. The schemes appear to be a normal part of someone's life. They manifest through that person's desire for love, security, or money. Once they have been unleashed, the demons take over and become a drive in the victim's life that they cannot control. The demons demand worship for themselves, and the people don't realize their desires have turned into idols until it is too late. Their passion for God becomes divided and diminishes into dying embers."

Sasson strained to look deeper into the darkness of the cave and pointed in that direction. "We saw a hooded person escape through there. So who is responsible?"

Kavo again studied the inscriptions. "These particular markings belong to a priestess from the old world named Divinica; she served the ancient demon Molech and many of his manifested representations. If she is here, she is not working alone. Dionysus is involved." Kavo lifted off the ground and spread his wings. "Come, we must alert the others."

～

"So you all understand what we're trying to do?" Ana asked her dance class.

The kids nodded. They'd gathered at her request for an early Saturday meeting. Many had given up their usual Saturday morning cartoons so they could be present.

Candice volunteered, "We're praying for the violence in the community to end and for God's power to come."

Ana smiled at their excitement. "Yes, and we're going to be praying regularly, leading up to the prayer march. If you guys want to be involved, we'll also be doing a fast. Let your parents know if you choose to participate. You can try fasting through a meal and praying during that time. We will also be doing a media fast."

Sean asked, "What's a media fast?"

Ana sat down closer. "I'll explain. With a regular fast, you don't eat food. With a media fast, you choose not to listen to secular music or watch entertainment for the purpose of praying and focusing on God."

"I can do that!" Brianna announced.

"Great! I'm glad you're so enthusiastic."

"Can we pray for the march before we start class?" Candice asked.

Ana nodded.

The kids bowed their heads as Ana prepared to pray.

"Excuse me?" A woman's voice cut through the silence of the room.

Ana turned and recognized the woman Mr. Stucco had shown around the centre. Ms. Woodstock's heels clicked on the dance floor. Her pale-blue business suit hugged her shapely figure. Her long, dark hair was pulled into a neat bun, and small glasses perched on her nose. She was strikingly beautiful except for the stern look she wore.

"Is this a religion class?" Ms. Woodstock asked.

"It's a dance class," Ana calmly stated. She noted that Ms. Woodstock had dropped her charming demeanor from her previous visit. The icy handshake they had previously shared and the sick feeling afterward rushed into Ana's mind.

"Keep this religious nonsense out of community sectors," Ms. Woodstock ordered as she adjusted her glasses and walked out of the room. Her heels resounded in the empty hallway.

The stifled silence afterward let Ana know the children had picked up on the hostility Ms. Woodstock had left behind.

"Who is that lady?" Christy hopped up and peeked out the door as if to make sure the woman was gone.

Ana waved the girl away from the door, afraid Christy would get sucked into the woman's obvious hatred simply by her standing there. "I don't think we want to find out."

～

Sandra and Cathy sat together on the patio of an ice cream shop. Kevin focused quietly on his ice cream as the women discussed recent events. More churches threatened by the popularity of Isaac's Well were pulling their support. Sandra was worried that the silly church politics would discourage Cathy.

"How can another church accuse us of stealing their members? That's so ridiculous!" Cathy laughed sarcastically. "Is that even a thing?

Sandra reassured her. "Don't concern yourself with it. We are often distrustful of what we don't understand."

Cathy was not satisfied. "But there is a war going on in the spirit. People need to be saved from hell."

Sandra patted Cathy's arm. "We have to keep praying."

Sandra turned to Kevin. "Are you okay, Kevin? You've been really quiet." Even though he had been coming to church each week, she could tell he still felt out of place—both here and at the church. *Maybe Cathy will soon realize how unprepared he is to be a husband. He doesn't even seem to care enough to get involved in the conversation.*

"All of this confuses me," Kevin started. "Pastor Mark said the greatest commandments are to love God with all your heart and your neighbor as yourself. I don't know much, but it seems to me that people have other agendas."

Cathy smiled.

Sandra was surprised. She hadn't expected that insight from Kevin. She had assumed he wasn't paying attention. "Seems you're learning a lot."

"Not fast enough!" Kevin shook his head. "I want to do right now, but I've been doing my own thing for years. I'm finding these bad habits are hard to break. Sometimes I only feel safe when Cathy and Beth are praying for me."

Cathy swallowed a spoonful of ice cream. "Everything will come together soon, I promise."

Kevin continued, "I feel like I've missed so much. I don't know how long it will take to get my life back on track."

Sandra was quiet. His honest sincerity stunned her.

"There's no hurry; take it one day at a time." Cathy suggested.

"Yes, there is, Cathy. You're pregnant. I have a lot of catching up to do. I hate to admit it, but I can't guarantee I won't have a relapse. What if you leave me for good?"

Cathy rubbed his arm and quoted Scripture. "Therefore do not worry about tomorrow, for tomorrow will worry about itself, each day has enough trouble of its own. We're in this together now. I won't leave you."

Sandra looked at Cathy and then Kevin. They were sweet to support each other, but she couldn't help but feel like Cathy was making an impossible promise.

~

Leah skirted around some empty chairs and found an empty area to sit in the sanctuary of the church. A special evening of prayer had been called with the regular members of Isaac's Well. A few people came in, looking exhausted. Her plan was working. People were worn out, and hopefully the work the Christians were doing would come to a quick end. Even she couldn't have anticipated the way her rumors had snowballed as they had spread from church to church.

Cathy complained, "People are saying that some of the miracles we've been seeing are not of God. I even got into an argument with someone about the purpose of the Holy Spirit signs and wonders we've been seeing in church. I didn't mean to argue, but I was just so angry."

Pastor Mark rubbed his eyes and sighed aloud. "Similar things are being said about our leadership—that they're following some 'false spirit.'"

Ana shook her head. "Another church dropped out of the march. We're losing a lot of our backing."

"My contact said that they wanted a bigger float for their church. They asked why some churches had bigger floats than other churches," Johanna added.

Ana threw up her hands in defeat. "This is just like what happened before the reconciliation. It's a disaster. Where did I go wrong?"

Will stood up and walked over to her. "Don't blame yourself. You have nothing to do with what's happening. The Enemy is just trying to get at us."

Ana looked at her hands. "Maybe we should call off the whole event, or someone else should take the lead. I don't know how to fix this."

Pastor Mark raised his voice over the growing murmurs. "Let's not make rash decisions, guys. We can't lose our focus here. I believe we heard from God about this, so we're marching—no matter how many churches stand with us."

Leah looked at Pastor Mark. "If this is of God, then why is there so much opposition? Maybe this is a sign that we should end it."

Will shook his head. "I don't think it's a sign we should quit. Opposition is sometimes a sign that we're headed in the right direction. We can't just fold every time something negative happens."

Leah continued, unwilling to give up so easily. "I don't know. Other churches are more established and have been around a long time and probably know what they're doing more than we do. Most of us are young. Maybe we should follow the example of the other churches. I mean they never thought of doing anything like this."

Cathy interrupted, "I don't know much about church establishments, but I don't think age and time have that much to do with being obedient to God. From what I've read, it seems like sometimes God uses whoever is listening—like in the story of Samuel and Eli. Samuel was only a kid, and Eli was a mature priest, but God had stopped speaking to Eli and chose to speak to the child."

Will nodded. "You're absolutely right. Spoken like a mature believer."

Leah shot back, "Are you saying I'm not a mature believer?"

"No, you're a defensive believer!" Owen joked.

Pastor Mark put up his hands. "Guys, stop this!" He looked soberly around the room. "We are in a battle, and we need to pay attention to is what's happening and leave no room for the Enemy. Remember what I spoke about at the reconciliation? Unity is the key. If the Enemy can tear that up, then he's taking ground we need to hold onto. We need to stay unified—both in here and out there," he said, as he pointed toward the doors.

Leah's anger smoldered, threatening to choke her.

Owen looked sheepish. "Sorry, Leah, I didn't mean anything by it."

Leah could feel her heart pounding as she nodded and looked away. Time was running out. If they went through with the prayer march, she could not do much to finish the things that Sakron had asked of her. All of the curses she and others had planted for years would be uprooted in a matter of weeks, and the consequences would be severe. She'd heard Sakron growl as she'd neared the elementary school. There was definitely another thick presence in that place now. Sakron forbade her to go near there again. A bigger disruption was needed. Tonight, she would ask Sakron who the others were. *I need help!*

∼

Silence enveloped Leah. Her skin was pinched with pain that emanated from the deep darkness around her. She yelled, but there was still only silence. A cold chain tightened over her wrist as she pounded her hand against something solid in the pitch-black space. She slammed her fist. Nothing. She pounded again.

Startled, Leah awoke in a cold sweat. She was completely tangled in her bed linens. Someone banged at her apartment door. She glanced at the clock. *3:32 a.m.*

She pulled off the covers and scrambled toward the door, running a mental checklist as she did. *Who would be coming this late?* She barely opened her door to peek out. A small smartly dressed woman wearing dark-rimmed glasses stared back at her. Long, shiny black hair fell over her shoulders. The woman pushed hard on the door and moved past Leah into the room.

"You ask questions, but don't expect answers?"

"Uh…sorry. Can I get you something?" Leah assumed she was the one who Sakron had sent to help.

"No." The woman walked back and forth. "I've come at your request for help. I'm here to inform you that the time has come to start phase two. You've been slacking off, little sister. The way things are going, you might as well quit now."

Leah sat down as a wave of anger brought tenseness to her entire body. "Look, lady, I don't know where you got your information, but I've been working really hard. I've been doing this by myself now for some time."

The woman stared back. Her silence caused Leah to feel anxious. She was strangely intimidating, and her eyes carried a ruthless look. The woman's obvious beauty did nothing to ease Leah's fear.

Who is she anyway?

The woman moved closer and looked into Leah's eyes, which shot icicles down Leah's spine. "I am Divinica, and I would advise you to watch your tone. I'm not one of your stupid little friends. I can strip you of your powers in a second. Don't think your demon Sakron will protect you."

Leah sucked in her breath at the mention of Sakron's name. She'd never met anyone who knew her demon by name.

Divinica coolly sat down across from Leah and crossed her legs. "Blood needs to be shed again. I know you have before, but a greater sacrifice is needed."

Leah's face drained of color. *I never told anyone about that.*

Divinica continued. "The land has been dry because of the prayers of our enemies. Only something big will fix that."

"I've done everything I know how to do. I'm not even sure how I've gone undetected for so long."

"Don't be naïve," Divinica spat. "You're not undetected. You're only allowed to remain under the wheat-and-the-tare principle."

Leah raised her eyebrows.

"Matthew thirteen?" Divinica's hands rested neatly over the knee of her crossed leg. "You mean you don't read that little black book you tote around? How can you pass for a Christian if you don't even read or understand the basic principles of the laws under which we also operate?"

She continued to explain. "Just as we have watchers, they also have watchers who feed them information. Never underestimate your enemy. Hasn't your demon taught you anything?" Divinica scowled.

Leah shrugged. She felt like an amateur.

Divinica glanced away. "I've gone to the community centre, and I've seen what they're doing there. The prayers of the children have a special strength. I've done everything I can do to convince that owner to sell the place to me, but he won't budge."

"What's so great about the community centre? Why is everyone so interested in it?"

"You've studied. What have you found?"

Leah hesitated. "Well, I know the centre was once a church.".

Divinica sighed. "It goes much deeper than that. But let's just say I have a bit of history with that place, and I'm eager to connect with my roots again."

Leah nodded even though she wasn't sure what Divinica was talking about.

"That girl Ana is indoctrinating the children with talk about God. Until they understand their power, we can use our present influences into their lives to gain entry and cause destruction. Some of the kids have no idea what it means to be 'set apart.' As long as they watch our television programs and listen to our music, we can activate curses on the music to control them. The brotherhood ensured we'd always have some access to young lives." Divinica whispered to herself. "We just need to know which points of entry are still available to us."

Divinica stood and began to pace again. She walked over to the bookshelf where artifacts lined the shelves. She picked up a figurine and studied it closely. As Leah looked at the small teraphim in Divinica's hands, she realized that the woman had picked up the small replica of her demon. Sakron had arrived in it.

Divinica looked back at Leah. "We will use what we know to cause nightmares. If we breed fear, their prayers will lack strength because they will be double-minded. For those to whom we have no access, we will have to use family members. Tonight, we'll unleash more demons into the city." She put down the statue and headed to the door. "We will leave now so we can move among the shadows."

Leah spoke up, trying to redeem herself. "I've been attacking the leader of the prayer movement, but I am not seeing any strong results. I've spread rumors about her, you know, like I've seen her with different guys in strange places. Something is protecting her."

Divinica stopped in front of the door. "A simple method of distraction will be sufficient enough to break her prayer covering, but don't let appearances deceive you. Only time will show the full effect of what you're doing to your little Ana." Divinica seemed confident. "Andrew's familiar spirit—the one to whom he was bound—is still around. We can still use it to get at him. Without a true master, he's still fair game. He has no protection."

How did she know about Ana's friends?

"I'm not so sure about that." Leah rubbed her eyes. "Like I said before, I've been trying for a while now."

Divinica smiled. "My watchers tell me all that I need to know, Leah. Some of these spirits have been here since the beginning." She extended her hands parallel to the floor as if measuring the presence of the spirits of whom she spoke. "They were here before the first people. I can feel the deeply embedded roots that have stood through generations. Once I tap into that power, no one will get in my way. We have many plans for this place."

Leah looked at the woman's beautiful, but dead, eyes. She wasn't sure she liked that idea.

CHAPTER 19

Backlash

"Put on all of God's armor so that you will be able to stand firm against all strategies of the devil. For we are not fighting against flesh-and-blood enemies, but against evil rulers and authorities of the unseen world, against mighty powers in this dark world, and against evil spirits in the heavenly places" (Ephesians 6:11, 12, NLT).

ANDREW HEADED FOR his car parked across the street from Megan's house. He opened the door and ducked into the driver's seat. The uneasy feeling that had started hours ago was growing stronger. He dropped his head to the steering wheel and closed his eyes. *This time I really messed up.* Not only had he blown it, but if Ana ever found out… Andrew sat back and covered his face with his hands.

What was I thinking?

In his mind he saw himself drawn by desire doing what he always had done. But this time he regretted his actions. There had been that moment to make a different decision…there was always a moment.

Andrew rubbed his face and looked out over the steering wheel. It would take him twenty minutes max to get to the nearest bar. The scent of alcohol was suddenly strong in his nostrils. He craved a drink—not just a drink—but one to put himself as far from this moment as possible. He turned the key in the ignition as the flavor of beer rolled over his palate.

Sasson stood nearby, waiting for Andrew. Much depended on his decisions. The whole earth yearned for the awakening of the sons of man to their glorious position.

How long?

A putrid smell permeated the atmosphere. The angel sensed the demon before he saw the pulsating parasite fawning over Andrew. Bacchus. His dark tentacles reached into Andrew's chest and caressed his heart, reconnecting former attachments. The demonic suggestions were growing stronger.

Sasson drew his sword and shouted a war cry as he ran toward Andrew. The demon's head shot up as Sasson entered the car. Sasson brought his sword down, piercing the spirit's rags before the demon had time to defend himself. The demon hissed as Sasson's sword slashed into the stretchy reptilian flesh, and, with a flash of light, Bacchus disappeared from the car.

A shiver ran through Andrew's body. He turned off the car and sat for a moment. The sensations that had been so strong were now fading away.

I don't want a drink; I don't want to go backward. What I did a few minutes ago doesn't have to lead me back to where I've come from. It stops here.

Andrew reached in his pocket for his cell and dialed Megan's number. "I'm really sorry for what just happened, Megan. I shouldn't have let it get that far."

Megan was silent on the receiver, but finally answered. "Andrew…"

"We need to stop seeing each other… It's wrong, and it's not helping either of us. I'm going to tell Pastor Mark what happened. I need help, and I can't get it by doing this."

"I know," she answered with a sigh.

His tone was confident when he added, "I'm going to give this Christian thing a real chance."

"What about me, Andrew?" Megan's voice broke.

After a pause, he answered, "I'm sorry. I didn't mean for this to happen…" *I wish I had thought of this before.*

Megan sighed again. Her voice was forced as she spoke hoarsely, "Fine. There's nothing else to say…I guess that's it." She hung up.

Andrew wondered what to do next. He ended the call and dialed another number. Ana answered.

"Hey, Ana, I was wondering if you could give me Pastor Mark's number. I need to talk to him."

Susan ran up beside Ana, breathing heavily. Ana noticed her hair was still black, but she had exchanged the blue tips for silver streaks this week.

"Where did you come from?" Ana smiled as Susan struggled to catch her breath. "You really need to get in shape. Maybe you should come to my dance class!"

"Ha, ha, ha." Susan laughed sarcastically as she straightened. "Something's wrong with Megan. We need to go see her."

"What happened?"

"I don't know. The last time I spoke to her she was crying and saying something about how Andrew had used her."

Ana felt her stomach turn.

"You know how she is about guys. She doesn't usually get attached, but this seems different. Now she's not returning my calls, and I'm worried. "

Half an hour later, Ana waited as Susan knocked on Megan's door for a second time. The door finally swung open. Megan looked terrible. She was wearing dirty, gray jogging pants and an oversized white T-shirt. Her hair was pulled up into a short messy ponytail. Her eyes were puffy and red; her face was blotchy. *Susan was right; Megan is not okay.*

Megan turned and walked away without a word. Ana closed the door behind them and followed Megan upstairs to her room.

The dog seemed excited to see them even if Megan wasn't. It jumped up on them and wagged its tail until Megan opened her door and shooed it out. She angrily slammed the door and stormed over to sit down on her bed. Her fury was unmistakable.

"What happened?" Ana could barely whisper as the knot in her stomach grew larger.

"I'll tell you what happened!" Megan shouted. "Andrew slept with me!"

"What?" Ana felt like she was going to throw up. "When?"

"Two weeks ago. He dumped me right after that," she stated frankly. "This is all your fault, Ana. He was using me to get back at you."

Ana was stunned and taken aback. "*My* fault?"

Megan stood and looked down at her. "Don't act like you didn't know what was going on." She paced the room like an interrogator. "I see through your phony little act. You think you're so wonderful. You act so innocent all the while wrapping people around your little finger. Andrew was so right about you."

Ana stared back, unable to speak. Megan obviously held some bitterness toward her. *How have I never noticed?*

"You think you're better than we are," Megan said, motioning toward herself and Susan. Then pointing at Ana, she said, "You think you're better than Andrew, and that's why you didn't want to date him. Isn't that what she told us, Susan?" She looked to Susan for support.

Susan just looked down as if she wanted to disappear completely.

Megan went on, "I really liked him, Ana. I thought he was a really great guy, but now he won't even talk to me." She burst into tears. "He just used me for what he couldn't get from you and then moved on."

Ana felt tears burning her own eyes as she reached for her friend, but Megan pushed her away.

Ana's insides went cold. Silence hung in the air. "I'm so sorry." She tried to bolster the frail friendship that was crumbling before her eyes.

Megan was unrelenting. "I've heard that one before. Seems you and Andrew have a lot more in common than you think. You're such a hypocrite, you know that? You pretended to be so great and act uninterested in Andrew. Meanwhile, you were going out with him behind our backs."

"It wasn't like that..." Ana's voice trembled. "Megan..."

"I'd like you to leave my room. I want you out of my house. Just leave me alone!" Megan finished, resolute.

Ana looked at Susan again, but Susan looked away.

Ana slowly walked to the door and opened it. Megan's dog wagged its tail as it licked her fingers before she headed downstairs. The dog whimpered in the background as she closed the front door behind her.

Ana's eyes burned with fresh tears. Megan's words had found new places to pierce as they echoed in her mind. *Why did Susan lead me into an ambush?*

Susan had sat in silence, which meant she agreed. *Is that how they really see me? After all the time I spent with them, prayed for them, and cared about them?*

Ana felt doubly betrayed. If this is what her supposed friends thought about her, then who could she really trust? Andrew had let her down, and her friends had abandoned her.

Ana walked back toward the bus stop, shivering and feeling cold inside although the sun burned hot in the sky. From this new vantage point, the last few months felt like a lie. She'd thought things were getting better with her friends attending church.

What else have I been wrong about?

～

Dionysus glanced behind him. The clientele of the Eclipse crowd dwindled as the night wore on. A few of the regulars ordered their final drinks for the night before they headed home. Dionysus sauntered down the dank passage. The loud music receded into a dull rhythm as it fell beneath the ground. By the time he reached the underground rooms, the only sound was deafening silence.

Below the underground tunnels and cement rooms, Dionysus' fallen ones gathered around him. Sakron came in and knelt before him.

Dionysus sneered. "What of your progress? Two territories for the bright ones have opened since the great gathering, and I have heard of nothing from you."

"We have been everywhere. Nightmare demons have been sent to inflict the children, but it's been difficult to find any who are not hedged about with prayer. We have been unable to access roots inside of them. The hospital even has a prayer covering these days!" Sakron spoke, half-defending himself and half-outraged. "I have sent out a call for reinforcements, but they need hosts and legal entry rights."

"That's it?" Dionysus growled, his primal nature beginning to crack through his usual handsome appearance. "What about your plan to take over Andrew again?"

"Since his familiar was uprooted from his family line, it can only get in occasionally. Our plan to use his struggle with lust worked perfectly on him. Then I sent Bacchus, the demon of drunkenness, to seal the deal, but a bright one interfered," Sakron sneered. "The bright ones are getting bolder. Andrew did not plunge into the downward spiral we had anticipated. Instead, he has become more secure than ever before. I miscalculated," Sakron finished apologetically.

Dionysus screeched, "The stakes are too high for you to miscalculate. Years of work will not be uprooted and destroyed because of this church!" As Dionysus swung around, his human face morphed into dark lizard scales and glowing eyes. "Within the space of half an hour, I saw one of my entry points closed because of their prayers. Waves of light have been passing through here and destroying my work. This is not how we should welcome the ruling goddess after her long wait. The ground must be desecrated before the bright ones gain more footing."

Dionysus turned back to Sakron. "Send that girl, Ana, a spirit of insecurity. Maybe she will reaccept it. If the other things we've done have been working, then this spirit should have no problem finding an old root. We must attack when she is weak. I want to attack her from every angle—destroying her completely." His snake-like tongue flicked in and out before he realized.

"Our root into Cathy is also gone," Sakron said carefully. "Dree is gone, and she has no desire to destroy herself. Nothing we are doing is swaying her hope. She bounces back as soon as we throw something at her." Sakron's gaze fixed on the floor. "She did not curse her seed at any time—even when we took away her mate. We're running out of time and options with her. Soon she will give birth to another generation of *them*. She killed her last one but has made no sign of ill-intent for this one."

Dionysus visibly brightened as an idea came to him. "Sakron, have you forgotten? We can still use the old roots of murder to attack her womb and her mind. Perhaps she will inadvertently curse her child. That will be another powerful blow, of course."

"For the others, send Havoc. Divinica can unleash him to create more discord and confusion." Dionysus thought about the spirit of insecurity he'd send to Ana. That would help, but he couldn't risk any more mistakes. "As for the girl, I will deal with her myself."

Andrew threw another pebble at Ana's window. She'd been avoiding his calls; hence, he was resorting to cliché attempts at getting her attention again—this time in the middle of the night. He was hoping that this 2:00 a.m. chat would help smooth things over. When she came to the window, he motioned for her to come down. She looked doubtful but pointed at the tree a few feet away from her open backyard and then disappeared from the window.

He walked over to where she had pointed and leaned against the tree to wait. She appeared a few moments later wearing jeans, a pullover, and flip-flops. Her face looked pale in the moonlight, and her curly hair fell over her shoulders. One look at her made him wonder if he had been too hasty in coming.

"Hey," she whispered hoarsely.

"Hey." He pushed away from the tree and walked toward her in long, slow strides.

"Why are you here at this time of night?"

"I came to apologize."

She frowned and narrowed her eyes. "Why? You're an adult; you can do whatever you want."

"I know, but—"

"I was stupid to think that anything could ever happen between us," she snapped. "Maybe the person you should apologize to is Megan."

Andrew stared at her for a long moment. The light in her eyes seemed to be gone. She looked entirely too somber, terrifying him. Instinctively he moved to embrace her because hugs solved everything.

"Don't touch me!" She backed away and raised her hands to prevent his coming closer. "How could you do this?" she asked, as tears filled her eyes.

Andrew didn't know what to say. *Why is she crying?* He had expected a religious reprimand, but not this. He stepped closer. "Ana, I tried to live like you do. I really did, but I didn't understand before. I'm not like you…I'm weak. I never wanted this to happen."

"No? It sure seems like it." Ana folded her arms across her chest. "You've been talking to Megan for a while now. What you do in your own time is your own business but leave me and my friends out of it." She dropped her hands to her sides.

Andrew's heart beat faster. He glanced around before stepping closer and whispering, "I don't know what you heard, but I didn't force her to do anything she didn't want to do. She invited me over to her place." Andrew stared back. He had hoped she would simply forgive him—no questions asked.

Ana shot back angrily, "Megan was my friend, and you came between us. I know you were just trying to make me jealous."

Andrew rubbed his forehead and closed his eyes. *I've never seen her so angry. How can I explain so she will trust me again?*

"Okay, I admit it. I was trying to make you jealous, but I didn't think it was working…" He paused to regroup his thoughts. "Ana, I was lonely. You didn't want to be with me; I needed something. I'm not like you."

"Don't you ever think of anyone but yourself?" she demanded hoarsely. She used her arms to hug herself as if she needed protection—from him. "Megan was weak, and you took advantage of that."

Andrew raised his voice. "Why are you defending her? She isn't who you think she is, you know!" He lowered his voice back to a whisper and said, "She doesn't seem to care about you. Believe me, she wasn't thinking about you! She talks about you and treats you like you're some kind of project." He tried to shake her out of naiveté. "You messed with my heart, Ana. All I wanted was you while you were happy to toy with me until someone better came along," he said referring to Will.

Maybe Ana isn't what I thought she was. She's probably just like every other girl. In reality, he wanted her to be like every other girl. Then it wouldn't matter if he lost her forever—even as a friend. He wanted her to feel some of the disappointment in which he was drowning.

Ana drew back as if she'd been slapped.

"You know that's not true!" Her face was simultaneously shadowed in outrage and hurt. Her hands suddenly balled into fists. "I told you I didn't feel right about the whole thing, and now I know why. I didn't *mean* to hurt you. I was simply confused." She stared down at the grass.

"Why is that acceptable for you but not for me?"

There was silence between them for a few moments. Hoping he was getting through to her, he reached out again to touch her arm. This time she didn't pull away. He watched as tears slid down her cheeks. In this moment she was as distant and unreachable as when she first ran out of the Eclipse, the first night he had seen her. She was like a special prize. He leaned in as if to kiss her, but instead, he tilted her chin up to look at him.

"Ana," he said softly. "I don't know my way back from here." He gently put both hands on her face, gazing into her eyes. She looked at him, startled by his closeness.

Andrew saw something then. He saw her vulnerability, her own needs. Maybe she could see that he did genuinely care about her or perhaps her stark eyes reflected his own hurt and loneliness, knowing he could say nothing that would change all that had happened.

She pulled away his hands, breaking the spell that seemed to be weaving around them. "Neither do I." She turned back to her house, leaving Andrew standing alone, staring after her.

～

Arrows flew everywhere, whizzing past Ana's head. She ran to the staircase of her home and tried to hide by crouching down low. People were walking and talking AMID the careening arrows, but few seemed aware of their peril. From her vantage point, she could see Andrew standing in the center of her living room, laughing and talking to her friends.

She tried to yell for Andrew to take cover. She screamed, but no words came out. An arrow pierced Andrew in the back, and he fell to the floor. Megan ran over to help. An arrow struck her in the heart, and she slumped over Andrew's lifeless body.

Ana looked down at her hands. They held a shield that was made of some

―――――

kind of thin metal. She held it up, but it was too flimsy to offer protection. Arrows were already puncturing it. She wasn't sure how long it would last.

She heard someone's voice and turned to see Will shouting to her from across the room. "Where's your sword?"

"What?" she tried to yell back over the noise.

"Where's your sword!"

This time the voice echoed and boomed, and she found herself awake in her bed.

Another dream.

"God, I'm so tired!" she prayed aloud. She turned over to grab her pen and notebook to write down everything she had seen and felt. She had always been a dreamer, but these dreams occurred so often that she was exhausted, unable to discern what God was trying to say. She sensed that she needed to pray. She leaned over and turned on her night light.

As she prayed, Ephesians six came to her heart. She needed to be reading the Bible, her Sword. She had been so busy with everything else that she had neglected the Bible. Her faith was getting weaker—the reason why the shield in her dream had been so flimsy.

Ana prayed for a while, but she felt no comfort. The stillness in the room magnified the emptiness creeping over her. Her friends had distanced themselves from her. Everyone was busy with their own life, and she was running out of people in whom she could really confide. Area pastors and church leaders continued to pull support from the march as rumors about them circulated. *What am I still pushing forward to? To revival? To unity? To end violence?* She didn't remember anymore. She pulled the covers over her head. The urge to run away and leave everything thing behind was getting stronger. Maybe she hadn't really been ready for anything again after all. She definitely didn't feel strong enough now.

❧

Ana searched through the church hallways, looking for Pastor Matthew. The concrete stairs leading to the basement were damp with puddles of water. Dim lights lined the corner of the corridor's ceiling. She spotted a nearby door and hurried over to open it. As she turned the knob, a pang of fear ran through

―――――

her body. Inside the room, Pastor Matthew struggled against ropes that bound him to a chair. His hands were duct-taped behind his back, and tape covered his mouth. His light-colored hair flung like straw over his forehead. Panic filled his eyes. The tape across his mouth puffed out as he tried to yell to her.

A man stood between them with his back to Ana. He pointed a shaky gun at Pastor Matthew's chest. Ana screamed, but her voice made no sound. She turned to see another man watching her from a dark corner of the room. Neatly trimmed, slicked-back hair framed a handsome, chiseled face. As his hands smoothed the cloth of his suit jacket, they morphed back and forth between the scales of a lizard and the appearance of a normal man. She gasped as his reptilian gaze met hers. His lips curled into a sneer as he moved closer.

Suddenly the young man shot Pastor Matthew. Ana screamed as the bullet pierced her mentor's chest. This time she heard her shrill scream. Pastor Matthew's body slumped lifelessly into the chair as the young man slowly turned around to point the gun at Ana. His menacing eyes seemed to intensify in color. Ana stumbled backward, groping for the doorknob. She turned and ran out into the dark corridor.

Hooded assailants tracked her as she ran. Her panic grew with every step through unfamiliar alleyways. She ducked through doorways, but nothing seemed to shake her followers. When a door appeared to her right, she darted through it and ran up a stairwell to the roof of a building. They were closing in on her. She turned from side to side, looking for a way of escape. Nowhere left to run. She looked up, lifted her arms and began to fly.

She flew off the building and into the clouds. She thought that if she looked down, she would see herself on that roof surrounded by her hooded pursuers. Instead, she focused up and up. She began to hear ringing as she flew higher and higher. The city lights below her dissolved into mere splashes of green. The starlit sky above opened to a bright, sunny day as she soared above trees, the beach and then the ocean. The wind streamed across her face as she listened to the roar of the wind. She would be safe as long as she kept flying. The ringing became louder and louder.

Ana snapped awake to the ring of the phone. Her heart pounded as she squinted in the darkness, trying to figure out where she was and why she felt like she'd been crying. *Pastor Matthew.* She groaned as she reached out from under her warm covers to answer her cell phone on the nightstand. She glanced at the clock as she sat up to see that it was almost five in the morning.

"H…h…hello?" she said, clearing her throat.

"Hi, Ana, sorry to wake you."

"Who is this?"

"It's Kevin. Cathy's been rushed to the hospital."

— C H A P T E R   2 0 —

By the Blood

"They triumphed over him by the blood of the Lamb and by the word of their testimony..." (Revelation 12:11, NIV).

S ASSON MET WITH the other angels in Ana's house. Aarao, Yonah, and Okelani had gathered with Kavo and some of the others. He was concerned about Ana. They all were. The attacks were becoming increasingly numerous.

"I think the best we can do now is to throw them off of Ana's scent," Kavo said, looking at him.

Sasson nodded. "She's been in the state of *agrupneo* for some time. This intensely watchful state is exhausting her. She's receiving revelation quickly and is on guard, but the dream demons have been running interference, trying to scare her. The doubt she carries about her calling is giving the Enemy an open door."

Aarao added, "But I don't think she's going to back down. She committed herself months ago to persevere through whatever comes."

"I know," Kavo agreed, "we will have to help her realize that it's her only option. Is there a deep enough reserve for her to persevere?"

Sasson nodded. "I believe so. We can use what we know to deal with these little fires and keep her hidden so she can recover. She only needs to put the puzzle pieces together in enough time." He turned to Yonah. "Ana is concerned about Cathy."

Yonah answered. "She's fine. They can't harm the baby; they're only trying to breed fear. The annals of prophecy say that this baby will live, and Cathy is growing increasingly mighty in the Spirit."

Kavo returned his attention Sasson. "No more interfering with Andrew. I heard about what you did for him. I understand why you did it, but he needs to fight the temptation on his own so the change will be a permanent one. When the time is right, he will be sent his own guardian. You must focus on Ana until she is out of danger."

Sasson nodded. "I will do as you command although I don't understand why he hasn't been assigned a guardian yet. He's finally made the right decision and is headed in the right direction." He couldn't hide the frustration in his voice.

Kavo insisted, "There is always a reason, so wait. We need to check into some things at the community centre."

"Zeb, instruct Daniel and his friends to start scouting the community centre."

"Will do." Zeb nodded. He and a few other angels disappeared.

"Aarao, encourage Sandra to increase prayer and fasting for Ana."

Aarao nodded.

Again Kavo turned his attention to Sasson. "We can hide her for a while longer, but after that she will have to be ready. The Enemy will be waiting for her."

～

Will stared at Ana in disbelief as she sat balancing on his porch railing. "Only three more weeks 'til the march, and you want to quit?"

The summer air felt fresh as the early sun's rays warmed the dew that sparkled on wet grass. The serenity of the morning was exactly the opposite of how Ana felt. She hadn't slept much. She imagined the neighbors still sleeping or lazing around their houses like she often did at this time.

Will seemed stunned by her news. He leaned dejectedly against the door frame of his house with his arms folded across his chest.

"Will, it's hard to explain, but I don't feel like myself. There's so much going on. I need time. I just have to get out of here and clear my mind." Feeling guilty, she smoothed the wrinkles from her jogging pants to avoid the look in his eyes. The grass and trees looked to be a much deeper green than usual, and she wondered if it was because of the combination of last week's heavy rain and the brilliant sunshine.

Will shook his head. "You're stressed. Take a day. Go home, get some rest, and you'll feel better tomorrow." He straightened, uncrossed his arms, and thrust his hands in his pockets.

He looked serene—standing there barefoot in his jeans and white T-shirt. He seemed confident and relaxed all the time and very much in control of his life. She envied that about him. "No, Will," she said as she shifted uncomfortably. "I'm leaving, and I need you to take over for me. I-I don't know if I want to do this anymore."

"Ana, you can't give up now." He stared at the wooden planks of the floor before looking at her again. "Everyone's depending on you and looking to you to lead the march. If you leave, I'm sure the youth and the kids will be really discouraged. We might as well cancel the whole event."

"Will, it's not that bad," she reassured him. "You'll be here helping."

"Yes, it will be that bad. Will you be back before the march?" Ana avoided meeting his gaze. In refusing to answer the question, she had unwittingly given him her answer.

Once again, he crossed his arms and stared at her. He leaned again on the door post, tilted back his head and sighed. "We've been in this together for the last couple of months. It's not time to quit."

"You'll take over for me?" Ana felt his frustration, but she was determined to go.

He sighed again. "You're not leaving me a choice."

"Thanks. Please let Pastor Mark know. I don't think I can face him right now." She hopped off the banister and squeezed his arm. "I'll contact you soon—when I get to where I'm going."

~

Cathy slept. Her arms cradled a chubby baby boy. Looking up at her, he giggled. She smiled at him and nuzzled his nose with hers. "I'll never let anything hurt you, my darling." She kissed him on the cheek. He smelled of baby powder and milk. Suddenly she felt icy hands on her arms. A grayish metallic-looking man stood in front of her with his eyes focused on the baby. She was paralyzed in fear.

The baby began to cry as a cramp ripped through her abdomen. She looked down and realized she was still pregnant. She screamed as she fought the gray monster for the baby in her arms. A fiercely bright light suddenly appeared behind the gray man. His dead, black eyes rolled sideways as he turned around to face the angel that had materialized behind him.

"Yonah!" the gray man growled.

"You've overstepped your bounds, Sakron," the angel spoke calmly and with authority. His wings arced as he drew a bright sword emanating light. Suddenly, two other angels appeared at his side, drawing their swords as well.

Cathy's limbs began to work, and she slowly backed away, holding the baby. The grayish man began to change before her eyes. He seemingly split out of his man shell and morphed into a tall beast—like a hunchbacked creature, covered by a thick, rounded shell. He lunged at the angels and knocked them over. Their swords clanged onto Sakron's shell and clashed with his sword.

Two additional frail-looking monsters materialized in the room and began fighting the angels as well. Cathy tightly clutched her son, her back against the wall. Her baby had fallen asleep during all the mayhem. His eyes were closed, and his fists fell relaxed at his sides.

Another man with dark, sandy-colored hair materialized beside Cathy. He smiled and gently stroked the baby's head. Cathy didn't recognize him, but he felt familiar. When He looked into Cathy's eyes, she could feel the intense love He had for both of them. She felt safe and secure. The man touched her head the same way he had caressed the baby. A strong breeze and brightness blanched the room. Her eyes stung from the blinding light. When she could see again, the man's face was in front of hers. His deep voice rolled into the room although his lips did not move. She closed her eyes.

My daughter, as it is with this baby, so it shall be with you. Stay in My loving arms, and I will give you rest though the storm rages around you. Fear not.

A sweet fragrance of spices filled the room. When she opened her eyes again, the monsters had disappeared.

❧

Kevin stood over Cathy as she rested in the hospital bed. He placed his hands on her stomach. "God, please don't let us lose this baby. I ask that Your blood would cover her and protect our child. I command that any evil directed toward her or the baby to be broken in Jesus' name." He heard a noise at the door and turned to see Beth, Sandra and Ana.

"How is she?" Beth whispered as they entered.

"She seems to be okay now. But she was in a lot of pain when she arrived last night. She was cramping and bleeding profusely. The doctors aren't sure what the problem is. They're running more tests."

Beth smoothed the hair from Cathy's face and then patted Kevin's arm. Sandra eyed Kevin suspiciously. "Did something happen to trigger this?"

Kevin shrugged. "Nothing…as far as we can tell. I've been up all night praying. She woke up a few times with nightmares. But that's about it."

Ana patted him on the shoulder. "We'll get out of your hair then and let her rest. But keep us updated."

"I will, but please pray."

Ana nodded. "Let her know we were here when she wakes up."

Kevin sat down and stared at Cathy.

◦

"How's Stephen?" Ana asked Beth when they were safely out of the hospital room.

"It's not looking good. He seems to be deteriorating." She blinked back her tears and smiled. "But I feel a sense of peace about everything. God is so good. I wouldn't have been able to survive all of this without His strength. I love Stephen so much. He's always had faith in God that I never possessed until this illness."

"Stephen and I have been just praying and loving each other. Our relationship is more intimate than ever before. I'm so thankful God sent Cathy when He did."

Ana stared at Beth and then looked at her mom. *How can someone going through so much still be so happy?* Beth obviously wasn't afraid anymore. With all that was going on, she wanted to be more like Beth and stop feeling sorry for herself. Instead, she felt powerless to change anything about her life.

Sandra tuned into Ana's thoughts. "That's beautiful, Beth. Sometimes I'm amazed by the way God does things." She turned to Ana. "I think we should be going. You have some packing to do." Sandra glanced at her watch.

Ana felt her cell phone vibrate as she and her mother entered the elevator. She looked down at the text.

I miss you, sweetheart. Come to see me today if you have a chance. I have something for you. Wella

Ana reread the text. She hadn't heard from Wella in a long time, but somehow Wella always had a way of knowing when something was wrong. She felt a surge of strength course through her for a moment. Just as suddenly as it had come, it was gone. "Mom, can we stop by Wella's house?"

"Sure, lead the way."

~

Leah walked down a few streets until she found the narrow alleyway—her old haunt. She cleared away some flattened cardboard boxes. The ground still had the faint stain of blood and etched markings. She stooped and lightly brushed her fingers across the spot where she normally offered small animal sacrifices. Divinica's words echoed in her mind.

Leah couldn't believe Divinica could ask for a bigger sacrifice than what she'd already given. It was impossible anyway. For that sacrifice, she would need to be pregnant again, and it was too late for that. Leah shuddered. Getting rid of her baby that way had seemed like a convenient option at the time… She blocked out the rest of her thoughts. It didn't matter because from what Divinica had implied, a baby sacrifice would not be enough.

What if I can't stomach such a task? Divinica Woodstock had made it clear she had no choice but to follow orders. The woman was not likely to be her new buddy in crime, holding her hand through any of this. If anything, she felt like she now had a new enemy. Divinica's fierceness terrified Leah. She had commanded her to secure a human sacrifice, one way or the other. Lately, Sakron had been of no help. He was almost never around, which was a great relief in some ways. She'd almost forgotten what it was like to feel her own real emotions.

Leah stood up and dusted off her hands. *How long will I be able to survive like this until I'm found out?* She sighed. If she were found out, then she wouldn't be forced to participate anymore. With each passing month, she realized she was sinking further and further into bondage from which she could never free herself. In truth, there was no end to the entanglements in which she found herself. But she had no time to think of such matters right now. Divinica was waiting for her.

As the priestess walked through fire toward the clearing, her dark hair and dress flowed as if driven by an unseen wind. A python spirit wrapped itself around her, its tail encircling her wrist. The snake spirit moved, silently readjusting its position a few times before finally slithering off to wait in the nearby bush.

The fire was as bright, and, at the same time, as dense as a forest. But this fire was different; there was no heat, and nothing was consumed as it burned. She walked toward Dionysus in the astral plane. Dionysus stood in the center of the clearing, dressed in a well-cut, gray suit. His dark and tattered wings spanned out around him. His eyes were little more than black slits in yellow holes. Although it was daytime, in this place between the temporal realm and the spiritual, everything was shaded by darkness. Objects waved with their own energy field, taking on an appearance far different than normal.

"Is the great lady ready for her appearing?" Dionysus extended his hand to Divinica.

Divinica strode slowly toward him and took his hand. Her skirt swished across the ground. "My lady will arise when everything is set. When the blood of an innocent is spilled during the final ritual, the goddess portal will have enough power to remain open to our side."

"She knows then that some of the portals have been closed?" Dionysus suddenly appeared distressed.

"Of course, everything here is reverberating in her realm. She will deal with the troublemakers at her appearing," Divinica answered with a sinister chuckle. The echo of her mirthless laugh was swallowed by the fire and mist.

"I will make sure the lady will have slaves and servants when she comes," Dionysus added.

"Yes, Leah and any others we can gather will make a good start for the lady when she is back in this realm. After I make the final sacrifice, I will rid Leah of her body. She will become one of the chosen—a high honor for her work, of course." Divinica smiled. "I will then add Sakron to my league of demons," she mused aloud.

"You and the lady shall have anything you wish. We will do our best to keep the remaining portals open." Dionysus folded his hand into a scaly fist. His face was visibly angry. "The prayers of the saints have done us great damage. The spread of their sanctification is keeping many from worshiping in our temples. Ancient orgies and murder are no longer drawing the audiences they once did."

"Just keep working. We cannot afford to give up when we're so close to her appearing." Divinica turned and walked to the edge of the clearing. She stretched her hand over the still-burning fires and then looked up. "Leah is here. I've prepared Havoc for her as you've requested. I must get back, but I will summon you again when the time is right."

~

Leah walked through the community centre parking lot and trudged up through the ravine and forest area. She finally brushed through the last bit of leaves and small bushes into a clearing where she had been a few times before. This small forest was not popular among people in the city. Stories of strange paranormal activity kept away most people. Leah smiled to herself. Of course, these stories were true, but fear had exaggerated them. Even Leah was amused by how ridiculous some of them had become.

When she arrived, Divinica was lying quietly, face up on the grass and dry dirt. She wore a long purple skirt and a loose white shirt. She resembled a young hippie. Her eyes were closed as if she were sleeping, but Leah knew better. Leah headed toward some nearby low bushes and sat down to wait and meditate to pass the time.

The afternoon was late when Divinica finally stirred. Leah was hungry and a bit stiff from sitting for so many hours. "Good, you're here," Divinica commented, refocusing her eyes as she got up and headed toward Leah.

Leah replied dryly, "Have been for a while."

"I have something for you," Divinica said, shaking her thick hair to the side and ignoring Leah's sarcasm. She reached around her neck and pulled off a red amulet. The gold chain dangled from her fingers as she released her hair onto her shoulders.

"What is that?" Leah asked as she studied the object in Divinica's hand. Divinica held up the chain in front of her. "Leah, I want you to meet Havoc." Divinica's voice was more pleasant than usual.

"What?" Leah looked confused.

"I'm giving you one of my demons to help you create distractions. All you have to do is wear this amulet, and he will do the work for you," Divinica explained, placing the thick-red gem of the necklace into Leah's open palm. "Wherever you go, take him with you in the necklace. He's very easy to manage and won't interfere with Sakron, your ruling demon."

"Why would I want another demon?" Leah stiffly asked, trying to mask her anger. "I already traded all of mine for Sakron, and that didn't help me much."

"Listen, Leah, I know you've been out here on your own, but you can't be that stupid. If you want to become stronger in this world, you will have to use what you already have to gain more power. I will show you a few things, but don't get any ideas about trying to take any of my demons."

Why would Divinica bother to mention the possibility of betrayal?

Leah was sure that if she tried, Divinica would make her suffer. Leah had no way to compete with someone as strong as her.

Divinica turned and walked back to where she had been lying down. She motioned to the space in front of her. "Come and sit here. Put on the necklace." Her words were forceful but sounded as smooth as glass. Leah was sure

Divinica was hiding something, but she did as she was told and put on the necklace as she sat cross-legged in front of her.

"Sakron has told me in the shadows that you already know how to soul travel. Why have you not used this to your benefit to discover new information?

"I'm scared. I've almost been trapped in the abyss several times already. I don't know how to do it without leaving my body unprotected."

"Havoc will help you with that. He will give you greater concentration and guard your body when you leave to spy on our enemies." Leah looked doubtful as Divinica continued, "You must tap into the ancient spirits by allowing yourself to be free of your body. If you hold onto the fear of losing your body, then you will never become great. I will show you how to invoke the power of the ancient ones using old meditations. You must increase your meditation time. Your body doesn't belong to you anymore, and you need to accept that fact. The old ones before us used cutting techniques to rid themselves of the thoughts of their body's welfare. You would do well to remember these techniques and put them into practice."

Leah cringed, remembering the gruesome things she had read and watched people do to connect to the spirit world. There was no end to the mutilation necessary. Leah's gaze searched Divinica's arms for signs of the ancient rituals. If she had cut herself, she could now see no trace of any scars on her smooth, olive-colored skin.

"I don't carry scars," Divinica said as she followed her gaze. "One of my demons is a healer demon. This kind is difficult to possess and requires more than you can imagine." She answered Leah's unspoken questions.

"I don't understand. The more demons I had before, the more torment I experienced. I thought I was going crazy. How can you talk so freely of having many?"

"I am not like you. I have embraced my pain and become one with it. The torment you speak of enduring is now a part of me. I'm not separate from it. I carry this burden in order to serve our master."

As Leah lay down, she felt herself grow cold. Time slowed down. Fear caused her body to tremble as the amulet glowed red. She felt herself falling further into herself while her soul lifted out of her body. She heard Divinica speaking. As Divinica's hand rested on her arm, Leah felt a burning vibration of pins and needles underneath it.

"It's time for you to step onto the front lines, little *sister*." The hint of sarcasm in the word *sister* did not bring any comfort to Leah. "Havoc will guide you there and help you return. I will help you concentrate using my abilities and guard your body. I want you to see what I have just seen. No turning back..."

Leah was forcefully ripped from her body. She felt burning and searing pain even though she knew that her body remained in the clearing in the forest. Next she was in one of the meeting rooms of the church, listening in on a conversation in progress. Such brightness filled the room that it hurt her senses. *Why can I still feel?* She noticed some areas in the room pulsed with light. *Are there men in the light?*

At the center of the pulsating lights, Daniel, Will and Elikai were deep in an intense conversation, sitting in chairs that faced one another.

Elikai said. "Will, I don't know if Ana has what it takes to keep organizing this. She seems to be getting more distant."

"She'll be fine! I think she just needs some time to herself to pray. We can keep her covered in prayer and pray about the other things that you guys have noticed."

Daniel spoke up. "I don't trust that girl, Leah. I don't think she's here for the right reasons. Elikai, do you remember when she used to attend when Ishmael was still leading? Her being here while all these things are going on can't be a coincidence."

Will waved at them. "Listen guys, we can't get drawn into a witch hunt or play a blame game. We need our full attention to be on God." Will looked back and forth between them. "He'll take care of everything else He wants to do, as we are obedient." Will crouched down, resting his arms across his thighs.

Divinica had been right. *They had been on to me.*

"Enough talk then," Elikai said, clasping his hands. "Let's pray." He leaned forward and bowed his head.

Daniel started, "Holy Spirit, we invite Your presence into this room."

Leah felt the room wave with power. The atmosphere began to thicken even more as the prayers grew even more passionate.

Daniel continued, "We delight in You, God! Our whole lives belong to You. We come in the power of agreement right now for the church and the march. We pray that the people of God would arise from their slumber and take back what the Enemy has stolen. Even more than that, Lord, we pray that Your kingdom will come."

Leah felt something cool and bright whiz past her head and turned to see the bright pulsating areas in the room begin to assemble. They joined together and began to form a protective shield around the young men as they prayed.

She blinked and saw herself lying alone in the clearing. She was slipping out of the astral plane when suddenly a bright-red demon appeared beside her. Havoc was unlike anything she had ever seen before. His fangs formed a wall of teeth in his mouth, and his eyes were deep, black holes. Scales of red armor covered his skinny bent body from head to toe, and he carried a black ice pick. Startled, she screamed, but the sound was silenced by the blankness of the astral plane. She silently observed, unable to make anyone aware of her presence. She was now a watcher.

Havoc laughed mischievously as he went to work, smashing things in the room in the astral space where he existed. Although not much was in the room, he smashed anything he could lay his red hands on. Leah knew what would happen next. Everything that he had touched would some-how stop "working" in the real world during real time. She wondered again if she always wanted this demon with her. As she watched him, she knew she would never be able to control him—even though he was linked to the amulet.

Elikai prayed, "In the name of Jesus, I command every spirit that is not of You to leave this room."

Leah was jolted and felt a powerful wave begin to dislodge her again. Havoc looked up from his work and toward the young men. He ran aiming his ice pick at the top of Will's head, ready to smash it with all his might. His blow met with a sword coming from the bright light. Leah looked on in shock as she saw the angel and the demon fighting above Will's bowed head.

Daniel said, "Guys, I'm sensing that something is not right. Can you pray in the Spirit as I pray?" Will and Elikai began praying in tongues as Daniel resumed praying. "We rebuke every spirit sent to cause harm on us and our church. We rebuke the spirit of destruction, and we plead the blood in this place right now."

All of the men suddenly rose from their chairs and started to walk around the room praying and singing in tongues.

Havoc and what looked like an angel wrestled back and forth before the angel finally overpowered him. Havoc was on his knees, holding his sword over his own head as protection from the angel. He looked over at Leah with fear in his eyes. He rolled away, and, in a last-ditch effort, he began to run toward her. When he was close enough, he jumped for the necklace. A large and final wave of light ripped her from the room. This time she didn't feel the pain and burning of the first arrival, but she heard the serene chime of crystal brushing against itself and felt a wintry blast of wind pulling her. The light grew brighter and brighter until the room disappeared in a flash, blinding her.

When she finally awoke in the clearing of the forest, it was dark; she was alone. She stared up into the newly darkened sky, unable to move for a few minutes. "I'll guard your body," Leah mimicked sarcastically. "That traitorous…" The ache behind her eyes felt like she had been staring into the sun.

In her astral travels, she had never actually seen an angel up close. Angels were impossible for people like her to see. She could sometimes sense their power, but rarely. Her relationship with demons maimed her from sensing anything spiritual.

What else is out there?

Leah sat up and rubbed her eyes.

What kind of power did these Christians actually possess? Clearly enough to send a powerful demon running to a weak human for shelter.

CHAPTER 21

Pressing In

"*Brothers and sisters, I do not consider myself yet to have taken hold of it. But one thing I do: Forgetting what is behind and straining toward what is ahead, I press on toward the goal to win the prize for which God has called me heavenward in Christ Jesus*" (Philippians 3:13, 14, NIV).

A NA WALKED UP to Wella's house after her mom dropped her off. Much time had passed since she had last walked up these creaking porch steps. Everything remained the same—like no time had passed at all. She could almost see herself sitting on the lined-up boxes and chairs where she and Pastor Matthew had often sat and talked. Everything was the same—except the flower pots sat empty, and Pastor Matthew was gone.

As Ana felt tears begin to sting her eyes, she quickly rang the doorbell. After a moment, a smiling Wella opened the door. She noticed Ana's tears and gently pulled her into a warm embrace.

"Oh, sweetheart, it's going to be okay." In her embrace, all the resistance inside of Ana began to melt away. She crumpled into Wella's plump arms and cried. Wella held her tightly as if a lesser grip would have left her unprotected. The faint smell of vanilla and cinnamon clung to Wella's clothes. At the forefront of Ana's mind were Pastor Matthew, the prayer march and the disappointments of the past few months. Wella's arms were a safe haven for her to rest and think about everything. After a few minutes, Wella patted Ana's back and held her at arm's length to examine her face. "Come inside, my dear, and have a seat. I'll make us something hot to drink." Wella led her inside and then motioned for her to take a comfortable chair.

Ana took in the familiar and welcoming surroundings. The room was alive with brightly colored furniture and pillows. Wella had often said that heaven would have lots of color, people and things, and she wanted to be surrounded with that kind of beauty now.

The walls were adorned with pictures of relatives and friends. The ones of Pastor Matthew and Wella were proof of the love they shared. She spied one of herself and Pastor Matthew on top of the piano. They stood smiling side by side in one of the meeting rooms at Good News Remnant.

After a few moments, Wella emerged from the kitchen, carrying a tray with two steaming cups of hot chocolate and a small loaf of banana bread. "Are you feeling better, dear?"

Ana nodded, rubbing her bare feet together on the familiar braided rug. Wella leaned over to cut the banana bread into thick slices and handed Ana a plate before settling into her plush, overstuffed chair. "I've missed you. Why haven't you come to visit me? We were friends too, weren't we?" She smiled and winked as she picked up her hot chocolate.

"I don't know." Ana looked away, suddenly ashamed. "I figured you would want and need some space."

"Ah—space. I see," Wella said as she lifted her eyebrows. She held the mug with both hands.

Ana added quietly, "I really did miss you."

"Well, how have you been? Busy at the church, no doubt?"

"Yes, very busy—too busy." Ana took a few bites of the warm and buttery banana bread, Wella's specialty. "Wella, I've been so stressed out lately. I'm not sleeping well, and things aren't going the way they were supposed to go. You heard about the march?"

"Oh, yes, the prayer march." Wella nodded again. "I've been hearing many things, sweetheart, from many people. I've been here praying for you, and God has been showing me things. Don't lose heart. There is much that you don't yet understand, but it will all become known very soon."

"I don't know if I'm ready to lead this thing, Wella. I've been having nightmares, and I have a bad feeling about this." Ana paused. "I feel like no one really cares what it's all about. The pastors in the area are pulling out of the march; rumors are being spread about us, and I don't know why. We're trying to do God's work, and I feel like the people who are getting in the way the most are Christians."

"Ana, sometimes people lose focus on what's important. Being distracted happens to the best of us. The key is to ask God to help you stay focused so that you don't fall into the trap of being offended with others."

"I don't know. I guess I expected everyone to want to do this with us, you know? Maybe I need some time away to clear my head."

"What were you thinking of?"

"Somewhere out of here. Maybe a hotel."

"I think I have a place where you could go." Wella put down her mug and stood up. "A friend of mine has a cottage about two hours west of here. I'm sure she wouldn't mind if you stayed there for a while."

"Oh, Wella, that would be perfect!"

"Why don't you let me give her a call and find out if it's available. But before I take care of that matter, I have something for you. Follow me."

Wella stood and walked in the direction of the study. Ana swallowed the last bite of banana bread, grabbed her mug, and followed Wella down the hall to Matthew's study.

Papers were scattered over the top of the ancient, worn desk, which was surrounded by shelves lined with his books. "Matthew was always working on projects that God had brought to his attention. Not long ago I was going through his papers, and I found a stack that talked about the community centre and the city. He even mentioned you in a few of them. Seems that he planned to have you get involved at the centre." She pointed to a particular pile on the desk.

Ana set down her mug and began leafing through the papers. "Yes, Pastor Mark mentioned that to me a few months ago when I started volunteering there."

"Well, it seems Matthew had given some serious thought to that place. He also did some spiritual mapping of the city. I thought that I had better give these papers to you before the march. I thought they might be of some use to you," Wella explained as they both bent over the papers.

Ana sat down and sifted through the papers. Among them were old newspaper clippings about the city, including stories of murders and kidnappings that dated back several years. Aerial maps of the city with red circles had date notations of when crimes had taken place. He'd also recorded weather anomalies and scenes where mutilated animals had been found.

Ana stared at one of the old clippings of a young girl about ten years old who had gone missing. She remembered hearing that story when she was in elementary school.

Wella leaned over her and looked at the clipping. "Did you hear about the young woman who went missing yesterday?"

"No," said Ana. Shaken from her thoughts. "What happened?"

"The authorities aren't sure. It seems she didn't come home from work. Her parents said that their daughter is always prompt, but yesterday she didn't come home, and they've heard nothing since."

Ana was silent. *More bad news.*

She sighed, "I hope they can find her." She took Wella's well-worn and soft hand in hers. "Why don't we say a prayer for her right now?"

"Great idea!" Wella smiled and patted Ana's hand. "Heavenly Father, we come before You right now and ask for this young girl's safe return home. We come against and cancel any scheme that has befallen her, and we pray that You will surround her in Your light and protect her. In the name of Jesus, we pray, amen."

Wella squeezed Ana's hand then reached out to touch her cheek. "Sweetheart, whatever you do, don't give up. You have a lot of support—even if you don't always see it." She gazed deeply into at Ana's eyes. "Something else really important you need to know is what your real weaknesses are. Be on guard against the kind that can pull you away from God and do not let it happen again. Otherwise, you'll be going round and around the same mountain again and again." She kissed Ana on the forehead. "You already have everything you need, my dear."

Ana tried to smile and nodded. *What does she mean? There's a lot I need and don't have.* Courage was only one of those needed intangibles.

Wella left the room to contact her friend about the cottage as Ana gathered the papers and put them in her bag. Within ten minutes, Ana was ready to leave. Wella wrote down all of the information for Ana and walked her to the door.

Wella smiled at Ana as she clasped her hands. "Listen, Ana, I want you to know that I'm truly happy. I really am. I'm full of joy and incredibly thankful for all of the years Matthew and I had together. We decided when we were young that we would live for God every day, and we did. I don't have any regrets. Even without Matthew, I'm ready to keep going because this is what we both wanted. We counted the cost. Now that doesn't mean just mean figuring out the things we'll gain in the end. Jesus already told us what was in store. Sometimes counting the cost means realizing what we might have to give up. I'll be praying for you, sweetheart. Take care of yourself, okay?" Wella patted her cheek.

Ana nodded although she wasn't sure she could get to that place Wella talked about, but she knew that place of acceptance was something she needed to gain. "Thanks for everything, Wella, I'm glad you're okay. I'll call you as soon as I get back from my trip." Ana slipped on her sandals and briefly hugged Wella.

"You'd better! No more of this *space* nonsense!"

∽

After a long quiet drive with her mom, Ana was relieved to see the cottage come into view. They parked in the driveway and walked up to the house. The countryside around the cottage was mostly wooded. Ana guessed by the look of the stone chimney that the cottage was a little old.

She reached into the mailbox as per her instructions and found a small envelope waiting for her. She opened the envelope and found the key and some important emergency phone numbers. The owner had even included a short note for her as well.

Dear Ana,

I hope you are able to rest and rejuvenate while you are here. I come here often for the same purpose. I'm glad to share the place with you. Call if you need anything.

God bless,

Roxanne

Ana folded the letter, stuck it in her pocket and then unlocked the door to the cottage. Sandra followed her inside into a small room with hand-carved chairs and a small table. A small open kitchen was adjacent to the living room. Although the place looked rustic, Ana was sure it had been renovated in the last few years. The fireplace had fresh wood stacked nearby, and a small, cushioned armchair was positioned in front of it.

"Looks cozy," Sandra said. She took a brief tour of the place, then kissed Ana and hugged her goodbye. "Keep the doors locked."

Ana laughed. "Mom…"

Sandra hugged her again, but this time she didn't let go.

Ana sighed. "I'm not dying. I'll be back."

"You sure you don't want me to pick you up?"

"Don't worry, it's a short ride to the main bus station."

After Sandra had gone, Ana opened the door to the bedroom and placed her bag on the floor next to the bed. She sat on the bed and studied its wicker base and soft, stuffed mattress. Against the wooden-plank wall was a desk with a small lamp. Ana unpacked her Bible and notebook and placed them on the desk.

Nothing was fancy about this place of refuge, but it had been tastefully decorated, giving a homey look. The big windows were covered with heavy blue curtains. Drawing back the curtains revealed a beautiful view of a sparkling brook and some lush trees nearby. She stood for a moment, gazing out. She would explore it after she had finished unpacking. She fished through her bag and pulled out Pastor Matthew's notes and clippings. Pastor Matthew had tracked weird events in Tehly for over ten years. He had circled the community centre and outlined a few sections of the city. *What had Pastor Matthew been doing?* Even after studying the papers, she knew she was overlooking something. Ana sighed. *This is hopeless.* Years ago, Pastor Matthew had made a mistake in choosing her as part of the team. She had no special talents and wasn't really gifted at anything. She couldn't even figure out what his notes meant. *Why did Wella give them to me?*

～

Kevin skipped onto the sidewalk and quickened his pace to the hospital. He had been going back and forth for days now. He was relieved that Cathy was doing better and would be able to go home soon. He had stayed up all night at times just to pray and fast for her and the baby. Though he didn't deserve it, God had answered his prayers. He was banking on what he knew about Jesus and His desire to help them. He was also banking on how good Cathy was. If God wasn't going to listen to him for his sake, then at least he would listen for Cathy's sake and the innocent child she carried.

When he arrived at the hospital, Sandra was already there, sitting next to an alert and vibrant Cathy. He waved at Sandra and walked over to the bed. Cathy had dark circles under her eyes, but she looked beautiful and was pleased to see him.

"Hey, babe! How are you feeling?" He leaned over to kiss her forehead.

"Umm—good," she replied, closing her eyes as he kissed her. "I slept well. I haven't been feeling any pain either."

Kevin smiled.

"Were you able to buy the things on the list I gave you to get ready for the baby?" Sandra interrupted.

"I got almost everything. The items are at my parents' house, but I'll move them over to Cathy's as soon as she gets to go home."

Cathy wrinkled her nose. "How did you afford it? You haven't been working for months now."

"Don't worry about it, babe. I promised I am going to take care of you."

"Did you get it from a friend?"

"No."

"Did you ask your parents?"

"No. They wouldn't have given it to me even if I had asked." He laughed. Cathy sighed and slammed her hand on her leg. "Kevin, I want to know. Was it something illegal?"

"Of course not." He looked at Sandra and then back to Cathy, embarrassed. "I told you I'm done with all of that—I sold my ring."

Cathy stared back. "The ring your grandfather gave you?"

"Yep."

Cathy's face fell. "But Kevin, you love that ring."

He shrugged. "I love you and the baby more. Anyway, I'm learning from the guys about what it means to be a husband and a father. The greatest thing I can do to show love is to sacrifice myself, or so I've been told." He flashed a quick glance at Sandra that only Cathy could see.

Cathy reached out to Kevin, and he bent over to hug her.

He smiled. "I'd do anything for you."

Sandra stood and turned to face Kevin. "Listen, Kevin, we can talk about Cathy's care once she gets home. She's going to need some help until she's a hundred percent."

Kevin noticed that Sandra looked pleased. *This is new. Is it possible she's finally starting to warm up to me?*

～

Cathy clasped Kevin's hand as they crossed the street toward her apartment. The beautiful weather had brought out the neighbors from the buildings around them. People stood outside, leaning over fences and sitting in lawn chairs. For the first time in a while, she walked down the street, smiling at everyone she passed. She felt happy. *This is how things should be.* She looked forward to spending time reading the Word, praying, and worshiping together as a couple. She studied Kevin. He was really a good man who loved her—of that fact she was sure. Even when he was on drugs, he had loved her, but now he would be able to show her real love. As long as he was committed to God, she didn't have to worry about many things to come. God would give them strength for whatever the future offered.

For some reason Kevin seemed unusually quiet. He'd grown a great deal in the last few months, and, as a result, her confidence in him and their relationship grew day to day. They had both committed themselves to live for God first—an excellent foundation for a good life together.

But would Kevin be able to abstain from drugs? What kind of home will our baby have?

If he relapsed again, it would be hard, but she was confident she and the baby would be all right without him. While she was in the hospital, Jesus had promised that He would work out everything—if she could trust in Him.

When they neared her apartment, Kevin took out his keys and opened the door. As it opened, Cathy smelled the familiar scent of her favorite candles. Her mouth dropped open in surprise. Candles burned throughout the dark room, and white rose petals had been sprinkled from the door to the kitchen table where she noticed a small box. As they stepped inside, Cathy stood silently admiring the beauty around her. "It's a good thing we didn't stop for that long horseback ride in the country *I* was planning."

Kevin laughed. "Everything is under control." He pointed to the fire extinguisher hanging on the wall. "That's in case I set your apartment on fire." He took her hand and led her to the table where a vase had been filled with long-stemmed white roses.

Cathy sat down at the table while he went to fill glasses with grape juice and returned to sit down across from her, leaving the filled glasses on the counter.

"Cathy, you're the most important person in my life after Jesus, of course." He smiled and continued fidgeting with his hands as he leaned over the table. "You are one of the strongest women I know, and I love you. We've been through hell together, but I know good days are ahead for us. When I had no purpose, I wasted years and energy, trying to make myself happy." He paused as he searched for the right words.

"You led me to Jesus and true life. I'm so thankful for that. Now I want to share that life with you and be with you always."

He stroked her hand with his thumb. "I want to be a husband and a father who will give of myself for my family. I'm going to take care of you and love you like you deserve to be loved. I want to be the man you have waited for me to become for so long."

"Kevin!" Cathy exclaimed and then smiled; her eyes filled with tears. Kevin lifted the box sitting on the table and opened it to expose a small ruby ring.

I can't believe this is really happening!

He stared at the ring for a moment. "I got you a ruby to remind us both of the blood of Jesus that cleanses us from our past and makes a brand-new way and a new covenant for our future. Without Jesus, neither of us would even be here." He stared at her as he whispered, "Would you do me the honor of becoming my wife?"

She grinned. Tears streamed down her cheeks. She gently placed her hands on Kevin's cheeks and looked into his eyes. "I love you too and trust you," she whispered. She stretched over the table to kiss him on the forehead and laughed. "Of course, I'll marry you!"

Kevin took her left hand and slipped the ring on her finger. He sat awkwardly staring at her and smiling. He kissed her hand. "I thought we could have communion together." He stood to get the bread and grape juice.

"I'd love to." Cathy giggled and wiped happy tears from her cheeks. She looked at her ring. It was a deep red, the color of redemption.

～

Ana's body flooded with pain. She was trapped in an empty cement cellar. The filth of the room emanated from more than what Ana saw with her eyes. It permeated everything, sliming the air and the cracked walls. Shadows passed through the walls, laughing and mocking her. On the ground beside her lay a needle and broken pieces of a mirror. All she could think of was the peace that would come if she could slice through her wrists.

The thought shocked her. She had never wanted to kill herself. She reached for the broken mirror on the floor and looked at herself. Light-brown waves instead of her black curls and green eyes wide with terror stared back at her. Her nose was dirty, and streaks of tears smudged her bruised face. A pale-yellow shirt contrasted sharply with the light-brown hair. She stared for a moment before she dropped the mirror that splintered into more pieces. Her sobs stole her breath. *There was one other way to end it. Mindlessly, she picked up the syringe and held it tightly.*

Her arms were covered with scabs and dark bruises marred the inside of her forearms. A cloth tied around her left arm caused her vein to protrude. She balanced her arm on the leg of her ripped jeans. She stabbed the needle in her arm. Piercing pain shot down her fingers and up to her shoulder, searing through the rest of her body.

Blood. Mine? No!

She panted in torment as her gaze focused up out of the room—above the jagged walls and broken ceiling and beyond the shadows. She once again looked into the eyes of Jesus, who was in His own time, hanging on the cross, while simultaneously watching the events in the dirty cellar.

His eyes. So much love.

Ana opened her eyes. She had been crying in her sleep again. The pain was still tangible and did not suddenly disappear upon awakening. The remnants of fear, pain and then love swirled in her heart. She gave herself over to the tears as she thought of the young woman she had been in the cellar. A woman full of hurt, regret and loss. This was another one of the dreams she'd had that night on the curb. This is what everything was about. God wanted to reach that woman. Ana wished she could help her. She prayed in the spirit. Maybe the girl didn't exist, but everything had felt as if it were happening to her. Ana wept. She wept for all of those who didn't know God's hope and love and were trapped in dark cellars. The grief was so unbearable she screamed. She'd never experienced this kind of intensity in prayer before. When she had no strength remaining, her prayer and tongues turned into groans. After a while, the grief dissipated, and peace flooded over her until she fell asleep again.

❦

Ana awakened to the buzz of insects outside of the cottage. The early morning heat seeped in, giving the room a woody, musky smell. She was still tired from her night prayers, but her thoughts turned to Cathy. She had panicked briefly when she'd learned that Cathy was in the hospital. The panic felt like Pastor Matthew all over again. Cathy was better, but the feeling of letting everyone down was still strong. Everyone she cared about seemed to be getting hurt. She wanted them protected. They should have been protected. Maybe it would have been better if she never followed Cathy out of the Eclipse. This life was full of contradictions. This fight meant giving your life and losing to win. You prayed for protection until something happened, and then you prayed for healing—if you could still pray at all. You were free—truly free—but a slave to Christ.

The weight of the work ahead of her felt like too much to carry. If the march went down in flames, its failure would be on her. She decided all she could do was fast until something happened. Food would always be there, but right now this is what she had to do. Maybe she could urge God to do something before it was too late. Even if He weren't going to answer, at the very least, He would have to take pity on her starving herself.

A week of no food passed. Her energy level rested at fatigue, and dull hunger was her new norm at the lower calorie intake she received from the diluted fruit juice. The fireplace crackled and sparked as she poked at the fire. She sat back in the cushioned armchair and readjusted the lap blanket. One of the effects of fasting was feeling chilled even though it was warm during the day. So once the sun went down, she was even more cold. For the most part, she pressed into prayer. Every hour of fasting felt like another small victory. Each morning was a new celebration. With each passing day, the insight she craved became clearer.

Some days her joy in God was so intense and the peace so real that everything else was colorless and empty. She felt like she could live like this forever. And at other times, she resisted the urge to go home, plop down in front of the television with a big bag of chips and forget everything. Leaving behind God's promises for her life and forfeiting her destiny seemed easier.

But then a thought occurred to her that she *could* leave it all behind, and God would still love her. With all the work aside, her identity was rooted in being His daughter. Love and acceptance were hers through Christ. She didn't have to twist God's arm to do anything. He *wanted* to do things for her. She didn't have to fear.

Another thought came. Her fear of rejection from Andrew had made her afraid to really let go for a good while. Fear of being alone was alive in her heart even though she didn't want to admit it out loud. All these issues were strains of fear tainting parts of her life. Until now, everything had been about her. Ana realized what Wella had meant about going around the same mountain. Her insecurity was her weakness which caused her to fall into the same mistakes with guys. Even though she hadn't dated Andrew, she still had invisible ties to him in her heart.

She prayed out loud, "God, take away my fear."

My strength will be made perfect in your weakness.

"I'm not strong enough."

All you must do is lean on Me. I will show you what comes next.

⁓

Grass patches protruded sporadically from the rocky hill. Ana held on and looked up. Healthy fear caused her to keep climbing. She placed her foot on a piece of jutting earth and pushed up. Her hand grasped for another patch of grass strong enough to hold her weight so she could pull herself up.

Almost there.

The hill was too steep. She looked back. How had she made it this far already?

The incline diminished as she climbed higher. The brown dirt and hard rock gave way to more patches of green until all she saw was a lush pasture on top of flat land.

As she topped the hill, a beautiful fountain came into view. It was warm, but near the fountain, snow covered the grass. She ran the rest of the way to get a drink of the crystal-clear water to quench her thirst from the most beautiful fountain she had ever seen. Layers of cascading water flowed, forming the shape of an invisible structure. Ana came close enough to take a drink. She found the water was sweet. She drank until her stomach was full.

Ana opened her eyes and stared into the predawn darkness. The dream message was clear; the hard part was over. She recorded the dream in her journal and then turned on her lamp. *Pastor Matthew's notes.* After a few minutes of rustling through the papers and comparing dates and locations, facts started to come together in her mind. Suddenly, all of the notes made sense. She went to the desk to make some additional notes.

~

Pastor Mark sighed and picked up his desk phone after an attempt to ignore the ring for the third time. Moments later, he was ready to hang up even though the conversation wasn't over.

"So you see why I just don't think it's appropriate?" Pastor Norman droned.

"Yes, it's perfectly clear, Pastor. You don't think Ana should be leading a prayer march because it doesn't fit with your doctrine about women in leadership."

"Ahem, uh…not exactly…"

"Then I must have misunderstood you."

"What she is doing is not biblically sound. We were warned of Jezebels throughout the Bible. I don't think this young woman is qualified to be leading men in this endeavor. If she wants to do a march with only the women, that would be acceptable," Pastor Norman continued.

Pastor Mark had had enough. "I'm sorry you feel that way. Let me know if you change your mind. I think standing together in unity for the sake of this city and putting aside minor differences—"

"This is not a *minor* difference. Have a good afternoon." The line went dead. Pastor Mark replaced the receiver.

A moment later, the phone rang again. "Hello? That was fast."

"Huh? Pastor? It's me—Will."

"Oh, sorry. I thought you were someone else. What's up?"

"It's Ana; she wants us to gather all the pastors and leaders who were involved with the march from the beginning—*ALL* of them."

"What? Why? It doesn't seem like it would be worth the trouble."

"I don't know. She said she wants to speak to all of them."

"When is she coming back? Did she specify a date for the meeting?"

"Two days before the march. She'll be home by then."

"All right. I hope she knows what she's doing."

"Me too."

———

Ana awoke to the sun's shining through her closed eyelids. She wanted to rest unmoving for a few more moments. She'd slept better than she had in years. After almost three weeks, the time had come to go home. Fasting wasn't going to change her all on its own, though the discipline had indeed created a capacity for her to grow and be strengthened. Still, she wouldn't be changed. God would use the relationships around her to do that. She embraced an awareness that God had pressed more of His love into her heart. Because of His great love, she would never walk away from what He had called her to do. And right now the time had come to return and fight. She felt strengthened in her spirit, but her joints were stiff, and her hipbones protruded because of the weight loss. The inside of her mouth felt grainy and dry, her saliva sticky from dehydration. Her stomach was sunken, and she could feel her ribs through her pajamas. She felt almost like a corpse. She would have to begin eating again, very slowly.

Ana stood and prayed around the room. The insecurity that had plagued her seemed nonexistent now. She prayed with force for everyone involved with the march and for her friends. The Enemy was working to keep everyone divided. She glanced again at Pastor Matthew's notes. She could pinpoint times and dates that the Enemy had unleashed specific attacks on the city, using death and sin to hold the land and its people captive. Kidnappings, rape and murder were only a few of the Enemy's tactics she had noticed. The time had come to break the stronghold the Enemy had set up. The time had come to gather the people of God and to show them what God had shown her.

Sasson studied Ana as she collected her belongings on her last day and began to pack. Dark circles shadowed her eyes, and her face looked haggard. Inside, she was radiant, and she was ready.

Cathy bounced up the stairs to her apartment. Her excitement made her feel lighter than usual. She needed to get out of her work clothes and get ready for her date with Kevin. Blood drained from her face as she approached her apartment. She froze. Her front door was open, and articles of clothing were scattered all over the floor. She inched inside and took out her cell. Her television and stereo system were missing. Broken glass crunched under her shoes as she surveyed the scene. She tried to control her shaking hand as she dialed, but it was no use.

She drew a sharp breath at the sound of the police dispatcher's voice. "Please come quickly; I've been robbed!"

CHAPTER 22

Freedom and Slavery

"There were those who dwelt in darkness and in the shadow of death, prisoners in misery and chains" (Psalm 107:10, NASB).

STILL NO ANSWER. Cathy clicked off her cell. Kevin was nowhere to be found. She looked at her hands. The shaking wouldn't stop. Her body felt weak with panic. Thoughts tumbled over each other in her mind. *Pray. I need Ana! Why is this happening, God?*

Now that the police had finally left, she started to clean up. Their comments about Kevin lingered in her mind. "Maybe he relapsed," one had said, "and took your stuff to sell for drugs. It looks like an inside job with no sign of forcible entry."

It was Kevin. Maybe what they are saying is true, and he couldn't resist his need.

But why is everything broken and so messy? Kevin had never done anything like this before, and why now? Why when he's been sober for so long? Has the pressure of marriage gotten to him? Cathy started to dial a different number. She didn't want to be alone in the apartment any longer.

~

Half an hour later, Cathy opened the door. Sandra's jaw dropped as she stepped inside.

"I was robbed," Cathy explained before Sandra could ask. By then her feelings of panic had subsided somewhat.

"What…?" Sandra seemed to be going through the same cycle that Cathy had just completed.

"The police were just here, but I am sure you can see why I don't feel like being here right now. They think Kevin is responsible for this mess, and I haven't been able to contact him. I'm not sure what to think. You don't think he'd do this do you?"

"Oh, Cathy, I'm so sorry." Sandra hugged her. "Let's hope for the best. I had my doubts about Kevin, but, to be honest, I think I misjudged him."

"I know you have never liked Kevin. I could tell by the way that you treated him." Cathy walked over and swept up more glass in a dustpan.

Sandra balked. "Cathy, it's not that I don't like him…he just reminds me of my ex-husband. I've forgiven him, but I still get angry when I think about how he left us." Sandra picked up Cathy's travel bag from the couch and walked to the door.

After emptying the dustpan in the trash, Cathy washed her hands. "Doesn't forgiveness mean that something in your heart changes toward the person?"

"Yes…but sometimes it's different."

"Different how?" Cathy dried her hands and grabbed her purse from the counter. "When I forgave Kevin for abandoning me, I felt my heart change toward him. I felt like God had healed my hurting heart, and I was able to see him in a different light."

They walked silently down the stairs. Cathy was slow and careful as she held the banister. Her earlier energy had now dissipated. Her pregnancy suddenly felt like a nuisance.

"You know what, Cathy? You're right. It's hard to let go of the anger. I've felt justified holding onto it all these years because I wanted to punish him somehow." She paused to gather her thoughts. "But all it's done is taint my opinion of men. When I really think about it, Kevin isn't like him at all. Kevin is a good guy, and he really loves you."

Cathy half smiled.

Sandra put Cathy's bag in the backseat of the car.

Cathy opened the passenger door on the other side, leaned on the roof and looked at Sandra. "Do you think Kevin had something to do with what happened to my apartment?"

"I don't think so, but we do need to pray. Something's definitely not right about all this."

~

Some familiar faces were among the leaders who had gathered in the mid-sized auditorium of Isaac's Well. A few of the leaders were wearing suits while others were dressed more casually. Ana was grateful for those who had shown up—even if the group was significantly smaller than when they had started. She had come straight to the meeting from the cottage.

Will, Pastor Mark and a few of the leaders from Isaac's Well stood against the walls, waiting to hear from Ana.

"Thank you all for coming today. I'm sure you're all wondering what is going on, so I'll simply start. Some of you may remember Pastor Matthew, who died about a year and half ago. When it happened, I was angry and confused, wondering how God could have allowed it."

"What does this have to do with the march, young lady?" one of the leaders spoke in a somewhat indignant tone.

"I'm getting to that. For the longest time, I didn't understand what was going on. But in time, it occurred to me that far too many evil things were happening simultaneously in this city for it to be a coincidence." She ran her fingers through her curly hair and pushed it behind her ear. "Pastor Matthew left his research, and I was able to prayerfully study it. He had uncovered a scheme the Enemy hatched to destroy our city."

Ana walked over to the chart paper in the front of the room. "The Enemy has been defiling the land with sin and then taking over areas piece by piece. The takeover starts with maybe a random act of violence in a place like this." She made a mark on the paper and pointed to it. "Then it's followed by other terrible incidents." She added more red dots that represented various other acts of violence. "The first random act of violence could even be in what's considered a safe neighborhood. Once he starts, he gains more legal rights to the area that attracts increasing violence. Then the evil spirits take and hold that ground. Eventually the whole area has a reputation as being a bad neighborhood." She connected the dots to show the area being sectioned off.

"We've been so busy fighting each other and criticizing each other's churches that we haven't noticed what's been happening. This destructive process can be completed in a matter of weeks, while in other places, it takes years. The Enemy has moved in and now occupies our city while we have been completely oblivious—gossiping and making judgments about each other and our churches.

A young man asked, "How do we know what you're saying is true about the city? We have no way of finding this out."

"There is a way. The violence usually increases in a given area over time. This is one of the largest cities in the country, and all you have to do is record where events happen and then examine the frequency of them over time."

"Why our city?" another man called out.

"You see, that's the issue; it isn't only our city. I believe this is happening everywhere. As Christians, we've been so distracted by other matters that we've practically handed over our cities to the Enemy. Prayer is our only defense, but that prayer has to be carried out in a spirit of unity to be an effective weapon against the Enemy's strategies. As long as the Enemy causes division, he has the right to wield power over us. If we humbly put aside our differences and pray, God promises to intervene. In that kind of atmosphere, we can see our city saved from these evil strategies."

A frail old man with deep wrinkles stood. "All right, what do you propose we do about it?"

"Many of you have heard strange rumors about supernatural things that have been happening in our church. I believe God has been preparing us for what's to come. In two days, we plan to begin our prayer march through the city and declare the name of the Lord Jesus Christ over the land. The focus of the march will only be prayer. We need to forget about every point of contention. We won't be having any floats or anything that will distract us from the main purpose of this march—prayer. We will have this march whether or not anyone joins us. We aren't trying to fight the generation that has gone before us or show any disrespect, but we need to do this together. I believe we started out well with the reconciliation. This march is of God, so please come and walk alongside of us. We need your help, and we need your wisdom."

One young man broke in. "I'm not sure about the validity of all that you're saying."

Pastor Norman added, "Our church has already started planning our own march."

Pastor Mark joined Ana at the front and placed his hand of support on her shoulder. "Well great, then hopefully when the time comes, we can rally around you guys for the kingdom."

Pastor Norman nodded and looked down sheepishly.

The older man with the deep wrinkles spoke up again. "What Ana's said is true. I've been prayer walking in this city for years, and I know that God is asking us to join together in this endeavor. I've been waiting for something like this. God spoke to me and said He was going to raise up people to walk with me."

Ana nodded. *Well God, it's in Your hands.* She had said exactly what He wanted her to say. Ana smiled. "Well, that's it. Please pass on the information to your congregations. Thanks for coming."

The people in the room started to clap.

She turned to her pastor. "Pastor Mark, will you close this gathering in prayer?"

"Father, we thank You for what You have shown us and for the work that Pastor Matthew did. Open our ears to hear what You're saying and help us know what our role is to be. In Jesus' name, amen."

A few leaders stayed to chat with each other. The gray-haired, older man with the deep wrinkles hobbled toward Ana. He looked about eighty, and his eyes were large and kind. He extended a frail looking hand, but his grip was strong.

"Thank you, young lady, for being obedient to God. I know this couldn't have been easy." His voice was weak. "I can see that God is raising you up as a leader to our generation. You will have our church's full support marching with you. We're going to kick some enemy behinds!" He patted Ana's shoulder and smiled.

"Great!" Ana was relieved. "We'll see you then." As he turned to leave, a few more people came to voice their own support. Ana couldn't help notice the sour look on Pastor Norman's face as he left without a word.

⁓

Yonah paced around Cathy in the living room. He had no doubt that she was stressed. Her thoughts came in jumbled waves.

Aarao came out from the kitchen and placed his hand on Yonah's shoulder. "We must begin preparing."

Yonah stopped in his tracks as his armor began to form on his porcelain skin. He closed his eyes and willed it to stop. He walked back toward Cathy and stood behind her. "She's not ready."

"She will have to be," Aarao concluded.

Sandra peeked out of the kitchen. "Stress isn't good for the baby. Try and do something else. Want to help me cook to take your mind off things?"

Cathy sighed and plopped onto the couch. "No, thanks. I cook best when I'm hungry, and right now I don't have an appetite."

"You need to eat soon; the baby needs food."

Cathy turned to look out the window. "We're fasting."

Sandra walked over to the couch and took Cathy's hands into hers." Don't be silly. I'm making you dinner, and you will eat." She patted Cathy's cheek. "It will be all right."

A key in the front door startled them. Ana swung open the door and stepped in with her bag.

Cathy quickly waddled to the door with Sandra trailing behind her.

"You're back!" Cathy threw her arms around Ana's neck and held on for dear life.

Ana voice was choked. "What did I miss?" She looked at her mother over Cathy's arms.

Sasson entered the room and walked to where Yonah and Aarao worshipped. Both of them were covered in armor, and the room was filled with light resting like dew on everything inside, intensifying and sparkling with each note leaving the mouth of each angel.

Sacrifice.

Everything was ripe for it. Sasson instinctively knelt as his own armor emerged. The three women gathered in the living room to worship. As the women joined in the melody the angels sang, Sasson noted the strained expression leaving Cathy's face. Tears appeared in its place.

Yonah could sense Cathy's thoughts, noting the struggle between feelings of abandonment and forgiveness. God was all she needed, but He didn't reduce the pain of rejection. Yonah placed his hand on her head as she began to weep. *Freedom.*

Cathy looked confused.

Freedom from what? Drugs?

She prayed for everything she could think of.

Yonah could feel the power flowing over her. The ravaged thoughts gave way to heat. Her heart burned as it connected with the Holy Spirit. Yonah removed his hand and opened his eyes. In all three of the women, the fire burned, streaming from them, and like a spark, ignited the droplets of light that rested throughout the room. The aroma of sacrifice filled the air. There was no mistaking the rare but pungent result of persecution offered back to the Lord in worship. That pleasant scent intertwined with the sweet perfume of the Holy Spirit. The burning light caused smoke to rise higher and higher.

ʂ

For the first time in years, Sandra finally understood what her lack of forgiveness toward her ex-husband looked like in her soul. She wept. She needed God's forgiveness for being so blind. Pain had gotten in the way of her prayers. Her discovery was pitiful and plain to see now; the justice she felt she deserved to punish her husband for leaving had done nothing but keep her wound opened and weeping—all because of pride. God's mercy and justice brought love and repentance, which He had been offering.

Her pride had closed doors and planted deep roots of bitterness within her. *Jesus, uproot this from me; I'm so sorry.* She wiped the tears streaming from her face. In her mind, she saw God's hand reaching into the busy weeds surrounding her heart and pulling out the roots one by one.

Each root came out with its own weakness attached: fear for Ana's future, pride along with its anger and arguments. Some of her instructions to those young women she helped were revealed as the controlling fear that it was.

ຈ

Ana lifted her hands in worship.

How can things be going so well and yet so badly at the same time? Here I am, back from an amazing time with God, renewed with purpose and vision while those I love are once again being attacked. Tears filled her eyes. She loved Jesus more than anything, and He loved her. He wasn't going to abandon them now. As she worshiped and prayed for Kevin, she was suddenly overwhelmed with grief for the city. It was like that night in the cottage. The young woman in the pale-yellow shirt flashed before her eyes. The city of Tehly was full of pain. The judgment among the churches added to it. The power of the Holy Spirit quickened through her body. She fell to her knees as the power within her begged for release. She started to yell as tears squeezed from her eyes. She felt no pain—only the sensation of being ready to explode consuming her.

Cathy knelt and grabbed one of her hands, and Sandra grabbed the other. Strength surged through Ana's body as the trio prayed in the Spirit. They were on the floor now only inches away. Ana groaned as the waves of heat surged over her and then began to decrease. But as Ana was becoming quiet, Cathy started to laugh and laugh until she was doubled over still gripping Ana's hand.

After a while when things subsided, Ana straightened and sat upright. Sandra was still singing and praying in tongues.

Cathy settled down and opened her eyes. "What happened?"

Ana shrugged. "I have no idea."

"It's called *prayer travail.*" Sandra stood and straightened her blouse. "When the Holy Spirit is praying through you, sometimes it's like labor. You must have given birth to something in the spirit."

Ana and Cathy exchanged looks.

"I was definitely not giving birth," Ana said with a laugh.

"I'm serious," Sandra said. "God must have wanted you to pray through something very important. Do you remember what you were praying about?"

"I felt impressed to pray for Tehly. There's so much sadness here with people in slavery to the Enemy. I was asking God to rescue us from the results of our sin."

Cathy smiled. "I heard the word freedom as I prayed for Kevin in the beginning. Then I had a vision of getting married and walking down the aisle to meet him at the altar. He looked so happy."

Sandra looked in Cathy's direction. "I saw Kevin with his hands tied."

Ana stood up and extended her hands for Sandra and Cathy to join her again. "Let's pray through this. We're getting clues as to what might be happening with Kevin. Maybe God will give us more clarity."

Sandra began "Jesus, our wonderful Savior, we ask that You send Your angels to locate and bring Kevin home. We ask for freedom from slavery, and whether it be from drugs or physical bonds, we ask that You would save him right now and show us what is going on. We plead Your blood, Jesus, that was shed for all of our sins. We plead that blood over the city of Tehly right now. Rescue us. Free us from the sway of the Enemy. Jesus, we speak life into Kevin right now."

Cathy prayed next. "We pray for his destiny to come forth. You love him more than I do, God, and so I'm asking You to do what You want with him. We belong to You. Let our lives be pleasing to You in whatever You want for us." Tears filled her eyes. "You are magnificent, God, and we will honor You with our lives—no matter what happens," she whispered.

～

Kevin awoke to an intense throbbing in his head. His vision blurred as he took in his surroundings. A broken chair leaned in the corner. White peeling paint did nothing to cover the cracked plaster spreading like fault lines throughout the room. The gray smudges that patterned the walls reflected years of neglect. He decided from the lack of windows that he was in some kind of cellar. He searched his memory, trying to recall what had happened.

The last thing he remembered was a struggle in Cathy's apartment.

Before that he had noticed a green car following him as he had walked there. He hadn't thought too much of it at first. He had gone up the steps and tried to open the apartment door but heard quick steps behind him. He recognized Greg, a drug dealer from the past he owed money to. Kevin had tried to reason with him and had promised to pay him back once he started working again, but Greg's guy had punched him and pushed him into the apartment.

He recalled fighting, things crashing around him and then nothing. Now his hands were tied behind his back as he lay in a crumpled heap. His past had brought him to this moment, and he could do nothing to fix it now.

He heard the voices of a male and a female from the room next door. He heard a woman's voice weeping, "Please let me go home. I won't tell anyone."

"No, babe, you're staying here. Look at'cha—you're stoned and messed up." Greg's voice mocked, "You're going to stay here until you pay back your debt to me."

"I don't have any money, and I already told you that if you keep me here, I'll never be able to pay you back."

"Shut up. You're going to pay back your debt to me in *service*. I have lots of plans for you."

"No!"

Kevin heard sounds of a struggle, then a loud slap and finally a thud on the floor.

"Why are you doing this? I thought you were my friend!"

"I don't have heroin whores as friends—only slaves," Greg replied and laughed. "When I'm done with you, you'll do exactly what you're told and when you're told." He heard more sounds of struggle. Kevin's head spun, and then blackness descended.

The sound of shattering glass stirred him out of his unconscious state. As he strained to listen, he heard soft whimpering and sobbing. "Hello, can anyone hear me?" he called.

The whimpering suddenly stopped.

"Anyone there?" he continued.

Footsteps shuffled to the door, and then it swung open. Kevin looked up and saw a young woman about 20 with long, light-brown hair, standing in front of him. She was barefoot, wearing ripped jeans and a pale-yellow T-shirt. Rough cuts and bruises lined her arms. She was pretty despite the tear stains and runny nose that smudged her face.

"I thought I was the only one here," she said, surprised.

"I think I've been here for a few hours or maybe a day. Can you do me a favor and help me sit up?"

She walked over to assist him in sitting with his back against the wall. Kevin noticed she had a piece of glass in her hand. When she saw him looking at it, she tossed it away.

"Are you okay?" She studied his head in the dimly lit room. "You have dried blood on your forehead around this bump." She reached out to gently touch his head.

He flinched. The skin around his eye felt tight and swollen.

"I could ask the same about you." He gestured to the bruises on her face and took in her appearance and lack of shoes. "What's your name?"

"Lisa. What's yours?"

"Kevin." He paused a moment, wondering if he should ask. "How did you get here?"

"I've been here for a few weeks. Greg's making me stay here to pay off my debt. I didn't mean to have a debt." She shook her head in regret. "He gave me free drugs for a while. Then one day I came here with him to get high, and when I woke up, he had another man here. He wouldn't let me leave; he said it was time for me to pay up."

She started to cry. "He hits me when I don't listen. I just want to go home." She sniffled. "Every day he gives me drugs and needles. I wish I had never started. I feel so stupid." Her green eyes seemed too dry for tears.

"Why don't you stop?"

"I've tried to go as long as I can. I'm trapped here, and if I stop now, he told me I could die trying to get off it."

Kevin nodded, understanding what she meant. Withdrawal was difficult on its own. He didn't want to imagine what it would have been like here without help. "I went through detox a while back and got off drugs. I've been clean ever since."

"I wish I could do that," Lisa admitted softly, looking down at her feet. She sat down next to Kevin against the wall and pulled up her knees. "I tried to quit before, but I gave up."

He nodded. "I tried to quit on my own once too. It didn't work. My girlfriend begged me to get help and support, but I thought I could do it on my own. I think I just wanted to be in control and still be able to do what I wanted, but I fell flat on my face. I went on a binge doing crack and drinking. When I think about it now, it scares me how far gone I was. If God hadn't helped me, I would still be there or dead."

Lisa looked at Kevin as if for the first time. "You believe in God?"

"Yeah, I do."

"Why?"

"I'm free from addiction because of Him; I have a real life now. Man, people think they're free when they get to do whatever they want, drink and do drugs, but the truth is that I was a slave. I had absolutely no control. I did what I thought I had to. I wasn't happy even when I did what I wanted. I tried to party and have fun to cover how I felt, but I was emptier by the day. Then one day I thought there had to be more to this life, and I went back home to see my girlfriend. She told me about Jesus, and at first, I was upset at her for changing without me, but then I saw how strong she'd become. She wasn't like the girl I had left behind. That girl was always looking to me for the answers. She needed me, which was one of the reasons why I liked her. I simply wanted to be important to someone." Kevin paused.

"When I came back, she had been praying for me, and she had all the answers. It took me a while to come around, but I discovered she was right. Jesus is all I want. When I gave my life to Him, everything changed." Kevin sat up straighter and tried to shift his weight. His tied hands had lost feeling all the way up to his elbows. "When I get out of here, my girlfriend and I are going to get married."

"If you get out of here..." Lisa added.

Kevin struggled with the rope around his wrists. "Lisa, do you think you could untie my hands?"

Lisa looked frightened. She quickly stood and backed toward the door. "I don't think I'm allowed. I can't afford to make him angrier." She tried to offer an explanation. "I'm probably not even supposed to be talking to you."

Kevin felt badly for scaring her. "You don't have to go; never mind about my hands. It's okay."

Lisa looked relieved and sat back down. "Why do you think you here?"

"I'm not really sure." He laughed dryly. "Same as you I guess…paying back old debts."

After a pause, she whispered, "How are we going to get out of here?" Her eyes were wide in the darkness. "At least one man guards the main door whenever Greg leaves, and I'm sure other people are there too. I'm really scared."

Kevin didn't want to admit it to Lisa, but he was also afraid.

The nearby doors and latches were being unlocked. Lisa bolted out of the room, closing the door behind her.

Kevin, now tired and thirsty, looked around the room and up at the ceiling. His hoarse whisper broke the silence around him. "God, please get us out of here. I know that You have the power to free us. Please protect us and watch over Cathy. Let her know that I love her. In the name of Jesus, amen."

$\sim$

Leah walked down the familiar path to Greg's place. Money bought his discretion and compliance.

According to Divinica, a blood sacrifice was necessary to hinder the work that the march would do. Despite their best efforts, the march had not yet been dismantled. The event was still on track, and none of the psychic readings they had consulted for the future were coming up in their favor. They were running out of ammunition.

Greg didn't mix potions in a cauldron, but his pharmaceutical products made him a sorcerer by trade. In fact, all drug dealers were sorcerers. In the spirit realm, she sensed the demons inside of him were like Sakron. Greg simply didn't know it. She was amused that he still considered himself a good person even though he had personally ruined a great many lives. Regardless, he was useful when she needed something done that would blow her cover if she did it herself.

She spotted him in the underground parking lot and motioned him with her head to meet near the wall so that no one else would see them talking.

"Did you get the package for me?" she asked.

"I got both of them." His blond hair was covered with a baseball cap. Although it was late afternoon, he looked like he had just gotten up.

"You can keep him there and do whatever you want with him. I'll give you $300 for the girl."

"Hmm, only $300? I think she's worth more than that. She's fairly innocent. You know, she's kind of growing on me."

Leah felt her anger rising. "Don't mess with me. I'm the one who told you to grab her."

"Yeah, but what do you need her for anyway?"

"Five hundred is the most I'm willing to offer. Otherwise, I'll find someone else to do business with."

"Listen, lady, I've been investing in this one for some time. I have other plans for her that could make me a lot more money."

"Fine, suit yourself. We'll see how long your operation goes before it's discovered. I'm sure the police would love to hear all I know about the unsolved murder involving a local pastor."

Greg looked Leah up and down. "Listen…whatever information you share will be linked back to you, sweetheart. Or maybe I should just start my new business with you." He stepped closer and reached out to grab her waist. He tried to push her up against the wall, but she quickly maneuvered out of his grasp.

"I would be incredibly bad for business. You have no idea." She could only hope her cold glare would entice him to back off. Greg was only a few years older than she was and not much taller. But she knew he could easily pin her if he wanted to. Sakron would not care enough to help her and would probably enjoy whatever sick predicament he found her in.

"I was just messing with you." He stepped back. "Just give me the money, and I'll bring her to you tomorrow night."

"I'll bring the money when you bring her to me in the forest near the ravine tomorrow night. And if everything goes well, I'll throw in an extra hundred for good measure." Her offer was meant to ensure he followed the plan. *Mistakes weren't an option at this point.*

"All right," he agreed as he reached into his pocket for a cigarette and a lighter. He had already lost interest in their conversation and turned back from where he had emerged earlier. "Later," he called as he disappeared deeper into the parking garage.

CHAPTER 23

Marked in the Spirit

"May your eyes be open toward this temple night and day, this place of which you said, 'My Name shall be there,' so that you will hear the prayer your servant prays toward this place" (1 Kings 8:29, NIV).

DAY TWO OF the march was underway. On the first day, a small group of about 30 had gathered, which consisted mostly of young people from the church. Some children from the centre had also shown up. They had met at the church in the morning so that Will and Ana could give everyone photocopies of the routes they would take through the city. The eighty-year-old pastor and a number of others who couldn't bear the extreme temperatures or walk easily had opted to stay at the church and pray in agreement for the rest of the day's march.

On day one, Wella reminded each of them to be on guard. To the natural eye, they were simply walking, but in the spirit, they were doing battle for the city. She had stayed behind to pray at the church.

Although most of the march would be done in silence, everyone needed to pray and listen to what God was saying. The plan was to meet back at the church for each evening to debrief and pray.

As the participants walked, they focused on certain spots, taking time to stand in areas and pray in the spirit as curious onlookers watched from their cars or houses.

On this day, a few extra people joined in to march. Sweat beaded on Ana's forehead. It was hotter than it had been in weeks, and the marchers did what they could to protect themselves from the heat. Ana pulled her T-shirt away from her body to create a breeze under her shirt, but it was useless. She glanced behind her. The parade of people walked, a few with fans in their hands, others wore tank tops or used extra shirts as head coverings. She wished she had brought something extra as well. A couple of the kids from the community centre rolled in and out of the group on their rollerblades and bikes.

Ana, Will and Pastor Mark had added a partial fast during the prayer walks by encouraging everyone to abstain from food in the mornings. The oppression in the atmosphere felt thick, and they were fighting back with everything they had.

Ana noticed Cathy near the back of the group. An umbrella shielded her from some of the sun's rays. Cathy's courage was unstoppable, especially in light of the fact that she still had received no word from Kevin. Ana said a prayer for his safe return home.

Will

Will walked a few steps closer to be near Ana. He had tried to stay close during the march. He was glad Ana was back. She seemed a little different. At only five feet two inches, she looked fragile, but she glowed.

He needed to make sure that she would be all right. She looked healthier now because she was eating again, but he sensed that she still needed a prayer covering since she was spearheading the march. They were midway through a green space near the high school when he glanced at her. Her face was grim, so he slowed his pace and reached out to take her elbow. He gestured for her to come away from the group then slowed his pace. "What's up?"

Ana looked up with hollow eyes, clearly upset. "I hear screaming and crying. I sense pain in this place."

He glanced around to see if anyone was listening to them and then looked down at her closely. "What do you mean?" he asked as he refocused on her.

She pointed to the ground under her feet. "Something happened here. Listen, can you stop the group? We need to do something extra in this area." Will shouted for everyone to stop. Pastor Mark and Johanna turned and walked back to where Ana and Will were standing.

To those who were within earshot, she said, "This is another part of the land where murder gave ground to the Enemy." The rest of the group slowly made their way closer. "We need to pray until something lifts from this place. Can I get some of you to worship softly while we pray and listen to what Holy Spirit wants us to do here?"

Johanna and Owen began to sing songs about the power of the blood of Jesus while others knelt in the grass to pray. After a while Elikai spoke. "I'm getting an impression of a lack of forgiveness and anger and curses being laid here. I think it has to do with the people who are related to the victims. We need to pray for them."

Will nodded. "I'm getting that too. God wants us to stand in the place of the perpetrators and repent."

❧

Ana asked, "Pastor Mark, would you lead us in prayer?"

Pastor Mark stood at the center of the group and lifted his arms as he raised his voice. "Heavenly Father, we stand now in this time to repent for the violence that took place here. We repent for the sin caused in this place that destroyed innocent lives. We ask for forgiveness for the evil that has been unleashed here. Let Your blood wash this place clean."

Will swayed as he took up the prayer, with his eyes tightly closed. "We also pray for the families affected by the violence and death. Heal their hearts, Father. Release forgiveness into their lives and homes, so the Enemy's roots here will be shattered and those who have partnered with the Enemy would break those ties."

Ana heard herself shout, "God, we declare that this is the day that the oppressed will go free and that justice would come to this city. We pray that every dark corner would be exposed, and that You would arise and free the captives!" In her mind's eye, she saw the chains of so many people. Holy anger arose as she thought of the price her Jesus had paid so that many could walk free. Jesus' blood had already bought back each hurting person. They simply had to receive His wonderful gift. The only one preventing them from receiving His gift was the Enemy. Suddenly she grew angrier, and tears filled her eyes. The injustice of it all struck deep pain in her heart.

"God, why should anyone suffer anymore?" Her voice broke as the truth filled her with emotion. "You came to set the captives free! You came! You broke every chain and freed us. Heal our lives. We declare freedom! Prison doors of doubt, fear, pain, evil and distress, we command you to be broken! Open and release the children of God! Father, release the armies of the Lord to do battle!" Her hands balled into fists as she became consumed with passion.

Sasson saw Rahos step closer to Johanna. Rahos waved his hand over her eyes and pointed to a small section of ground nearby. Sasson looked over to where Rahos pointed, and he saw a geyser. The small piece of ground had already been marked by some kind of godly spiritual activity. *Great!* Sasson watched as Rahos whispered into Johanna's ear. *"Now."*

Johanna suddenly stopped singing and faltered back. She shook her head and looked over to the spot Rahos had shown her. She waved to Owen, and he followed her. Soon everyone was standing over the "geyser." To the people praying, it was only a spot of grass, but Sasson knew what was coming. Everyone still sang, but now as Johanna began to sing in tongues, a charge of power caused her body to shake.

In the spirit realm, Sasson witnessed the havoc they were creating on the ground level. The heavens bent like a plastic sheet and touched down to the place where they worshipped. The geyser opened and began to spray. Ministering angels began to step out of the sky where it bent to join them and surrounded the area. Each had an assignment and disappeared in a flash to accomplish it.

Demon spirits of misery and violence came out of the ground screaming as they lost their hold and were pulled into the abyss. Some were centuries old, and others were the result of recent events.

Angels flew in and out of the group, joyfully joining into the music. As the song and prayers ended, the sky snapped back, releasing the tension and returning to normal.

☙

"I'd like us to plant some Scripture here," Johanna suggested after they had sung, "You'll Come" by Hillsong. "We're prophetically replacing the past that was buried here with the truth of God. Isaiah 58:6 comes to mind." She cleared her throat and raised her voice. "I'll read it now."

"Is not this the kind of fasting I have chosen: to loose the chains of injustice and untie the cords of the yoke, to set the oppressed free and break every yoke?" (NIV).

After she had finished reading, she quickly jotted it down on a piece of paper. They found a patch of earth where they could dig, and Daniel began to make a hole. When it was deep enough, they dropped the folded piece of paper in the ground and covered it.

Ana prayed, "Lord, thank You for shifting the atmosphere here. Let Your Word spring up from the ground and let healing and deliverance come to Your children. In the name of Jesus, amen."

〜

The afternoon light flickered in a haze through the curtains of Ana's kitchen. Everyone had gone home to rest, break their fast and get ready for the evening prayer meeting. Ana sat reading her Bible and enjoying the air-conditioned break from the heat when someone knocked on her door. A sheepish Susan stood looking through the window in the door. Ana opened it and stood there waiting. She hadn't seen Susan for weeks.

Susan smiled. "We missed you while you were away, Ana." Ana's happiness at seeing her friend failed to erase the sting that surfaced in her heart.

"I had to get away to clear my head," she answered cautiously.

"I'm sorry about what happened before you left." Susan searched Ana's face. "You know how Megan gets when she's angry. I didn't want to get in the way, though I didn't agree with what she said. You've always been a good friend to both of us, and we love you." She put her arms around Ana, hugging her tightly. "You know that, right? I wanted to tell you that day when she was yelling at you, but I'm such a coward. Then when I tried to reach you again, you'd already left. Your mom told me when you came back."

Ana sighed. "Susan, why don't you come in?"

"Oh, I can't stay," Susan said as she wiped sweat from her forehead. "I have to go see Megan. She's still not doing very well." She looked around nervously. "But I know she's sorry after the way she treated you. She's just stuck on her pride. I don't think she thought it would be hard to win over Andrew. You had nothing to do with what happened." Susan leaned against the door and playfully tugged Ana's curly hair. "She was just jealous because, no matter what she did, he was still more interested in you. She'll get over it." Susan shrugged. "I'm not sure why she hasn't yet."

"Well, I miss both of you too. I'll go to see her in a few days. Keep me posted."

"All right, see you soon." She hugged Ana and was gone.

〜

The day's debriefing and evening prayer had just ended. People got ready to leave, but as Ana helped clean up, she noticed a few of her friends talking among themselves in hushed voices.

Andrew stood with another group of people she didn't know quite as well. She'd heard from Cathy and Destiny that Andrew had been at church every day that the church was open. She had heard that he had met with Pastor Mark to talk and pray, seeking help with working through his issues, and apparently taking his walk with God more seriously since he had slept with Megan. Though no one said as much, it was also clear that Megan hadn't been around at all.

Ana and Andrew hadn't yet spoken since her return. With so much going on, she had forgotten. She wanted to tell him she was no longer angry and understood that he had simply made a mistake. Holding that over his head when Cathy had made the same mistake months ago wasn't fair. Ana found it hard to wrap her mind around everything that had followed, but she missed her friendship with him.

As she started to walk closer to her friends, Pastor Mark pulled her aside.

One look at his strained-looking face told Ana it was serious. "Ana, Johanna had a very strange dream the other night. I know it's some kind of warning, but I'm not sure what it is. I think you should hear it." He motioned for Johanna to join them. Johanna looked up and quickly excused herself from another group.

As Johanna neared, Ana said, "Mark says you had a dream?"

"Yeah, I wasn't going to say anything because I didn't want to scare anybody, but Mark thinks it's too important to ignore. The night before last, I woke up frightened with chills around four in the morning. I was dreaming that I was on my way to the church when I unexpectedly saw a dark-gray pillar of smoke in the distance. This smoke was so thick you couldn't see through it to the other side. The billows were dark and solid. Suddenly, I saw a beautiful woman riding the pillar of smoke like a horse over the skyline. In the dream I was so scared that the woman would see me, and I didn't want her to. I ran the rest of the way to the church and tried to point out what the woman was doing. Then the woman became aware of me and turned and looked right at me."

Johanna's face was blank. "Ana, at that moment, I felt doomed. The next thing I know her foot was on the ground in front of me, and then I woke up." Johanna shuddered and hugged herself. Pastor Mark put his arm around her and pulled her closer. "It felt so real. I think something is coming, and we really need to pray against it."

Ana frowned as she focused her attention on what Johanna said. The woman riding on the pillar of smoke could represent so many things. Perhaps she was a demonic principality of some kind...or maybe she was simply a distraction. She wanted more time to pray into it so she would know for sure. She nodded. "Okay, then let's pray into it right now." They all joined hands.

₠

"I'm telling you something shady is going on there." Daniel was trying to convince his listeners as Ana joined them after praying with Mark and Johanna.

"What do you mean?" Elikai whispered.

———

"It happened again," Daniel explained.

As Will joined them, Ana questioned them. "What are you guys talking about?"

Destiny answered, "Daniel says that something is going on at the Eclipse. He's been having reoccurring dreams about the place."

Ana nodded. "I wouldn't be surprised. I was there a few times with my friends over the past year."

Daniel joked, "My Ana, weren't you a busy girl while you were away?"

Elikai smiled and looked at those around him in the circle. "Why don't we go down there tonight and blast that place with the love of Jesus?"

"I'm in," Ana immediately agreed.

"Me too," said Destiny with a nod.

Owen joined them when he overheard Destiny's words. He leaned into the conspiring group. "Whatever's going on here," he said seriously. "I want in."

"It's settled then. Prayer, prophesy and love," Will stated. "Tonight, we bring the kingdom to the Eclipse."

Andrew was standing nearby when he heard the familiar name. "What about the Eclipse?"

———

CHAPTER 24

Oil of Joy

"...*To bestow on them a crown of beauty instead of ashes, the oil of joy instead of mourning, and a garment of praise instead of a spirit of despair. They will be called oaks of righteousness, a planting of the* Lord *for the display of his splendor*" (Isaiah 61:3, NIV).

1:30 A.M.

AFTER SEARCHING FOR a while to find parking, Andrew followed Will's car into a parking lot not too far from the Eclipse. Destiny, Ana, and Elikai exited Andrew's car to meet Owen and Daniel who had ridden with Will.

Andrew appraised everyone's outfits. They all looked nice—as though they had tried to look like they had used very little effort. The guys each had settled for dark jeans and fitted shirts of some sort, except Will who wore a buttoned-down shirt. Elikai had tied back his long dreads to the base of his neck. Destiny wore tights, heels and a dress with her crimped unbraided hair pinned up. Ana wore fitted black jeans and a blouse that fell off one shoulder and was cinched in at the waist with a belt. Her black curly hair had grown out now and was past her shoulders.

Andrew glanced at Ana out of the corner of his eye. He had picked her up after Elikai and Destiny. He was tempted to pick her up first so he could talk to her alone but decided against it. He knew she had to stay focused, and he was trying to learn to put others' needs above his own.

Tonight she looked gorgeous though—sweet and simple. Was she checking out Will? Maybe he had imagined it. He compared himself to his rival. Will looked like he hit the gym regularly whereas he himself was tall and thin and a little deprived in that area. He figured he could take him in a fight though. He couldn't picture Will's fighting dirty. With one more glance to size up Will, he decided that he would be ruthless. *When have I ever had to compete for a girl?*

He pushed that thought from his mind and tried to focus. *God, heal my heart.* After a moment, he directed his attention back to Ana. "So what's the plan?" He fell into step with her as they walked toward the Eclipse.

"We go in and just mingle, pray and discern what God is showing us. If God leads you to speak to anyone, go for it."

Daniel came up behind them. "Okay, let's pray a covering before we go in that we won't be seduced by what's happening inside."

They stopped walking and gathered in a circle in front of a store a few doors from the nightclub. After praying, Andrew, Daniel and Elikai led the way into the Eclipse. Will, Ana, Destiny and Owen followed close behind.

Inside, loud music pumped from the speakers as people danced and walked around holding their drinks and mingling. As they walked inside the Eclipse, Andrew felt awkward. He was sure someone would guess what they were doing point from the dance floor, and maybe even shout, "The Christians are coming!"

But few even noticed their entrance. Andrew split from the group to find tables.

Andrew noticed that Elikai and Daniel started a conversation with a thin young woman. They were clearly more comfortable than he was, even laughing with the woman. He'd never been uncomfortable here before, but he was here for different reasons now. Andrew headed to the bar to order something to drink. Leaning against the counter to wait for his Sprite, he turned around so he could observe those around him. He found it really tough to focus on God in that atmosphere. He remembered the days of dancing and meeting girls, the fun, the thrill, and the excitement. Those days weren't far gone enough yet for him to feel okay in this atmosphere.

Even though he missed certain parts of his old lifestyle, he didn't miss the emptiness. Things were harder since he'd gotten serious about his relationship with God, but he felt a new kind of peace and a hope for the future that he'd never thought possible.

When the Sprite he had ordered came, he scanned the room for Ana who was sitting with Destiny and talking animatedly. She seemed happy, telling a story that caused Destiny to double over laughing. She seemed so happy—so very opposite from that first day he had seen her sad and looking cute as she sat sipping her soda while her friends had taken over the dance floor. He was thankful that he'd gone over to speak to her even though things hadn't turned out the way he'd originally hoped. Who would have known he would be here for any reason other than to drink or pick up girls?

He had expected Ana to be thrilled by his attention that night because most girls were. Had she been, he would have been able to manipulate her emotions. He smiled, realizing how dumb he had been. In the end, she'd been stronger than he had ever imagined in her commitment to God, and she had given him a hand up out of the pit of his meaningless life.

Someone suddenly came and stood beside him, interrupting his thoughts. "Hey, Bro, long time no see!" Greg raised his hand and brought it down to grab Andrew's in a handshake that ended in a partial hug. Andrew was caught off-guard and confused by the friendly greeting from a guy with whom he had only casually socialized in the past.

"Hey! Greg! What's up?" He leaned back against the bar.

"Not much, man." Greg leaned back as well with his elbows on the counter to face the crowd. "I haven't seen you around here in a while."

Andrew nodded. "Change of scenery."

"You found a new place to party?" Greg asked curiously.

"Something like that; I'm a Christian now," Andrew found the words strange coming from his mouth.

"Yeah, right…you? *A holy boy?*" Greg raised his eyebrows and lifted his hands to feign praising God.

"Yeah, man. I've been saved now for a while," Andrew continued undaunted by Greg's attitude.

"Then why are you here?"

"A few friends and I came to hang out and pray."

"Why would you come here to pray?" Greg laughed. He turned around and motioned to the bartender.

The bartender took Greg's order.

Andrew gulped his soda, suddenly feeling awkward. "People need prayer everywhere, Greg."

Greg raked his fingers through his blond hair. He seemed suddenly agitated. "Can you pray for me?"

Andrew hid his surprise. "Sure, what about?"

"I don't know, man. I just think I need some prayer. Things have gotten out of hand and out of my control." Greg whispered, "Some crazy stuff is going on…" Greg glanced around as if to make sure no one was listening.

The bartender brought him back a beer.

He took a long swig of his beer then leaned in close to whisper, "I've been having these crazy dreams and seeing monsters and like…ghosts fighting. Sometimes the dream feels so real, I feel like I'm going crazy."

The scent of beer hit Andrew full in the face before Greg added, "I think this place is haunted." He looked Andrew in the eyes to see if he would think he was crazy too. "I never used to be afraid of anything, but I'm wondering if I should cut my losses and get out of this place." He took another gulp of beer. "Business has been slow for the last few months anyway. People owe me money…" Greg continued, watching the crowd, and now drinking slowly.

"Maybe you should lay off the beer," Andrew jokingly said.

Greg looked behind him at the bartender and then back at Andrew. "Man, I'm serious."

"Okay…uh, I'll pray for you. Want me to do it now?"

Greg looked relieved. "Yeah, I need a *holy* boy like you to pray for me. I can't pray for myself. I'm too evil; God would laugh in my face."

"That's not true, Greg. God still loves you—no matter what you've done." Andrew pointed at his chest. "I'm living proof of how much God loves people like us."

Andrew closed his eyes to pray. He could sense that Greg was really frightened. *If someone like Greg is scared, should I be worried too?*

❧

Will took a break and sat down with Destiny and Ana.

Teasing, Ana said, "Look at you! Social butterfly, and here I thought you were shy."

"Me, shy?" Will countered. "No way. I make friends easily." He smiled, feeling a secret satisfaction that Ana had noticed something about him.

Ana shook her head. "I don't know. You don't usually have much to say. I had you pegged as the strong, silent type."

Destiny laughed. "Honestly, Ana, Will talks all the time." She looked at Will mischievously. "But I have to admit, he has been really quiet since he got back from school. Do you have something on your mind, Will? Hmm?" She giggled.

Will stared back. "Nothing worth mentioning." He cleared his throat to divert attention from the heat rushing to his face. He looked at Ana, "What about you? You seemed so standoffish when I first met you."

Ana's eyes grew wide. "Oh! I'm sorry if I appeared that way. I had a lot on my mind."

"Well, I'm glad I met you, and that we've become friends." They smiled at each other for a long moment.

Destiny looked between them. "Should I leave? I'm starting to feel like a third wheel."

"Sorry," Will shifted the topic again. "You ladies picking up on anything?"

"Well, since you asked," Destiny leaned in and whispered. "I'm sensing a lot of sorrow, but I'm not sure if I'm picking up people's emotions or something in the atmosphere…" After a pause, she added, "It's hard to tell in here."

"There's definitely something here," Ana said, confirming Destiny's suspicions.

Will nodded in agreement. "I was talking with Daniel, and he said that he thinks some kind of spiritual stronghold here keeps people captive and disillusioned."

Ana sipped of her drink. "Let's all gather again in about fifteen minutes outside. Can you tell the guys?"

Will stood. "Sure! Be back in a few."

⁊⁑

Elikai and Owen were talking in another corner of the club when Will joined them.

"Where's Daniel?" Will asked as he strolled up to them.

Owen rubbed his forehead. "I don't know."

"He left a while ago, looking for the bathroom. Maybe he got held up." Elikai said.

Owen patted his stomach. "Can we leave soon? I'm so hungry."

"Ana wants us to meet outside to pray in a few minutes. Why don't you buy something here?"

Owen waved off that suggestion. "Nah, too expensive. I'd rather starve."

"Then starve you will," Elikai said patting Owen on the back. He turned to Will. "Speaking of starving, you and Ana have been getting pretty friendly there lately, huh, buddy?" Elikai slapped him on the shoulder. "You planning on asking her out tonight?"

Will looked away. "Nope, I don't know where'd you get that idea."

"Hey, I'm not the only one who has noticed…I think the only person who hasn't noticed is Ana." He turned in the direction of Ana's table. "And she'll probably find out soon enough if Destiny has her way."

Will looked at the floor. He hadn't anticipated people's figuring out his feelings. He still wasn't sure what God was saying, so he didn't want to say anything to Ana.

Maybe I need to back off a bit more.

Daniel popped out of the crowd and cut through the dance floor to join them. "Guys…"

"Where did you go?" Will asked.

"I went looking for the bathroom and got lost." He motioned for them to come in closer as he tried to whisper but ended up almost shouting to be heard over the music. "But I found this door that led to what looked like a tunnel."

Andrew joined them.

Elikai stared at him. "Where'd you find that?"

"Well, like I said, I went to find the bathroom, and I kept sensing this strong, creepy feeling—like someone was watching me—so I went to find a more private bathroom."

Owen asked, "You think it could be spiritual?"

"Not sure, but I just felt like I should look around, and that's when I found the door. Someone had obviously tried to cover it with a curtain and had even put a cabinet in front of it, so I almost missed it. Something about the way the curtain drooped caught my eye. The door was locked, but when I peered through a crack, it looked like it led to a tunnel. Everything downstairs feels really old and ancient. It reminded me of a cave."

The young men were silent.

Elikai said, "Wow! Good thing you're nosey. Maybe we should call the police. Sounds pretty shady."

"I don't know what I'd say though." Daniel frowned

Will began. "Well, now that we're all here, let's tell the girls what you found. They wanted to meet up to pray again; I'll call them."

❧

Ana, Will, Andrew and the group gathered outside not far from the club. After debriefing, they began to pray. Some prayed in tongues.

Destiny spoke with authority, but sounded weary. "I know some of us are feeling the heaviness and finding it difficult to pray, but we need to push past this. The Bible says that we are light and salt, so let's shine brighter in this darkness."

Ana added, "All we have to do is focus on how beautiful and great our God is."

The group joined hands and began to pray, this time with a renewed fervency. The tune to "Wonderful God" repeatedly came to Ana's mind so she began to sing.

Will prayed out loud. "Father, You are a God of love and peace. Release

Your light on this land. Only You know what goes on here, on how many levels and where it will lead. Lord, shine Your light in this place."

Passionately Destiny whispered, "We ask You to help everyone in this club to find You. God, that those searching for meaning or validation will find it in Your arms. I pray that true joy will fill this place as people are drawn to You. Let Your presence come down, Lord."

Ana added, "Let Your glory come, Jesus. Shatter the evil kingdom that the Enemy is trying to establish here."

Daniel lifted his hands toward the heavens and closed his eyes. "Lord, release Your angels into this atmosphere to do battle for these lost ones. Surround us now, Lord."

❦

Sasson looked up at the angel who suddenly joined them. He stepped into the concealment dome that the angels had created around the prayer warriors.

"What are you doing here, Rahos?" Sasson looked around. "Is Johanna here?"

"No, but I have been sent," Rahos answered. "The Lord has told me to prepare the land."

Edon looked perplexed. "So soon?"

Rahos nodded and turned toward the club. He lifted his arm as his wings began to spread wider than the circle of teenagers praying. He began to grow right before the other angels' eyes until he was three times his original already large size. The angels commenced to lift up their hands and continued to speak praises to Yahweh as Rahos raised his arm and began stirring the sky above the Eclipse. The air around them thickened as a vortex formed and funneled down toward the ground.

Angels wielding swords were the first to come through the portal in the vortex that Rahos had created. These angels had been called from many different nations, according to the cut of their armor. Immediately after coming through the portal, they positioned themselves around the Eclipse as others went inside. Next, an angel carrying a golden scroll came through the portal. He was not dressed in battle clothes as Sasson had expected but was robed as a royal messenger complete with the golden sash around his waist. The messenger went inside the club. Last to come through the portal was a large angel carrying a large silver vial in his hand. His face stretched into an enormous, playful smile. He saluted the angels standing in the circle and then turned to enter into the Eclipse as the portal closed behind him.

After a few minutes, Ana and her friends stopped praying and waited in silence before Will said, "Amen."

Daniel spoke up. "I had a vision of a guy in the club wearing a blue shirt and jeans. I want to go back in and look for him. Anyone want to come?" He raised his eyebrows as he looked around, hopeful.

"Yeah, let's do it!" Destiny said.

The rest nodded in agreement.

Once in the Eclipse, the team spread out to find the man in the blue shirt and jeans. Not surprisingly, more than one guy in the room was wearing a blue shirt, though in different shades of the color, and a couple of them were wearing jeans. After a few minutes Daniel signaled the group to come to him. He was speaking to a young guy wearing a blue button-down shirt and dark blue jeans. The young man listened to Daniel and nodded as the group joined them at the table.

"Hey, guys, this is Jonathan. I was telling him I had a vision a few minutes ago with him in it. I asked him if we could pray for him and see what God might be telling him, and he said we could."

Jonathan nodded.

Elikai and Owen grabbed some chairs from other tables for the girls to sit on. The rest of the group stood or crouched low. Ana remembered they'd been taught to split up into smaller groups to pray, so as not to overwhelm the person for whom they were praying. However, Jonathan seemingly liked having lots of people around him and seemed comfortable and outgoing.

"I really appreciate you guys praying for me." Jonathan's face was animated. "Today I was asking God for a sign that He was real and then wow! Here you are!"

Destiny smiled. "God always takes time out to show us how important we are to Him. I'm sensing that God wants you to know that He loves you very much." Destiny closed her eyes, focusing on what else God wanted to say. "At times you've felt that you weren't good enough for God to love, but He says that you're just what He wants."

Daniel took that as a cue that she was finished prophesying and jumped in. "God has seen your pain in the last little while, and He says that He is the only One who can heal that pain and satisfy your heart. You need to be lost in Him, and He will heal and restore every part of you and give you joy." Daniel paused for a moment as something else came to him. "Jonathan? Is something wrong with one of your hands? I feel God wants us to pray for your healing."

Jonathan's eyes opened wide in surprise. "Yeah! A few weeks ago, I was drinking, and my girlfriend and I were in a car accident on the way home. I hit a tree. I hurt my wrist, and it hasn't healed from the injury. I hate myself for being so stupid. She was really upset and broke up with me. She won't even talk to me so I can apologize," he explained, looking down.

Elikai asked, "Is it all right if we gently touch your wrist and pray for healing? We know God heals because we've seen it happen before."

Jonathan extended his hand, and they leaned in to touch his wrist.

Ana began, "We pray that Jonathan's wrist will be healed right now in the name of Jesus. We rebuke the pain and command the nerves and tendons and everything else to be healed. And I also pray, God, that You would show Jonathan the mysteries of Your love."

Elikai continued. "Jesus, we release the manifestation of Your trade with us; our sickness for health and strength, and we loose healing over Jonathan's wrist in the name of Jesus." He looked straight at Jonathan. "Can you test your wrist?"

Jonathan rolled his wrist in his other hand, massaging it at the same time. "It feels somewhat better, but it still hurts." He sounded a little disappointed.

Ana nodded. "That's okay. We'll pray some more."

Destiny prayed, "Father, let Your healing power come now as we bind this pain. We also release Your light and joy into Jonathan's life."

Owen looked around the group and opened his mouth now that no one was praying. "Father, I thank You for what You're doing in Jonathan's life. I thank You for his healing and for Your faithfulness in leading us to him today."

Jonathan jumped up and knocked over his chair. He grasped his wrist. "The pain is gone!" he exclaimed.

They all burst out laughing as Owen slapped him on the back.

Destiny asked, "Are you sure?"

Jonathan's face was stunned. "Yeah, I'm sure!"

Daniel grinned. "Let me tell you about the God who healed you."

As Daniel pulled Jonathan aside to tell him about Jesus' saving power and pray for him, the bouncer headed toward them, and he didn't appear happy. As people wandered off the dance floor, a crowd had gathered around the team.

A young woman pushed her way into the circle. "Hey, can you pray for me too?"

A friend of Jonathan's searched their faces for answers. "Are you guys psychics or something?"

The bouncer reached them and announced, "I'm going to have to ask all of you leave."

Andrew protested, "We aren't doing anything."

Will came up behind him and gently pushed him in the direction of the door. "Come on, it's not worth arguing." He turned around and smiled at the group. "If anyone wants prayer, we'll be outside."

Andrew started laughing like Will had just told a joke. He clutched Will's shoulder. Will was already laughing too, and he doubled over in hysterics when Andrew fell to the floor.

ஃ

Ana knew it was the power of the Holy Spirit permeating the group. God's peace and joy flooded her in a new way. She'd never been drunk but imagined the elated intoxication she experienced at the moment was better because she was in full awareness of her senses and of God's heart. There was nothing she could do. People continued to join them and watch as each of her friends were touched by God.

The bouncer looked skeptical as he watched them on the floor, making no move toward the exit.

Ana could barely catch her breath; her belly ached from laughing. Destiny writhed on the dirty floor. Ana slapped her hands to her knees as they both howled in laughter.

Someone watching yelled out, "What kind of drugs are these guys on? I want some!"

In the spirit realm, diamonds of light burst into the smoky club every few moments as more angels with swords began to materialize in the room, making their presence known to the powers of darkness. Their brightness in the realm overshadowed the strongest spotlight as demons who had been busy at work scattered. Sasson drew his sword and swiped at demons running for cover. The demons scarcely noticed as hands and claws clasped over their pain-pierced ears.

"Stop mocking us!" one screeched.

Okelani ran at Incubus/Succubus as it tried to ooze back into the human to whom it had been attached. The demon was having difficulty as his host neared the group. Okelani used the moment to pry off the demon. The other guardians were doing the same.

Chaos ensued in the room as the angels and demons fought. The laughter had many effects on the demons. Some were stunned. Those furthest from the group tried to flee as the sound stabbed into their ears.

Sasson knew Dionysus could hear the commotion from below the ground, but he wouldn't dare show his face. Sasson was glad for the spiritual mayhem. It was about time; this place needed a good cleansing. He laughed and moved around the room with the others. He ripped down hanging webs and illusions that were used to cloak what was really happening in the club.

The large angel poured his vial of oil in the spiritual realm over those who would come close enough to see what was happening to the group. He exuded the joy of the Creator and danced through the room as he swung the vial over many heads. He poured more on Jonathan. The messenger angel took his position next to Jonathan and opened his scroll.

Jonathan's hair was soaked with sweat at the temples as he laughed. Then he began to speak words he had never before heard.

> *"The Spirit of the Lord GOD is upon Me, because the LORD has anointed Me to preach good tiding to the poor; He has sent Me to heal the brokenhearted, To proclaim liberty to the captives, and the opening of the prison to those who are bound; to proclaim the acceptable year of the LORD, and the day of vengeance of our God; to comfort all who mourn, to console those who mourn in Zion, to give them beauty for ashes, the oil of joy for mourning, the garment of praise for the spirit of heaviness; that they may be called trees of righteousness, the planting of the LORD, that He may be glorified"* (Isaiah 61:1-3, NKJV).

The messenger angel then rolled up the scroll. Each word spoken materialized as an arrow released into the spiritual realm, reaching a specific human target. Some of the arrows went straight through the floor to unseen places. A few people shrugged at the message and returned to what they had been doing in the club while others stood transfixed with tears in their eyes.

Jonathan struggled to stand and regain his composure. Although he continued to laugh, tears were in his eyes. Sasson knew that in time Jonathan would understand what had happened to him.

The bouncer's walkie-talkie barked a few muffled commands. He turned to the crowd. "Ladies and gentlemen, the Eclipse will be closing early tonight. We need everyone to leave now!"

A few moans from the crowd preceded their heading toward the exits. As if to emphasize the bouncer's words, the spotlights were turned off, the room went dark, and then the main lighting was turned on full blast.

As the holy laughter began to ebb and cease, Ana and her friends picked themselves off the floor. Destiny half-carried and half-leaned on Ana as they collected their belongings and looked for the guys in the chaos. Ana, still heady, giggled when she spotted Will and Andrew helping each other rise from the floor on shaky legs.

Ana and the others stepped from the air-conditioned room into a dense wall of muggy night air. People were already gathering to ask them questions. The group divided into pairs to tell people about Jesus and pray for those who asked.

They were mid-prayer when police cruisers arrived without lights and sirens. Ana watched Daniel walk over to them. She assumed he was going to tell them about what he had discovered earlier. A few moments later, he rejoined the group.

"Apparently they already got a call about the place," he said to Elikai as he joined his friends.

Owen commented, "Looks like the owners called them to get rid of us."

"No, they received a call before this. They want us to clear out of here. They're going to look into it."

That night many new angels joined those who became a part of the kingdom of God and broke free of the kingdom of darkness. Jonathan was one of the first to give his life to Jesus.

Sasson looked at the empty first floor of the Eclipse; with the lights out and the windows dark, it resembled a large, gaping monster. The evil that had been hidden for so long was being exposed under a great light. More police were arriving. God was already working underground. Dionysus would be furious at what had taken place. Sasson was relieved to see dark spirits abandoning their territory as they floated away from the building. Now the prisoners held in darkness would be freed. Sasson looked into the sky. The day of battle was nearing, and people were being positioned into the purposes of God.

The roll of distant thunder gurgled behind the gathering clouds. The remaining people outside of the Eclipse ran for cars as a brooding dark curtain filled what had been an open starry night. Heavy droplets of rain began to fall, beating like fists upon the dry ground.

Behind the thick cloud, a scuffle ensued. Beams of light penetrated through the darkness. Swords clashed, light and dark angels fought, pushing and taking stabs at each other. A final blow sent them hurtling in opposite directions. The layer of film opened and released one angel with a crack of lightning. He fell toward the earth unconscious for only a few seconds before he was awakened by another roll of thunder. He stopped, hovered, remembered his mission and then turned to disappear in a flash, bent on seeking his target.

CHAPTER 25

High Praise

"Let the high praises of God be in their mouth, and a two-edged sword in their hand..." (Psalm 149:6, NKJV).

THE EMPTINESS IN the pit of Kevin's stomach was different from the emptiness he experienced after becoming accustomed to fasting. There was no promise of a late-night dinner or pancakes the next morning. The only the question to be answered was when this nightmare would come to a close. Exhaustion from starvation weighed down his body. Even the water Lisa had managed to sneak him did little to fill the deepening chasm in his stomach.

The cuts on his face had stopped bleeding. The bruises on his face felt like numb holes tightening each time he blinked. He rolled from side to side to keep the blood flowing to his arms. The stinging pins and needles in his hands had long since disappeared and were now replaced with throbbing numbness. His pants raised a faintly pungent scent of dried urine. The escape of oblivion was tempting. Kevin fought in his mind to stay focused on God and Cathy.

He guessed that nearly three or four days had passed since he had been captured, but having no windows made it impossible for him to know. Sleep, an often-evasive friend, proved faithful to woo him into another world, breaking up the hours spent in pain and hunger. But his friend never stayed long enough, and Kevin would reawaken to his living nightmare.

The urge for crack warred within him. The feeling of being high teased him. *You gave up me for this?* His back pressed against the cement wall. He fought against the mocking voices of his mind with earnestly murmured prayers for Cathy, the baby, Lisa and himself—his moment-by-moment ritual to keep away panic and despair. He had cried, wondering if God would ever again answer him.

How can I stay faithful to pray when deep down I feel like I deserve all that is happening right now?

Hope seemed to whisper goodbye each time he fell asleep. He wondered whether or not he would awaken to find that his time had run out.

Kevin snapped awake to gunshots resounding through the hollow underground chambers. *I'm going to die!*

The door flew open as flashlights and voices flooded the room. "Anyone in here?" a male voice boomed. Kevin faintly heard himself mumble as he squinted up at the source of the sudden brightness. Hands fumbled to turn him over and cut the rope that had rubbed raw welts into his wrists. He was lifted onto a gurney and rushed from the room. As he was rolled toward the exit, he caught a glimpse of a paramedic's kneeling over a motionless Lisa before he blacked out again.

As the damp night air rushed over Kevin's face, he opened his eyes. He was lying on a stretcher, and a light drizzle of rain sprinkled his face. Ambulances, a fire truck and police cruisers filled the area in front of the Eclipse.

As he felt the bump of being loaded into an ambulance, the paramedic noticed that he had opened his eyes. "He's awake!" the attendant yelled.

He felt a presence beside him and opened his eyes again. A police officer in rain gear leaned over him. "What's your name, sir?"

The paramedic peered at him through fogged-over wet glasses.

"Kevin Noter."

"The young lady we found in the room next to yours is still unconscious," the officer stated. "Do you have any information that can help us identify her or what's happened to her?"

"She told me she was on heroin," Kevin said, trying to focus his racing thoughts.

A second paramedic nodded his head. "What's her name? Do you know if she has any allergies?"

Kevin shook his head. "She was kidnapped and held against her will; we both were. I don't know much about her. All I know is that her name is Lisa."

The police officer looked from Kevin to the paramedic. "I'll go pull up info on missing persons."

～

Sasson walked along with the silent prayer warriors. Their determination for day four of the prayer march was not dampened despite the rain that continued to fall since from the previous night. He smiled as he looked into the tired, red-rimmed eyes of those who had been at the Eclipse the previous night. They were truly exhausted, but their excitement was unmistakable because new people had joined their ranks today, including Jonathan.

At least the rain was good for something; the heat wave that had blazed over their heads during the early days of the march had finally broken. T-shirts soaked in water had now been replaced by umbrellas that bobbed over heads as well as colored raincoats adorning the crowd. The younger kids had even abandoned their other means of transportation for old-fashioned walking.

Sasson was impressed with the way the numbers grew as every age group and ethnic background gathered together as one body to walk through the high and low parts of the city. Each day they would travel to where they had left off, car pooling and being bussed to the "hot spots" that needed prayer.

The "hiddenness" shield he and the other angels had created kept the prayer walkers' work hidden from the eyes of onlookers. Seemingly, a bunch of people were simply on their way somewhere.

❧

Kavo and the others watched as the incense-carrying angels descended and ascended above the group of walking warriors. The carriers gathered the prayers and escorted them into heaven to be placed into golden bowls. True prayers gathered weight, but the prayers of the insincere held no substance. This process required fearless and totally repentant hearts. Kavo wondered if the majority of prayers from these people would be enough to tip the scales in order to accomplish what God wanted to do.

Something needed to change the quality of the prayers into the sweet heavy incense Kavo knew they could be. Kavo motioned to Sasson signal him to begin what they had discussed.

Sasson walked among the children, whispering into their ears. A few of the kids from the community centre walked together near the front of the group. They had learned how to pray and were eager to flex their spiritual muscles. They whispered among themselves, and it wasn't long until Sean made his way to Will.

Will found Ana to relay the message. "Some of the kids feel that we need to pray in the vicinity of the community centre. One of the girls remembered she used to dream about it."

Ana considered the request for a moment. "Let's go. I would like to pray about a few things there as well." Turning to the front of the group, she yelled, "Kids, lead the way!"

A large train of people stepped forward and filled the back parking lot of the community centre. When the majority of the group arrived, they began discerning like they usually did when they prayed and listened to the Holy Spirit. People paced back and forth praying in the Spirit, singing and standing. After half an hour, they gathered together again.

Ana spoke from under her umbrella. "I'm really sensing a lot of resistance in the Spirit to our prayers. I'm not sure why."

Daniel suggested, "Maybe we should plant some Scripture here too. This place is very important to this side of the city. I feel like what happens here will affect many other things and places—kind of like an epicenter or something. I can almost see the connections in the spirit that extend out of here."

Ana agreed. "Let's ask God to show us what Scripture we should declare over this place."

After a few moments, one of the boys from the dance class spoke up. "I think we should use the Scripture where God told Joshua anywhere his foot would step would be his. Anyone know where that one is found?"

Flipping quickly through his pocket Bible, Will replied, "Sure; it's from the book of Joshua—1:3."

"You still carry one of those?" Andrew snickered as he scrolled through the Bible on his phone.

Will rolled his eyes and shook his head.

"Here, write it down." He handed Andrew a pen and a small piece of paper.

Ana called out, "Okay, while he's writing down that verse, I want us all to join hands and pray in the Spirit for a few minutes."

As they prayed, Elikai began trembling. Owen noticed, and when he placed his hand on Elikai's shoulder, they both began to tremble as the Holy Spirit ministered between them. Tears filled Elikai's eyes, and he began to prophesy. "The Lord says that my people have prayed, but they have not humbled themselves or turned from wickedness. If my people will humble themselves to each other in love, freedom will come in this place. Repent, My people, for this is the thing that I'm calling you to do. No longer will each man work for himself, but you will join together. Turn to Me. I'm weighing your hearts." Elikai wept as he spoke the words. Ana felt sorrow over the words and began to personally repent for her own times of division in her heart.

Others responded by crouching down despite the rain to humble themselves physically before God.

Ana repented for the negative way some had responded to the march. Personal agendas had kept many from joining. Kavo listened as church members found each other and confessed rumors they had heard and the hidden matters they had kept in their hearts.

The incense that continued to rise became unmistakably clear and weighty. Kavo smiled. It was working; the incense was good. The spiritual realm began to shake as the earth split, and more of the crystal kingdom sprouted up around the community centre and shot downward, creating deep roots into the ground.

Leah lay still on the floor, trying to meditate. The rain had kept her at home. *No way! I'm walking in that!*

Every hindrance she had used was having no effect. She was certain that she could do nothing more to wear down Ana. All she could do now was wait for further instructions and brace herself for what was to come.

Sakron was too busy with his own secrets to bother with her. Each night Leah had witnessed Havoc leave the amulet as well. Who knew what he was up to? Things were frightfully quiet. She was scared. She felt the silence—the kind that seemed peaceful before something loud and frightening jumped out at you.

Stephen

The hospital room was quiet with the steady hum of breathing and beeping monitors. The rain outside drummed heavily against the windowsill. Stephen lay unmoving, but his mind was alert, rolling through the years of his happy marriage to Beth.

Beth will be able to survive without me. Her new friends seem to be a great support to her.

They had been praying for him for a long time. How he wished he could tell them how glad he was that they were there. He had peace about dying. The last few months had been agony physically, but a deep sense of peace filled him, knowing that the love of his life would be fine. All through the prayers, his condition had not improved. But the prayers truly touched his heart each time Beth and her friends had joined together on his behalf. He believed Jesus had the power to heal him. Although he couldn't speak anymore, Stephen decided what Cathy and his wife had said was true. Jesus was the Son of God, and He loved him. He had not always enjoyed the strongest relationship with God, but he had started believing in Him years ago.

Stephen also knew he wasn't sick because God was punishing him. Whatever happened, Stephen was thankful for God's sacrifice of His Son.

Stephen's eyes rolled under closed lids. He wanted to understand more about the Son of God who had taken on sickness, torture and pain all because of love. This concept of dying for the one you love was easy to understand.

Wouldn't he die for Beth in a minute? Wouldn't he take on her pain if he could spare her? Hadn't Beth wished she could do the same for him? His darling Beth would have rescued him from the pain of cancer if she could have borne it herself.

Stephen's mind wandered over the many beautiful things he had seen his wife do over the years. Pictures unfolded over pictures as he thought of her inner beauty. As he gazed inwardly, scrolling through his memories, he saw the brightness that had been shining over each scene of his life. That brightness filled his body with a sense of deep warmth.

Suddenly he became aware that the brightness he was experiencing was not coming from his thoughts but from inside the hospital room. He lifted his heavy lids. Everything in the room looked the same—nose tube for oxygen, the monitors, and a bright and shining man…

Stephen was startled. As the man slowly approached and reached out to him, Stephen could feel heat creep over his body as the pain in his lungs and chest floated away. The man stood over him and smiled. Stephen was able to smile back.

"Who are you?" Stephen mumbled, trying to force words from his dry, weak lips.

"*I AM*…" the man's voice echoed. The dazzling figure pulsed with a bright light and then simply disappeared.

~

"Kevin called!" Cathy screamed up the stairs in her excitement. Sandra and Ana bounded down the stairs to hear her news. It was later in the afternoon after praying at the community centre. Ana was getting ready after her nap. Her energy levels had not fully recovered after the fast, and the walking each day was steadily taking its toll on her mind and body.

"Where is he? What did he say?" Sandra asked, clutching her knitting needles as she stopped near the bottom of the stairs. In her rush she had dropped her ball of yarn, and now it continued bouncing down behind her. Ana managed to miss the ball, but unable to stop on such short notice, she abruptly bumped into her mom.

"He's in the hospital for observation and dehydration," she explained.

"He was kidnapped. He was being held in a cellar somewhere beneath the Eclipse for days with nothing to eat or drink. The police raided the place the night of the rainstorm!"

"How did they know he was there?" Ana asked.

"Someone apparently tipped off the police. He was with that young woman who had gone missing a few weeks ago!"

"Praise God!" Ana could feel herself begin to tear up as she thought of her prayer with Wella.

"She's in bad shape though. She was addicted to heroin and tried to kill herself, but apparently the paramedics got to her in time."

"Did they capture the kidnapper?"

"Not yet, but they did arrest a few dealers and found a large stash of drugs. Apparently, an underground drug business was going on there. I'm so glad Kevin is safe. I need to get to the hospital now!" Cathy looked restless.

"Hang on a minute, and I'll give you a ride." Sandra put down the knitting needles on the kitchen table and reached for her keys.

∾

"Kevin?"

That sweet voice he thought he'd never hear again! "Cathy!" Kevin choked out, finalizing the realness of his rescue. *This is reality. I really am here in the hospital.* He couldn't wait to see Cathy's face. He looked up weakly as she finally settled on his bed and stretched out her arms to embrace him.

"I'm so glad you're okay!" She kissed him all over his face, careful to avoid the bruises and cuts. "I didn't know where you were—or what happened," she said between sweet kisses. She stopped talking and nuzzled his neck.

"We have to stop meeting like this," he joked, gesturing around the hospital room.

She looked into his face and sighed. "I didn't know what to think, Kevin, but I'm glad I didn't give up on you."

Kevin stared silently at her face, taking in the moment he thought he'd never have again. He'd literally prayed like his life depended on it.

He smiled. "Me too."

∾

The repentance mode lasted for a day before the final ordained day of the march. The personal, yet corporate, repentance had shifted the collective scales so that the prayers were quickly filling the bowls in heaven.

The zealous humans sometimes didn't know when it was time to end and time to shift. But that was what the angels were there for.

Kavo likened the effect of the repentance to pushing a car downhill. Once the momentum had started, the pushing became unnecessary. *Joy* spilled over, and people found it difficult to stay in the repentance mode.

News of the raid on the Eclipse had spread, strengthening the resolve of the marchers. They silently prayed forth their own promises in the community, while uniting hearts, believing for the greater promise of what God was bringing into the city.

Kavo declared what the other angels already knew. "It's time to take your places!"

~

On the last day of the march, everyone prepared for the praise fest. Ana spotted Wella in the crowd. Wella's hair flowed loosely over her shoulders. She wore a bright-green summer dress and carried two dancers' flags. Ana could not remember the last time she had seen her friend wearing a summer dress, revealing her plump arms and legs. But Wella was radiant. "There you are, my darling!" Wella swaddled Ana in her arms. "I've been looking all over for you." Looking at the crowd, she began to muse about the event. "Oh, Ana, Matthew would be so proud. I know he must be cheering in heaven with that great crowd of witnesses."

Ana smiled. "I hope so."

Wella winked, smiling mischievously at Ana. "Hope you're ready to kick some enemy derrieres today."

Ana reached for a dance flag. "You know I am." She winked back, "hand me my sword."

Johanna

Rahos stood beside Johanna as she stretched behind the stage. Musicians and dancers were already crowding toward the front for the praise rally.

People worshipped as the speakers blasted the first of the bands' worship melodies.

Pastor Mark led the people in shouts of victory. Dancers waved and twirled their colorful flags from side to side. They whirled and danced to the music as the people sang.

The sun was hot, and the air was fresh in the park beside the parking lot of the community centre. Mr. Stucco had given them permission to hold the rally on the edge facing the ravine that led to the forest.

The children from the community centre performed a marvelous dance together. After their dance, the time had come for Johanna to take the stage and follow with a choreographed solo dance. She jumped and swayed to the music as she focused on Jesus' victory in the city.

For weeks she had worked hard on the dance. Now, she stomped and danced, swiping her arms as she fought invisible foes. The choreography began to fade, and she became one with the music as the Holy Spirit moved her. She extended her leg and reached for the sky bending far back. Her body swooped and bent, contracting arms, running and leaping. She was suspended, held in time as she saw herself dancing before the throne of God. As she danced, she was entranced with God's beauty. She paused before her feet seemed to take her into another rhythm, another step. Beads of sweat formed on her forehead, but she did not want to stop. Her breath moved in rhythm, simply another part of the dance.

As she whirled and moved over the stage, she signaled some of the other dancers from other churches. They took her cue and as one began circling around her in a spontaneous flow.

❧

The Holy Spirit surrounded the dancers on the stage, anointing swirled and poured over out everywhere. Worshipping angels materialized in the spirit realm between the dancers. They flowed in the same movements with even more reverence before the throne. They bowed and leaped, intertwining with the dancers. The dancers held hands with invisible partners.

Colors and light arched out, dazzling and shimmering all over the stage and into the crowd. Rahos and the angels heard each color as it released its own deep bell vibration. Each sound joined with the other colors and became a harmony. The unearthly melodies shot heavenward over the skyline in every direction.

Rahos' gaze followed Johanna in admiration. He paused and tilted back to look into the distant sky, listening again. Drawing his sword, he glanced at the other angels who were following suit.

The armor of both Okelani and Kavo' came to the surface of their skin. Ram's horn trumpets suddenly sounded faintly in the distance. The sound grew louder and more frequent until they heard one single blast—loud, long and powerful.

In the angelic realm, above the crowd, the sky quivered. Shock waves of portals opened. Swift flying angels burst though the portals into the atmosphere carrying swords, hammers and banners. They landed everywhere.

Holes full of light filled the heavenlies. Deep into the chasms of light were glimpses of heaven from where the angels had been sent. The angels gathered in ranks and under banners, according to their assigned warrior teams. When Sasson, Kavo and the other angels stood together, a new angel had now joined their ranks.

Sasson was the first to notice the angel. "We've been waiting for you."

"I was detained," he answered, sounding breathless. ""A principality was holding me back. I fought my way free and finally landed here."

Kavo wondered when the breakthrough had come and asked, "When did you come?"

"The rainstorm; I've been with Andrew ever since—preparing him."

"Glad to finally have you with us." Okelani stepped forward, touching his sword to the new angel's sword. "What's your name?"

"I am called Adara."

～

Ana jumped up and down and danced as Holy Spirit increased on her. She raised her hands. So much joy flooded her that she wanted to jump out of herself to worship God. Her body seemed a cumbersome barrier between her and the fullness that was ready to break through. Deep within, her senses exploded with an awareness of the love of God.

Responding to the urge, she prayed in tongues with a new force that she had never known. A change came in the spiritual atmosphere. Rushes of heat surged from her inner man. God was quickening something to her. She knelt.

Pray and worship in this holy moment. I am demolishing the work that the Enemy has been trying to set up. I have heard My people, and because their hearts are turned to Me, I will show My glory in this place!

Sasson and Okelani looked up. Another large angel came down slowly, carrying a bright cape intertwined with rich colors that resembled fire. Sasson pointed in awe as he recognized the familiar angel.

Kavo shouted, "Matthew's angel! I haven't seen him since Matthew went to join the other saints in heaven."

Sasson nodded, remembering his old friend.

Dunamis, Matthew's angel, carried the mantle to Ana and placed it on her shoulders. As it rested on her, she shook inwardly like she had that first night on the curb—completely unaware of what was happening around her. The mantle lay brightly over her shoulders and then dissolved so that it was no longer visible to the angels. Dunamis flew over to the others.

"I'm here to help carry on the work that was given to Matthew and is now given to Ana." The angels nodded at what that they had originally suspected.

Suddenly Dunamis looked up, sensing something afar off, then shot upward and disappeared with a flash.

"This is only the beginning," Okelani noted.

In the forest, Divinica moved gracefully, chanting and lighting candles as she poured dark ash onto the ground. She outlined the sacred symbols that would pull the goddess through the portal. Her fingers were quick and steady, realizing there was no time for errors. She could already feel the shift in the atmosphere along with the booming bass that travelled into the dark forest beyond the center. The power of the last portal was dwindling. Soon it would close like the others.

Leah stepped into the clearing and recognized Divinica's slender figure as she sang and swayed, circling her feet in the dirt like a dancer. She looked young but seemed old. There was an agelessness about her. Leah admired Divinica's beauty and her smooth, pale skin that contrasted with her dark, straight hair. As Divinica finished the last of the chants, she finally turned, as if sensing Leah's presence. Crushed and broken flowers were scattered in the dirt after the ritual. Leah studied the symbols on the ground before she spoke. "Sakron told me to meet you here," she said cautiously.

"Yes, I told him to summon you to help me with the ritual. I know what you did, Leah."

Leah stared back. Divinica's gaze bored a hole through her mind. "You can't hide anything from me."

A tremor ran through Leah's body as she spoke, trying to sound casual. "What are you talking about?"

Divinica paced in a circle. Her bare feet were covered in ash and dirt. Even with the dark smudges on her petite feet, Leah noticed how perfect her toes seemed. Purple nail polish was smoothed on each nail bed.

Divinica spoke slowly. "Here we are…" She raised her hands to motion around her. "…out in the open. The rituals are done, and we no longer have the blood of the innocent to finish the calling forth of the goddess. You forget, little sister, that your demons report back to me. I know all about your little phone call to the police. You were very silly. I can't imagine what possessed you, dear. No matter. You will stand in her place."

Leah felt the blood drain from her face. Her body became cold and shook. Leah turned to run, but her feet were frozen. Her body was being drawn toward Divinica by an invisible force.

Leah's ruby amulet lifted from her throat and pointed toward Divinica. The cold links of the necklace pulled, rubbing against the back of Leah's neck as it propelled her forward.

Divinica stood motionless staring straight into Leah's eyes with fierce concentration. Leah struggled as Divinica spoke into her mind.

Sakron and Havoc will lead you to me. There is no use fighting. If you come willingly, I will slit your throat before I use the rest of you.

Leah screamed inwardly; her mouth refused to open as her body continued to betray her—drawn forward against her will. She felt like a sleepwalker in a bad dream.

"There is no need to fear, Leah," Divinica spoke soothingly. "You will become one with the goddess—a slave for eternity. You will be one with pain and agony. They will no longer frighten you."

Divinica grabbed Leah's hand and led her like a child the rest of the way into the centre of the marks on the ground. She placed her on the ground and rubbed ash on her forehead. Divinica looked above the trees in the direction she had been chanting. She focused on it for a moment and then nodded. She looked down at Leah again and stood up to chant. "You're not the kind of blood we wanted, but you'll have to do."

Leah lay helpless. Tears streamed from the corners of her eyes. Wisps of hair clung to her temples. Terror and panic were trapped behind her senseless and unmoving eyes. Divinica used her knife to carve the same symbols that were on the ground into Leah's arms. Blood streamed from the wounds and began to intermingle with the dirt. Leah screamed inside. *There is nothing I can do now. It's over. No use in fighting to get free.*

Her chest pounded as she continued to cry. *No one loves or cares about me enough to be looking for me now.* The most that she could hope for was that it would all be done quickly. She thought about at least escaping the pain somehow and wondered if she could focus enough now to meditate and leave her body before the worst of the rituals took place. *Havoc was supposed to help me with that.*

She remembered the day she had received him and had expected greater powers. All she had realized that day was that even demons are afraid.

Jesus—this had something do with Him. Was He actually stronger?...Why me? Where is His love now? No one has ever wanted me...Jesus? Leah felt the air deflating from her lungs like an old balloon. Her body shut down from shock.

Leah choked as vomit burned at the base of her throat, reviving briefly as Divinica began piercing her neck. *Jesus, help me!*

The knife stopped abruptly as Divinica studied Leah's face for a moment. She suddenly jumped up, wielding her knife in all directions.

———

Leah knew she did not have much time. She was blacking out and would soon be dead. Already she felt herself being drawn up and out of her body. Maybe the meditation was working. The light was getting brighter, and the awareness of the pain in her body was diminishing. She welcomed the release but instead of black nothingness, she awoke to shining light.

~

The heavenly host had gathered. Dionysus, ready to do battle, had summoned all the demons and spirits of darkness in the city to be ready. As in ancient times, Dionysus fought to do damage to as many angels as possible. Only now more angels were in the city then he last remembered. He turned from side to side, seething in disgust and…terror. *Someone was responsible for this and would pay.*

He flew from one spot, stabbing his sword into one angel, talons tearing into the flesh of another as he searched the crowd. He spotted Ana kneeling from afar.

Her! He dove in her direction.

🐍

During the celebration, a hooded man had fixed his gaze on Ana. He pushed his way slowly through the crowd as his dazed stare darted left and right and returned to her. His hands pushed deep into his pockets, with one finger resting lightly on the cold gun. As he maneuvered around many dancing worshippers, people bumped into him unaware of his lethal intent. He started to shake as sweat dripped inside his sweater.

He drew closer, secretly clutching his gun, now his finger was poised on the trigger. He licked his lips and paused. Finally, within close range, he slowly drew the gun from his pocket and pointed it at Ana.

———

CHAPTER 26

Light and Dark

"Where can I go from your Spirit? Where can I flee from your presence? If I go up to the heavens, you are there; if I make my bed in the depths, you are there. If I rise on the wings of the dawn, if I settle on the far side of the sea even there your hand will guide me, your right hand will hold me fast. If I say, 'Surely the darkness will hide me and the light become night around me,' even the darkness will not be dark to you; the night will shine like the day, for darkness is as light to you" (Psalm 139:7-12, NIV).

LEAH LOOKED DOWN at her body and saw four large bright beings surround her with their swords drawn. *Are these angels?* Above her, through a portal streaming with darkness, she saw a huge image of a woman even more beautiful than Divinica. This larger-than-life woman howled as she desperately tried to reach Leah through the portal. Then her face suddenly began to morph. The beautiful, almond-shaped eyes turned black, and her long lush hair began to shrink up as if it had been singed with fire. Her face became pale red with deeply embedded scars. Blood dripped from the fangs of the now-hideous monster when it tried to pull itself through the portal.

Like a kite free from its controlling string, Leah could not resist the draw she felt toward that portal as it began to close. One of the brightest and the largest of the angels stood between Leah and the portal, preventing her from going in.

"Dunamis! Watch out!" another angel called. In a massive effort to free itself, the creature clawed a chunk of flesh from the Dunamis' arm. He grimaced but turned and swiped his sword into the portal, immediately releasing Leah from its pull and continued to use his sword to beat back the ugly creature's talons.

The other angels formed a circle around Divinica as she screamed obscenities. She stamped her feet, creating a dust cloud of ash and dirt around her long skirt. Sakron and Havoc were nowhere in sight, and her own demons remained hidden as well. She cursed the angels, trying in vain to slash them with her knife. She broke free from their invisible barrier, thrashing about wildly to run from the forest. In her haste she knocked over two of the candles.

In front of Dunamis, the hideous monster morphed back into a smiling, docile beauty, beckoning Leah one final time. Her loose curls bobbed up and down before the portal finally closed.

~

Something's not right!

Will looked up, scanning the crowd. His heart raced when he saw the hooded person pointing a gun at Ana. In the split second he had spotted the gun and the hand to whom it was connected, he instinctively sprinted toward the assassin, covering the distance between them at full speed.

"Ana!"

§

Deep in prayer, Ana opened her eyes when she heard screaming. She saw the gun aimed in her direction. People yelled and ran around her.

This isn't happening. She screamed.

§

Okelani slammed his fist into the ground, bending both space and time between Will and the shooter.

313

Before Will realized what happened, he was already diving at the gun-man's chest and tackled him. The bullet cut through the air as the gun arced and fell to ground—hot but harmless. Screaming people ran in all directions. Security guards ran from the outskirts directly into the centre of the commotion.

Sasson simultaneously lunged, his sword drawn, at the possessed hooded man and knocked Dionysus right out of him. Angel and demon smashed into each other as swords of light and dark clashed.

"Get out of my way!" Dionysus snarled as he forced his wings from his back and tried to fly back toward Ana.

Sasson's own wings flapped and propelled him forward. He felt power coursing through his large wings with each beat. "Leave her alone. Stand down!" Sasson yelled, grabbing Dionysus' leg before he could flee.

Dionysus stabbed his sword downward at Sasson. "She will die for this! I will inflict her life!" He finally freed himself and again dove toward Ana.

Sasson headed him off and blocked Ana before Dionysus could reach her. His shining wingspan fully spread, completely hiding her from view. He held his sword on guard, bracing for another onslaught.

"You have no authority!" Sasson declared as his sword clashed with the demon's sword. This time he pushed back with all his might to prevent Dionysus from coming closer.

Dionysus grunted as he slashed at Sasson's chest, puncturing his armor.

From behind the warriors, Okelani ordered sternly, "That will be enough, demon!"

"This doesn't concern you, guardian!" Dionysus hissed, turning around and then jumping high enough to hover over them.

Okelani now infuriated, took another broad and powerful swipe, cutting into the demon's leg. "Anything that concerns my charge concerns me!"

More angels of light began to gather around their enemy Dionysus.

Seeing that he was outnumbered, he flew higher and bolted in the other direction. His angry howl of defeat trailed off behind him.

Catching his breath, Sasson spoke. "Thanks for the help."

"Don't mention it," Okelani replied. "Let's go; there's still much to do."

❧

Ana knelt, stunned and unable to move in the chaos that surrounded her. She watched in disbelief as Will slammed the gunman to the ground. Elikai came out of nowhere, snapping her back to reality when he grabbed her shoulders and literally lifted her up from the ground. He took her hand and pulled her, on stumbling legs, through the scattering crowd to take cover under the stage.

❧

Will struggled as he tried to pin the writhing hooded man. The perpetrator moaned as Will again slammed him against the ground. The man's eyes flashed wildly in their sockets as he tried to fight back. The gun lay within his reach on the pavement.

Owen scrambled to kick the gun out of the way before a security guard finally picked it up. Will and the assailant continued to roll on the ground. The man, now lucid, threw a punch at Will, attempting to free himself. Will dodged the punch and slammed the man against the ground again and again. Then he raised his fist.

The man groaned, "Will, stop!"

Will's clenched fists involuntarily halted at the sound of his name. He blinked in disbelief as the bruised hands of the would-be assassin tried to wrestle Will's grasp from the throat of his hooded sweatshirt.

Will stared down. His open mouth formed words, but he made no sound. The security guards pulled them apart as Will finally found his voice. "Ishmael…?"

∼

The forest was dark in the spiritual plane. The trees all swayed with a life of their own under the forces of good and evil.

Dunamis' large body shone again in the darkness as he looked lovingly at Leah and spoke. "You are loved; choose Him."

At that instant Leah felt the warmth and love radiating from the angel. He cradled Leah's spirit body in his arms and carried her down to place her back into her cut and broken body. Flames gathered and licked up the rest of the demonic symbols on the ground, illuminating the clearing.

Smoke filled her nostrils as she once again became aware of the piercing pain and the heaviness of her body. The reality and brightness of the angels in the spirit realm began to fade as she once again experienced the world through her normal five senses. A man's voice was calling through the forest.

"Hello, is anyone in here?"

The distant voice sounded familiar to her. She could hear her heart thudding in her ears as her pulse throbbed, weakly pumping blood from her sliced wrists. A wave of nausea came over her, and then everything went black.

Mere minutes had passed before the sound of the police sirens could be heard in the distance. Ana paced in the silence behind the stage for what seemed like an hour before things settled down enough for the officers to find her and take her statement. She wanted to stay there, because even now, everything seemed so surreal. But God's power was still strong upon her, filling her and surrounding her with a deep sense of peace. God was doing something great in this place, and she wasn't going to back down from doing His work. After the questioning, she excused herself and stayed there to pray. After a few moments, she found Pastor Mark and asked him to have everyone who still remained gather at the church.

This is the last time I pay attention to some dumb dream.

Andrew crunched over broken tree branches as he swatted the hovering mosquitoes, landing and sticking to his sweaty neck. Overhead the birds chirped as Andrew worked his way deeper into the forest.

With a lawn chair and a cool drink, this might not be so bad.

This was the first bit of silence he had experienced all day and mosquitoes or not, he was actually starting to enjoy the tranquility of silence. He had more to think about these days, including his growing discipline in prayer and study of the Word, his relationship with Pastor Mark, and his stupidity with Ana. Lust and alcohol were a terrible combination to battle, but each day he felt more serious regarding his life and his decisions. He realized that chances were he would not stop being drawn to Ana, but every day he had a deeper understanding of what made her so remarkable.

Pastor Mark's advising him to be accountable to the other men of the church offered him a new kind of safety net. He believed that one day the holes in his heart would close, and he would be able to love the way a godly man was supposed to love. Ana was right. For a long time he could only think about his own wants—never realizing how his choices affected those around him.

He decided that he would have to lean on God and obey whatever He told him to do. And he had definitely been hearing stuff. Last night he'd dreamed he'd walked in the forest and found a precious jewel. *Maybe God wants to make me rich because I'm trying to be good now.*

He was reminded of the dream when the band struck up one of those tear-jerker torture songs. Being aware of how messed up he was did not help his cause. In full recognition of his weakness to this new strange form of public humiliation, Andrew had decided that today not one salty droplet should escape his eye. He had turned toward the forest, heading in the direction of this dream treasure hunt.

A woman's scream abruptly interrupted his thoughts. A short distance into the forest, he saw a figure sweep past in a blur. "Hello?" He walked five paces when suddenly he noticed bright-orange flames and billows of smoke wafting through the trees. He heard more rustling and the loud crackling of branches crashing as they fed the fire. He cautiously stepped closer and was about to turn and run back the way he had come when he spotted a body lying in the clearing. Recognizing Leah's lifeless body crumpled on the ground as the fire raged around her, he jumped through some bushes that had yet to catch fire. Andrew ran to Leah and stomped out the flames closest to her body.

※

Sasson and Okelani stood with Ana, watching the outcome of the commotion as a breathless Zeb materialized behind them. "The last of the Enemy's portals have closed in the forest. Yonah, Dunamis and Adara are already there. Andrew was sent to find Leah, but he's going to need reinforcements. There is a fire," Zeb finished.

Sasson nodded to Okelani. "Notify the others. We'll meet you there."

◈

Once he had smothered the smaller flames around her, Andrew quickly knelt to try and put out the ones smoldering in her clothes and hair. He burned his hands as he ground her hair into the dry dirt. He coughed as the smell of her scorched hair filled his nostrils. Parts of her clothes were charred black and smoking. She was bleeding from wounds on her wrist and seemed to have blotchy blisters on her legs from the fire. He lifted her head into his lap. "Leah!" he gently slapped her pale cheek.

Nothing.

He coughed and wheezed as smoke filled his lungs. The fire was spreading, and the black smoke was becoming too thick to see through. His eyes stung as he tried to roll her onto his back. Blood smeared his clothes. He knew he should be strong enough to lift her frame, but the dead weight made her seem twice as heavy. He knelt on the ground beside her to sling her body over his shoulder. As he rolled her onto his arm, a pendant around her neck gleamed, suddenly glowing red. He blinked again, staring at it.

Must be the smoke and fire.

Finally, he lifted her, awkwardly carrying her as he stumbled along a pathway leading out of the forest.

Whatever happened before I got here had to have been gruesome.

As Andrew staggered under her weight to the edge of the forest, his lungs burned with exhaustion. Smoke made him cough continuously. He was surprised that the music from the praise fest had ended early. When he reached the edge of the parking lot he dropped to his knees panting. He saw Daniel point at him and start to run toward him. Paramedics followed close behind, Andrew felt like an eternity passed before they reached him and relieved him of Leah's weight.

◈

When Kavo arrived, the fire had already consumed a sizeable portion of the forest behind the community centre. Kavo had no doubt that the flames would soon make their way to the building itself, and that was not an option. Dunamis, Adara and Yonah joined arms and started to spin, Yonah beat his wings, creating momentum.

In a few moments Sasson, followed by Zeb, Okelani and a few more angels appeared and joined the circle. They spun, beating their wings to create a vacuum that almost completely smothered the flames.

Firefighters arrived on the scene and surveyed the burnt trees and grass. One firefighter turned in a circle, scanning the area, and asked. "What do you think happened here?"

"It looks like the fire somehow burned itself out."

Another firefighter dropped his ax to the ground. "Must have been some kind of weird fluke with all this dry brush available to burn."

"Probably. Let's finish it off."

~

Kavo and the angels flew out of the forest to rejoin the rest of the heavenly host that had gathered to fight. They flew above the clouds and into their own realm. A messenger angel flew back and forth in the heavens, blowing the ram's horn and continuing to sound the alarm.

As Kavo and the others zoomed upward in their warrior team, their armor fully re-emerged through skin. The guardian angels and warrior angels each took up newly assigned weapons from the heavenly armory before surging back into the earth's atmosphere.

With the commotion of the shooting and the fire, the worship in the earthly realm had come to a halt. However, in the spiritual realm, the music continued as beautiful melodies reverberated through the stratosphere.

A constant flow of angels directed by the Holy Spirit streamed into Tehly to different areas of the city. They continued to tear down demonic scaffolding hidden underground as well as the beginnings of the satanic towers that protruded from the ground, invisible to the human eye.

Swords and hammers cut apart demonic strongholds. Dionysus left behind his human counterpart and fought in his demon form with his age-old sword. Even his scales were unable to reflect the light that around him. His demons fought desperately to hold up the falling structures, to no avail. Everything crumbled around them as the ground began to shake with the force of the angelic hammers.

He watched while demons looked on with dread as the last pieces of the scaffolding lay in pieces on the ground. The foundations of their mischief had been dislodged and were now disintegrating piece by piece. Demons floated around in confusion, unsure of what to do next.

"It's not over!" Dionysus hissed as he turned toward Sakron who hovered nearby.

Sakron breathed heavily when he spoke. "Our brethren have started to flee. We must fight now before our numbers are too low."

Dionysus turned and screamed at the demons who were still following him. "Fight!"

The last of the demons rushed forward toward the angels as a single unit.

§

Under the instruction of Pastor Mark, the worship team boldly reassembled at the church. They started worship with the song "Lowest Place," and praise and worship to God resumed in full force. The people danced and sang with renewed vigor. Moments later, Ana took the stage to lead everyone in prayer.

Without a shred of shyness remaining, she shouted into the microphone, "Father, You alone deserve the honor and praise. You said there would be joy in the laying down of our lives, and we release that joy into this city. We release Your joy into every church, into every school and institution." She lifted her hands. "We declare Your peace in our city. The Enemy's work is being exposed right now, and we boldly command every evil spirit to flee in the mighty name of Jesus!"

§

As the congregation continued to pray and shout praises, the ground shook with great force in the spiritual realm. Sasson and the angels glowed with electricity, able to feel the vibrations in the sky while battling the demons.

Sasson looked at the angelic army. Lightning bolts streamed from them as they marched forward against the demonic horde. The angels walked forward together as one, surrounded by a lightning storm that caused Dionysus and his demons to stumble and fall back over each other. Indecision grew among the demons as they began to cast curses on each other, passing the blame on to each other for what was happening.

———

The heavenly host continued to move onward with outstretched arms holding swords and hammers at the ready while a large, shining, transparent hand pushed back the forces of the Enemy.

The angels flew out of the line and attacked again. Sasson found himself in the center of the battle. He turned to see Okelani and Kavo fighting off several demons. Swords clashed, feathers and scales flew. The enemy no longer possessed any hope.

Sasson flew up at a demon and clanged his sword against the demon's rusty armor. As their forces wearied of the battle, the cursing demons began to retreat, flying in all directions. The large shimmering hand resembling the sparkling edge of the ocean. The hand pushed back the demons and separated them from the fight, rolling them back like sod, as dark billows of smoke covered them. They rolled back farther and farther, ultimately disappearing into the abyss with faint shouts of confusion and profanities until the sky was clear of them.

CHAPTER 27

Vision in the Night

"In a dream, in a vision of the night, when deep sleep falls on people as they slumber in their beds, he may speak in their ears and terrify them with warnings" (Job 33:15, 16, NIV).

A S THE INTENSITY of the prayer diminished, Ana suddenly felt deflated. Now she was sure she had finished what God wanted her to do. She walked down the black steps of the stage, noticing Cathy and Beth standing nearby. Both women were smiling and in deep conversation. As she headed toward them, she noticed Kevin with a familiar-looking older gentleman who were heading their way. She couldn't place the older man until he came to stand next to Beth. *Stephen!* And now he was a picture of perfect health!

Cathy hugged Ana after seeing tears well up in her eyes.

"I heard about what happened earlier. Are you okay?" Cathy held Ana at arm's length to look her over.

"Yes, totally fine. Thank God!"

Stephen and Kevin joined them. "Stephen, you look amazing!" Ana's tears refused to stop. "I don't know why I'm crying; I'm actually very happy."

Ana's insides felt exposed and raw, yet relief flooded through her. *Things are finally working out.*

"Thank you for all your prayers." Stephen hugged her tightly.

Even after he had released her, Ana couldn't stop staring. "I can't believe what I'm seeing."

"Why not? You believe God heals, and that's what He's done for me. I'll never live my life the same way again." Then he turned to hug Beth. "I haven't felt like this in years."

Ana turned to Cathy. "Why didn't you tell me?"

"We wanted to surprise everyone. I only found out myself a day ago."

Beth shrugged. "The doctors weren't going to release him because they wanted to do more tests…we still have to go back for more. They are in absolute shock over there!"

Stephen interrupted, "I already told them what happened. Jesus walked in and touched me. If they can't believe that explanation, then that's their problem." He winked and then smiled.

Ana turned toward Kevin, glad to see him looking better. "Where's your new friend?"

"She's still detoxing in the hospital. She'll be okay though. We went to visit her earlier. She seems happy to be free from that prison, but she's still very withdrawn."

Cathy nodded. "We're going to spend some time with her later to try to help her process some of what she's been through. She will have to join the hospital's counseling program."

Kevin agreed. "She was there way longer than I was. I'm still not sure what happened that night we were discovered along with the others. "

"God answers prayers. We know that!" Ana beamed at each of them. She wiped her eyes. God had done the impossible for all of them in the past few months. She sensed today there had been several victories and there would be more to come. A sense of reassurance fell over her.

Cathy frowned. "Do you think any of the ambulances are parked here at the church?" She bent over and clutched her stomach. Her face had taken on a somewhat strained look.

"I'm not sure, why?" Beth looked around.

"I think the baby is coming." Cathy started to rub her stomach as blood drained from her face. "That was a strong contraction. I have been having mild contractions since earlier, but now they're getting much stronger."

"Now?" Kevin shouted, grabbing Cathy's arm and placing his hand on her back.

She swallowed. "My water hasn't broken yet, but I think I should get to the hospital."

Beth patted Cathy's hand. "I've got my car."

In the hospital room, Leah fought through nightmares in her subconscious. She knew her body lay still, disguising the turmoil that was keeping her from awakening to reality.

Outside her room, two police officers were questioning Andrew.

"I told you already. I was taking a walk in the forest. I saw her lying in the clearing near the fire…I went to help her." Andrew hands were damp, and his armpits prickled with nervousness. *My story doesn't even sound believable to me!*

"Do you know this young lady?"

"Yes, she attends my church."

"Why did you go into the forest?"

"I don't know…I just felt like I needed some quiet." Better not mention the dream.

"In the middle of a concert?"

"It wasn't a concert—"

"Do you know of anyone who would want to harm her?"

"No. You will have to ask her that when she wakes up…I don't know her that well."

"Okay, sir, that's all the questions we have for now. Don't plan any trips outside the city for a couple of weeks until we can sort through this situation."

Andrew raked his fingers through his hair and sighed, glad to be done with questions. He stood and walked past Leah's room, peeking in before leaving. *She looks so helpless lying there.* He felt sorry for her. Her blood still covered his clothes. *I can't go anywhere looking like this.* He turned away, deciding it would be better if he came back to check on her in the morning after he had cleaned up. He glanced back at the police officers who were talking and comparing notes.

As he came around the corner of the corridor, he bumped into someone who was in a rush. As he felt the woman falling, he quickly reached out to steady her. He caught her arm and quickly pulled her back toward him before she could fall.

"Hey, sorry about that…"

"Andrew? What are you doing here?" He recognized Ana's voice.

Andrew met her shocked gaze. "I found Leah in the forest unconscious. I came with her in the ambulance and had to stay for questioning."

"Oh, my! What happened?"

"Don't know, no one does. We'll have to wait for her to wake up. Whatever it was…it was very disturbing."

"Will she be okay?"

Andrew shrugged. "The doctors said she's stabilized, and they took care of her wounds. They're not sure why she isn't waking up. Maybe it's the trauma of whatever happened out there." Andrew shrugged.

"Oh," said Ana with a shudder.

When Andrew saw how shaken she was, he pulled her into the circle of his arm. "She'll be fine."

Ana looked up at him and then stepped back. "Actually, I'm glad you're here. I wanted to speak to you about what happened before… I didn't get the chance to—"

He put up his hand to stop her. "Ana, let's leave it in the past. I know I'm a jerk. Megan is still not speaking to me."

"No, I only want to tell you that I'm sorry about the way I acted. I know you regret what happened, and it was a mistake. I was so confused by my own emotions. I feel like I could have supported you better as—a sister-in-Christ."

Andrew was shocked by her words. "Ana, you don't know what it means to me to hear you say that!" Tears burned his eyes. "I'll make it up to you."

"It's not about me. You have your own relationship with God."

Andrew didn't care what she said. He wrapped his arms around her again, pulled her to his chest and hugged her tight.

At that very moment, Will came up behind Ana, carrying some Chinese takeout. Caught off-guard, Andrew suddenly released her from his embrace. He was self-conscious about the blood on his shirt.

Ana turned to face Will.

Andrew felt guilty—as if he had been caught doing something wrong. He knew feeling that way was dumb since Will and Ana weren't dating, but something about being around them made him feel out of place.

"What are you guys doing here anyway?" Andrew acknowledged Will with a nod.

Breathless, Ana said, "Cathy's in labor, so we came after the march. Will gave me a ride, and Mom will be here any minute."

Will eyed the blood on Andrew's shirt. "Looks like everyone had an intense day. You good?"

Andrew tensed and clenched his hand into a hidden fist. *Why does Will's concern annoy me?* "I'm fine; the blood isn't mine. I was just heading home to get cleaned up." He stepped back. "I'll be back in the morning to check on Leah. Ana can explain." He said goodbye to Ana and waved at Will.

"Come on, Ana, you must be hungry," Will said.

She snapped out of her thoughts and followed him.

Andrew turned back and watched them walk away.

◞

Ana had just finished eating with Will when she spotted Pastor Mark walking down the hall. Will stood up as he approached.

Pastor Mark greeted them both with a hug "How are things going here?"

"No baby yet, but she's close. Mom and Beth are both with her now."

"Any word on Ishmael?" Will asked as Pastor Mark settled into a chair next to them.

"Well, it's the strangest thing. The police are still trying to find the underlying cause of it. From what I can gather, a bit more seems to be going on then what we thought. Although, I have to admit that I'm not even sure what I should think."

Ana glanced up in confusion. "What's happening?"

"I just came from the police station, and by the way he was acting, Ishmael seemingly doesn't remember anything that happened." Pastor Mark leaned back in his chair and crossed his ankle over his leg. He rolled his head on his shoulders as if trying to wake up. "Ishmael was quite distraught when he found out what he'd done. He was crying and carrying on about being framed. All he remembers is being attacked by Will. Some blood tests were done on him to determine if drugs had something to do with it."

Will frowned. "How could he try to kill someone? He's been gone all this time and now this?"

Ana stared off for a minute. "This is completely crazy. Why would Ishmael try to kill me?" She stared at Will as she once again processed the afternoon's events. "You ran at a man with a gun; you saved my life." She shook her head. "Thank you. I don't know what would have happened if you hadn't noticed him. Weren't you afraid?"

"Honestly Ana, I don't know what happened. It's beyond me to understand how I knew the gun was pointing at you. I didn't have time to think. I just saw the gun pointing at you, and the next thing I knew, I was on him. It all happened so fast…I'm not even sure if I ran. I must have blacked out in panic or something."

Pastor Mark nodded. "Let's just give glory to God for today. We must have really shaken some things in the spiritual realm with allthat intense worship and prayer. Now Ishmael is back—unfortunately under sad circumstances, but we'll get to the bottom of it." He leaned forward to whisper. "Despite what's happened, I believe today was a victory in many ways. We need to keep praying."

He leaned back in his chair again and smiled in satisfaction. "It's nice to see all of you guys supporting each other like a real family. You're here for Cathy as well as some of the other members."

Will and Ana looked at each other. "Do you mean Andrew? Did you see him when he left a while ago?" Ana asked.

"No, I was talking about Megan and Susan. I saw them a few minutes ago at one of the concierge desks. I assumed they were here for Cathy."

"Nope. We haven't seen them at all. They must be here for something else," Ana said to herself. Megan was still avoiding her.

Pastor Mark looked puzzled. "Well, was Andrew here to see Cathy? I didn't think they were that close."

Ana sighed aloud. "No, he was here for Leah. You won't believe what happened…"

～

Divinica drove to the outskirts of the city. She wouldn't meet with Dionysus until the Christians' prayer shield came down. The highway was dark as streetlamps became fewer and farther between. Things had not worked out the way she'd planned, but it wasn't over. Unless they had been dislodged, she fully expected before the month was out that at least some of the demons wandering in the abyss would be drawn back to the city like moths to a flame.

Their roots were hidden, and nothing could be done about that. No one knew why they were there or how to get rid of them. The others would wait until they were summoned.

Since her cover was still intact, she would be able to get into the city again. A simple spell over Leah using Havoc and Sakron would buy her just enough time. Dionysus would wait and waltz right back in with the others. For now, she needed to lay low. The church had managed to destroy her attempt at bringing in the goddess this time.

She had been buying time for decades. She was not as old as the ancients, but she had gained strength over her travels. Next time she would go deeper and bypass the Christians' knowledge. She would not and could not fail the goddess again. The goddess had now been waiting for quite some time, and Divinica knew she would not wait much longer…

～

Ana walked through the hospital corridors. Where is everyone?

Cathy's baby was on its way. She wanted it to come into the world with great celebration. After all, that is what they had planned. And she had been assigned to do the decorations.

Ana continued walking down the hall, carrying balloons and streamers when, all of a sudden, she noticed a tall, muscular man standing in front of her.

He smiled and looked down at her. "A pleasure to meet you, Ana," he said.

"Have we met before?" He did seem familiar.

"Yes, we have, and we will meet again many more times."

"Oh?"

"Because you have a great work to finish—this was only the beginning," he continued. "You and the body of believers have birthed something great and strong in the spirit, which must be nurtured or else it will die."

"That's so sad—to speak of death when we're here to welcome someone into the world." Ana sensed the gravity of the man's words.

"I know it's hard to hear, but you will understand when the time is right. Listen, Ana, and keep listening. Your friend Leah is in danger and needs to be set free. Will you help her? At any cost?" Ana focused on the man. He was so tall.

What's wrong with Leah? Something had happened to Leah? Ana thought. She nodded. "Yes, I will help her. I'll help anyone in need, just as I promised."

"I remember," the tall man replied.

What happened to her?" Ana asked.

"Don't you remember?" The man looked concerned and quickly peeked behind him before focusing again on Ana.

Leah, blood…the blood on Andrew's shirt.

"Yes, blood is the answer," the man spoke quickly. "Always remember the power is in the blood."

"Did I say that out loud?" Ana squinted in confusion.

"No, you didn't, but look at your hands." Ana looked down and noticed that the decorations were gone; she was now carrying a Bible. She blinked, and the Bible flickered and turned into a sword.

"What you have been given, Ana, is not small; use every weapon you have to fight in this next season. You will not be fighting alone…"

Ana reached out to touch the man as a halo of light enveloped him. Smooth white wings on his back slowly arced upward as her hand passed through him.

She looked past where he had stood and saw Kevin running down the hallway, shouting, "It's a boy!"

She jolted awake.

"It's a boy, Ana," Will said softly. "Wake up." He gently brushed her hair behind her ear and straightened in his seat, forcing Ana to lift her head from his shoulder. She hadn't realized she had fallen asleep in that position.

A beaming Kevin stood in the waiting room.

At the news her mom closed her magazine, stood up and hugged the excited new father. "Praise God! Congratulations! You must be so proud. I'll go get Beth and Stephen."

Will stood to slap Kevin's hand and pat him on the back.

Ana squinted up at Kevin as she sat up. "Congrats! When can we meet your son?"

"Cathy's resting, but you should be able to see him in a few minutes. I was just holding him. He's so cute… What a miracle!" Kevin smiled.

Ana suddenly remembered her dream. "Does anyone know what room Leah is in?"

Will shrugged. "Not sure, but we can find out. What's up?"

Ana rubbed her eyes and stood. She smoothed her tousled curls back behind her ears and met Will's eyes. "I had a dream. We need to go pray for her…"

~

Sasson, Okelani, Dunamis and Aarao stood in the hospital with their charges gathered around Leah.

"You were right, my friend," Sasson said to Aarao. "With these ones, a battle is always looming on the horizon, but there will be many victories too. Hopefully, Ana will remember everything I told her in the dream."

Aarao placed his hand on Sandra's head. She had joined hands with Will and Ana, and she was praying in the spirit. "Two generations going strong."

Okelani smiled and flashed Sasson an exaggerated wink. "And many more generations to come!"

Sasson laughed and cautioned. "I believe that remains to be seen, Okelani. Don't get ahead of yourself because nothing is written in stone."

Okelani grinned. "You are sure the annals of prophesy don't say something about that?"

"You may have to check in with Adara. I'm sure he'll have some words on the matter." Sasson looked amused.

Dunamis circled the group in brooding silence and waited while the humans prayed. After a few minutes, he went to rest his hand on Leah's head, covering her eyes.

Leah's eyelids began to flutter. She slowly opened them.

"Hey, look! She's awake," Will whispered.

"Will, go get the nurse," Sandra said.

"Yes, ma'am."

Dark circles shadowed Leah's eyes in her pale face. Her gaze shifted wildly then narrowed in confusion. Ana stepped closer to the hospital bed and ran her hand over Leah's head, smoothing her brown hair back from her face. "It's going to be okay, Leah. You're awake now."

THE END
OF BOOK ONE

For the latest news on future books

from Nana Abraham,

sign up for her newsletter at

www.nanabraham.com

www.ingramcontent.com/pod-product-compliance
Lightning Source LLC
Chambersburg PA
CBHW020934260626
47169CB00006B/1719